SIGNIFICANT LOSS

SIGNIFICANT LOSS

David Brierley

ORION

This is a work of fiction. Names, characters, place and incidents
are either the product of the author's imagination or used
fictitiously. Any resemblence to actual events or locales or
persons living or dead is entirely coincidental.

First published in Great Britain in 1994 by
Orion
An imprint of Orion Books Ltd
Orion House, 5 Upper St Martin's Lane, London WC2H 9EA

A CIP catalogue record for this book is available from the British Library

Extracts from The Book of Common Prayer, the rights in which are vested in
the Crown, are reproduced by permission of the Crown's Patentee,
Cambridge University Press.

ISBN 1 85797 085 3

Typeset by Deltatype Ltd, Ellesmere Port, Cheshire
Printed in Great Britain by
Clays Ltd. St. Ives plc

For Ulrike, with love

PROLOGUE

THE SEPTEMBER SKY at daybreak hesitated between rain and sunshine, but turned high-blue, warm and serene. They were blessed with a fine day for the funeral.

Inspector Stewart Wilson had brushed his uniform, wondered briefly about a suit and tie, then decided, against the wishes of his wife, to pay his last respects in official garb. It was no more than Kevin deserved. The young fellow, their nephew, an up-and-coming broker and would-be hot-shot, had been more or less working with him, investigating Lloyd's, when it happened. All very unofficial and most definitely not in Kevin's best interests. A good lad, Kevin.

Yes, wearing the uniform was the least Stu could do. Nothing and something.

Of course, his wife and her sister Jenny blamed him for Kevin's death. He had promised them, insisted that there was no danger: now this. In their eyes, the guilt was his.

Someone at the top was to blame. Of that, Wilson was sure: this was not merely fraud, this was murder.

They stood around in Jenny's modest terraced house and waited, embarrassed by each other's presence, surprised by the shafts of yellow light through the thin curtains; the other mourners had yet to arrive, and the black limousines. They were Kevin's only relatives: his mother, Jenny, his aunt, Rosie, his uncle Stu, bonded and separated and somehow shrunk by grief. None of them had been able to sleep.

The doorbell rang and Stu Wilson ushered their guests inside, making introductions and easing silences with small talk. Yes, the weather was perfect. The old school friends, mostly from the soccer team, the pretty and strangely prim young women, Kevin's starchy colleagues from Lloyd's, gathered in lounge and hallway, trying to remain decorous, serious, mournful. Young men and women under thirty; they were, Stu saw, at the fine age when life was only for living. He thought, sure as hell, Kevin would have wanted to see them all laughing; the lad had had a talent for friendship, a talent for laughter. Yet he sensed they were glad to see the undertaker arrive, a sombre master of ceremonies.

Rosie had wanted a church burial, Jenny had agreed; so Kevin, an out-and-out unbeliever, was to be interred in consecrated ground. Stu did not bother to argue; there were so many other battles to fight.

Their black limousine followed the slow black hearse to the church; behind them a line of cars had formed. Rosie sat beside Jenny, who still needed tranquilisers and was biting her handkerchief; the sunlight slanted across her face, revealing her eyes behind sunglasses to be bloodshot and grief-rimmed. She had been groomed to an improbable elegance by Rosie, so that everything was just as her younger sister thought right. Stu's uniform felt slightly uncomfortable, as if he had gained weight or the garments had shrunk, but he was glad of his decision: the uniform helped him to avoid excess emotion, sloppiness.

From the rear of the limousine, he turned to look at the convoy, the briefly-seen faces in the reflecting windscreens, the black ties, the dark suits; he tried to put names to faces and failed. He had spoken to an older woman, a Mrs Sanderson, who had muttered about having been Kevin's teacher, and to an elegant lady, Mrs Montfort, blonde and expensive, who said she had worked at Lloyd's with Kevin; the other women were much younger. Then he was surprised to see Ray Marchwood. Kevin had started a new job at Lloyd's only days before he died, working for Ray and his brother Robert. He was driving an old-fashioned sports car in British racing green, and Stu wondered how much Ray knew, then tried to bury the thought, sick and tired of Lloyd's of London. He had spent over a year investigating the world-famous insurance market, the cornerstone of Britain's presence in world financial markets. He had often heard such phrases while he fought vainly to prove the obvious. Now this had happened. Perhaps this too was obvious and unprovable. He would see.

He wound down a window to let in fresh air. Minutes passed, the car ticked onwards. Feeling his palms moisten, he searched his wrists as if looking for his pulse.

4

The vicar was waiting for the coffin and its bearers, greeting the mourners at the church gate of St Christopher, a brick church with a square tower that rose to a forceful spire. The coffin was light on Stu's shoulder; the bearers moved easily through the porch into the nave, placing the coffin on a metal stand beside the altar. The vicar quoted scripture as they silently attended to their task.

Whosoever liveth and believeth in me shall never die . . .

Jenny, Rosie and Stu took their places in the pews at the front, near the altar steps. Behind them, the other mourners took their seats, in a whisper-filled silence.

The vicar read a psalm, then they sang a hymn, accompanied by an organ that blared out imperatives that did not help the haphazard congregation find full voice.

Glory be to the Father, and to the Son, and to the Holy Ghost . . .

Sunlight fell through the stained glass windows, bringing a glow to saints, knights and heraldic blazons of long-dead benefactors. There followed a eulogy to the dead man, tragically cut down. The vicar spoke as if he meant what he said, though he had never met Kevin, not to Stu's knowledge. Rosie had briefed him well.

I am the resurrection and the life, saith the Lord . . .

They rose to sing. Stu stood next to Jenny, with Rosie to hand on the other side; there had, he reflected, to be a way, with dignity, for the living to let go. If this was all they had, the best man could fathom, so be it. The organ resounded and Stu suddenly sensed the extent of the church, heard the music test every pew, every window, every pillar and every stone with its force.

Else what shall they do which are baptised for the dead, if the dead rise not at all? Why are they then baptised for the dead? And why stand we in jeopardy every hour?

They prayed. Then another hymn was sung, the voices were louder; now the bearers were asked to come forward, to carry the coffin to the churchyard; the way was uneven, but they shuffled onwards until they reached the grave, where white slings were produced and the light pine-clad box was lowered, effortlessly.

The howl of fire engines and ambulances, the blazing warehouse that awful night, were vivid in Stu Wilson's brain. Since then he had not slept or only dozed, to waken after garish dreams, leaden with his regrets.

In the midst of life we are in death . . . O holy and most merciful saviour, deliver us not into the bitter pains of eternal death.

There was a light wind, birdsong, the gracious movement of sun-lit leaves, chestnut, oak and beech. It was difficult to register what the vicar said, even though he had a clear, high voice. Rosie held Jenny's arm. Stu stood to one side.

To forget his anger, his sorrow, his guilt, his plans, his hopelessness, Stu again contemplated the mourners, their faces, expressions, their silence.

He tried not to hear his own thoughts: this is an outrage, this will not pass unnoticed, I will not leave Kevin unavenged. Yet the words were whispered by the wind, even as he tried not to hear them. Trees shifted, outrage, a blackbird trilled, outrage, a cloud let them move into the shade.

Of course, he was not well. He tried to look at the faces, and realised with disgust that he was seeing his sorrow in theirs. Jenny and Rosie bowed over the grave.

There was Ray Marchwood, black tie, grim expression.

Mrs Montfort, dark blue suit, dark glasses, curiously distraught.

The older woman, very tired. A fine face. The schoolmistress, Mrs Sanderson.

People bent to throw earth on the grave. The end of a friendship, end of a love. It was a ceremonial.

Forasmuch as it hath pleased Almighty God of his great mercy to take unto himself the soul of our dear brother here departed . . .

As the group round the graveside started to dwindle, he left his wife and his sister-in-law to their thoughts, he turned to thank everyone for coming, shaking hands by the churchyard gate.

Three fresh-faced blokes, who worked as stockbrokers, Forex traders, City types in striped shirts, said a gruff goodbye; they had been on holiday with Kevin, in Spain. Then there were some fellows from Lloyd's, who had worked with Kevin on a computer system; Stu nodded, said nothing.

A couple of young women, who did not appear to know anybody, shook his hand. 'Goodbye, thank you for coming.' An odd thing to say.

The older woman, Mrs Sanderson, once Kevin's head-mistress; had been to see Kevin recently, she said, 'about Lloyd's'. Stu contained his surprise and asked for an address and telephone number; he had some questions.

6

Then there were friends from Kevin's school, some more pretty girls. His mother Jenny had always insisted: 'Kevin is so shy.' Not, evidently, with everyone.

Suddenly, Ray Marchwood offered him a thin hand. He looked up, for Ray was a tall man, and saw thin, tired features which almost broke into a grim smile. To Stu, Ray had been just one more of his adversaries over the last years. The backroom genius, brother of the greatest broker in the market, joint owner of a leading private brokership, a gold mine. Now, when Ray spoke, Stu was surprised: 'Shouldn't have happened. Money is one thing, this is another. Something will have to be done.' His brother, Robert Marchwood, was sorry not to pay his respects; he had been taken ill abroad.

Stu wondered what this might mean, looked at the proferred hand, which contained a card: Raymond Marchwood, Finance Director, Knowle & Co, Brokers at Lloyd's of London.

Mrs Montfort had slipped away, without a word.

Suddenly, they were just the three of them, standing beside their uniformed chauffeur, Jenny and Rosie and he. They took the limousine; he would walk home, alone.

BOOK ONE

ONE

STEPHEN GROTE, CHAIRMAN of Lloyd's of London, was in excellent spirits. Not a man to let a few problems sour his pleasures, he was strolling towards Covent Garden, he could see the Royal Opera House and felt cheered. Even though the cool spring evening threatened rain, even though there were problems, nothing could detract from the pleasures of his favourite opera, *The Magic Flute*.

The problems, however, might be termed a crisis; after the performance, they would have to be discussed.

To that end, he had invited his friends to the opera. He had obtained tickets that were not to be had, at a price which one ought to refuse to pay – for a performance which everyone wanted to hear. This ensured his friends made themselves available. If he personally also had to pay the fees of the Queen of the Night, then so be it; that was expected from him as a director of the Opera House, the head of a billion-pound business, as the chairman of the most exclusive club in Britain.

During the day, he had wondered about Alec, Alexander Wilmot-Greaves, and Henry Stone, but he heard nothing, nor expected to do so, until after that evening's performance.

It was with some relief that he saw the headlines on the newspaper stands as he and his party approached Covent Garden: BODY OF BANKER FOUND. He let his guests stroll on without him while he bought the newspaper. This final edition was dominated by a late surge of the stockmarket, but on the second page he found an article about the death of a prominent Italian banker, who had been drowned in St Katherine's Dock, by the Tower of London. An accident, apparently.

Grote peered over his half-moon reading glasses, stared along the street at the Opera House whose colonnaded façade gleamed under powerful lights. Donna, his wife, and their friends had already disappeared inside.

The article reported that the banker had worked for the Holy See. There was no mention of Lloyd's of London so it appeared at least one problem had been solved. It remained to deal with another, one that had plagued Grote for decades: Robert Hugh Marchwood, chairman of Knowle & Co. Inside Lloyd's, Marchwood had a formidable reputation as broker and deal-maker; outside he was famous for receiving a salary of ten million pounds a year. One would have thought, Stephen mused, that Robert Marchwood earned enough from their little agreement, and would keep his word.

Yet the darned fellow could not be trusted.

That was a matter for later; time was pressing now, so Stephen threw the newspaper in a black metal bin.

Outside Covent Garden, there was bustle, excitement, as black cabs or chauffeur-driven cars drew up. Everyone was in evening dress; on the pavement, behind metal barriers, press photographers gathered, waiting for royal snaps; next to them were a couple of policemen. Stephen entered the foyer, where Donna, his elegant American wife, greeted him with a kiss on the forehead. She was slightly taller than he was, one of those women whose intelligence and wit lend grace and beauty to their middle years. An expert in British antique furniture, Donna worked for Sotheby's; they had married just a few years earlier, both for the first time, and were considered a happy couple.

Bells rang; the performance, a royal occasion, would commence in fifteen minutes. Stephen Grote enjoyed all the pomp; it was good to feel in the thick of things. At Covent Garden, there were friends to meet, backstage gossip to hear. When the opera house throbbed, it was a wonderful place.

For Stephen, a man in his late fifties, there might seem little left to achieve; he was rich, happily married and he moved in the best circles; as chairman of Lloyd's, the most prestigious, if not the largest, City institution, this was inevitable. Yet he was entering an age when other doors looked certain to open, and he had not, as yet, been offered a knighthood.

The evening had started well. The pre-show trattoria had been delightful; his guests appeared on time; there was laughter and fine wine. Now they were to see and hear world-class performers, enjoying top-flight fees, who should sing accordingly. The conductor was Sir Gregor Stanislas, the East European who over two decades had turned Covent Garden into one of the great opera houses of the world.

Thanks to their mutual friendship with the diva Mercedes Valldemosa, Stephen had attracted a reluctant Stanislas to London and liked to claim, with a smile, that this was his greatest achievement. Nevertheless, there was always more that could be done. The Opera House was permanently short of money. There was a long list of good causes needing cash: a roof to mend, dressing rooms to upgrade. Government grants never sufficed. There were plans to develop the Opera House, and Stephen Grote was determined to see them through; the best singers deserved the best facilities. London deserved the best.

He contributed freely out of his own pocket. Without children, married to a woman of independent means, he was happy to provide – though never as much as Covent Garden might like. He constantly tried to persuade his friends from Lloyd's to dig deep. God knows, they could all afford it. Yet it was not without its risks, as he was aware, having recently signed a large cheque to cover the fees of the Queen of the Night. There were only two or three on the circuit whom Stanislas considered adequate in the role, yet opinions were divided about this one. Stanislas did not apologise for his mistakes.

Leaving their friends in the stalls, Donna and Stephen rushed to their seats in the royal box and found their neighbours present and very correct: Lord and Lady Sankey, the supermarket people, and Sir Simon and Lady Samuelson of the banking dynasty. There were smiles and handshakes; Donna had long known the Samuelsons as distinguished collectors.

Below, Stephen could see the awkward figure of John Devies, the deputy chairman of Lloyd's, who had a gammy leg and had to shoe-horn himself into a seat with his walking stick. This impediment had not prevented him from being a top-notch helmsman in his day; now he was an elder statesman, who chaired the Royal Yacht Squadron in Cowes.

Had Alec Wilmot-Greaves arrived? He had not made it to the trattoria and Stephen had good reason to worry. He could see the red hair of Neil Fortescue and the hand of Tony MacNulty, gesturing to his wife with his unlit pipe. Henry Stone was nowhere to be seen, but they had met at the trattoria and Henry seemed to be bearing up. Stephen hoped that Alec had not had a funk.

Problems, problems.

The opera was being broadcast live. Under bright lights a bald man talked to a television camera, then the chatter and laughter of the audience seemed to diminish, the prince and princess arrived, Sir Gregor Stanislas walked onto the podium to loud applause, the audience rose and the national anthem was played.

The lights dimmed. The overture began and despite himself, Stephen's thoughts wandered from the opera – to the dead Italian banker, to the evening's impending meeting, to the damned Monet which he wished Marchwood had never demanded and he himself had never desired. Finally, he spotted Alec Wilmot-Greaves in the stalls, peering through thick glasses at the stage, and exhaled deeply, relieved.

During the interval, the Grotes went with the Sankeys to the bar, leaving their friends to their own devices. Donna, despite republican misgivings, mustered a curtsy when she was presented to the royal couple. It was all very jolly and Stephen scrupulously avoided mentioning the Queen of the Night, who had turned a high G into the croak of a wounded frog.

After the final curtain calls, the carnations and the applause, Stephen's party met and divided: the men left the Opera House to talk business, their ladies departed for Mayfair where the men would join them for a night-cap. This was clumsy and anti-social, but could not be helped. The men were so busy, so booked out, but they simply had to meet. They had had similar, impromptu meetings in Cowes, in Baden-Baden, in Zurich, in New York and on the Côte d'Azur; people would fly around the globe, to make one key decision.

This was never done over the telephone. Not only would it have been stupid; it was forbidden. Stephen had long ago established the rules of their game: discretion, simplicity, security, control. Over the years, each word had acquired a meaning of its own, the force of law.

Covent Garden was a favourite rendezvous; there they had access to a large, anonymous building near the Opera House, the Freemasons' Hall. Here they could talk, undisturbed, at a moment's notice.

Stephen and his friends belonged to the Who's Who of Lloyd's of London, they ran the market's steering committee, traded around the globe, dominated the day-to-day business of the insurance market, determined the flow of billions of pounds of business. Outside Lloyd's, they were prominent City business-men, discreet eminences; Stephen Grote wined and dined select members of the financial press, Henry Stone attended inter-national conferences to discuss the world insurance scene, John Devies was an old Whitehall hand, dealing with the DTI and parliamentary committees. They were all fervently committed to free trade in financial services, to breaking into the closed Japanese market, to promoting the City and Lloyd's throughout the world. That much was to be expected; but they did not advertise their power and wealth. Not only would that have been vulgar – it would have infringed Grote's rules.

Stephen Grote and John Devies were the first to arrive at the Freemasons' Hall. They had changed the actual meeting room at the last minute. A simple but habitual precaution, followed even inside the Hall, which was not a public venue.

Their conversation moved from Mozart to money; the value of their share portfolios continued to rise, beyond all reason.

Devies stroked a ruddy cheek, leaned on his silver-topped cane and said: 'You know, old man, one stock of mine has doubled in the last month. Called Cole & Harrison. New man moved in, something of a hot-shot, apparently. Know what they make?' Devies liked to chop his phrases; he had been in the Guards before joining Horcum and turning it into the largest British brokership.

Grote, who had a remarkable memory for detail, shook his head, shamming ignorance. Devies enjoyed his little joke. 'Women's hair-dryers!' he said. 'Natural growth market, I'd say.'

They both chuckled and Devies repeated the joke to Neil Fortescue, a tall red-haired man who smiled convincingly. Fortescue headed the London office of the largest broker in the world; he and Devies dominated the billions in premiums placed at Lloyd's every year. They could make and break people at will, and they enjoyed each other's jokes.

Fortescue was just off the plane from New York; after a record year he had been celebrating in expense-account Manhattan, with an expense-account girlfriend. Yet he had returned to London on Concorde for the meeting. An ambitious man, Fortescue was seen in the Lloyd's market as Grote's natural successor, which did not greatly endear him to the older man. They were the worst best friends in the world.

Grote placed two small, electronic devices on the baize table that stood in the centre of the room. Two green lights went on; they were so sensitive that a cleaner with a walkman in the corridor outside would change the lights to red. Discretion was imperative.

A short, dark, moustached figure arrived and took a seat beside them at the table: Henry Stone owned a top Lloyd's agency, Williams, Stone & Co, and was sometimes suspected, erroneously, of being the richest man working at Lloyd's. He was an excellent linguist and dealt with their business in continental Europe.

The pungent smell of pipe tobacco accompanied Tony MacNulty into the room. Grote frowned but, as always, welcomed the chairman of Wordsworth, a long-established Lloyd's agency. MacNulty was flustered. 'Sorry I'm late.'

Everyone nodded and smiled. They all knew MacNulty was having difficulties with his wife. Formal greetings were exchanged.

Stephen Grote glanced at his watch. It was getting late and Alexander Wilmot-Greaves had still not arrived.

Finally, the tall, bald man with thick glasses who had been the late-comer in the stalls entered and Grote exchanged a quick glance with him. Wilmot-Greaves nodded solemnly, an affirmative. He was the smartest and highest-paid underwriter in Lloyd's. Now he had shown that he had steel in his character, too.

John Devies entertained them with the grim details of Grote's expensive sponsorship of the frog. Stephen was unamused and vowed to have words with Stanislas, who had booked her.

Finally, Wilmot-Greaves removed his heavy glasses and said: 'You've all seen the newspaper.'

Stephen Grote smiled and all agreed that the task had been well executed, with a minimum of fuss.

'I've spoken to our friends at the Met,' Devies said, not choosing to name names. 'It will be treated as an accident. The fellow fell off a boat. Happens all the time in Cowes. A short, sharp hearing in the coroner's court.'

They could all imagine the coroner's conclusions. The banker, Claudio Scrivano of Banco Cristòforo, must have been under extreme stress, probably pressure of work. The poor chap, clearly half out of his mind, had stumbled in the dead of night from the quay in St Katherine's dock. Grote thanked Wilmot-Greaves and Stone for their work, while Devies hoped that this would bring an unhappy story to a close.

Grote deplored violence; it was crude, and mostly unnecessary. However, losses of thirty million pounds and more had been sustained by friends of friends, who took a less rational view; Scrivano was a thief on a grand scale, and worse, a man who had threatened to talk.

Wilmot-Greaves coughed, then said, in a gruff voice: 'We should not forget Marchwood.'

At the name of Robert Hugh Marchwood, Grote turned to Neil Fortescue: 'Remind me. Remind us all. What did we agree with Robert Marchwood at Baden-Baden?'

Robert and Raymond Marchwood were the most famous duo in Lloyd's, the Marchwood brothers who owned and ran Knowle & Co. The flamboyant Robert struck the big deals, threw parties and uncorked things, while Ray kept the business ticking over, the office working, the small deals flowing. Money flooded in, million upon million; they were a phenomenon.

Fortescue flushed at Grote's question. 'In return for the oil rig deal, they were to leave us and our business alone: no data collection, no surveillance, no police and "no accidents".'

The list, which was known to everyone there, was still galling. Wilmot-Greaves got in first, denouncing Robert Marchwood who – just for fun, for no reason at all – had sold him a pup. An 'accident', à la Marchwood: an insurance deal that turned very sour.

'A wilful attempt to ruin my reputation,' Alec spluttered. The anger was shared. Everyone round the table knew: Marchwood had done these things just to prove he was smarter than the rest. And there had been so many such 'accidents' that this meeting had had to be called.

Devies leaned on the walking-stick held between his knees: 'Now it's Ray Marchwood who's up to his tricks. He's back collecting data.'

Information – about ships, planes, cars, property, anything Lloyd's cared to insure, about prices and claims – was the key to the insurance market. Their mastery of that market meant using this information to their advantage – 'picking the ripest plums from the tree', as Grote liked to say. But records had to be kept, records which could not be eliminated, and with them someone could research which plums went into which pockets. This information was their great weakness; it could be used to destroy them.

'Hacked into the databank of the Horcum computer,' Devies went on. 'Neat trick, apparently. No damage worth mentioning.'

There was a silence. Grote looked at Henry Stone, who spoke slowly, giving each word due emphasis. 'Last night we were informed that Marchwood has a close friend in the police force, the Serious Fraud Office, an Inspector Tomlinson. Yes, Derek Tomlinson. The man who heads the Wansbeck investigation.'

Wansbeck had been involved in a dirty takeover battle; the investigation was going nowhere fast, but this was not considered a recommendation for Tomlinson.

'Not a friend of ours,' Devies muttered.

'No data collection, no surveillance, no police and no "accidents",' Wilmot-Greaves repeated Fortescue's words, grimly. Marchwood was clearly not leaving them or their business alone.

It was Fortescue who commented: 'I sometimes wonder why we ever bothered with the man.'

Of course, everybody knew why. Everybody knew also that something had to be done; too many of the Baden-Baden agreements had been broken. A motion was proposed, seconded, carried unanimously. The man would be taught a lesson. Not a lesson in the Scrivano manner, that was too drastic, but a lesson nonetheless.

An hour later they were all in Mayfair with their womenfolk, drinking Grote's finest champagne.

Two

THERE HAD BEEN a phone call. Late last night.

Robert had left home this morning as usual, before seven, without mentioning the disturbance in the small hours. Thérèse Marchwood, sitting in the kitchen beside black coffee, thought about Robert's words on the telephone, low, angry, something about Baden-Baden, about trust, about money.

They made no sense at all.

She had first met Robert in Baden-Baden, at a congress in the German spa town. A petite, stylish woman in her early forties, Thérèse was a Swiss francophone. She looked out onto the freshly greened trees, the mown grass, damp from the light morning drizzle and thought: in Zurich, there could still be snow lying on the ground. In Baden-Baden, too.

She was not accustomed to telephone calls in the dead of night. But one should not complain. She had no right.

For many years, Thérèse had been an interpreter, at home in five languages; now, by any standards, she was fortunate to live at Golden Rain. A grade-two listed building with sash windows, portico and Georgian aspect, Golden Rain had been so named by a Victorian owner who had enthusiastically planted laburnums to the rear of the house, splashing sprays of summer yellow among the older oak, beech and horse-chestnut.

She overturned her coffee, knocking grounds and sugar across the table. She had heard glass breaking.

Golden Rain had outhouses, greenhouses, the old stables where Robert kept his cars; there was the new swimming-pool and gymnasium, which was double-glazed and triple-safe. Yet there was so much glass, there were so many gadgets, there was always something to go wrong, to break and repair. It was the curse of the property-owning classes: last week, the heating people, the week before, the decorators, next week, the security people.

But today was the gardener's day off.

Thérèse picked up the white orchid she had bought for the sitting room, its roots and plastic soil contained in a white art-nouveau bowl; she stepped curiously into the hall, her heels clicking precise echoes on the marbled floor. She stopped. Suddenly the weight of the tall, thin orchid between her white hands felt like lead.

She was not alone.

She turned back to the kitchen, screamed, dropped the orchid at the feet of a man in a Balaclava mask.

Hands grasped her. There were two men, dressed in black. She fought, then despaired. They could do anything, absolutely anything with her. Another scream opened up inside her, unable to burst out. Her eyes were bound tight. There was a bag over her head, her hands were tied, she was carried as if she was nothing at all into the kitchen, no, into the downstairs cloak-room. She heard steps, steps, doors slamming, the wind, water. Thérèse sobbed without sobbing, screamed in silence.

THREE

GOT A JOB, got a job, got a job.

The underground carriage rattled in the dark, rattled down to London town, the rattle echoing between scratched grey formica walls, through dirty, viewless windows. Above, black nobbed hand-grips dangled like shrunken heads.

Got a job, got a job, got a job . . . Kevin Vaughan was, despite it all, pleased. Not ecstatic, pleased.

Another underground train passed close by, a flash-flicker of passing lights. The rattle asserted itself again, the noise he had heard now for two years, morning and evening, five days a week, forty-eight weeks a year.

It was something of a miracle. Not just a job. After a couple of years at Lloyd's he could even boast of having a career.

He had planned nothing, he had intended to pluck guitar strings, kick a football and watch the world go by. He had not had what one might call a career plan.

He owed it all to Ray Marchwood, that much was certain, and to his mother, who had forced him to go round to see 'Uncle Ray', a friend of hers whom she had known forever. Which was odd, really. The man had billions, but lived like you and me.

'Jenny sent you, then?' he asked, when Kevin appeared on the doorstep. 'Well, come on in. I'll get you a coffee, if you fancy one.'

Ray's sitting room was modest, painted white; there were two hessian-covered sofas, white bookshelves, white pictures, an off-white carpet and newspapers scattered on the floor. It was the same size as the living room at home, yet it appeared twice as large.

'Take a seat.'

Biscuits and coffee; neat.

'Do you want a job?' Ray asked.

The standard question. Yes, of course, definitely. Always.

'Why did you leave school?' Ray adjusted his wire-framed glasses. 'Why didn't you go to college?'

Kev drank from his mug and bit into a crumbly biscuit. 'Do you have a degree?'

'No,' Ray said.

Kevin just had to leave school. His grades were a surprise. At the Spring Road Comprehensive, nothing fitted, everything leaked, nobody worked. Kevin had had seven English teachers in five years, the last had been a woman who knew about rat dynamics and the reproductive system of the fluke worm. That, at least, was what she claimed.

'Jenny tells me you did well in maths,' Ray prompted him.

'Yes, I'm interested in computers . . .'

'For playing games?'

Kev hesitated, considered the bookshelves, which contained books on photography and some brightly coloured science fiction paperbacks.

'You bet. And the old bag . . .' he corrected himself '. . . My maths teacher showed us how to write programs.'

Ray drank his coffee, asked about school, asked about his mother, asked how she was doing.

Kevin felt quite pleased with himself. He had done his bit, given it a go, he could tell his mother he had tried like crazy, that Ray was well-disposed, but lived in a different, slightly white world. Believing that his interview was over, Kevin changed the subject. There was not a record, not a CD, not a cassette in sight. 'Don't you like music?' he asked.

Ray smiled and fetched a record player that must have been forty years old, a plastic-covered box with a fabric speaker-grille and three knobs.

'For some reason, I like old record-players; I collect 78s – Charlie Parker, bebop, that sort of thing. Louis Armstrong, too.'

Kevin was transfixed by the sight of brown paper record sleeves, thick plastic disks and a changer which dropped the records with a thud onto a turntable. All the records bombed, in those days.

Yet the music was something else. That man Parker could play; his 'Slow boat to China' was one of the fastest Kevin had ever heard.

Before he left, Kevin looked long and hard at Ray, at the white room, at the small collection of photographs on the mantelpiece; a young girl, a middle-aged man, a middle-aged woman, some black-and-white shots of two boys in school uniform.

Now he knew those photographs were mementoes of the Marchwood brothers, Ray and Robert, joint owners of Knowle & Co, a top private brokerage. Ray earned eight million a year and his brother ten; there were people who said that Grote, the chairman, was jealous because he only took a million, but then you had to remember the dividends from his family firm, which were two or three or four million a year. Besides, Grote had married money. So there had to be some other reason why Grote and the Marchwoods did not see eye to eye.

Yet Ray was a nice guy, even if he was an enigma. It was a miracle that he had fixed up a job for Kevin; and it was a miracle, too, that Kevin had taken to Lloyd's. Insurance, previously, had not loomed large in Kev's plans.

Blighter, his new boss, treated him with respect because of Ray. Or, at least, with as much respect as your average well-spoken thug like Blighter can muster. On his first day, Kevin had received a lesson from Blighter, otherwise known as Alan Denbigh-Wright Esquire, Lloyd's underwriter. Many in Lloyd's had nicknames and Mr Denbigh-Wright had been given an apt one: he was truly a blighter.

Yet he took the trouble to explain to Kevin what the thousands of people in the room at Lloyd's were doing.

'It all started out in a coffee shop three hundred years ago, and the basic principle has remained the same since,' the Blighter told him. 'Insurance in Lloyd's is an agreement between two gentlemen, based on trust. Three centuries ago, a shipowner who wanted to insure his boat would come to Lloyd's coffee house. He would ask one of the gentlemen there if he would repay his losses, should his ship sink, and what price he might demand for such a guarantee. They would haggle until they had a deal. Then the owner would pay a premium and receive a signed undertaking from the gentleman to cover the potential loss. The gentleman had to trust the owner to reveal all the risks of the voyage and the owner had to trust the gentleman to pay.'

Kevin said, straight-faced: 'So you're an old-fashioned gentleman, really?'

The Blighter appreciated a joke at his own expense, laughing loudly. Then he said: 'As an underwriter, I do exactly the same job as the gentleman in the coffee house, and I make money by taking more in premiums than I pay out in claims. Brokers act as middlemen for the shipowners and agents act as middlemen for the people who back underwriters like me. There's thousands of them, mostly rich, known as names.

'Because risks are much larger than in the past, the brokers spread each risk by dividing it among several underwriters. They, in turn, try to limit their exposure to any one potential loss, to any one disaster.

'Nowadays, each underwriter is backed by millions of pounds. I represent four thousand names who have formally pledged two hundred million, which I risk on their behalf. I could lose money, but I seldom do.'

Kevin knew that names stood to lose everything if a man like the Blighter made a serious mistake. Indeed, there was no limit to what his names might pay. Called unlimited liability, this was unique to Lloyd's.

'I suppose we *could* lose money,' Blighter said. 'But we never do.'

This was true: the Blighter seemed a one-way bet. The names just knew that they got cheques, fat cheques from the Blighter, for doing nothing. In return, the Blighter earned nearly a million a year. Everybody was rich and became even richer; Lloyd's was wonderful.

That conversation had taken place two years ago. Kevin was given the title of junior underwriting clerk and allowed to watch, listen and learn while sitting near the Blighter in the underwriting room. He discovered how Blighter earned his money – he bullied, browbeat and bruised to strike a good deal. And he had both the experience and the mathematics to separate the good from the bad.

Kevin decided he was going to bust a gut; he saw money did not smell. He had no desire to struggle like his mother, who after his father had left them often hid when the milkman called. With his first pay cheque, he bought himself two new suits, striped cotton shirts, silk ties, and a pair of leather moccasins. He went into debt.

To show his worth, he helped update the computer which kept track of the Blighter's deals. He started evening classes, worked evenings. His aim was an external degree in computing and accounting from the City University. His old head teacher, Mrs Sanderson, always said that he had a knack for numbers. The secret of the best brains in Lloyd's was mathematics; the Marchwoods were brilliant mathematicians, the Blighter, too.

Every so often, Ray Marchwood appeared in the queue of brokers waiting outside the open office, called the box, where Blighter and his team worked. In the underwriting room there were hundreds of such teams, which were called syndicates.

'Don't think you're going to get away with anything, Ray, just because of young Kevin here . . .' Blighter said. 'The price has to be right. Now, what's your problem?'

It might involve insuring a tanker, a cargo, a building; invariably, the price *was* right, a deal was struck and Ray could stroll off to other underwriters, who would follow the Blighter's lead. Ray brought excellent deals to the Blighter, which explained Kev's presence in the box. One favour deserves another. Just like the gentlemen in the coffee shop.

Lloyd's was unique and very British; a peculiar, clannish, male world: an odd place with odd rules. It took time to adjust, to recognise the gods among the men, to understand the politics. This was crucial.

You had to know that Marchwood, Devies, and Fortescue were the top-flight brokers, men who brought the big premiums and big risks to the market; you had to know that Blighter and Wilmot-Greaves were the hardest-headed under-writers; you had to know that MacNulty, Grote and Stone were the top agents. An agent like Grote not only advised names which syndicates to back with their money, he ran top syndicates, too, and employed his own underwriters. Grote was the grandest of the grand; people spoke about him in hushed tones: the chairman did this, thought that, said the other.

After Kevin's first year, there had been a small pay rise, after his second there had been promotion to data processing clerk and £15,000 a year, which would have seemed like a fortune before he'd heard of Denbigh-Wright, Grote and Marchwood. Even so, life was looking up: the rattle in the underground trains took on a new meaning: earn a bomb, earn a bomb, earn a bomb.

FOUR

THE KING OF Love my shepherd is,
Whose goodness faileth never:
I nothing lack if I am his,
And he is mine for ever.

Five hundred children sang, more or less in time, more or less in tune.

Mrs Cornelia Sanderson beamed at them, the young, entranced faces turned towards her, the blue pullovers and white shirts, more or less clean and tidy. Every so often, every once in a while, Connie allowed herself a private indiscretion; she admitted how much she loved them all, the difficult as well as the bright, the tough as much as the quiet. Now, watching the mouths open, she felt for them all, adored their more or lessness.

Ron claimed she would have cared less if they had been able to have more than the one boy, Jonathan, who was now grown-up, doing frightfully well in Australia. But she had been in the teaching profession too long to be an over-the-mooner. Children involved work too – her patience was not what it should be, she had no angelic nature and, with grey hair and an ample girth, cut no angelic figure. Nor was she always cheerful; the smile involved effort, she forced herself, she forced others.

There were, however, things to show for all the effort. After ten years of wrangling over money, fighting for good teachers to stay, encouraging the disheartened, after years of building and renovating, she had held together the fabric of Lime Grove school, reduced class sizes, improved the teaching; despite an inauspicious catchment area, the school performed consistently better than its neighbours.

Perhaps she and Ron could spend Christmas in Australia with Jonathan and the grandchildren. They had been invited often enough, but Ron always claimed he was too busy, that he could not leave the garage for too long. No, she was going to insist – this year, it was to be Christmas on the beach!

Mrs Sanderson made the day's announcements; there was a final prayer, the children filed out, singing 'Shalom, shalom, until we meet again' to the honky sounds of the school piano. Then Jill, her deputy, came in, looking bleak. She insisted Connie accompany her to the office. There were two police officers, a man and a woman, waiting for her and there was bad news. About her husband. About Ron.

FIVE

STU HAD BEEN summoned.

A deep breath and Inspector Stewart Wilson walked into the grey-walled office with a wide plate-glass window. The boss. A glance upwards, the wave of a pen-clutching hand.

'Hello, Stu, take a seat.'

'Thank you, sir.' Relations were still cool between the inspector and the chief inspector, after an acquaintance that had lasted nearly two decades. You do not, Wilson reflected, choose who works with you; you just have to get on with things as best you can; avoid complaining to the wife.

With Stonecot, things had not worked well. Even after all these years, the Hilton affair still divided the two men; at the time, Wilson had been an inspector, a man headed for the heights, while Stonecot was his sergeant. All that had changed; Stonecot had been promoted until he seemed certain to become a chief superintendent, while Wilson had been moved around, given a uniform, allowed to stagnate. Buried.

Stu Wilson did, however, love the job. So he stayed, survived a stint with the traffic police, boredom interspersed with terror; waiting for the worst, waiting for stupidity or sheer bad luck to produce the carnage that became statistics. Wilson had been overjoyed to be transferred back to the CID, even if it was in an Essex force under Stonecot.

After the Hilton arrest, a commander from the Met told him: 'You'll never work for the Met again.' Wilson had laughed in the teeth of his cliché; pull the other leg, friend. Unfortunately, the cliché had proved true as clichés often do. Even so, he had clawed his way back from the dead.

'I've some news for you . . .'

Another breath. Stu could see that the chief inspector had

found a new role for him, with a little help from his friends. A change of life, the onset of gold-watch time, perhaps.

At least he had a decent pension to look forward to, after his nearly twenty-years; he was still fit, despite the stress, the long hours, the sheer difficulty of the job; indeed, his reputation was high, higher than it had ever been. Internally, that is. He was considered as sharp as anyone in the local CID, certainly he was sharper than Stonecot. This was not, it had to be admitted, always to his advantage.

Last week, the judge had praised him for his work, the prosecution team presented him with a black legal bag, the case had even made the national newspapers. The blokes had loved it; there had been a binge at the local curry shop where he ate and drank too much.

He had got away with that. His mate and second-in-command-in-crime, Sergeant Keith Peters, known by everyone as Keef, had found the taxi that had taken him home. Wheels were a Keef speciality.

'Mrs Rainsley wants to see you,' Stonecot said. 'In fact, she wants to give you a job.'

This was a bombshell. Mrs Rainsley was director general of the new, revamped and reformulated, high-tension anti-fraud unit, and every copper was entitled to be cynical about the Serious Fraud Office, given its poor record.

'Congratulations, Inspector.'

Stonecot doubtless thought he had exiled Wilson for life. 'The SFO is very keen to hear from you about the Marchwood affair.'

Wilson smiled. That, at least, was good news. He thanked Stonecot for his support and looked forward to working with him in the future.

Stonecot almost smiled, then said: 'You're a darned good copper, Wilson. But watch your back.'

After decades together, this was more than unexpected. Was Stonecot worse or better than he had thought?

Everybody had their own views about the biscuit tin, as the SFO was called. Wilson saw the resemblance at a glance. A discreet grey metal box, which might once have been used for a biscuit selection, had been placed in a London street, somewhere between Euston Station, the British Museum and the Royal Courts of Justice. Where layers of biscuits might have been, windows had been fitted, floors built, elevators installed, and Mrs Rainsley.

A QC in her late forties, the new director general had been brought in to sharpen up the SFO, which she had promptly enmeshed in two high-profile cases, involving complicated take-over battles and the obscure workings of the free market: Irwell and Wansbeck. Irwell, a widget-maker wanting to take over a mobile phone manufacturer, had paid thirty million in 'fees' to its 'friends' who bought its shares and sold those of its target, so it could be certain of completing the billion-pound deal; Wansbeck, a chemicals giant, had also used 'friends' to hide the failure of a massive rights issue after it paid over the odds for a pharmaceutical company.

Rainsley had put the City on trial.

There were mutterings that all was not well, mutterings that the cases had turned into a legal nightmare. So Wilson did not quite know what to make of the fact that he had been chosen by the DG personally.

'I've read your file, Wilson. You seem to make a thing of catching fraudsters. We need men like you around here.'

'Thank you, DG.'

'I also see from the file that the Met considered you a troublemaker . . .'

The Hilton arrest, twenty years on. They really had stitched him up. He would never forget the scene, dozens of big-wigs, judges, bankers, businessmen, policemen, arriving outside the Park Lane Hilton in their grand cars, while he and his team of five waited and watched, front and back. Finally, a Rolls arrived, their man stepped out, smelled the fresh air, stretched and walked elegantly through the foyer. Wilson watched him take the lift to the fifteenth floor restaurant. He followed moments later, with Sergeant Stonecot, in the service lift, leaving two teams of two at the lifts downstairs. They had to get it right: they did not want to be searching the Hilton late at night, knocking round broom cupboards. Finally, they saw him take his seat – and not just him, there was commissioner X, deputy chief constable Y, High Court judge Z, all since gonged, pensioned and buried. Stu Wilson, a newly married man with the best of his life still before him, had been cock-a-hoop, grinning at Stonecot amidst the bustle of cooks and waiters; and then he asked: 'You on?'

Stonecot nodded and they strolled out with a couple of waiters, arriving at table number three to nab their man, hobnobbing with the Met's finest. Their man was given five years for theft and receiving stolen goods, but returned to civvy street in three, thanks to good behaviour. Wilson's behaviour had led to him being buried, well, all but.

He did not bother repeating the story to Mrs Rainsley, who peered at him through large, round, owlish glasses and insisted: 'I expect you have matured since then.'

He had no alternative but to smile and nod.

The DG pushed a file towards him. 'You will help with Wansbeck and Irwell, but your main task is to look into this. I think you are familiar with the case.'

Wilson nodded and smiled and pretended to be charming again; opened the buff file and saw a picture of Mr Robert Marchwood, posing by an ornate fireplace like some lord of the manor, beneath a painting by Claude Monet.

A picture that had been stolen recently.

SIX

THE POLICE WERE a worry to her.

Robert had bought a dog, a German shepherd, had appointed a live-in housekeeper married to a live-in handyman and gardener, had acquired a surveillance system which dotted the house with body-heat sensors and panic buttons. The thing screeched at the drop of a hat.

So Thérèse need not fear the unknown footstep.

Above the mantelpiece, she had placed a great gilt mirror with wooden foliage and pierced scrolls, a golden-faced putto smiling down from the architrave.

So Thérèse need not miss the Monet that was no longer a Monet.

To the police, Robert had insisted: 'I'm sure it was just a cheap imitation. A daub.'

Yet she knew it was a masterpiece; a great work by a great painter; she knew he had loved the painting, too.

To her, when it had arrived, he had said: 'It reminds me of Baden-Baden, it reminds me of you.' She had even taken pictures of him beside the hearth, posing in the affected manner of a nineteenth-century nobleman. They had laughed and laughed about that, for Robert lacked affection, despite his wealth.

She had told Inspector Wilson none of this. Robert did not want her to. She was not sure she understood. Something to do with insurance.

That night, on the telephone, he had mentioned Baden-Baden. Whom had he talked to? Had he known what would happen? No, she did not believe that. He, too, had been surprised and upset.

Often, when she saw the mirror that replaced the Monet, she

remembered the Baden-Baden congress, their first days together. There had been an exhibition, devoted to paintings of Rouen cathedral. The exhibition poster still hung in her study: *Monet und die Kathedrale zu Rouen.*

After their first lunch together, Robert had seen the poster and said: 'OK, let's do it!'

She took his hand. They fairly ran to the exhibition hall in the Kurpark, she had to phone and switch translation duty from that afternoon. Robert was waiting with tickets and catalogues, having somehow circumvented the queue.

On display was one of the classic impressionist series, the same Gothic façade painted from the same room, the same window in different light, in very different colours: blue-purple, orange, red-brown, crimson, blue-grey, turquoise. There were no crisp outlines, the form of the building was revealed by contrasting colours, implying sunlight, implying mist, the onset of dusk.

Robert said the paintings were beautiful, their colours almost too gorgeous, but he was baffled by the repetition.

Perhaps, he said, Monet knew he had a winning formula – this was industrial production, taking advantage of the market! She laughed. But he was suspicious that everybody claimed to be wild about the pictures, that people fell over themselves to buy them; he said it was just fashionable.

But he asked: 'Do you really love the pictures?'

'Yes,' she said, and meant it.

After an hour or so wandering round, admiring, they withdrew, as everybody did, to the modern café whose plate-glass windows overlooked the willows and gravel paths of the Kurpark. Robert had a cup of tea, refused all cakes (Thérèse never feared a slice of Black Forest gateau) and started a mock polemic, joking about Rouen Cathdral in blue and purple, in orange and yellow, in red and pink, in white-grey and black, Rouen Cathedral in a snowstorm of paint.

In the catalogue, she found an explanation of sorts: the cathedral had a stone reality that was contrasted with the insubstantial, infinitely changeable light – without which, there could be no perception.

This did not satisfy him either, but no matter. He wanted to see her that evening, even though he had an important meeting.

'We'll eat afterwards,' Marchwood determined, then added

33

gallantly: 'You are a delightful lady and I would be very grateful if you would care to join me.'

She hesitated. He was attentive, he listened. She did not, however, know if she liked him – this was a man whose work was money, whose life was money. Her life was different; she was frightened of being bored.

'Do you not want to play roulette?' She tried to deflect his interest. Baden-Baden had a casino.

'I don't gamble,' he said, 'not really.'

'What does that mean?'

'Playing the casino is for people with more money than sense. In the long run, you're bound to lose.'

She agreed. She suggested they eat at the pizzeria; she would pay. He nodded. A simple meal could make him happy, she liked that.

'Good meeting?' she asked, when he appeared at the restaurant that evening, obviously drained.

'Tough, very tough. In fact, we had something of a row. At least I'm not late and at least we have a deal.'

'Do you want to talk about it?'

He shook his head, and they ordered some middling-to-awful wine. Surrounded by potted plants and extravagant Chianti bottles, they ordered too much food, drank too much, laughed too loudly.

Then it was bedtime. He made sure she was impressed.

He slipped away early from the conference. Perhaps that meeting had blown everything for him. Certainly, the conference did not matter to him. She did not even know who he was. Chairman of Knowle & Co – what did that mean?

She was glad she did not have to know more.

Two weeks later, one Friday evening in Zurich, he knocked on her door. 'I was passing by.' People just don't do that sort of thing, not in Switzerland. She had arranged a dinner party where everyone was speaking German; she was sorry, nervous and embarrassed; he nodded, gave her a package, smiled and went away.

She did not open the package until they had all gone and the dishwasher was humming.

In the package was a Monet sketch, bought from the Galerie Beyeler in Basel. A sketch of Rouen. A copy, of course. Yet, when she looked closely, she was not so sure.

She rang his hotel the following morning. He was gone. Later there was a letter for her, handwritten on the notepaper of the 'West Europa Bank/Banque de l'Europe Occidentale'. He had enclosed a return plane ticket, first class, to London, departing next weekend. 'I would love you to come.' She hesitated, caught the plane, and soon she was flying twice a month to London.

Of course, she knew he was thinking of marriage; of course, she knew he was a rich man, and her life would be radically changed. She liked her independence, enjoyed her career, loved Zurich.

Nevertheless, she was surprised when he proposed to her. They were talking, just chatting, in the car; he described his first marriage, its excesses, its inadequacies, its infelicities – which were no better and no worse than any marriage, anywhere.

'I think it fell apart because of my son.'

Then he told her about Rowan, whose mind had been scrambled in a sailing accident. He had failed; he had not been able to cope; instead, he had run away from grief.

'If we should . . .' He stopped himself, shook his head. 'Look, what I am trying to tell you is that we have had a wonderful time together, that you are a beautiful, intelligent, kind woman . . .'

The sentence ended with a question: would she? He did not, however, want children.

She almost giggled. Until this juncture, he had handled every occasion with skill; now, at the critical moment, he was less in control. She said she was most flattered that he should ask; she did not know the answer; she did not aspire to be a mother, not at her age. Even if her answer was negative, she was grateful for the time they had spent together.

She returned to Zurich, to her job and to her perfect, but small flat with lakeside views. A month later, she said yes.

Her father did not like the idea, when she told him. There were scenes in the kitchen of the chalet, their family home, father shouting at daughter. What did anyone want so much money for? He had had a good life with nothing! Thérèse exploded. She was nearly forty now, and could do what she wanted! This was the man she had fallen in love with! Her father wagged an irate finger: 'C'est plutôt de la rage!'

More like rabies than love!

Of this, Robert was not aware.

Throughout the arguments, discussions and welter of bad feeling, her mother had been a great support. A brick, as the English say, ever willing to trust houses. Maman had accepted her daughter's choice, wishing only that she might have chosen earlier, with more chance of grandchildren – she already had six. So the priest was told and persuaded, the Church was more than persuaded and, finally, it all happened.

When they returned from their honeymoon in the Bahamas, Robert said: 'I've a little something for you. A present.'

Golden Rain now boasted a new picture in the dining room: a Monet, a landscape called the Vallée de la Creuse. She was astonished. The picture was stunning; a triangle of bright water burning its way through dark, somnolent hills. It contained a force, a presence beyond words.

She did not know what to say. Why had he bought it? How had he bought it? It must be worth millions. Where had he obtained the picture – they did not, after all, grow on trees? Had he bought it through work? Was there a deal?

He left her questions unanswered.

'It's a present. For you and for me. A memento of our time in Baden-Baden, a perfect start to a perfect relationship.'

Now there was a policeman who dropped round, asking questions. She knew what she had to say. She told Wilson: 'As far as I know, the painting is just a daub, nothing, not a Monet; that is the truth.'

Inspector Wilson never hid his disbelief but always thanked her when he left.

SEVEN

IT WAS SIMPLY a nightmare.

The new job in the SFO was more difficult, the change of scene more painful, than Stu Wilson had ever imagined.

Weeks drifted by. Stu became more and more frustrated, because nothing happened or nothing was allowed to happen. Or so it seemed. He had exchanged a busy police station for an air-conditioned tin box where everything was just slightly askew. A nightmare.

Because he could not blame somebody, a person, he blamed the place. It was being re-organised. People were being moved on, sacked or retired, new people with new ideas and new furniture moved in.

Stu was a new person, with a new desk. He ought to have been happy. He was, however, wise enough to see that pretty soon he too would become an old person with an old desk.

Unfortunately, everybody was trying to stop him doing his work. There was no shortage of daft jobs, the two cases where he served as bag-carrier: Irwell and Wansbeck. Apart from watching the mess grow, he obeyed several masters. None of them cared about stolen Monets.

Mrs Rainsley had assigned him mainly to the tender mercies of Inspector Derek Tomlinson, head of the Wansbeck investigation; but there were plenty of others ready to have him check statements, documents and prepare lawyers' files for court. Lots of files.

This was not Stu's idea of fun.

Millions were being spent on the two top-drawer cases, largely on lawyers and accountants. A new courtroom, complete with television screens, had been constructed for Wansbeck, ensuring some good would come out of the affair: the first trial with in-court entertainment. Stu could see half the guys did not understand the case. Convincing a jury promised to be exciting.

Stu wanted to avoid the mire, but Rainsley seemed to have other ideas; she pointed him back to Tomlinson. Anything Stu could do about the Monet had virtually been blocked.

He moaned to Tomlinson, a square, testy man, who merely shrugged his shoulders and put more nonsense in his in-tray. Between them, between Rainsley and Tomlinson, he was being strangled. He complained to Rosie, who told him to stop treating his job as his life and asked him to work less; so he went to the chess club during the week, pushing wood more often than normal. Unlike some coppers, Stu did not solve his frustrations with drink. Finally, he booked an appointment with the DG, to complain. He knew it was a risk, but life, as he liked to say, had deadly consequences.

People got wind of the meeting; Tomlinson summoned Stu to his office, gave him a funny look. 'Dare I ask you, Stewart, what you intend to say to the DG?'

For once, Stu saw the minefield. He was polite, bland, almost friendly and said nothing. He had his reasons for seeing Mrs Rainsley, muttered something about the Revenue.

In fact, this was true, as far as it went. He needed to hold the Inland Revenue at bay. He knew they were screaming to get at Marchwood. Free Monets – otherwise known as 'gifts in kind (worth millions)' – were not allowable under any rules known to Her Majesty's Revenue Service.

Mrs Rainsley agreed to help; she rang the head of the Revenue, in Wilson's presence, obtained his consent and promised a covering letter.

'Inspector Wilson,' she said. 'That's settled. Now I want you to find out what this picture means for Lloyd's. If millions of pounds are being paid as bribes, it means there's something very large to find. You have a month.'

Wilson threw himself into work. It had been a professional theft. A bit brutal. The thieves had worn gloves and masks; according to Mrs Marchwood, one was taller than the other, both were taller than her. Thanks, dear.

Forensics had found no prints, nothing around the mantel-piece, nothing on the cellar skylight; gloves, gloves, gloves. Cigarettes had been found in the woods to the west of the front lawn, but they could have belonged to anyone who did not wear lipstick. The thieves had probably taken the picture, wrapped, over the fields behind the house to a car waiting in some side road. Nobody had seen anything, no footprints. There was, on that side of the house, nobody to see anything. Squirrels and horses. They had had hours and hours to get away; Mrs Marchwood had been found by neighbours, who had called the police. It was probably a contract – a theft to order. Somebody rich had wanted the picture.

Wilson felt everything pointed to someone close to Lloyd's; this was the world of the Marchwoods. They entertained a great deal; hundreds of people must have seen the painting, must have seen the old-fashioned security system.

Interviewing the Marchwoods had been more frustrating than profitable. It did, however, confirm Stu's suspicions. Mr Marchwood insisted he had not acquired a Monet. It had been a gift, a private matter. It was not insured. 'It was not signed. To me, it looked an unimpressive daub.'

'Which you hung over the mantelpiece.'

'My wife admired the picture.'

A Monet, which everybody knew was a Monet, suddenly became a canvas with paint splodges. Mrs Marchwood claimed that she was confused, that she had thought this, then that, that she really, really did not know. She showed Wilson a photograph, which he accepted gratefully, which went into the green buff file, which he locked in his left hand office drawer, one evening before disappearing for a chess match.

The following day, the file was gone.

He rifled through every drawer, through every file, through his briefcase, just to see that there was no mistake. There was no mistake.

He made himself a cup of tea using the kettle at the end of the investigations room. Steadied himself. Until that moment, he had felt, well, unloved, ill-at-ease in a strange office; now, at least, he knew that he could afford to trust nobody.

He made a few quick-fire phone calls; within an hour, he was drinking another cup of tea, with Mrs Marchwood. Unless he was successful, here and now, he could forget everything.

He repeated the obvious questions, the ones he had discussed, again and again, with the lady and the lady's husband. Now Thérèse Marchwood was alone.

He asked: 'Who gave you the picture?'

'Business friends of my husband, I believe.'

'You believe?'

'That is what Robert said. You have heard him say so yourself. The picture was something and nothing, a little gesture from someone.'

'From whom?'

'Business friends from Lloyd's, I suppose.'

'I suppose so.'

'If you are finished with your questions, Inspector . . . ?'

Stu Wilson sipped tea, admired the antique-studded living room, then played his trusty gambit: 'Don't you find it odd to be married to an Englishman?'

She shrugged her fine shoulders. She was a very fine woman. Exquisite was the word that sprang to his mind.

'Where do you come from?' He could almost hear her sigh, but he had time to kill.

'I was born in the Jura and worked for many years in Zurich. I consider myself to be European.'

He looked at the fine clock on the fine mantelpiece: ten minutes to twelve. The call was due at noon. He found her remarkably sweet-tempered, and was sorry to put her through this.

He plied her with silly questions: did she prefer London to Zurich, what were the differences? The English countryside to the Alps? No, he had never seen the Alps. He lingered. Did she have pictures?

'I suppose I will have to complete your education, Inspector.' She rose, went to a drawer in a wall cabinet, and produced some photographs.

'Scenes from the continent of Europe,' she murmured, with more than a hint of impatience. She showed him a picture of the Jura valley, where she came from; this was the valley of the Engadine, where she went skiing. . .

The telephone rang. He excused her, and she went into the hall; it sounded like a discussion with an insurance salesman. Stu had no time to grin, he rifled through the drawer, through the packets of photographs marked: 'Golden Rain'.

When she returned he was standing by the window.

He apologised for taking so much of her time. She had been charming and he looked forward to visiting Zurich, some day. She smiled: 'Zurich is a special place.'

40

No sooner was he inside his car than Keef was on the telephone from the Essex station. 'How did it go, Stu?'

'Fine.'

'I had the dame eating out of my hand. She was just dying for a new life policy.'

Stu Wilson told him not to boast: 'See you soon.'

He stopped at a motorway service station, took a deep breath and pulled his prize from his breast pocket. Flipped open the packet. Yes, lots of lovely pictures.

Back at the Essex station, Sergeant Keith Peters, helping out unofficially, was his usual restrained self: 'Let's see what we can do, Chief. Let's see what we can do.'

The prints were distributed within days, to all ports and airports. Someone, somewhere must have seen the Monet. It was not something one could forget.

EIGHT

IN THE MIDDLE of a dinner party, Donna Grote was called away to the telephone. A transatlantic call from Sotheby's in New York. Stephen Grote looked across the table at the Lemkes, at Mary-Ellen, Donna's sister, and Marshall D. Lemke, her husband. He apologised on Donna's behalf.

Marshall was a lawyer who had worked at the American Embassy for years; he was rather too forthright for Grote's taste. Mary-Ellen, a decided woman in her fifties, did not stand on ceremony, either. Not Grote's type, not quite.

Relations between the Grotes and the Lemkes were fraught. It was as if a late marriage could have no meaning. Of course, she had told her sister things, that the physical thing did not matter. In many respects, it was better than being young, surrounded by nappies, woken by crying babies. The Lemkes refused to be convinced.

This dinner at Stephen's Mayfair home was another sacrifice, another attempt to keep things afloat among the Chippendale furniture, silver candelabra and antique vases placed in antique niches.

'They've sold the Van Gogh, the Doctor Gachet, for sixty-eight million dollars,' Donna gushed, when she appeared. The sale would ensure the success of Sotheby's summer season, which was just starting.

'Impressionists must be the best investment around. They just keep on going up and up,' Marshall said, then added, looking at Stephen: 'They're just about the only thing you don't have, I'd say.'

The brothers-in-law contemplated each other.

'Darling,' Mary-Ellen said. 'Stephen hasn't missed out on impressionists. He just doesn't collect them.'

Stephen smiled and Donna seized the opportunity to move everybody back to the living room for liqueurs and coffee. With a brandy in his thick-fingered hand, Marshall changed tack, talking about world trade and the City. At the Embassy, he had argued for decades over the fine print of world trade agreements, particularly the banking clauses; yet he was also the CIA's banking expert in London. He never spoke openly about this task.

Even Donna, who really liked him, thought Marshall had been boorish over dinner. Perhaps he had been drinking before driving over. Certainly, he seemed more excited than usual. Above all, she felt, he was unjust – if a major piece or collection was destined for auction, Mr Stephen Grote, chairman of Lloyd's, was always among the few to be invited to a private viewing. He was a true connoisseur.

It was one of the great disappointments of Stephen's life that he had failed to re-purchase the family estates at Hanbury, when they became available in the 80s, because of his financial disaster à la Marchwood, which had cost him millions. Hanbury would have enabled the collection to become both extensive and well-displayed. Instead, the five floors of the Mayfair house were full to over-brimming; there was almost too much to admire in the space available.

It was a Kent display cabinet that had first brought Donna here. A week after meeting Stephen at a private showing, Donna had paid him a visit, to show him an exceptional William Kent cabinet, with mirror-interior and gilt ornamentation. The reaction was instinctive. 'Ah, a Kent'. He named a sum, larger than Donna had any right to expect at auction; she rang the vendor, there and then, and the deal was struck. Bond Street was suitably pleased. From then on, the contacts had become more frequent, he invited her to dinner parties with Lloyd's friends and colleagues, showed her his patrician Zurich house, on the north side of the lake.

One evening, after a visit to a Covent Garden *Don Giovanni*, his behaviour had been, well, unusual and abrupt. The following day, he begged to see her, despite her busy schedule, appeared with a bouquet of carnations, fell on his knees and asked for her hand in marriage. She accepted gratefully and now the Kent cabinet which contained some of the Grote watch collection was part of her own household.

43

Marshall had remained unimpressed with the love match. Mary-Ellen was altogether more pleased when she heard the news: Donna was to marry the chairman of Lloyd's! Her family, the Warrilows of Ohio, was entering a sanctuary of high Englishness! Mary-Ellen had, for many years, been a member of Lloyd's, a name. A few years back, Marshall had joined. And they had just discovered that the Vice-President of the United States of America was a name. So it was mighty chic for all Republicans to love the Brits.

Marshall had only discovered that the Vice-President was involved in Lloyd's when Washington started to worry. Washington did not like the idea of unlimited liability, that a future president might be bankrupted. So Washington officials had been talking to him about getting some purchase on Lloyd's, possibly doing a deal to extricate the Vice-President.

Marshall had examined the relevant files, which gave off an unpleasant odour, and seen the problem, one which could become his own. Now he looked at the mirrored cabinet, took a large swig of fine cognac and turned to Stephen: 'Why don't you get Mary-Ellen on the Lloyd's steering committee? Our guys have long wanted representation and Mary-Ellen is among the slickest operators I know.'

'And that's the truth,' Donna commented; Mary-Ellen was joint head of their family trust. This might be the long-desired solution to their in-law problem. She caught Stephen's eye and he acquiesced gracefully.

'I'm sure that Mary-Ellen would be just the right person for the task. I'll see what I can do.'

Donna rewarded Stephen with a kiss. This was, however, the sort of lukewarm, watery answer that unfuriated Marshall, even when Stephen was saying what he wanted to hear.

NINE

KEVIN VAUGHAN DID not know why he had agreed to this; he must have been out of his mind; but Uncle Stu had talked to Aunt Rosie who had talked to his mum, who had insisted, not for the first time, that blood was thicker than water, that family was family. So Kev had agreed, but only because he respected his Uncle Stu, even if he was a policeman.

So here Kevin was, wearing his latest work clothes, pinstripes, black loafers and wide lapels, admiring the home of the Essex Knights Chess Club.

This was a concrete pre-fab with windows, chairs and desks, which stood beside the bowling green and the rose garden. Charming. There was a group of middle-aged blokes who stood around while some lads played chess raucously, hammering a double-faced clock. Kev wanted to be elsewhere.

He knew he was breaking the rules by being here.

Once the Blighter had pointed to the opaque glass walls of the underwriting room and proclaimed, touching his nose with his forefinger: 'These walls would not dare to talk to outsiders, young fellow. When you leave this room you keep your mouth shut, your eyes closed, your mind pure, old son.'

After watching the Blighter for a couple of years, he knew Lloyd's was not finger-licking clean, but neither was the kitchen table. He had to eat.

He was tired, though. Perhaps that was why he had relented. He hated to admit it, but he was well and truly drained. That very evening, he should have been at head office, installing the new machine. A month ago, Tony MacNulty of Wordsworth had called him in from the box, waved a pipe in his direction and asked if he would like to work for head office on the new computer.

45

This was a big break. Situated in an alleyway near Lime Street, Wordsworth desperately needed a new machine to control and process everything in one centrally organised system; the existing system simply did not work. So this was a golden opportunity; he would work alongside the finance director and MacNulty.

Inside Lloyd's, MacNulty was a top-notch man, an Olympian. He had turned his firm, Wordsworth, into a leading Lloyd's agency, and had become the market's best-paid man. That was Kevin's ultimate goal: the board of Wordsworth and a six- or seven-figure income.

Unfortunately, even though the new computer, leased for two hundred thousand a year, would improve the Blighter's paperwork beyond all recognition, the Blighter had only let Kevin leave the underwriting box under protest. But MacNulty, the boss, had the final word and the dream of a smart new flat in Docklands, near the City, moved closer.

Lloyd's of London was a different world to the one inhabited by his mum, his uncle and Essex Knights CC. Kevin looked at the chess players and was almost shocked to see so many hard luck stories. Just then, his uncle arrived. Stu looked elegant, immaculate, in an old-fashioned way. You could tell he had been in the navy, he never slouched.

'This your club, then, Stu?' Kevin asked.

'It's a good place to meet. Fancy a tea?'

'No, thanks.'

Stu directed Kevin over to a table with set, board and clock. 'Still know how to play? The worst thing that can happen is you might lose!'

Stu set up the pieces, allowing Kevin white. A variant of the Queen's Gambit Accepted developed on the black and white board between them.

To justify his fascination, Stu explained how the game had taught him patience, to observe others turn their intentions into action; it helped him through his wild twenties, when the sight of a harbour on the Pacific rim meant more than just a decent meal. It taught him calm.

'Nowadays I play once a week here. And at weekends for the Essex team. Keeps me sane and out of Rosie's hair.'

Fair enough. Kevin nodded, rubbed a snub-nose, and con-templated the havoc set to engulf his position.

'What do you think of Lloyd's?'

'I think I shouldn't be here.'

'Doesn't surprise me. This is a good place to meet.'

At this, Kevin contemplated the Essex Knights, a horde of middle-aged addicts. He said: 'What do you want to know?'

'Have you heard that Robert Marchwood had a Monet?'

'The Monet?' Kevin grinned. 'Sure, Marchwood had one; for a time there were jokes doing the rounds in the market: Marchwood has Monet to burn.'

Wilson winced. Despite discreet enquiries at Lloyd's, nobody had mentioned this. He was frustrated: 'Nobody at Lloyd's will tell me anything.'

'The only market in the world where the insiders know everything and the outsiders nothing,' Kevin said, borrowing a favourite Blighter expression.

'What does that mean?'

'Well, look at Grote. He's supposed to police the market, ensure everything is fair-play and jolly hockey-sticks, but has a huge slice of the action himself. Just think of the temptation . . . and that's true of all the big guys: MacNulty, Devies, Stone, Wilmot-Greaves . . .'

'And Robert Marchwood?'

'He's different. So is Ray. They're not on the ruling committee, for one thing. For another, the Marchwoods and the rest are at each other's throats.'

'Why?'

Kevin shrugged his shoulders, stared glumly at an impaled king and resigned: 'Another game?'

'Sure. Do you think the Grote gang had reason to give Robert Marchwood a nice impressionist masterpiece for his fireplace?'

Stu received no answer. He talked in a patient whisper about the future, insisted that Kevin should take care: 'Just find out what you can. This looks like a massive fraud to me. Given the money involved, they will be dangerous.'

His nephew pushed a shock of blond hair from his forehead, rubbed his nose again and saw that Stu was not joking. So they agreed lines of communication and other madness.

'I don't know why I am doing this, Stu.'

Stu smiled. 'Don't ever ring me at work,' he said. 'Or if you absolutely must, call yourself Danny, Danny Shuttleworth.'

Kev finally broke into a broad grin, then stared at the

chessboard, and was not surprised to see his wild sacrificial play had been refuted. He wanted to leave, sharpish.

He commented: 'I think you've a bloody nerve.'

Stu smiled. Sure. The next day Stu left early for the Isle of Wight. It was, of course, his day off. Because of a lead, a good lead, he was sacrificing a day at the chessboard. But since some kind person at the SFO had raped his Monet file, it seemed almost normal to work on his day off. Whatever happened, he was not to lose this game.

In the Solent, the mist would not lift, and solitary yachts, the regular ferries and hovercraft, occasional geese flying, drifted in and out of grey silence.

He had not been followed. He drove to Ventnor, a small Victorian enclave perched on a cliff above a beach and promenade. He parked and entered a white promenade café with formica tables and red plastic chairs, waited.

'Sounds like World War Three, next door.'

Stu Wilson stood and shook hands with Jim Welsby, a senior customs and excise man; a tall, robust figure. They were the only people in the café; next door, they could hear the high-tech scream of the amusement arcade. There was an undeniable out-of-season emptiness.

'My cousin's place,' Welsby said, with an apologetic grin, gesturing past the till. There was a figure in the back room. They climbed dark stairs, until they were in a room overlooking the sea, the boat-dotted strand and the sad remnants of a Victorian pier.

'You took care . . . coming here?'

Stu nodded.

'This is a small island. Among boating people, everybody knows everybody and you can't move for people from Lloyd's. They insure everything, of course. And there's the certificates, too.'

Lloyd's issued certificates proving boats' seaworthiness and value; the sea was very much Lloyd's business.

Welsby hesitated, looked out of the window.

Stu waited. He had just issued the photograph of the Monet, nothing else. No other information.

The sea was grey, the sky was grey, no horizon.

'Drugs is our game, you see, not art,' Welsby observed. 'Mostly boredom, unless you like messing about in boats. A bit of terror, every so often. The sea.'

Stu stayed silent.

'Well, the boss and me's out in one of the motor launches, just to be out of Cowes, you know. Then we see MacNulty's boat, one of his boats, actually, anchored west of here. We stop for a drink, like, nothing special. John Devies is on deck and he and the boss are thicker than thieves . . .'

'Devies is chairman of the Royal Yacht Club?'

Welsby nodded. 'MacNulty his deputy. My boss runs the whole excise operation. So when he barged in, they couldn't really afford to stop him.'

'What was the boat?' Stu was taking notes.

'It was MacNulty's ketch, an ocean-going affair, all the modern gadgets, radar and more radar. Not really sailing, I'd say . . . So then we're standing in the stateroom and I sees this picture, like.'

Welsby produced the blown-up photograph, which had been torn into eight pieces and reassembled with tape.

'You're sure?'

'I thought it was good at the time. I gives the picture a real good look. It's not the sort of thing you find on a ketch, even a fancy one.'

'Did anyone say anything?'

Welsby hesitated: 'Tony says, his uncle done it. And the boss treats that as a joke.'

'When was this?'

'Twentieth of May last year. I checked in our logbooks; there was nothing happening about the time, so in it went. They were on their way back from France. There was three of them: MacNulty and Devies and another bloke.'

'You weren't introduced?'

'Not proper. It was all a big joke.'

Stu listened, carefully, intently. He would need more photographs to identify the third gentleman. Then Welsby, who had seen police duty, stated: 'I'll only give you an affidavit if you really need it.'

'I need it now. No, yesterday.'

Welsby snorted, then said: 'I don't know if you understand. I found the photograph by chance. In the boss's waste-bin. He must have remembered too.'

Stu looked at the table. Welsby had carefully taped the pieces of torn photograph together. They did not lock like jigsaw pieces, but offered a collection of bits.

He shook hands and left.

Kev was the first to read Stu's report, which showed that MacNulty, Devies and a third man had smuggled a Monet into the country.

Finally, Kevin said, 'The picture could be a pay-off for so many things . . .'

'Yes.'

'Billions of pounds flow through Lloyd's every year, billions in premiums, billions in claims, billions are invested short-term or re-insured elsewhere. You only need to tweak the system just a little, here and there . . .'

The second to hear was the DG. She smiled ever so sweetly and said: 'Lovely, Wilson. This will turn rough.'

BOOK TWO

ONE

IT WAS A dry, breezy night; thin, low clouds, turned copper-amber by street lights, sped across the October sky.

In the City of London, a chauffeur-driven Rolls-Royce halted by the Royal Exchange; a man wearing a mackintosh descended and entered an empty passage that would be thronged with futures traders during the day, strode past the statue of John Julius Reuter, founder of the news empire; then he crossed a silent road, extending his step as he followed the curtain-wall of the Bank of England, glanced around before turning into Throgmorton Street, where he disappeared inside a narrow passage through a wrought-iron gate.

The man was nobody, going nowhere, seen by no one.

A swipe with a security card let him proceed. A narrow staircase, lit white from neon strip-lights, rose steeply to a bare corridor, here, there was an unusual door, a camera, a card-reader and code-pad. Another swipe, then Stephen Grote entered a five figure code. The door opened.

Inside, another white-walled corridor, a shift-system clock and cards.

This was the small services division (cleaning, storage, security) operated by Horcum, the British insurance broker headed by John Devies, the deputy chairman of Lloyd's, famed for his silver-knobbed canes. From the street, the offices seemed old-fashioned, cheap, and because they were deemed necessary by the chairman, backed, as always, by his managing director, nobody dared question their right to exist. Their budget was, however, much higher than any audited figures indicated; a cleaner here could apparently earn, thanks to overtime, as much as a good broker. Of course, few cleaners elsewhere have degrees in electronics and computer science.

Even at this hour, the sparse office hummed.

Only in the room at the end of the corridor was there some semblance of luxury: a large dining table, leather seats. There were boards, drawings, jottings on the wall, no pictures.

Stephen Grote was only slightly late that Thursday evening, yet every close friend, apart from Tony MacNulty, was there: John Devies, Neil Fortescue, Henry Stone, Alexander Wilmot-Greaves.

Greetings.

John Devies, who always chaired these meetings, tapped the floor with his cane; it was late and he was eager to consider reports from surveillance and from finance; and Tony MacNulty figured also on the agenda.

Neil Fortescue stroked back his red hair and lit a cigarette; first he wanted a word about fun and games.

'In recognition of my services to the American insurance industry . . .' he began, and everyone smiled, 'I have been given a Lear jet for business and personal use. I hope to make a maiden journey with some friends this weekend, unless Stephen has any objections. I'm looking for suggestions.'

Unlike the others, Fortescue did not own or have a large stake in a Lloyd's business, but being a director of a major American corporation provided perks the others could not quite afford.

Suddenly, everybody had a suggestion to make. Gstaad, the South of France, Lago Maggiore . . . The English weather had been notably grey recently. The choice was clear: John Devies had a palace down on the Cap d'Antibes, they could free up Saturday and Sunday for a quiet trip, to enjoy the late sun.

'Tony will have to be asked. In case he is available,' Devies said. 'And if so – who he would like to show the Med.'

Recently, despite his marriage, Tony had developed a deep and meaningful and unique attachment to a very special young woman. Called Susan. Just like the one before last. This was, however, not the nub of the problem. The reason for their doubts was that Tony was becoming too attached to the bottle and everyone knew that he and Robert Marchwood were close.

'There's a new fellow in the Blighter's box,' Alex Wilmot-Greaves wondered, removing his heavy, horn-rimmed glasses. 'Now, what's the young man's name? Anyway, Ray Marchwood got him the job, with Tony's help and approval.'

'That proves nothing; it's not a hanging offence to do a favour,' Stone said crisply.

Stephen said: 'Nobody is suggesting that it is; we all like and admire Tony, but we dare not let him become unsound.'

Alec agreed: 'Perhaps half of Tony's profits derive from Marchwood. He has enjoyed an unblemished service.'

There was a silence while all watched Fortescue carefully extinguish his cigarette.

Friendship, they all knew, had its obligations as well as its rewards. Claudio Scrivano was the most recent friend to prove unreliable.

It was agreed Tony would be watched and that his relationship with Marchwood was a problem. Alec Wilmot-Greaves immediately rang the Blighter, one of their friends from the Lutine lodge, on his mobile phone; the Blighter was at a Guildhall dinner and would see Alec at the Savoy, later.

To prove that a fondness for a good bottle was not a sin, John Devies toasted Tony; the second wine from Latour that he had brought succeeded in cheering the party. Heathcote had a good store of claret in its cleaning division.

Fortescue lit another cigarette and worried about the record level of the stockmarket: 'Either I'm mad or everybody else. Do you think it's time to sell?'

'Things have run ahead of themselves,' Wilmot-Greaves grinned, sipping his wine.

Stephen Grote smiled. They had learned their lesson.

Some fifteen years ago, they nearly met with disaster. It was a time when everything had become excessive, even by Lloyd's standards. The Revenue was very curious, their accountants were groaning, money was turning up here, there and everywhere. Everyone could see fortunes were being made and spent, which nobody could explain.

Dickens, Andrew & Pont had been the final straw. DA&P was a Lloyd's agency run by two friends, Andrew and Pont who were among the best brains in Lloyd's. They had not been content to oversee the agency, to make good money. Instead, they plundered the company as if it were a private gold mine; insurance money was sent overseas, to Monte Carlo, Gibraltar, Bermuda and Grand Cayman, to brass-plate companies which they surreptitiously owned. The money mounted up hidden in offshore accounts, and within four or five years the duo stole forty, fifty million pounds, quite an achievement; this was the 70s, a time when not every Tom, Dick and Harry was a millionaire. At a time when Grote was not yet chairman.

It was inevitable that the money would be missed, yet the duo were unusually greedy, clever and stupid. They expected the yawning cavern to remain undiscovered. They were wrong.

Lloyd's spent the 70s cleaning up the mess, limiting the damage, dealing with politicians and police. Stephen Grote told his friends: Another DA&P and they would be finished. No more excesses. It was Alec Wilmot-Greaves who brought the matter to a head, who tried Grote's patience so sorely that his famous calm and equanimity turned to fire and brimstone. Wilmot-Greaves allowed a helicopter to fly him round the Alps, even had it wait for him in the air while he sunbathed in the penthouse suite at the Gstaad Palace, near to Grote's own Alpine retreat.

This was DA&P style, this was too much. Stephen Grote drove over and strode into the Palace as if he owned the whole, improbable place and bawled Alec out in front of the staff: 'Get that chopper out of the sky, move your head from the clouds and your rear from here. I'll see you in London! Otherwise, you're finished.'

A showdown ensued the following week, here, in this room in the heart of the City; Grote sacked pilots, sold planes and boats. Other tempers glowed, some egos were very sore, but people fell into line. From then on, there were simple laws to be obeyed, Grote's laws: discretion, simplicity, order, control.

The force of Grote's anger, because it was so unexpected, had impressed; his rationale was accepted: ever greater wealth beckoned. And to avoid another DA&P, everyone had to watch everyone else.

John Devies opened another bottle then summarised the latest news from services division, the clean-up of Cristòforo. The bad news was, as ever, left till last: 'Despite our little warning in the spring, hardly six months ago, despite our repeated hints that collection and surveillance were not on . . .' Devies paused, gathered breath. 'We believe Ray is storing and collating data about DA&P. It is possible he has obtained records from the US, details of bank accounts, money transfers.'

There was a silence.

So DA&P could again become a major problem. It was part of a past they wanted buried and forgotten. They wanted, too, to end the feuding with Marchwood.

Wilmot-Greaves pushed back his heavy glasses, incredulous: 'I really do think that Robert Marchwood has learned his lesson. Nobody likes to lose a Monet . . .'

Stone, the most injured party, was irritated: 'Do you *know* that Ray has records? The French and the Italians are actively forgetting the Cristòforo. So much has been eradicated . . .' He drew back his black hair, frustrated at the aggravation.

'We have to be sure,' Fortescue nodded to Devies. 'The Christòforo is still so sensitive, especially because of the links with DA&P. And if anybody worked out the truth about Scrivano . . .' He looked at Wilmot-Greaves and Stone, who avoided his gaze.

Their past could not be extricated from their present. Each one of them had a history recorded in slips, fiches, in money transfers and contracts, held in banks, lawyers' offices and Lloyd's, that were not theirs to burn.

Every past is blemished, yet history at Lloyd's tends to be more remorseless than elsewhere. Contracts signed twenty, thirty years ago were returning to haunt syndicates; this was happening with asbestosis and other pollution claims. Billions were being lost, as a result. By the same token, misdemeanours could return to haunt them.

If need be, they could have Ray Marchwood stopped, but this was the last option, the final resort.

'The police files on DA&P were as clean as possible, but someone has investigated them,' Devies said. 'That need not matter. Since Ray tried to break into the Horcum computer we've moved the information to Tony at Wordsworth. The bulk is hidden among the data in the Lloyd's computer store.'

Fortescue exhaled smoke: 'Can this be a problem? The computer store is well-guarded and the data is spread very thinly among the records of all syndicates.'

'Ray could do it,' Stone insisted; he had seen some of Ray Marchwood's work from archive material, then added, with a wry smile: 'I do hope Tony keeps on top of this, now.'

'Tony will be told,' Alec Wilmot-Greaves promised. 'So that he understands. And Ray should be warned, again.'

Grote looked over his half-moon glasses at the faces round the table: 'I think that's no longer enough. John and I have already authorised unofficial action against Knowle. Two of our fellows are going in tonight. We simply have to see just what the

Marchwoods are up to.' This was a high risk move. Neither Stone nor Wilmot-Greaves was happy. Yet Grote insisted. 'We warned them barely six months ago; we took tough action, repossessed the Monet; now we half-sense another problem, but we have to know. It is time, also, to look at the Marchwoods' relationship with MacNulty. Any betrayal strikes at the heart of our interests.'

'Sure,' Fortescue agreed, ever the hawk.

Wilmot-Greaves was contemplating his spectacles; he said: 'Tomorrow, on Friday, we have an opportunity to act officially, to underline our position. Robert Marchwood will meet the Lloyd's committee. I see no need for more action.'

'We simply have to know, to be sure,' Devies insisted. Grote nodded, waiting, watching Wilmot-Greaves, who finally shrugged his shoulders. Then the others assented.

Devies moved on. He had a file in his hands, stamped: Serious Fraud Office. He opened it, to applause and laughter. A photograph purloined by an SFO friend.

Yes, our Inspector Wilson seemed to be having a little difficulty with his investigation. A case of the vanishing photograph of the vanishing Monet.

Fortescue remarked, jauntily: 'Friends at the Met say the name Wilson should ring a bell: it was he who pulled off the Hilton raid.'

Stephen Grote looked at Devies. Neither of them had forgotten that particular occasion.

TWO

IT COULD NOT be long before a tree near the house succumbed.

The wind was whipping horse-chestnut, aspen and beech, oak and laburnum. In the woods and copses belonging to Golden Rain the trees stood their ground. Yet the storm had started to stampede the bushes and shrubs, to give branch and leaf a brief freedom, visiting violence upon the world.

Robert Marchwood stirred in bed, to find his wife almost frantic. 'The wind is slaughtering trees,' she said.

Despite tiredness, Robert smiled. The break-in had been a shock, she had not recovered, even though six months had passed; he understood.

After she had spoken, they did not sleep, listening to the roar of the wind. She slipped closer under the duvet, her small body shivering against his chest. They had had words last night. Robert returned late after a rugby dinner, one of those loutish all-male affairs. The English liked such things, she did not understand, no wonder they had an unfortunate reputation abroad. Years ago, Robert had played for the Old Staplefordians, an old boys' team, so he simply had to get drunk with them, every so often. Thérèse had lashed him with her scorn.

A two-hundred-year-old oak drove them out of bed. At first, it sounded as if the house had been hit by a bomb, then they heard broken glass falling from the greenhouse.

Robert rose to survey the damage; in the dark, in the wind, wearing overcoat and pyjamas, barely able to stand, even he felt unnerved. He did not dare investigate, but returned carefully along the gravel path and was glad to reach the house and entrance-hall. There he found a sudden silence; it was as if he were returning home after a break-in, uncertain whether the thieves were still at large in his home.

He dismissed the thought. He had had the best security systems installed since the robbery. Thérèse was snug upstairs; the Hughes, the new housekeeper and her husband, were in the annexe, watched by a German shepherd-dog. Even so, the wind was extraordinary.

The damage did not matter. Lloyd's would pay.

After a cup of tea, he returned to his senses, could joke about trees that went bang in the night. Thérèse, saucer-eyed from tiredness, did not laugh.

For a month or so, ever since Inspector Wilson ceased to visit, she had not mentioned the Monet, but it still preoccupied her. Now she asked him: 'What had the theft to do with Baden-Baden?'

He responded calmly: 'Nothing, why?'

He knew she did not believe him; she had overheard the late-night phone call from Tony MacNulty; she had had to lie to the police which he had seen her do, without hesitation; yet she would continue to probe him about why, when and where. His firm reply meant that she would wait and try later.

The storm did not matter. He would not let it matter. The Monet mattered, the break-in, but Thérèse would forget. He would watch, wait and see; the war with Grote and friends was not over.

'Cheer up, darling,' he shouted to Thérèse early next morning as he strode to the stables in the dark, fighting the buffeting wind. He stabled rather than garaged his cars, his favourite toys, engineered wonders of steel, aluminium, paint, plastic, glass and leather.

He chose the Mercedes, black, teutonic; it was solid, it reassured. He placed his black calfskin briefcase on the passenger seat, filled with his papers. Claims and potential claims. Many of the great disasters of the world, real or imagined, went through this small black bag.

Forty minutes later, Robert opened up the offices of Knowle & Co, an air-conditioned suite in the shadow of the Lloyd's building. His habitual good mood was fully restored.

He was early for work. The white clock above the empty reception desk stated it was half past six. Friday morning, and his car had swept over rain-glazed deserted roads. The wind seemed to have abated.

Outside, in Leadenhall Street, Marchwood heard sirens, the whine of ambulances. He looked down the corridor to his and Ray's personal office suites.

Something was wrong. Ray's door was open, but Ray was not there. That was the one office that always had to be locked.

Quietly, Robert placed his briefcase on the floor, then, quite absurdly, he took the gent's umbrella that hung on a deserted coatstand, tiptoed down the corridor and entered the reception room of Ray's suite. Nothing. He pushed the door to the inner sanctum, where Ray worked.

Nothing.

Or at least: there was nobody there, the room had its usually unholy mess of computer hardware and software, printers and flow-charts; a desk covered with papers and diskettes, a paper dart. Marchwood saw nothing untoward in the chaos. He walked to one corner, lifted a floor tile, peered down at the safe.

Perhaps he was becoming paranoid. He retreated with his umbrella hooked over his arm, a very proper gentleman. Outside, he let the umbrella drop in the corridor. They had rattled him, taking the picture.

He recalled that night six months ago, when the telephone rang. It was some time before he recognised Tony MacNulty, calling from a call-box; the usually precise speech was drink-slurred, washed by the noise of passing cars.

MacNulty had warned him that the friends had decided he had broken the Baden-Baden agreement once too often. He had argued, knowing it was useless, knowing he would just have to wait and see; MacNulty would not tell him what was planned. All MacNulty could do was warn.

Marchwood had been grateful for the call. He knew Tony was breaking every rule, risking much; he would be dealt with severely, if the others discovered.

Once again the family business was under threat. After the war, their father, Rex Marchwood, had joined a Mr Knowle, an old Lloyd's hand who ran a tiny brokerage bearing his name; Knowle sold out, except for a minority stake, and retired. To the brothers, the brokerage was home from home, their father's firm. They joined it in their teens, as two young clerks. It was an exciting time; London was emerging from the Blitz, from rationing. The world came to Lloyd's, there was money to be made, it was fun to be young – until, one morning, Robert walked into the chairman's office and found his father hanging stiffly from a pedimented bookcase. It was a sight that haunted them both, even decades later.

Neither accepted that he had committed suicide.

After his father died, Robert found a leather overall and Freemasons' insignia, medals and suchlike. A host of people turned up at his father's funeral, men his mother had never met; his father had led a life apart.

'Never cross the Freemasons,' Rex Marchwood had warned his sons, just weeks before he died; it was a comment they had rarely heeded but never forgotten.

Nor had they forgotten how they had rescued the ailing business from the brink after their father's death. Over the decades they had turned Knowle into the most remarkable private company in the City. In 1987, it made profits of forty million pounds, after paying Ray and Robert a combined salary of eighteen million. The founder, Mr Knowle, ancient but still going strong, had received dividends of twenty million in ten years from his stake. This phenomenal success was due to a series of deals which Robert Marchwood brokered throughout the Lloyd's market, culminating in the legendary oil-rig deal. This vast deal, which structured Lloyd's exposure to the North Sea, saw Marchwood dividing risks and premiums from the oil companies between Lloyd's syndicates. Only by working together, with the 'friends', could this multi-billion pound deal be brought off; it was this deal that had been struck, in essence, at Baden-Baden; it brought millions to all concerned and a Monet to Marchwood's Georgian home.

The lost painting was a small, yet insistent source of annoyance. It made Marchwood certain that he and Ray were not just going to roll over and die, whatever the friends might hope.

Marchwood heard his younger brother struggling with the front door; Ray did not expect to find the offices of Knowle & Co unlocked, not at this hour.

Marchwood padded into the tape room, leaving Ray to find him. He stared at the Telex machine ticking over, at the overnight market reports feeding through on Reuters. It seemed just another day in October. Tokyo down, Hong Kong steady, Singapore ahead, then news of storm damage in central and southern England. It sounded as if he had been lucky to reach the office.

'Robbo? Still gambling on emerging markets?' A bespectacled man, with short, unruly hair and a pale, drawn face peered at him from the tape room door. This was Raymond Howard Marchwood, finance director and deputy chairman of Knowle & Co.

Robert snorted, tearing off the report rolls.

'Worried are we?' Ray dropped his briefcase and coat somewhere. He disapproved of Robert's investments in the Far East, because they were a high-risk gamble; neither of them understood the culture nor the market.

'No.' Robert gestured at the tapes: 'They reckon London'll drop like a stone today. Jitters about over-heating.'

'They've been saying that for months.' Ray managed their personal blue-chip portfolio, whose value had doubled to eighty million in just three years.

Ray removed and cleaned his metal-framed glasses. 'What is Mr Grote planning?'

Robert said nothing. He could see Ray was nervous; he had not forgotten the Monet incident nor the warnings. Ray was a man who took life in his stride; a natural observer, he watched the world about its business, that was both his job and his nature; by reacting rationally to change, by calm prediction and calculation, he made money. In Lloyd's, Ray was universally accepted and admired; he had once supported the Liberal Democrats, a mistake which had been forgiven if not forgotten.

Nobody had a bad word for him; whereas Robert, whose politics were conventional, was not universally admired.

'Been in your room, yet?' Marchwood asked, not bothering to reply. Grote was a matter for later.

'No, why?'

'Take a look.'

There was a pause.

Ray left swiftly and returned even quicker. 'Have you been at my computer terminal?' He was whispering.

Robert shook his head.

They both turned to the door, as if they had heard something. There was still the chance that an intruder was in the office; aside from the front door, there was the fire exit, linked to an awesome alarm.

They strode into the main office, heard the cosseted calm of abandoned word processors, saw flickering computer terminals, chairs and untidy desks. Robert crossed the spacious, open-planned disorder, to see if someone was hiding among the dividing-screens and plants and desks.

Nobody. Then nobody's footstep.

The brothers looked at each other.

Robert requisitioned the umbrella again and they tiptoed into the corridor on the far side of the reception desk, where there were sundry offices. A stockroom door was ajar, Robert kicked it open and fumbled with the light switch. Nothing. Along the corridor, they heard someone running, they had no time to turn before the fire-door alarm filled the offices with deafening noise.

'Leave him, Robbo.'

Robert disregarded his brother, charged down the corridor, round the corner, to the fire door. He grasped at the metal handle, the door swung back. He took the steps down the emergency staircase two at a time, one flight, two flights, then stopped; his quarry was already two floors below, he peered over the metal banister rail, the emergency door at street level crashed open, slammed shut.

He exhaled, looked at the umbrella and laughed, loudly, before retracing his steps. He entered Ray's room. His brother was finger-tipping his way through his computer: 'Everything still in place?'

Ray grunted. 'Whoever it was, spent the night here, hacking into our system and data-banks. You disturbed him because you arrived so early.'

'A professional.'

Ray laughed and then said: 'Sure. But it shouldn't surprise you. First, you mug Grote, then Wilmot-Greaves, lose them millions, for no reason at all, just because Grote is bad news, just because they deserve a kick. Now he's taking his revenge.'

Robert did not want to hear this, he turned to watch curtains of rain sweep across the window. Yet Ray was not finished: 'The Monet has gone, our friends are crawling over our office and our business, there are police investigating. Just because of your distaste for Grote. Forget the past, get on with the present.'

'It is you who insists on data collection,' Robert observed, in his most measured tones, despite his anger. 'Even though they object.'

'You agreed we had no option. It's our last line of defence. If ever it came to all-out war, we could shoot back.'

Robert frowned. 'Did our intruder open the safe?' he asked, finally.

Ray shrugged his shoulders.

Robert returned to the tape room. He would tell Ray later about his conversation last night with Inspector Tomlinson, at the Old Staplefordians' reunion dinner. Tomlinson was a rugger chum who had joined the Serious Fraud Office; over the years he had helped them where he could, with copies of archive material, information about DA&P among other things. Last night, Derek had merely had a warning for him: 'They're after you, my boy. Our man Wilson has you in his sights. Watch out.'

Thanks a million, mate, Robert had thought. If it's not the friends, it's the police.

Ray entered the tape room, still looking less than happy; he adjusted his glasses and said: 'Look, if they try to cane you today, pull down your trousers, be polite and take it like a man. We have to get out of this mess.'

Rolls of paper churned through the printers, Reuters was producing yards, rather than inches, on felled trees, blocked roads, upturned lorries, disrupted trains and unroofed houses. The weather was moving eastwards and worsening, the gale turning into a hurricane. The stockmarket was edgy, a slide had started, the FTSE-100 was already a hundred points adrift only minutes after the start of trading. Ray looked at the tapes without seeing. He turned to Robert: 'Whatever they say at the meeting, take it like a man, you hear. Otherwise, we're finished.'

Robert saw the shadow of their father in Ray's expression and nodded, despite himself.

THREE

SHE COULD WELL be ruined, for all she knew.

Connie Sanderson lay in bed and listened.

For six months and twenty or so days, she had not slept soundly. She would wake at five or six, then fail to slip back into the shadow of the sleep she had left.

Ron had got up as normal, gone to work as normal, died of a heart attack in his office at the garage. She had last seen him at breakfast, alive; it seemed impossible to imagine him dead. When the police had told her, she had not cried, she had not believed. She was at school, school assembly had just finished. It seemed impossible that anybody should die when the children had just filed into their classrooms and lessons had just started, it could not happen. Yet it had, it had.

Tonight, it had been worse, she had woken even earlier; the wind was throwing itself at the house. In the middle distance, things thudded and crashed; glass was broken, a slate went on a heavy journey.

She switched on a light. It was four in the morning. Just too early. At five or six, she could look forward to seven; at seven, Ron had always brought her tea; at seven, life began. When she woke early, despite a sleeping tablet, she knew that seven would never be the same. She had to keep a grip on herself; she had to sleep.

She clicked out the light, and took a deep breath. She had rehearsed the pep talk before, telling herself how much she had to live for, how good her health was, how fortunate she was to be headmistress of Lime Grove, how nice it would be to see her son Jonathan, her rather sweet daughter-in-law Arabella and her grandchildren when she flew out to Australia for a month's stay next summer. Jonathan had flown back for the funeral, for two days, then returned; family and business called.

66

She dozed off, woken again by the welter of events outside. She turned her pillow. The house was too large for her, she had had no time for the garden, none whatsoever – she had a school with six hundred pupils to run, the estate of a dead husband to wind up, a garage and Bentley dealership to lick into shape, that was more than enough, truly.

Then there was the small matter of Lloyd's.

She had discovered Ron had joined Lloyd's without telling her, a year before he died; the papers were all kept at the garage; when she read them, she was first astonished, then angry. She could be ruined. Unlimited liability, pay until there is nothing left – the very idea!

Sleep was impossible, now. She turned on the radio, without rising, waiting for the news. The weather forecast was notably bad, but the South East appeared to be no worse than anywhere else. Across the country, trees had been uprooted, slates dislodged. She had to sort out her affairs. That Friday morning, she had an appointment to see a Mr MacNulty, a Mr Tony MacNulty, who represented Ron at Lloyd's. Apparently, a Mr Robert Marchwood, who had bought a Bentley from Ron a year ago, had introduced Ron to MacNulty, who ran a large Lloyd's agency. This much she and her lawyer had pieced together. Ron had had to juggle the value of their assets just to join; he had claimed to have one hundred and fifty thousand pounds in addition to the house and garage; this was not true. In fact, to raise the money, he had deposited a piece of paper at the bank which entitled Lloyd's to receive one hundred and fifty thousand from the bank, if his syndicates made a loss, and further entitled the bank to sell the house to recoup the money. To accomplish this little trick, Ron had not used his usual bank, which would have been worried, given the garage's debts, which were also secured on the house. She was now a widow living in a twice-mortgaged home.

It was madness; Ron had joined Lloyd's for all the wrong reasons, just to be a member of the most prestigious club in the country. He would have loved the final induction ceremony in some grand room within Lloyd's where he had been told he could lose everything, that he had unlimited liability; it did not matter that he would pay for his syndicates' losses until he had nothing left: he was joining the right people, entering the right circles. Ron was a lovely man, but he could be a dreadful fool and a terrible snob.

She was appalled by the risk. The idea you could earn money for old rope, for nothing, was deeply suspect; she only knew one way to have money, through hard slog.

Ron was different. He suffered from delusions of grandeur, due perhaps to the public school education and a stint as a RAF pilot, after the war. He certainly had flair, but he believed life owed him the substance to match, the broad acres of wheat, the listed building, Sanderson Hall. Oh, they had rowed about his snobbery; Connie had no pretensions, she was what she was – pretty, at one time, and bright as a button. She had become a darned good schoolmistress, she had no grounds for shame.

For Ron, things were different.

He had lied to her. In retrospect, this saddened her more than anything else. The lies about Lloyd's, the lies about the garage. His business had never earned as much as he had claimed. Seeing the books for the first time had been a shock, it confirmed how deluded he was. He had wined and dined those who enjoyed talking about fine wines, fine foods and fine cars, though the distance between fine words and a fat cheque could stretch to infinity. If business was good, Ron sold one new car and traded a couple of secondhand models every month, making decent money on repairs and maintenance. Yet business had been slack for ages, even in a boom. The county set – the stockbrokers, bankers, lawyers, judges and farmers he fed and watered – tended to buy German, the so-and-sos.

Above all, she was astonished how little Ron earned, how much he lived from hand to mouth; after decades in the business, the garage was groaning from debts of nearly four hundred thousand pounds. This did not seem to have mattered; Ron paid himself three or four times as much as he should, drove a Bentley himself, ate out regularly and expensively, played golf, hunted. She looked at the figures and guessed that selling the garage would just about eliminate the debts. Her accountant agreed with the assessment; she would be left the house, her pension and a few investments. That did, however, leave her exposed to Lloyd's.

What a fool!

Despite her anger and confusion, she still smiled when she thought of him; his bravado and braggadocio. She looked at the clock; it had turned seven. She would take a shower, then make herself a cup of tea; she was determined, for Ron's sake, to put her world to rights.

She would make MacNulty beg for mercy.

FOUR

KEVIN VAUGHAN WAS in an extraordinary state that Friday morning. Home late, he had barely slept, he was so high, so tense. He had to get to work, had to phone first. At Liverpool Street station, he burst out of the train, rushed upstairs, through long corridors, over an endless escalator, until he found an out-of-the-way telephone booth.

'It's Daniel.'

'Where are you? Have you got it?' the voice asked.

'It didn't work out, sorry. I've no time to explain. I know I should have rung last night.'

There was a hesitation, before Stu said: 'That's fine. Just take care, take it easy.'

'See you.'

Kevin put down the phone. He felt like an idiot – and a hero. He still did not know why he was taking such a risk.

At first, things had gone to plan.

He had stayed late at head office, in the computer room at Wordsworth. As agreed. Waited for everyone to leave.

During the day, the first batch of data had been switched onto the new banks, from the old computer. If there was any evidence of malpractice, it would be in these records.

Once he had checked the front door and adjoining offices, Kevin had produced a blue diskette from his wallet and started to run the program it contained, a spreadsheet which he had tweaked for his purposes. The internal phone rang. He cursed. This was not possible, everyone had left.

He waited, then relented. 'Hello, hello.' He tried not to sound irritated.

'Sorry to disturb you.' It was Alice Montfort, personal assistant to Tony MacNulty. His secretary, really. Kevin looked at the stupid computer, whose cogitations were chewing time. Blank screen, apart from an hour-glass ikon.

'Would you come into Tony's office, for a moment? Thanks.' The tone did not allow a negative answer.

Mrs Montfort was a smartly dressed, fleshy woman, in her early forties. She dominated the Wordsworth head office, often acting as MacNulty's deputy while the boss was unavailable. Kevin had soon appreciated the fact that, without her, the office would not work, and that, without her, MacNulty would not know what went on. So he was always friendly, always made a little joke, always made sure she felt loved and appreciated.

He could not, however, be sure of his success.

Alice Montfort had a tart manner. She always dressed formally, wore suits, matching two-pieces in shades of grey, blue and, occasionally, black-brown tweed. All very proper and rather expensive. To match the suits, there was a range of silk shirts and black patterned stockings; Kevin had noticed the stockings, even tried a joke about the patterns: 'Today is Monday, so Monday means circles.' Her reaction had not been favourable.

Even so, he hoped that she would have put in a word for him with MacNulty or, at least, not undermined his position. After all, MacNulty had the power to make Kevin an underwriter like the Blighter; he could give Kev the full backing of the Wordsworth agency: administer his paperwork, supply capital through its names, advise on underwriting strategy and help with the authorities. If he thought Kevin had the talent, if Kevin's face fitted, Kevin could be in clover.

So Mrs Montfort had to be handled with care.

He stopped his computer program, pocketed the blue diskette with the evidence, hurried along the corridor, through the central reception area, to MacNulty's room. A glance at the front door revealed a key, presumably everything was locked. Oh, God.

He straightened his tie, knocked on the door to the chairman's office.

'Yes?'

He was expecting to have to lift some furniture, move some files, unblock the photocopier, whatever.

'What are you doing here so late?'

He hesitated. 'I'm just your average workaholic.'

She did not smile. 'Well, can you help me, please? I did this, this afternoon. Tony will brain me if he finds out . . .'

She had removed a book from the shelves and accidentally knocked over the glass picture frame with MacNulty's family photos. It had smashed; she had rushed to Oxford Street after work, acquired a replacement, but now she was all thumbs.

Kev nodded, smiled, removed his jacket, placing it carefully on the plain red cotton sofa beside her pinstriped blazer. The room, in anonymous pine, was silent, the spotlights glinting on the metal picture frames.

Then, success. He managed to flip back the clips holding the broken glass pane, and gave her the glass, which she placed in a plastic bag. He worked free the pictures, some colour, some black and white, some professional, some nasty instant-camera snaps. MacNulty and kids and blonde wife. The house, the high-tech boat, the other boat, the school uniforms. He laid them down carefully on the desk top while Mrs Montfort placed the plywood backing in the bag, then freed the replacement frame from its packing. It was fortunate Tony did not possess a sophisticated taste.

He waited for her to undo the clips on the new frame. Damn, her fingernails. He smiled and again succeeded.

'Where's Tony?'

'Oh, out with his wife, thank God.'

Now the photographs had to be placed, face down, on the glass and masking paper that framed the photographs. The first attempt was unsuccessful; two pictures slipped, one boat was left sailing towards the ceiling.

'Damn,' she said again. The lighting was subdued, which did not help. 'You can go home if you want. I'm sorry to drag you into this. It's just . . .' She gestured, as if he must understand.

Kevin was no longer tense. He shifted from one foot to another, looked at her bowed head, her face slightly obscured by her red-brown hair. On the other side of the room was a large pine cupboard.

She caught his gaze and whispered: 'The main safe's inside the cupboard. Hidden behind the gin bottles.'

Kevin did not know what to make of this; he said: 'Oh?'

'Just what are you doing here, at this time of night?'

He shrugged his shoulders.

'There!' Suddenly, she was triumphant, smiling; it was fixed.

Standing beside her, Kevin was surprised by her face; it seemed both older and more beautiful than he remembered. Yes, the frame looked fine now. MacNulty would never notice.

Then she surprised him with a kiss.

'That's for being such a nice spy!'

To his great embarrassment and annoyance, he blushed.

It was only much later, the next morning, that he noticed the diskette, with his program, was gone. It only needed Tony to find it, he would see at once he had been prying, then he was finished. Finished.

FIVE

A BRONZE ORMOLU clock, signed Breguet à Paris, struck seven with an insistent, pinging chime.

Donna pretended to sleep, but heard Stephen switch on the radio.

'. . . A gale warning for shipping, issued by the Met Office today, Friday the thirteenth of October, at o–seven–hundred hours GMT. There are warnings of gales and severe gales in all areas . . .'

She groaned. They had been late to bed, Stephen had returned late in a difficult mood from one of his many meetings; she had seen her sister Mary-Ellen; then things had started banging about, doors, windows, the wind against wall and wood and pane; there had been no hope for sleep. What a night.

A pillow dropped on her face; roused, Donna returned it into his midriff; Stephen responded by placing a big kiss on her forehead.

'I'm sure glad your mood has improved since last night,' Donna said.

Stephen smiled: 'We all have our problems.'

She looked at her husband: 'What's today's meeting about?' She yawned and started to search for her dressing gown.

Stephen, sitting on the end of the bed, suddenly looking wan, said: 'Oh, I don't recall, it really is not up to me. I'm just chairman, remember.'

She smiled, ruefully. It was easier to lie than tell her the truth. Until Mary-Ellen had told her last night, she had not really known that there was a difficulty with this Marchwood guy. 'Mary-Ellen said you were going to discipline him.' Meaning: Marchwood.

'You know that cannot be my decision.'

She sensed that the discussion angered him, that if she pressed him there would, eventually, be an outburst of rage; this discovery, that Stephen could be provoked, had amused her at first, until she found that his temper could produce days of thunder and lightning. This she preferred to avoid; so she diverted her gaze, to the wind and the weather thrashing against the windowpane.

Mary-Ellen had taken Donna to Chinatown for a meal, just to tell her about Marchwood. It was becoming a habit; since Mary-Ellen became a committee member, she clucked over Donna like a hen with a chick.

Mary-Ellen claimed there was a mystery. Stephen Grote and Robert Marchwood had known each other for nearly thirty years, the two most important guys in Lloyds yet they had rarely worked together. This intrigued Mary-Ellen so much that she started asking around. One old-timer had hinted at bad blood between the two; he told her that Grote had known Marchwood's father, Rex, and that there had been merger talks between them.

'So what?' Donna had asked. So nothing.

For years, the two men had avoided one another, until their firms became so large, they simply had to do business together. Then, eight years ago, Marchwood had knowingly offered an appalling deal to an unsuspecting underwriter employed by Stephen. Re-insurance of American buildings, a major risk, yet one that could be very sweet. Most of Lloyd's business from the States, its largest market, was re-insurance; a re-insurer insures the original insurer to reduce the latter's risks. In this case, Stephen's syndicate was to protect several American companies; one depended on the broker, should he suspect anything was wrong, to speak his mind.

At the time, Marchwood had seemed trustworthy.

So Stephen told his underwriter: 'Do it.' Those two words had cost millions; one of his best syndicates was swamped by losses, its names lost money and, worst of all, his reputation was sullied. As a result, the stockmarket flotation of his family firm had to be postponed; his dream of buying and restoring Hanbury Hall, the traditional home of the Grote family, had to be shelved.

The deal was a disaster; Stephen had been suckered. Empty tenements, desolate apartments in New York, Boston, Los

Angeles and Baltimore were set alight as Marchwood had certainly known they would be – down-at-heels claiming on their worthless homes from their local insurer, who had been reinsured by Grote's syndicate. The claims bled his syndicate, its names, his reputation, white.

This was, in Mary-Ellen's view, all very mysterious.

'Everyone thinks it was deliberate and nobody knows why,' Mary-Ellen said. 'Did you know?'

Of course, Donna had known nothing. Now in the light of morning, she admired Stephen's unshaven face; he was proud, too proud, and hated to make mistakes. If that was all, she forgave him. She took a shower.

Stephen Grote listened to the sounds of water inside and outside the house. He was wide awake, but drained.

Donna emerged from the bathroom and told him, 'By the way, Sotheby's are entertaining the police today. It seems a major painting has been stolen. With everyone else away, it seems that the Warrilow girl will have to help.'

Having worked for decades to build up her reputation as a leading expert at Sotheby's, Donna had kept her maiden name, Warrilow, for professional purposes.

Stephen strode into the bathroom and dampened a face cloth to wipe his face and hands. Then he re-appeared, curious about her tale, with a towel cloth in his hands, carefully drying each finger.

'A theft? What's that all about?' he asked.

'Oh, it's a very interesting case, but it's all a secret,' Donna teased him. 'All I can tell you is that the inspector's coming round today. An Inspector Wilson.'

Stephen did not say anything, he just looked. Donna knew this meant something, could not, however, decide what.

The name of the inspector accompanied Stephen Grote's thoughts as his chauffeur-driven Rolls swept down Park Lane, along Piccadilly, round the National Gallery and down the Strand towards the City.

By the time he reached Lime Street the stockmarket, inscrutably, had fallen through the floor.

SIX

MRS MONTFORT WAS as brisk as ever. 'Mr Vaughan, you are very late. Mr MacNulty wants a word.'

Kevin was not only late, he was exhausted. The weather was not much fun, either. 'Can I grab a quick coffee first?'

'I'll bring one in.'

'That's service,' he said, and she smiled, a quiet triumph. He steeled himself for the worst.

He stepped into MacNulty's office with a fixed smile. He expected to see the blue plastic square on the middle of Tony's desk, glowing.

In fact, there was nothing there. Just the pens MacNulty used for signing papers. Alan Denbigh-Wright lay moderately crumpled on the red sofa. He raised a hand in silent greeting, and Kev nodded, looked at MacNulty.

'Ah, Kevin, good morning or should I say . . .' Tony gestured with his pipe at his watch. He was as white as a sheet, not at all his cheerful self.

Without invitation, Kev took a seat and offered his sob story, about the underground, the storm. He looked at the framed photographs. Nothing untoward that he could see.

But there was a problem. Kevin waited, his right hand cupping his left elbow.

Finally, MacNulty asked: 'How often do you see Ray Marchwood?'

Kevin could have answered perfect civilly: they met every other week, at weekends, they were both computer buffs and liked to talk jargon. Perhaps that would have been fine.

Instead, he answered dourly: 'That's my business. What I do in my own time is my business.'

MacNulty said nothing, looked at the Blighter.

'You were here late, last night.'

'Working.'

'That's no tone of voice to adopt here.'

Kev exploded. 'You have no right to interrogate me. I was trying to make the mainframe work; I tell you, it was not my idea to acquire crud hardware and crud software. The stuff will be out-of-date before it is installed.'

MacNulty hesitated; Denbigh-Wright laughed lightly. Kevin turned to look him in the eye. He bristled with innocence, though he knew he was guilty. Finally, he demanded: 'What has my relationship with Ray to do with anything?'

He had a right to know if people were making false insinuations behind his back.

MacNulty responded coolly: 'If you want to succeed at this agency, I would suggest that . . .'

A list followed.

Kevin was, quite suddenly, aghast as Tony and the Blighter spoke, in the harshest tones, of himself, of his attitude. Everything about him seemed to be a mistake of some sort. Before, he had been worried that he would not succeed by ability alone. By the time the pair had finished, he felt certain he would not.

Perhaps he was just rattled.

'I'm sorry,' he apologised. 'I've been working very hard, it has been a frustrating time recently, the computer has not been working well.'

They did not smile. He told them about Ray: every so often, the two of them would have a tea and a chat, he would pick the great man's brains, that was the long and the short of the matter. 'He's known me and my mother for as long as I can remember. We're not family, but he's a close friend . . .'

'Yes.' MacNulty let his doubt hang in the air.

'What's the problem? After all, Ray provides . . .' He was about to say: much of our best business.

'Oh, nothing, nothing, young man,' MacNulty said, with a wave, clearly lying. 'You have to remember you're working for Wordsworth now.'

Kev shrugged and nodded. Difficult to forget.

'No problem,' the Blighter said, standing beside him. 'Let's be off. There's work for you to do back in the box.'

Mrs Montfort arrived with coffee for them all, bringing

much-needed relief; Blighter joshed with the lady, while Kevin added milk and sugar.

In fact, Denbigh-Wright was wrong; there was no work. All eyes were on the Stock Exchange: shares had gone into free-fall. The weather seemed to have triggered everything; houses with lost roofs, cars crushed by falling trees, roads and rail lines blocked, the whole mess seemed to have undermined the confidence of those sophisticates whose hopes and fears were reflected and amplified in share price movements. At least, that was Kevin's theory.

Terror or lethargy had struck the underwriting room; usually chock-a-block at midmorning, it was empty; one lone broker wanted to place insurance with their syndicate. The Blighter, untypically, waved him away and they tinkered with the computer terminal instead. Then the Blighter decided they should trot off to see John Devies, the deputy chairman, a sailing friend.

There was quite a crowd in Devies's office, all gathered to watch his Stock Exchange screen, which showed price movements as they happened. In computer jargon: in real time. Kevin wondered what unreal time might be and his thoughts wandered to Alice Montfort.

This was an opportunity for Kevin to meet the Great and the Good, to make a favourable impression: Grote, Wilmot-Greaves, Stone, MacNulty, Fortescue and others stood around, watching the television, some were drinking. All the prices were red and falling, everybody talked in low tones as if their net worth had died.

The Deputy Chairman approached him, leaning heavily on a stick: 'I hear the Blighter has a bright young fellow working for him. Enjoying things at Wordsworth, are you?'

Kevin nodded keenly and Devies continued: 'Good outfit, Wordsworth. Can I get you a gin and tonic?'

'No, thank you, sir.'

He smiled at Devies's weather-beaten features. Denbigh-Wright had brought him here for a purpose, which he could not quite fathom, he had had a bruising interview, for no apparent reason; he felt empty and tired. Perhaps they had, after all, found the diskette.

SEVEN

STU CURSED HIS luck.

He had an appointment at Sotheby's with a former curator at the Courtauld Institute. Instead, a striking, tall woman, Ms Donna Warrilow, told him the news: 'My colleague, I'm afraid, has been detained in Paris. Nothing is landing at Heathrow at the moment.'

First, Kevin on the phone, nervous, and now this. He looked at his black case; the darkroom guys had worked all hours and achieved miracles with the photographs he had purloined from Golden Rain, producing a fine set of pictures, both slides and prints, of the Marchwood-Monet.

Donna Warrilow then said: 'Although my field is English art, I do help my colleague from time to time . . .'

This offer was gratefully accepted and they entered one of the buildings off Bond Street used by Sotheby's for small exhibitions, minor auctions, renovations, valuations and short-term storage.

The viewing room was reasonably well-appointed, reasonably friendly in unfussy hessian, and offered thick, comfortable armchairs. Outside there were drab corridors where tables and commodes entered and pictures left.

Ms Warrilow was a dark-haired, American woman given to languid gestures and a flashing smile. She rifled through Wilson's slides in silence, click, click, click. Then she sorted among other slides, comparing his picture with those certain to have been painted by Claude-Oscar Monet, *peintre*.

This lasted for some time. Despite the noise of the projector fans, Stu could hear the wind bluster and blow outside. He was on edge; he had to be sure the picture was genuine; if not, he had already made a fool of himself.

'Well, what do you think, Inspector?'

'You know what I think, otherwise I would not be here.'

'If I tell you that is a Monet, will you tell me the owner's name?'

'I thought it was my job to ask the questions.'

There was a pause.

'Well, late 80s, clearly one of the absolutely wonderful river series. One of twenty-four, I believe, ten of which, more or less, were painted from this vantage point.'

'Sure?'

'Sure I'm sure, Inspector.'

She flicked the projector controls, to change the pictures, pointing to details, structure, brushwork, the restricted palette. For someone who claimed not to be an expert, she was good. Wilson had to admit that the resemblances were marked between a Monet-Monet and a Marchwood-Monet.

'Aside from which, it's a work of genius, one of the best of the series. A remarkable discovery,' she said finally. 'Not in Wildenstein, Inspector?'

'One of three recorded as lost,' Stu Wilson announced, not to be outdone. He had, of course, consulted the four-volume *catalogue raisonné* by the Jewish art dealer.

Donna Warrilow concluded: 'It is very unlikely to be a forgery; it shares with the other canvasses the uncertain perspective, the forceful assimilation of the terrain in blocks of mottled colour, the ambiguity of the landscape . . . Now, I guess, you're worried about the provenance, Inspector?'

He laughed. 'And price at auction?'

She seemed to ignore the question: 'These things do, occasionally, turn up, as if from nowhere. One can't know, but my guess would be that this work had been gathering dust in a Soviet attic or vault for seventy years.'

She explained that Russian collectors – notably Sergei Shchukin and Ivan Morozov – had bought heavily in Paris at the turn of the century: the impressionists, Cézanne, Matisse, Picasso. Their collections, the finest and largest in Russia, became the property of the state after the Revolution, the backbone of the Hermitage's unparalleled French collections. There were, however, other collectors, such as Shchukin's brothers, who had proved unwilling to sacrifice their prized possessions to the onward march of history. So they hid and hoarded and waited for *glasnost*.

'Yep, the evil empire,' she said. 'The Soviet order breaks down, things start to turn up. If you have nice dollars, you can find and buy. I know one or two people who have gotten themselves bargains.'

Stu was prepared to be convinced; the story appealed to his distrustful nature. Even a quiet landscape, seen through a man's eyes, had lost its innocence.

'Could you make a guess at a price?' he asked.

She replied: 'Well, Inspector, I would guess three to four million at auction. Especially after the Gachet sale, even without a friendly face or pretty flowers. It's just such a great view. Let's say four million minimum.'

He was stunned into silence. Marchwood might have been right, perhaps he had just been given a daub – painted by Tony MacNulty's uncle. Yes, a series of blotches worth four million pounds.

Ms Warrilow repeated: 'For a canvas of that quality, in that condition, from that era, in the present market, four million ought to be conservative. A keen collector might pay twice that. Now, Inspector, who's the lucky owner?'

She could smell a potential deal, evidently. He shook his head, smiled at the decidedly elegant Ms Warrilow, pocketed the slides and made his way out of the building. Still dazed by the numbers, he stepped into a bleak Bond Street. He would need another opinion, of course. He had to be definite – otherwise the game was over.

EIGHT

CONNIE SANDERSON HAD waited, had been forced to wait, until she felt outraged.

Mr Tony MacNulty, chairman of Wordsworth & Co, apologised for the delay; he had had a little crisis to deal with, a personal matter; he hoped she had been given coffee and biscuits. She forced herself to shake his hand and smile, before stating her case: 'It was only following my husband's death that I discovered he had become a name at Lloyd's. Under the circumstances, I want to withdraw at once.'

There was a silence, while MacNulty compressed the tobacco in his pipe, struck a match, puffed. He enunciated his answer slowly, precisely.

'Mrs Sanderson, I'm sorry if your late husband did not inform you of his decision to join the Society. We are, you will appreciate, a financial institution, not responsible for names' matrimonial circumstances.'

Connie glanced at the family photographs; MacNulty evidently had four or five children, mostly in the throes of private schooling, a large house somewhere, an extravagant yacht, a blonde and not-so-young wife. The office itself was bare and bland. Grey clouds moved across the sky, occasional rain flung against the glass, resounding like hail.

MacNulty reminded her of the vicar at her church; his ponderous manner suggested close contact with the Lord, a deep concern both for the eternal and for the right word. She watched horrified, silenced, as MacNulty expressed his everlasting regret for Ronald's death, then touchingly recalled how he had met Ronald through a mutual friend – Robert Marchwood, the broker. Laying aside his pipe, he said: 'We played golf together and then I took Ronald for an afternoon's sailing in the Solent. I must say Ronald was exceedingly keen to join Lloyd's. He realised this was an opportunity not open to everyone.'

Connie knew none of this, but could imagine, vividly.

'This still does not alter the fact I want to leave.'

MacNulty expressed his understanding for her position; it was a terrible blow for anyone to lose a husband after a long and happy marriage; but really, in these trying circumstances, one should avoid hasty decisions.

He sighed. 'I'm afraid you are committed to both this year and next; you cannot leave until the year after next.'

She did not know what to say. He explained that Lloyd's operated a three-year accounting system; she was locked in.

'But you really should not worry. Your syndicates, let me see, are run by Mite Leven, Annan and Salter. These are a good, solid bet.'

'Why was Ron not placed on the Wordsworth syndicates?'

MacNulty cleared his throat and said: 'I'm afraid they are oversubscribed.'

She looked out of the window. 'The fact is, you do not face the same risks as me.'

'Come, come, my dear lady. You really are being far too emotional. I, too, am a name and have unlimited liability. In two or three years' time, you will be thanking Ronald for finding you another source of income.'

Connie felt tired; more tired and sad than she had felt for a long time; it was the cumulative effect of sleepless nights, the sudden absence of someone close whom she felt she could rely upon; she looked at Mr MacNulty, and felt unsure; he seemed plausible, polite and informative, if slightly patronising. Ronald had already pledged everything to him. It was not necessarily MacNulty's fault that she distrusted him. Perhaps the pipe was to blame. Perhaps she was kicking up a fuss for no reason. The conversation turned to the appalling weather, the terrible unreliability of public transport and the meeting was over. MacNulty accompanied her to the door, and shook her hand.

They bumped into a young man with another, older man waiting for the lift. It was only when the young man said hello, that she recognised Kevin Vaughan. She returned his smile and said: 'You're looking well.'

He nodded and they fell into a pained silence in the lift. She did not want to pry; Kevin Vaughan had been an absolutely angelic ten-year-old, now he looked, well, sharply cut in a sharp suit. He certainly had come a long way from his school days.

She breathed a sigh of relief as she reached the wind-lashed street.

NINE

TO MARKET, TO market.

Robert Marchwood braved the blasting wind and the scything rain, to make a headlong dash to Lloyd's, to Lime Street, waving a largely useless umbrella. He reached the entrance canopy, a suspended barrel vault in glass and steel, passed two security guards, and entered the lobby outside the lifts. Now he was safe, if not entirely dry.

He pressed and waited, almost languidly, for one of the glass-walled boxes that scaled the external walls of Lloyd's.

Before he had left their office, the stockmarket had entered free-fall. A 20 per cent loss in three hours; Ray had telephoned their stockbroker, who talked gibberish, unable to think; all of a sudden, confidence had cracked, the market seemed to be throwing itself off a cliff. Everybody blamed the storm, the hurricane-force winds had unleashed a panic; now, the world was full of many sellers and few buyers. All they could do was watch.

Ray managed their private share portfolios. According to Ray's computer, which tracked the market in real time, their shares had fallen by 17.67 per cent that morning. They had just lost fifteen million pounds in two hours.

Fortunately, the bulk of their money – Knowle's cash – was invested in gilts, which had risen. Anyway, it was just paper money – the gains of the past two years had been eliminated, so what?

Nevertheless, Ray's face had been drawn as he listened, on an open line, to their broker's dealing room; the main market was following the options market down; the trading room buzz fell silent as the blue chip stocks dropped again. It was not an exciting sound, unless you were listening to your fortune evaporate.

The lift doors opened, Robert entered, pressed the metal button marked twelve, and looked out into the City as it spun away beneath his feet. Mansion House, the Bank, St Paul's appeared in the grey middle distance; Baring Brothers, Deutsche Bank and Commercial Union loomed larger, darker, to his right. He was impelled upwards, alongside pillars of concrete and steel and sheets of glass.

Not for the first time, Robert wondered what his old man might have made of the place. Idle speculation; he had never known his father well enough to know his mind.

He himself was sceptical of the new building, the old one had been cramped, but cosy. Ray, of course, liked the new, almost without qualification. Technology run riot. As so often, Ray was in a minority – there were all those jokes about Lloyd's having started out in a coffee house and ended up in a percolator. It had taken years and years and years to build. Then nothing worked; there did not seem to be a glass pane which did not leak; but, slowly but surely, everything was put right; it became the new market place. Robert saw great variety in the building: a mixture of cathedral, ship, oil rig and rocket launch-pad. It was difficult to understand; each part was supposed to proclaim its purpose, yet the whole eluded definition.

The twelfth floor was Grote's empire; so many flowers, so much marble, so much mahogany. The blooms, placed on antique furniture, were overwhelming, spray after spray: roses and lilies, orchids and dahlias, an unending burst of colour, even in the grimy depths of winter. Millions had been lavished on the marble. A national mausoleum for the unknown revolutionary, perhaps. A tomb for the unknown name.

Robert coughed. It was hard not to feel intimidated.

Here, the building seemed to say: this is the force of money. The weight of wealth imposed itself, the columns and vaults and friezes promised security and probity. They proclaimed: your money is safe with us, we are the truth. No wonder communists adopted, without any irony, the grand style beloved of fascists.

He presented himself at the reception, mentioned his name to two gents in uniform. He smiled; he could not believe how well he felt; 20 per cent of his share portfolio gone, the family business, the effort of a lifetime, threatened with closure, and still he could smile.

He grinned at Fortescue, who flushed to the roots of his red hair, then greeted him: 'Hello, Robert. The committee is ready to see you. I hope we haven't kept you waiting.'

They entered the committee room, the inner sanctum, transported from the depths of Wiltshire, a white plaster ceiling with roundels and rosettes, plaster wall panelling, a fireplace, five curtained windows; in a high-tech building, on the twelfth floor, it seemed an implausible joke, but it always impressed the new members, who had to swear to the committee that they understood they might lose everything at Lloyd's. Nobody ever backed out here, it was here that all names said they did not mind losing everything.

Robert started shaking hands. Devies, Wilmot-Greaves, Stone, MacNulty, the main blokes. Mrs Mary-Ellen Lemke, an American sister-in-law to Grote. Delighted to meet you. This was the Marchwood charm offensive.

Stephen Grote entered and Robert hastened over to him: 'Hello, Stephen, I'm so pleased to see you. It's been a long time. This weather is such a pain.'

Grote agreed, with a smile. 'On such days, it's best to pretend that the wind and the rain do not exist.'

'You might sell the idea to the Met office.'

They both laughed.

'Remember me to your brother,' Grote said and moved on.

'My regards to Donna.' Robert had decided: either he would survive and thrive or Stephen would know the reason why.

TEN

THE BLIGHTER HAD collared Kevin Vaughan and insisted on lunch at Bells Brothers' wine bar, the one near Liverpool Street station with wood-and-glass partitions, chunky sandwiches and extensive wine list.

Kevin hated the idea, but accepted eagerly.

The bar was crowded and raucous, even on a day when most people were bonded by super-glue and super-losses to their trading screens.

Denbigh-Wright thought this was just the place for a man-to-man talk.

'Young man,' he said, when they had settled at a small wooden table in a dark corner with sandwiches and a bottle of 'we're-not-working-this-afternoon' Sancerre. 'Young man, you have a bright future.'

Kevin remained gracious. 'Thanks.'

A sandwich was pointed in Kev's direction: 'You know the form. You have brains, you can work hard, you have potential, but don't . . .' he slurped at the wine, mmmm, good, very good, a little grassy, then helped himself to another sandwich '. . . don't screw the chairman's secretary in the chairman's office.'

'Mrs Montfort? You must be joking! Was that the reason for the show this morning? Honestly!'

These sandwiches are good, very good, fancy some more? Beef and horse-radish? The Blighter ignored Kev's protest, ignored the ruck around the bar and appeared with another plate of sandwiches. Probably filched someone else's order.

'Before a black-tie dinner in the Guildhall, I happened to see lights in MacNulty's room. So I let myself into the offices with my universal key. I heard voices, where there should not have been voices.'

89

'It's not true! I was helping her with some work!'

'Calm down. I haven't told Tony, not this time. But everyone is very, very touchy. They'd kill you if they knew.'

Kevin checked and paused. He was risking his entire career, not just a pay rise, not just a car, not just promotion. This deal with Stu was utter madness. Why help the police when they are too dumb to help themselves?

'Look, I'm sorry . . .' Kevin recanted.

'Just don't do it again. At least you sleep on the right side of the blanket, unlike others I could name.'

The Blighter laughed, then lowered his voice: 'There's one hell of a bust-up about Marchwood . . . You know and I know that Marchwood makes much of our money; his business is our business; MacNulty is terrified we will be blown away if and when Marchwood explodes. The man is just so unreliable . . . We just cannot afford any mistakes.'

Then Denbigh-Wright yawned; he had been in the office early, talking with MacNulty, relaying the message from Alec Wilmot-Greaves about Kevin's connections. Tony had been bitter, but not surprised: 'We will not sack Kevin, not yet. That will only make our friends more suspicious.'

The Blighter did not repeat this frank statement. Kevin looked at him, said nothing. Suspected.

'You should think about joining the Freemasons; I know the Lutine Lodge would welcome you. People would know you are one of us.'

Kevin nodded, just to appear right-on, then headed for the Wordsworth computer, just to appear to be busy. Now, where was that diskette, that program? He did not know where MacNulty might be, he would have to ask Mrs Montfort, to see if the coast was clear.

She was nowhere to be seen.

He would travel home late, in any case. He tried ringing his mother, at home; the phones were engaged or the lines were down; he started, once again, to look for the fault in the head office computer network.

The receptionist brought him the lunchtime mail; there was an internal letter marked private and confidential.

He ripped it open. It was signed by MacNulty; a computer program had been found on a blue diskette, an explanation was demanded and a meeting late that afternoon. In view of the weather, MacNulty was staying overnight in a hotel in Bloomsbury.

Kev knew his boss had a flat in the Barbican, so this was odd. Perhaps Tony had changed his mind, perhaps he would be given the bullet. No, probably.

He rushed through the office, past the receptionist, to Tony's room. Locked. Mrs Alice Montfort had disappeared.

He rang the hotel in Bloomsbury. A voice confirmed: Yes, a suite had been booked in Mr MacNulty's name. No, Kevin did not want to leave a message.

He peered outside; the office building had been placed, by persons unknown, in a gigantic car wash. He had several miserable hours to kill.

ELEVEN

ROBERT WAS LATE. He was always late, damn him. Veronica Cantor looked at her watch, three o'clock, paced up and down the small room in the Great Standard Hotel, lit a cigarette, smoked briefly, then pulled the net curtain aside. She did not curse the terrible weather, the wind and the rain. Instead she said to herself: damn him, damn Robert Hugh Marchwood.

The Great Standard Hotel enjoyed a handsome position within the City of London: between the Guildhall and St Paul's in the west and Liverpool Street station in the east, there was no other significant luxury hotel. Such was the boast of the hotel brochure. Yet the room was small, impersonal, with one large bed, an ageing television set and fixtures acquired during the 1960s, when plastic fascia were considered modern.

Once the hotel had owned one of the finest wine cellars in the country, laid down before phylloxera ravaged Bordeaux vineyards and Flanders mud changed the world. Now the hotel was mainly interesting as an object of speculation; in the boom and bust cycle of London hotels, the key was to buy when prices were rising, then sell before they started to fall. The canny had made fortunes out of the Great Standard, without changing a thing; unfortunately, guests tended not to return. Even so, Robert Marchwood, a man of habit, was an honoured guest here.

Usually placid and self-possessed, Veronica was seething. Her hand dragged through her jet black locks. A tall, angular young woman, she might have been in her late twenties. She wore a black suit, with a pleated skirt, white high-collared blouse and uncompromisingly flat shoes. Everything expensive, nothing showy. She held a promising position in the Lloyd's press office and was called deputy press officer; she worked for Stephen

Grote and for three years she had drunk champagne with Robert Marchwood at the Grand Standard.

The wind drilled rain against the window, washing away the view of the station's arching roof.

The door opened. Robert brought flowers and excuses and wine. Her rage evaporated, while the rain fell and the wind threatened to suck the glass from the window frame. Outside, the trains huddled beneath the station roof, delayed.

Marchwood switched on the radio beside the bed. Raising her head, Veronica felt this was brutal. But he was worried about his shares. He looked dark and sombre beside her. He was worried about Knowle, worried about Lloyd's.

She let her head fall back into the pillow. 'Will you have to leave soon?' she asked.

'The call of duty. I have to speak to my brother. Perhaps we could spend the evening together. I don't think I will be travelling home tonight.'

'Perhaps. Grote after you, again?' She had heard about the committee meeting.

'In a manner of speaking, yes.'

She laughed; he laughed. He switched off the radio, turned of the world's woes, and kissed her. Her beauty was heightened by the disarray of her black, pleated dress. Long, long legs. He touched her calf, drawing an irregular line to her knee, over her smooth, smooth skin.

He was fond of Veronica, genuinely fond; they had often had a chuckle together. Nevertheless, he felt their relationship had reached its natural term, he could not say why, perhaps it was Thérèse, perhaps it was age. It had been wonderful while it lasted. There was no more champagne in the bottle.

For months he had sensed this, felt unable to say. Not that he feared Veronica's anger, she would probably say what others had said, often enough, about married men. That they were all selfish rotters and only women knew how to cry. It was probably true, but it was not for him to change the world.

He disappeared into the bathroom, leaving her alone.

By his jacket, on the floor, she saw a white envelope, a letter without addressee, and, out of sheer bloody-minded curiosity, she opened it.

The letter stated neither to whom it was sent nor from whom it came, and bore the heading, underlined and in bold: FINAL

WARNING. Underneath, there were five numbered points, expressed cryptically. Number one read: Baden-Baden to stand. Number two: No data collection, no surveillance. Number three: No police.

The bathroom door opened, she slipped the letter into the bed clothes. 'What has the committee decided?' she asked.

'Oh, to throw out Ray. He will no longer be allowed to enter the room. Confined to head office, after thirty years.'

'That bad?'

'They'll throw me out next.'

'Why do you bother? After all . . .' Her voice trailed away at the sight of his blank look. His work was his life.

She apologised, she had opened an envelope she had found, her mistake. She proferred the letter and was surprised to hear him give a short laugh. They looked at each other and he kissed the slightly unreliable Veronica Cantor.

'Don't worry,' he said. She knew he forgave her because he liked her; she had seen him lose his cool when others pried. 'Don't worry, it's a love letter from God.'

Outside, there was the sound of something crashing to the ground, metal rather than glass. No, it was just the wind. Even the walls of the hotel seemed to vibrate. He sat on the edge of the bed. She placed her arms round his shoulders and kissed his neck.

'I have bad news.'

Ominous. He waited.

'I'm pregnant.'

He turned and looked at her angular, intelligent face, her fine body and her long, smooth legs. Her black hair. There was a silence.

He managed to say: 'I don't know whether I should congratulate you or commiserate.'

'Congratulate, I think.'

He kissed her. 'Congratulations, darling,' he hesitated. 'What are you going to do?'

'I'm sure. What do you want?'

He shook himself. 'So you want to keep the child?'

She started to make a protest, but her voice trailed away, as she worried she might sound insincere. She had seen the baby on the ultra-sound, turning somersaults inside her stomach; yes, she wanted to keep it.

'Are you going to marry what's-his-name?'

This was a reference to her official boyfriend, a stockbroker tied to his screen. She shook her head.

In truth, she was terribly vague, except that she wanted the child. She was surprised by her own resolve.

'It's your child.'

Robert gasped. 'You always took precautions.'

She informed him, gently, that they sometimes did not work.

He turned to the closed window, where the curtains moved. He felt baffled, rather than angry. He thought everything had been clear, they had had an arrangement.

'I'll make sure you have everything you need.' He meant: money.

'Is that all? Do you not want children?'

'I had a son once.'

He did not continue, nor did he state the obvious: he was married.

She started to cry; he looked at his hands, the window, the weather. She washed her face in the bathroom, swiftly restored her make-up, picked up the flowers, smelled them, let them drop in the wastepaper bin, and left. He looked at the door, at the letter with its warning. For once, his bravado had been no more than that; his whole world seemed to be falling apart.

TWELVE

STEPHEN GROTE PURSED his lips and essayed a whistle: Papageno's aria with the Glockenspiel. Fortunately, he was in his twelfth-floor office, alone.

It had been a good day, a darned good day.

Sure, he had lost some loot. Fortescue was going out of his mind over just one stock. Stephen's broker had rung, wetting himself about some twenty or thirty of his stocks, poor man. Well, these things happened. 'In the long run shares always come right,' Stephen said. Yet he thought: in the long run, we're all dead.

Nobody likes losing money. Nobody. Once Marchwood had carved ten million out of Stephen's forty or fifty million, nothing much in the scheme of things, but it still hurt like crazy. His plans for Hanbury House had been thwarted . . .

The committee meeting had been terrific; the report on Marchwood had been spot on, Robbo had been found guilty of negligence towards himself and Wilmot-Greaves, the fellow had been well and truly nailed; all their friends had had their say, Mary-Ellen had had more than her say, and Marchwood had looked as if he had tried to chew the front bumper off a Rolls.

It was unusual for Marchwood to have been so silent. No quips, no rude asides, no jokes – usually, Robbo lacked seriousness, a clever schoolboy, a sneaky fellow. A rogue and rotter like his father. A final warning had been given. Fortescue had slipped him the letter.

Now Stephen had some time to himself, he let his leather studded armchair take the weight. He tried to ignore the weather, forget his shares; he wondered what Donna and Inspector Wilson might have decided. He pressed a button on his telephone console and found Donna in her Bond Street den.

'Darling, do you fancy an evening at Covent Garden? The Royal Ballet are performing.'

'Stephen, you've just got to be crazy. Haven't you heard about the weather?'

This annoyed him. 'If it's not one thing, it's another. If people are not whingeing about their shares, then they rabbit on about the bloody weather. I'm sick of it.'

'I'm so sorry I even dared to mention it. Do you want to talk about Marchwood?'

'Donna, forgive me. Yes, your sister was in fine form; Mary-Ellen knew how to deal with Mr Marchwood.' He chuckled. 'How was your meeting?'

'Fine. The police inspector was real cute.'

'Ah, really? And what did you decide?'

She laughed and he could see her smile: 'Oh, a Monet is a Monet is a Monet.'

He laughed too, long and loud. What the police couldn't find couldn't come home to haunt him.

'Darling, it wasn't that funny. I'll catch you later,' she said and rang off.

He ordered a pot of China tea and rewound the finest clock in his twelfth floor office, his Thomas Tompion. This was a small, private Friday afternoon ritual, solemnly performed; he loved the clock. Tompion was the man known as 'the father of English clockmaking'. It was true, even if a cliché; Tompion had made significant technical advances, yet his clocks were remarkable also for their fine and decorous style.

'There is something about the tick of a fine clock,' he would claim. It suggested a hidden order, a force that might, one day, tame the mess.

His secretary announced: 'Mr Devies will be along shortly.'

Stephen's other great horological hero was Harrison, a cantankerous carpenter from Lincoln. Harrison was the first man to produce a timepiece so accurate and robust that sailors could determine a ship's position. He received a prize from Parliament for 'Discovering the Longitude at Sea', but was later shabbily treated for his pains. He saved many lives at sea, many cargoes, much to the benefit of Lloyd's, and Britain.

Stephen's delight in clocks and watches had induced him to write two elegant monographs about Tompion and Harrison. This had effected his election to the Worshipful Company of

Clockmakers, and led to other honours, including a trustee-ship of the Fitzwilliam Museum in Cambridge.

It was apt that the Harrisons were preserved at Greenwich on the Thames. This was the site of the first astronomical observatory (where a pair of Tompion pendulum clocks stood beside the telescopes) and a hub of British naval power, the place where world time was unified – around the meridian that passes through the observatory. But if the world's time was still based in London, insurance, merchant shipping and sea power were no longer; yet there were significant residues of Britain's world-encompassing greatness: marine insurance was still dominated by Lloyd's; the Baltic Exchange, where shipping and airline capacity was bought and sold, stood directly opposite, in St Mary Axe. The world's oceans were no longer a pond ruled by the Royal Navy, by they still contributed to London's wealth, still paid a tribute to Lloyd's.

Clearly, the glory of the nineteenth century was not sustainable in the twentieth. Two wars, hard-fought and hard-won, had curtailed Britain's power. However, there were traditions of greatness which remained; Grote saw the Lloyd's agent in every port, Lloyd's system of global marine surveillance, as unsung examples.

His family, also, could look back on a good, if not noble tradition. Like so many of the great City dynasties, like the Rothschilds, Barings, like the Lombards and Fuggers before them, the Grotes were émigrés, who arrived, made good and were assimilated. The Grotes, Stephen liked to say, were 'darned good, but only middling darned good'.

In truth, he himself had risen as far as any of his forebears.

He poured himself another cup of Oolong, when Devies stomped into his room, shook his cane at the window, and flicked a remote control switch. A television screen appeared in a wall cupboard.

'. . . The news is dominated today by the hurricane-force winds that have brought chaos to Britain. Dozens of lives have been lost, possibly hundreds . . .'

The report rolled on, in grim detail. The Cabinet was sitting in emergency session, a Government source had described the devastation caused by the storm winds as 'without precedent'; a state of emergency was expected to be announced shortly. The east coast, from Norfolk to Aberdeen, had suffered severe damage, many low-lying areas had been flooded, with rivers bursting their banks. Pictures of forlorn sandbags. Deaths from falling trees and collapsed buildings. Police, fire and ambulance services overwhelmed.

'At sea, the effects of the hurricane have been savage. Many ships are in difficulties and there are reports that oil installations have suffered serious structural damage. There are fears for the lives of platform workers and reports of fires. The weather is so treacherous that maritime rescue services are out of action until conditions improve.'

Devies was white: 'I have been told that a rig has blown.'

Grote picked up the telephone and asked his secretary: 'Could you get me Chichester please? And could we have a fresh pot of tea? Thank you so much.'

The news from Chichester was worse than expected. The maritime surveillance room, Lloyd's eye on the seas of the world, was in uproar. Maydays had been received from five North Sea oil rigs, there were reports of deaths and untold destruction. Gusts of 170 and 180 miles an hour in Forties Field. One rig completely blown-out, others ripped out of the water by gas explosions. Oil everywhere; oil burning, oil polluting, death in the North Sea. Yet the information was inadequate; the rigs did not respond when called; it was horrific, but nobody knew just how horrific. Nobody would really know until it was over. Until it was time to count the missing and call them dead. Until it was time to pay.

Grote asked Devies: 'How many are ours?'

Devies shrugged his shoulders. 'Perhaps all of them.'

They both knew Lloyd's was the prime insurer of the North Sea rigs; in the mid 60s Hurricane Betsy had routed oil installations in the Gulf of Mexico, and had taken many in the market to the brink and beyond. Stephen remembered it well; a close friend had killed himself. This could be far worse. Twenty billions, thirty billions. The figures were so large, they meant nothing.

He talked to someone who blamed the meteorologists. They had predicted bad weather, force 10, but not force 14 or 15 or worse. Stephen pointed out it did not matter. The rigs and platforms were designed for certain stresses, certain dangers. The hurricane had simply exceeded the expectations of men, the economic imaginations of mere mortals. Even if they had known, there would have been little they could do.

99

Finally, Grote replaced the phone, poured Devies and himself a cup of fresh tea, stared at his Tompion. 'Well, now we'll see whether this is the end of Marchwood.'

THIRTEEN

CONNIE SANDERSON TURNED the car into the drive. She did not stare, she simply tried to look at things as they were.

The journey home had been hellish. The radio was full of dire warnings: do not go outside until you really must, only in an emergency should you undertake a journey. Yet everyone had to get home, having left for work, this was plain ridiculous. They should have been warned, in the morning, then people would have known what to do.

She switched off the ignition. She was not going to cry. She opened the car door, stepped out and was drenched by wet squalls. Tiles continued to fall from the roof, smashing into her rose beds, the clematis was filled with red-brown debris and sections of the side fence had been blown flat, leaving a toothy battlement. The sycamores and pear trees swayed and curved, she could hardly stand, hardly see; a fir had exploded into a neighbour's dining room, stoving in the glass frontage and the first-floor bay.

Another tile fell from somewhere, landed with a crash nearby. She hurried into the porch, fumbled with her keys.

They had bought the house together, when Ron had inherited from his parents; she had instantly liked the place: spacious, with a large garden, built in the thirties with a reassuring black and white mock Tudor façade, surmounted by a large pitched roof with eaves and oriel windows. It was not a mansion, but, for her, it had been more than enough.

She opened the door, to find water dripping into the hall from the upper floors. A Chinese vase, filled with dried flowers, had been dislodged from the hall table and smashed; water ran down the gilded mirror behind the table; she looked upwards, and saw water running out of the landing lamp socket. The loft must be awash.

She picked up the telephone. Dead.

Another slate fell, then she noticed an unfamiliar noise: the house was whistling, a loud, variable whistle. This was the wind buffeting and blustering through the roof. She walked down the panelled entrance hall, opened the cupboard under the stairs, grasped a torch.

In the event, she need not have bothered. The loft was as bright as her dining room, there was water and tile dust everywhere, the glass-wool insulation was soggy; she coughed and coughed. The gaping holes looked larger from inside than from below; she discovered vistas she never knew the house offered, she looked out over her rear garden, to empty meadows and the distant motorway, jam-packed, headlight to tail-light. Rain poured in, accompanied by the whistle-howl wind. There was little she could do, the whole house would have to be redecorated.

She descended, returned with some plastic sheeting, a plastic bucket and mop to protect things as best she could. Before her eyes, half a dozen slates lifted and fell into the rhododendron beside the patio. Her much-cherished garden was in a sorry state; the trellises were chasing each other over the lawn, one tree, a pine, had been decapitated.

She set about mopping the worst of the water, but it was an impossible task, squalls of wet entered just as she finished; the air buffeted her, her hair was drenched, she was in her best suit. She had just ruined three hundred pounds' worth of clothes, she looked at the water stains, the grime and red dust. Her blouse was beyond redemption.

She started looking through the old furniture, the packing cases and trunks, picking valuable pieces. The task was hopeless, but she stuck to it. She lifted wet sheets, stumbled on the corner of a particularly heavy bedstead, admired the solidity of a chest of drawers that one day might be fashionable again, covered it with plastic to deflect the waterfall.

Then she lifted a cover, looked more closely at a dusty heap of pink-painted bars, a small mattress, a slatted base, a headboard bearing the picture of a teddy bear. Ron had not thrown it away, though he had promised, promised; she wept into the wind-borne dusk.

FOURTEEN

SOMETIMES, YOU WONDER what your family is doing.
For weeks, months, there was no problem, no sweat, then you
hear something on the news . . .

Five people had been killed in London by falling objects, by
tiles, by a tree. Stu Wilson was worried. What if Rosie, what if
Jenny, what if Kevin?

The house was dark and empty.

Wilson fought with key and lock, opened the door and
stumbled drenched into the hallway.

He was a hero; he had made the journey home. Three hours
for a journey that usually took one. He had heard the news again
and again. A state of emergency had been announced, the army
had been called in, the stockmarket had slumped. An unreal
terror. The oil rigs, well, that was terrible, distant, another
planet – but a tree, a tile, my God, even a plant pot.

He wanted to see Rosie. She would laugh at him, that was
fine. He parked the car in the garage, though he might still have
to see Kevin. He was worried about Kevin. They had to have a
word or two.

Someone had been at his desk, again. Kev had to take care.

Rosie was not there. The library ought, by rights, to have
closed early and allowed staff home; so she was probably in the
next road, talking green politics with a neighbour. He hoped
so.

First, it had been the church, then it was the church youth
club, and finally, it was the Green Party. One way or another,
Rosie would save the world.

During the last election, she had been out on the streets,
campaigning, distributing leaflets in the shopping precinct.
And all the guys at the station had seen her, and all the guys had

had their say. Yes, he was writing organic reports, recycling ideas, creating compost.

Stu did not necessarily disagree with Rosie; the church or the youth club or the Great Patagonian elephant were, as far as he was concerned, worthwhile causes. It beat watching television. Flicker, flicker, your life's gone by.

The street lights half-lit up, stuttered, then switched off. Where was Rosie?

He flicked a switch and was relieved to see a light go on. Just then, Rosie herself arrived, wet, energetic and cheerful. A particularly wet hug. She had indeed been nattering with her ecologically sound friend, sitting in the dark, waiting for sanity and electricity to return to the world.

Yes, the library had closed early; she filled him in on the latest gossip and intrigue between the bookracks. He helped her out of her wet things, propped up her wet umbrella in the hall, then walked into the kitchen, switched on the heating, filled a kettle.

It was good to be home.

Sometimes, Stu wondered what people thought families were for – after years in the force, he had heard so many terrible tales, seen such terrible behaviour, from people who supposedly belonged together: bruised wives, bloodied babies . . . Well, well. It was beyond his comprehension, yet it seemed to get worse, year in, year out.

He wished he could just switch off when he came home, but he needed to get things off his chest. This had made things difficult for Rosie. He only had to see one thing during the day and the evening was finished. Too often they sat in the kitchen and cried over the things people did. Nobody was responsible. Nobody had the time or money or energy to care about the baby or gran, even though the neighbours had said and seen and warned. The police had been round a week earlier and noticed nothing. Oh God. Sometimes, he felt there had to be a way to say: NO!

He had found a dead child, badly beaten, once. He had made sure the parents went down, but he had solved nothing, it would all happen again – there were no easy answers, to pretend prison was more than the best of a rotten set of options was stupid. Money would help, sure, but there was just not enough money to put the world to rights. Never would be. To his mind, you had to take responsibility for your own patch, in your own life;

you had to make people responsible for their lives, their children, it was the only way.

They had not been able to have kids of their own; when the time came, she wanted to adopt, but he was never at home and would not, he felt, have been a good dad. They aged into a sort of permanent truce, where harsh words and raised voices were not allowed. Rosie became more active in the local church, helping with the youth club, then, more recently, 'environmentally conscious', which meant the Green Party and vegetarian food. Fine, fine. On Sundays, though, he insisted on meat. He liked to see a joint on the table. Besides, it was an excuse to invite people round, to uncork the old sherry bottle. He usually only drank on Sundays, with friends, since his stint with the traffic police.

With hindsight, she had been right and he had been wrong. They should have adopted. It would be nice to pick up a daughter from school, that sort of thing. Play football with a lad; he had often kicked a ball around the park with Kevin, helped out when Jenny was over-over-protective; but Kevin was not his son.

He carried a freshly brewed pot of tea into the lounge where Rosie had already taken a seat in her favourite armchair; she was watching the news.

A small, self-important man was being interviewed. Mr Grote, in front of the Lloyd's building.

'Is it true that the damaged or destroyed rigs are insured at Lloyd's?'

'It is too early to be precise. Lloyd's pioneered the insurance of the offshore industry, so several of the rigs will be . . .'

'Do you think that the market will be able to cope? Initial estimates suggest losses might be as high as twenty billion pounds . . .'

'Whose estimates?'

The interviewing voice was silent.

'No matter. Clearly, this is a terrible disaster, but I have no doubt that Lloyd's will meet its commitments.'

The wind was defeating the microphone.

'Thank you, Mr Grote . . . We return from the City of London to the North Sea, from where we have just received our first pictures, taken from a Shackleton reconnaissance aircraft this afternoon. This is what remains of the Piper Belle rig . . .'

The film showed a ramshackle scaffolding, made of crazed steel pipes and a metal box, burnt, blackened, still burning. It looked like one of those toys people use in films. This was not real. Even Stu, who had spent so much of his life at sea, who had seen the devastation caused by waves and wind and water, found the images hard to believe.

'The helipad has disappeared, one of the cranes has been washed away, the drilling derrick is buckled and broken; half the superstructure is missing . . .'

Evidence of a huge explosion. Workplace for two hundred men and women. Stu was glad he did not have to break the news to anyone. Rosie was silent.

He walked to the sideboard, picked up the telephone, dialled Jenny's number, noticed that the phone was dead.

Rosie said: 'Been dead since lunchtime.'

There were reports of large oil slicks, of pollution over miles and miles of sea. She sprang up from her chair, and crisply switched off the television. She would rustle up something to eat. She seemed cheerful, he knew, because she was upset. These things were too much to take. He had been involved with a multiple pile-up once, mayhem in fog, on the motorway. There was nothing you could say.

'What do you fancy?'

'Anything,' he said. 'How am I to get in touch with Kevin?'

'Tonight? You can always drive round to Jenny's.'

He explained about the picture and its valuation.

'Well, I hope you are not putting him at risk. People think differently when so much is at stake.'

Stu laughed and pulled his chess set out of the sideboard, then set up the pieces, which were based on Romanesque figures found on the Isle of Lewis – squat, strong, with startled eyes. It had been a gift from Rosie on their twentieth wedding anniversary – a surprise, because she never played. He placed some cuttings beside the chessboard and played through Kasparov's recent games against Karpov, marvelling at their control and violence.

FIFTEEN

CONNIE WAS TIRED, but no longer wet.

A candle burned on the kitchen table. Walter and Lucy, neighbours who had lost their front room to the errant fir, had come for a candlelit supper with a difference. Walter had brought a primus stove, Connie scrambled eggs and provided hot cups of tea.

The wind had dropped to a gale, and they whiled away the time telling each other jolly stories. Walter, who was a lawyer, had a fund of yarns about deaf or senile judges, stupid policemen and even more stupid crooks; Connie responded with children's sayings and doings, with stories about her local council and teachers' gossip; Lucy restricted her contributions to an occasional hearty laugh. It was all so jolly that Connie regretted they had not seen more of each other. Ron had played golf with Walter every so often, but Walter had never spoken about his wife. They knew that Lucy had long had her problems, that much was well-whispered, but nowadays she worked for a mental health charity which maintained hospices for sufferers from depression, a good thing. The tea was less of a good thing, being warm and very bitter; they cheered up the awful brew with a tot of rum, and tried to work out where they should sleep the night.

'You can stay here, there's no problem,' Connie said. 'Now that Ron's gone, there are hundreds of beds. At least one or two ought to be dry.'

'I always thought Ronald was one of life's artists. Made it all look so easy,' Lucy said. This irritated Connie – what did she know about Ron? They hardly ever met, apart from drinks at Christmas or the odd summer party. Waved, of course, exchanged pleasantries in the drive. Smiled.

'Yes,' Walter agreed, with a chuckle. 'Ron was one of those chaps who made living an art. He was never at work, not that I saw. I would drive past the garage four times a week, say, on the way to court. Every so often, I popped in. But he was never there. Finally, the chief mechanic told me not to bother during the day; it was not worth my while; the boss was always out. I would have given my right arm for a routine like that.'

Lucy laughed, too. Connie looked at her dry-scrubbed hands, with her marriage rings, then she rose to make some more tea. The candle went out; they fumbled with matches, hot wax and a new packet, until a steady flame burned once again.

Sixteen

A BORED MAN at the hotel reception in Bloomsbury did not bother to look up from his newspaper. Yes, second floor.

Kevin Vaughan steeled himself. The stairway was clean, wallpapered in floral swirls with a dark, patterned carpet. The hotel was larger than one might imagine, forged out of two rather grand terraced houses.

Number 15. He knocked, and the door opened.

Mrs Montfort had been wearing a red silk shirt, no jacket, prim blue skirt, gold ear rings. Plain black stockings.

'This yours?' She held a blue diskette in her hand. She closed the door, he muttered something . . .

Now she was wearing a white towel dressing gown.

He finally found his latest pair of City shoes, one beside the television set, one under the dressing table, nearly a hundred quid a throw, the pair built for eternity. His suit was a mess by the mini-bar, he thought about a hanger, by rights a wooden hanger, there were those metal things, which rattled like an out-of-tune guitar in the wardrobe, at last he found his silk tie on the floor, beside her dressing gown. Yes, one hell of a rush. Sort it out later.

They showered together.

He was speechless, so she talked about herself and, for once, he listened. Her life was, well, a bit chaotic. She was divorced, without any children; her husband had run off with another man. Still, she had a reasonable life, a flat, nice holidays.

He fiddled open the black soap case with the fake hotel crest, so that she could lather herself; he admired; her body was generous, but not over-generous. She was especially beautiful to touch.

Lying on the bed, later, somewhere between half-dry and

half-wet, Kevin made some sort of protest about his job, his career. He remembered Denbigh-Wright's words.

She laughed, lightly. 'Oh, don't worry, I won't say anything. Besides, Tony is just playing you along.'

'What do you mean?'

'Even the Blighter went to somewhere like Eton, didn't he? You don't stand a chance.'

In a couple of years, Kevin would have a degree. Yet he saw the danger; even if he had the brains, the clients would not like his London accent.

Yes, she said, that was the argument MacNulty would use against him. There had been someone else, who had been blocked, for the same reason.

Stuff MacNulty. She giggled at his silence, and he could see, at least, that he had made her happy. For a time.

'I suppose there have not been many girls in your life?'

He responded swiftly: 'I suppose there have been many men in yours?'

'Not that many, actually.'

'I'm boring, too.'

They both laughed, for no real reason, which was as good a reason as any. He decided it was time to raid the mini-bar, so he rose, while she switched on the television.

'Oh, look, there's Grote . . .'

'What? Where?' He was still struggling to find a beer in the fridge. For her, there was Liebfraumilch at champagne prices. What a rip-off.

'. . . We return from the City of London to the North Sea, from where we have just received our first pictures, taken from a Shackleton reconnaissance aircraft this afternoon. This is what remains of the Piper Belle rig . . .'

The Piper Belle. One of the Blighter's little numbers. Kev stared at a badly chewed tin box.

'Oh, well, that's this year's bonus gone.'

The television continued with the names of four other rigs that had been severely damaged by the hurricane. Kevin recognised the names, the Blighter was lead underwriter for three of them, that much he knew, because he had recently fed the data into the computer; this was part of the great Robert Marchwood oil rig deal that had made so many in the Lloyd's hierarchy so very rich. This was the deal that he had been trying to investigate with the program on the diskette that now lay on the bedside table, beside his watch.

He switched off, poured Alice a glass of awful wine, helped himself to a glass of beer. Chink, chink. To Kev and Alice. To the lost billions.

The room was nondescript, modern-bland, but she glowed, propped up in pillows, a counterpane across her lap. 'Has Wordsworth lost money?'

'I guess so.' He explained: based on the data he had seen, the Blighter had insured the first tranche of the rigs, perhaps as much as one hundred million, that would drive the syndicate into loss. But he reckoned the damage was strictly limited – that would be true of Stone, of Wilmot-Greaves, of Grote, the top dogs. It was his hunch that, over the years, they had made hundreds of millions in premiums. Others would have to pay the open-ended commitment.

'Who?'

'Depends how Marchwood split up the deal,' he said. 'I guess: the syndicates of Mite Leven, Annan and Salter.' He laughed: 'And Robey, probably, in the Cronin syndicate. All bluster and no brains: good old "Ropey" Robey.'

Robey had only got the underwriter's job, so they said, because he was an old friend of the chairman of Lloyd's, because they had worked together, years ago; he was also known as a good shot and went hunting with Alec Wilmot-Greaves.

If a broker offered the Blighter a really dodgy deal and he was in a goodish mood, he would send the guy on to see Annan, a man only rumoured to be alive, with the comment: 'Always interested in out-of-the-way propositions, our Mister Annan. Try Mister Robey, too.'

Sometimes, Blighter would say, seeing Mite and Leven together, 'Sometimes the weak exist so the strong can get stronger.'

And Salter's nickname was 'The Mine'. It was known that Marchwood had mined there, very profitably. That was his business and Lloyd's was a free market; the names who did not work in the market had not a clue.

'Did you see the file on Mrs Sanderson?' he asked. Alice had not, but remembered the appointment that morning. 'Tony keeps personal information locked in his cupboard, and anything sensitive in the safe, such as hard disks.'

'And gin.'

'No, that's in a box file, under D for drinkies.'

Kevin smiled: 'There are hard disks in the safe?'

'The removable ones, I would have thought you knew. There are sticky labels on them: asbestosis, DA&P, Baden-Baden. God knows what it means.'

He did not know that either, but he did not say anything. The hard disks were, effectively, mobile data banks. Did they hold evidence of a deal between Knowle and Wordsworth? Or of a marketwide deal between Knowle and the Lloyd's hierarchy? Was one of the disks marked Marchwood? Could this confirm his hunch about the oil rigs?

He had intended to wave Stu goodbye; now, his curiosity was aroused.

He surprised the receptionist, wishing him a very good evening. The street outside the hotel was calm and silent. Kevin walked for five, ten minutes, past the shadow-filled exterior of the British Museum, a temple barely lit by street lamps.

Finally, he managed to hail a taxi. The driver muttered, then drove in silence to the Bank of England. From there, he headed north on foot, before doubling back, through St Mary Axe, to Lloyd's. The streets were deserted, there were few signs of the storm that had blown so forcefully earlier, newspapers, assorted rubbish lay in the gutters.

The Wordsworth offices were dark, one solitary security guard manned the reception desk, guarding the whole block. Kevin walked round the block, waited, waited, the man did not move, he knew him vaguely, finally he strode up to the desk, with a broad smile, showed his pass, admitted he had forgotten a present for his wife, then failed to sign his name in the book. See you later.

One lift was working. He took it to the fourth floor, to the front entrance of the agency. There he paused, considered the keys that Alice Montfort had lent him; finally, he tried the largest and most imposing and was in luck.

The point of no return.

SEVENTEEN

THE PHONE RANG.

It took some time for Stu Wilson to notice.

He and his chess pieces were moving through impenetrable depths. It was late, so late that Stu hardly noticed the silence outside. The wind had gone, had been swallowed by some awesome beast of the night.

Rosie had retired to bed hours ago, taking a book, while a tenor sang melancholy arias in the background. Their evenings together were often this way: quiet. He could see the old-fashioned record-sleeve on the sideboard beside the black sound system. The tenor had been famous twenty years ago, but had since disappeared God knows where.

He turned the record over, for a third or fourth time, he liked to simplify at this time of night, then the telephone rang. The engineers must have mended some lines. A blooming miracle. It was Kevin, excited as hell, though he said very little. Called himself Daniel.

They agreed to meet in Capri, which was more an old joke than a code name. Stu looked at his watch; it was way past midnight, why not meet tomorrow? Kevin insisted. Stu relented. The things he did, sometimes.

The main roads had been mostly cleared, but many minor roads were impassable – except by bicycle. So Stu pumped up his bike tyres, checked his lights and then filled his old whisky flask; this was heroism beyond the call of duty. He left by the lane behind the house.

The night was mild and calm, his breath left barely a trace in the air as he cycled round trees, branches, smashed fencing; his route took him past rows of darkened houses, shuttered shops, under the railway arch, past the station, on and on he pedalled, suddenly enjoying the exercise. Everywhere, tiles had been dislodged, lay smashed in driveways and gardens, gables and chimneys had disappeared, one house appeared to have lost an entire roof. Telephone wires were down, one or two telephone poles uprooted. Hard to believe that the wind had abated, hard to believe that such a wind had been there.

Everyone, it seemed, had gone to bed. The clear-up could begin tomorrow.

Capri was not an island basking in Mediterranean sunshine and the aura of Roman emperors. Capri was only a name for a row of three lock-up garages beside a high-rise block, built by a 60s brutalist, which proclaimed the perfection of abstract thought and the grey reality of concrete. Whenever Stu drove past the block, he almost heard the people's pain.

Yet Keef, his sergeant from the Essex shop, had an affinity to the place. He rented the garages to keep and maintain his growing collection of Ford Capris. They often met here, to talk shop, to criticise the powers that be and wonder about Stonecot's leadership. Stu used the place to meet contacts and store information; the garages were overlooked by the flats on the first two floors, reserved for old couples. Two grannies, supplementing their pensions, kept an eye on the place.

Stu opened the small door inset in the large, central door, parked his push-bike inside, switched on the lights and waited.

The sound of high-pitched bike brakes. It was Kevin, in a good mood: 'Your friend has naff taste.'

He pointed to the white wonder, Keef's pride and joy, a 200 horse-power Capri with turbo-charged engine, wide wheels, speed stripes and leather seats. Otherwise, the lock-up was a heavy-duty workshop, with blow-torch, electronic tuning gear and God knows what else. Seemed a funny hobby for a cop, until you realised that a Capri had been the set of wheels to impress the ladies hereabouts, twenty years ago.

'Keef still dreams of his time in a Capri,' Stu explained. He locked the door: 'Were you followed?'

'Don't be ridiculous!'

Stu explained. His desk had been turned over again. During the day someone, with a key, had been through every drawer. It had to be a senior colleague, maybe two. Stu poured Kevin a whisky.

'Where did you ring from?'

'Phone box.'

'Told no one?' Kev shook his head. Stu continued: 'Look this is very big, very big indeed. In twenty years in the police force . . .'

Kevin did not need to be told: 'That's why I rang.'

He placed a sheaf of photocopies, a computer print-out and some computer diskettes on the car bonnet. The diskette returned by Alice was there.

'Hell. Now I don't know where to begin.'

So Stu started the whole thing off. The Monet, a painting worth five million pounds, had been given to Robert Marchwood, chairman of Knowle & Co. Why?

'To stitch up the market. MacNulty and his friends needed Robbo to rig the market.'

'Who are MacNulty's friends?'

'Stephen Grote, John Devies, Henry Stone, Neil Fortescue and Alec Wilmot-Greaves and a host of minor gods such as Alan Denbigh-Wright. Do you know he asked me to join the Freemasons?'

Stu shook his head: 'Why did they need Marchwood?'

'With him they could control the market, with him they could determine the way risks and premiums are distributed. Without him, it would not work.'

Stu was not sure he understood.

Kev tried another tack: 'Five billion pounds flow into the market each year as premiums; the friends work together to take their cut – just two to three per cent would clear one hundred million pounds a year.'

'How?'

'They direct the best business to themselves. Blighter's syndicate is stuffed with friends, they have the largest exposure, with most of the capital pledged. There are other syndicates. It adds up to a top quality income, millions and millions of pound worth. Lloyd's is being used as a private money-machine. And the Monet was just petty cash for services rendered.'

'Proof?'

'This diskette,' Kevin picked up the blue square of plastic snaffled from his pocket by Alice, 'details the relationship between Knowle and Wordsworth in respect of the oil rigs. It's not the whole picture, just part of the picture. But you can see that the good business goes to Tony, thanks to Robbo.'

'And the overall picture?'

'It might be on the hard disks in Tony's safe. There's one marked Baden-Baden, where they have an insurance conference each year; one year, I reckon, they met there and cut the deal on the rigs.'

Stu mused, then said: 'That's where the Marchwoods met. In Baden-Baden.'

'In any event,' Kevin went on, 'the hard disks will only give you the overall pattern of the deal. I think you have to go to the Lloyd's data store to see the full story, to see the detailed workings of the rigs deal, to see the friends (and Robbo) sorting the wheat from the chaff.'

'That's surmise.'

'Sure.' Kevin shrugged his shoulders. 'Lloyd's is one hell of a complicated casino. It's the complexity which gives the friends their chance.'

Stu helped himself to some whisky. His thoughts turned to the Monet, a masterpiece – in this context, it was just nothing. So the swindle was worth, well, a hundred million a year? It made Irwell's illegal arrangements with friends and admirers look like chicken-shit, yet in the biscuit tin there were two dozen guys working full time on the Irwell bid. Of course, Lloyd's was fiendishly tricky: these guys were not just tough, they were exceptionally smart; they had turned crime into art.

Wilson pressed Kevin again: 'Can't we prove this? What might convince a jury?'

'Hold on. Do you know a Connie Sanderson?'

Stu shook his head. Kevin handed him photocopies he had made of her file.

'My old headmistress. I reckon she's bust. Taking the risks, so the other guys could take the money.'

She was not on Blighter's syndicates, but she was on Mite Leven, Annan and Salter – all dominated by business from Marchwood. Awful rig business, bound to explode.

'The Blighter won't explode?'

'Profits will be eliminated this year, maybe next year, too. But the billions to be paid will be paid by others.'

Kev ran through the information on the diskette and print-out: the relationship between Blighter and Robbo, between Wordsworth and Knowle. One sweetheart deal after another. The same pattern, year in, year out. There was a master deal somewhere, there had to be.

'The whole deal will start to unwind slowly, during the next months and years, as people are burnt and bankrupted.' But you had to know what you were watching.

The garage smelt of oil, cleaning solutions, of car dirt; it was cool inside, colder than outside.

Stu and Kev looked at the pile of information, the data. All that effort, all that risk, yet both knew it was not enough, there were too many guesses, too many questions unanswered: who had stolen the Monet? Why? They needed proof of a master deal; fingerprints, something signed, something that you could actually see. They were close, but the closer they came, the greater was the chance of the evidence disappearing; Stu had already lost one file. It was risky to inform the DG, impossible not to.

Kev was cold. 'Stu, I have to go.' He made his final offer: 'Raid Wordsworth's offices. In MacNulty's safe, there are several hard disks, aside from Baden-Baden, they are marked asbestosis and DA&P. They contain, I guess, the patterns of other deals between the friends and Marchwood. But let me get out first.'

'Leaving Lloyd's?'

'Leaving you, Stu. This is far enough. I have to think of myself . . . Just look at this place. Can you ever see this coming to trial? Who would ever testify against Grote or Marchwood? There's so much money riding on this, do you think the SFO will let you turn Lloyd's into a crater? . . . I wish you all the best, but I have a life to live.'

Stu nodded at his nephew; he turned away and heard a bike being wheeled away, heard the door being unlocked, then quietly shut.

There were few people and few places Stu trusted. There was this collection of old scrap and nearly classic cars, the chrome exhaust pipes and bumpers hung overhead, they would keep his secrets. He wrapped the information that Kev had brought in a plastic bag and hid it inside the car seat that was, for some reason, fixed high on the wall. It already contained pictures, slides, addresses. An affadavit; in Ventnor, armed with every conceivable photograph, talking to Welsby, the customs man, Keef had struck pure gold.

Then Stu noticed that Kevin had not taken a single sip of his

whisky. Well, down the hatch. It was past midnight and he
wasn't driving.

BOOK THREE

ONE

A GREY DAY in July, warm, muggy, smudged with rain.

The newspaper vendor in Pall Mall was still selling the early edition of the evening paper, bearing the headline: UPROAR OVER LLOYD'S LOSSES. Despite billion-pound losses from last October's hurricane, Lloyd's chairman Stephen Grote had told the annual meeting of names that Lloyd's would survive and flourish: 'We have experienced three hundred years of trials and tribulations and, I may add, greatness . . .'

Beside the stand of the Pall Mall vendor, between Piccadilly and St James's Park, a cab stopped, and a raincoated man from Whitehall descended, bought a paper, then hurried along the pavement, entering the four-square cream-white building that overlooked Waterloo Place.

Along the upper edge of its façade ran a frieze copied from the Parthenon. This reminded the visitor of Lord Elgin, who wrested the marble original from the Turk, and served as a tribute to Phidias's fifth-century masterpiece and to Athena herself, goddess of wisdom and war.

For a century and more this building had housed the Athenaeum, a club for scientists, lawyers and writers, for the eminently civilised. The hubris of the comparison between the Parthenon and the Athenaeum, between fifth-century Athens and nineteenth-century London had not worried the Victorians: they were not alone – Paris and Berlin also each laid claim to be the Athens of the North, as they stretched after possessions and empires overseas.

The man from Whitehall left his raincoat at the cloakroom, passed a portrait of Darwin on the staircase, then entered the library, where Thackeray wrote several novels, though not, it is said, his best work. The library at this hour was empty, except for one middle-aged man reading a newspaper.

'Hello, Bill,' our man murmured. 'Dreadfully sorry I'm late.'

'Don't worry, old man. Thought you would be in severe need of one of these.' William, from Downing Street, gestured at a waiting whisky and soda, cigar in hand. 'Had a chance to catch up on things without interference from the blower. And to indulge a little.'

Nigel, for that was the name of our man from Whitehall, smiled, dropped his leather bag, newspaper and umbrella beside a chair and took a seat.

'To the whole bloody mess.' He raised his glass.

'To the mess.'

There was a silence while both sipped their drinks; Nigel looked round, as if to be sure that they were alone among the books and periodicals, the aged, leather-covered furniture, the high bookshelves.

'I can confirm the Treasury is feeling the pinch,' he said.

Bill placed his cigar on an ashtray. 'That bad . . . ?'

'Think of a number between ten and twenty, take its square root, move the decimal point eleven places to the right . . .'

Bill laughed.

Of course, they both knew there was something of a problem. Black October had holed the Exchequer's finances, and left the Government reeling. Sterling had plummeted – the loss of revenue from the North Sea would open large budget and trade deficits – while the costs of the North Sea clean-up and of increasing unemployment would be high and long-lasting.

Nigel sipped his whisky and sighed: 'The little men with the calculators reckon the storm will cost the Treasury thirty billion, spread over three years . . .'

'Equivalent to the annual bill for the Health Service,' Bill added. 'Fun and games, fun and games.'

Both men had heard Whitehall, in the quietest possible way, screaming. The new budgets, the new targets looked hideous. Nobody was sure that cutting and slashing made sense, even if it was practicable, with the economy threatening to disappear into a hole.

'Give or take a billion. Lloyd's has taken a hit of ten billion,' Nigel said, gesturing at the newspaper. 'At least.'

Bill raised his eyebrows: 'That's not what Mister Grote said. Read my lips and all that. A little dicky-bird tells me there may be a problem on the other side of the Atlantic, too. So watch this space.'

'Another?' Nigel asked, pointing his glass at Bill, who smiled and nodded. He was in luck: a waiter on the stairs took their order.

'Yes, bleak's the word.' Nigel returned to his seat, answering a question that had not been asked: 'All budgets revised downwards since last time. God knows what we shall do with the steaming fiasco at Lloyd's.'

'Natural fertiliser, my boy, spread liberally to green the set-aside acres of England.'

They smiled. 'My lord and master was all for horsewhipping the cads,' Nigel said, 'after he discovered bankruptcies could mean by-elections before the general election.'

Bill drew at his cigar. 'His Greyness rang the head of the SFO, Mrs Rainsley, last night. Entre nous, the White House has been troubling his sleep. They would like to see action.'

Nigel pondered this. 'The police can't stop MPs going bankrupt.' In the Victoria Street bunker Nigel and his master had frittered away time, idly wondering what if this, what if that, what if the other; the only certainty seemed to be that, once bankrupted, an MP must resign.

'No,' Bill mused, languidly, watching the cigar's ash grow. Even he did not know what his master had wanted. 'A meeting at Chequers has been pencilled in for August. He will hold fire until he has seen Grote.'

They both knew that there had been arguments about what Lloyd's should pay towards the oil catastrophe. Besides, there was this outcry about the losses within Lloyd's, claims that the market was run for the benefit of the insiders, all unproven.

The waiter entered with drinks, nuts and a round of sandwiches.

Nigel said, after the waiter had disappeared: 'The City is running rings round the Government at the moment. Neither Irwell nor Wansbeck are coming up with the right publicity . . .'

They smirked. The complexities of Wansbeck had even sent judge and jury to sleep. Nobody understood quite how it worked, but everyone saw that forming secret pacts to buy chunks of companies was not the right way to make money.

'A bloody mess.' Nigel stroked his chin and, for once, spoke his mind. 'Good fun for the lawyers . . . The PM has to move, doesn't he?'

Bill picked up a sandwich. 'I think he's desperate to know what to do.'

They were silent for a time, playing through alternative responses, the political advantages, economic disadvantages or vice versa. The choices, frankly, were limited, in certain areas hopeless. For six months, they had met here on alternate evenings to confer and suggest, and watch the economy slide. There was only one strong card possessed by the Government, the weakness of the Opposition; now there was some desperate talk of a war, an overseas escapade. They would have to wait and see and, if need be, pray for something short on body-bags and long on good publicity.

TWO

A STRANGE CAR stood on the gravel drive of Golden Rain, one of those little boxes on wheels, with a white-and-black Swiss CH sticker and Zurich number plates.

Robert Marchwood observed that they had a visitor or visitors. Had Thérèse warned him? He could not remember, he thought he would have, had she done so, but he was not sure. Recently, he had felt as if he was only half-awake; it was this darned virus.

The drive compacted slightly under his crisp footsteps. She could not be far. The hall lights, drawing-room lights were on, a cold spread was prepared in the kitchen – various breads, salads and cured meats. He left his briefcase on the chair beside the hall table, then made his way up the main staircase.

'Thérèse?'

On the landing, with its solid, white-painted doors in deep doorframes, he suddenly heard distant voices and laughter, sounds that seemed to boom along some tunnel. He turned and saw nobody, deceived by the weird acoustics of the house.

He opened a bedroom door, almost fell over an unexpected suitcase, then stood at a window overlooking the pool.

Thérèse and a male guest, in the swimming-bath. He could see her in the water, laughing, catching and throwing a bright beach ball, turning, then swimming a few strokes, once the ball had escaped her grasp, only to be beaten to her goal by a fuzzy-haired gent wearing an absurd bathing-cap. They were both laughing.

He went downstairs.

'Ah, Robert.' Thérèse was apparently delighted to see him. 'Robert meet Urs, Urs meet Robert.'

Urs, a man of medium height and build in his late 30s, waved from the middle of the pool and flashed perfect white teeth.

'Urs is an old friend from Zurich. You know, he's the tame architect I talk about.'

Robert, too, smiled and nodded. Urs had apparently rung, just that afternoon, on the off-chance that Thérèse might be at home, and Thérèse had invited him, simple as that. Robert agreed, it was no problem; he had friends round all the time.

They dressed, while he went in search of a grand cru Chablis from Les Clos. 'None of your over-priced Swiss nonsense,' he said, bearing his prize.

Thérèse laughed: 'Robert prefers over-priced French.'

To honour Urs, Thérèse had had the dining room prepared by the housekeeper, but Urs insisted on the kitchen; he liked kitchens, theirs was particularly fine. That, at least, was what Robert gathered, when they were all seated round the kitchen table. It was a gathering, where gesturing proved more viable than the spoken word. Urs spoke German and reasonable French, but abominable English, comparable in awfulness with Robert's love affair with the gallic tongue.

Thérèse rattled away animatedly in three languages to both of them, while preparing fresh croutons, two salad sauces, slurping wine and making Urs a peppermint tea in an unglazed teapot she had brought from Switzerland. Robert just gawped at her energy. Do real men drink peppermint tea? Well, Urs looked real enough, and he would drink some wine later. He said: 'I remember I saw Robert once in Zurich, we were having a dinner.'

Thérèse smiled, but Robert did not: he remembered that weekend in Zurich, the way he had had this woman on his mind.

The wine was good. The dog started to bark outside, there were voices; Robert excused himself and rose to find the Hugheses, his handiman and his wife, on the lawn, staring at the dusk.

False alarm, apparently. Robert returned to the kitchen.

Urs explained that he had taken a sabbatical to study low-cost family housing. In Britain, this meant visiting Docklands, a council estate in Newcastle, Glasgow and a range of other oddities.

'Docklands is a mess,' Robert said, reducing the length of his sentences. 'No sense to it.'

He could see that Urs itched to enter into a grand theoretical lecture, but was overwhelmed by the demands of English. He left them together with a full bottle, pecking a kiss at Thérèse's cheek; he smiled at Urs.

In the hallway, he stumbled for no reason. The darned virus.

Not that he had been ill, he had simply not been himself, he had felt out of sorts for weeks. The doctor had diagnosed a virus, one of those nasty things that plagues everybody, for no good reason, then disappears. Nothing the wonders of medical science could do.

Just keep taking the vitamin C tablets, get plenty of rest. Robert had nodded and was moderately obedient. He took the tablets. They did no harm and might do some good; there really was no reason for concern.

Thérèse found him in their white marble bathroom at three in the morning, half-naked, looking puffy-eyed and wan.

'What's the matter, darling?'

He shrugged and grumbled. He really did not know. She gave him some water, went to find his pyjama top and a dressing gown; when she returned, he was scrumpled on the floor beside the bath.

'It's nothing, nothing at all.'

Thérèse struggled with his bulk, until he was sitting in the bedroom in a white wicker chair that had seen happier days.

'I'll get a doctor.'

'No.' His retort allowed no disobedience. She pulled on his pyjama top, wrapped him in his dressing gown, wet a sponge and wiped his face. Robert smiled and she kissed him on the forehead. He had just blacked out for a moment, that was all. Nothing serious.

He asked for a cup of tea, without milk or sugar, which he found refreshing. Thérèse slipped down the stairs, to the kitchen and filled a kettle. Outside, it was quiet and damp. Her reflection in the kitchen window was gaunt.

'Could be rain, could be fine,' he announced cheerily, when she re-appeared with the tray. He had already rearranged table and chairs so that they could sit together. They kissed, as if nothing had happened.

He looked years younger than a moment earlier; whatever it was, appeared to have passed, his boyish face reminded her of the good times. There was a silence, then she poured the tea.

He had disappointed her; perhaps she had expected too much, perhaps she had expected more than anybody had a right to. In so many ways, she was living the life of a fairy-tale princess, she had everything anyone could ever wish for and more besides – but she had worked, she could still work, to earn whatever she needed. She had not married for money, for luxury and all the associated baubles. It was, however, pleasant to be surrounded by beautiful things.

They were there, all around her, with hidden little hooks, contractual arrangements. On her off-days, she thought like this. In fact, she thought more and more this way.

One thing, however, was certain, she had definitely, certainly, sincerely married him for what she thought him to be; she had chosen a firm man with definite character, had admired Robert's power, his sense of self and his love of romance; perhaps, indeed, she had loved him. As close to love as she ever dreamed she would be. It was that sense of something special that had uprooted her, not far off her fortieth birthday, from home and career.

Now, she was not sure who he was. This was not just a difference of languages, of temperaments, of age and sex; she was truly uncertain. So her feelings became less secure. True, she was not really the typical wife of a rich man – the former stewardess, model or actress that many seemed to choose. Coffee mornings and chitchat about hairdressing and infidelity were not her thing.

When she remembered his impulsive generosity she flushed; yet when she remembered his tantrums, his lies, she was shocked that she had become so weak. Would things have been worse with Urs? Would things have been better?

Robert was as white now as a sheet of fine writing paper.

They talked, quietly, amid the chink of cup and saucer. She ran her hand through his hair. Perhaps, perhaps.

The house was still, there was no wind, not a pane rattled. The bedroom was lit by two subdued bedside lamps. He had drawn the curtains. He looked at Thérèse, her hair was unkempt from sleep, her face strangely white without make-up; in a way, he preferred her like this, almost young and blushing. There were laughter lines around her eyes. Things had not been easy; work was demanding, Lloyd's was in uproar, his firm needed attention.

He said: 'I cannot afford to be ill.'

Thérèse was irritated. What was his work? They had spent a

weekend at Ascot, she had been on her best behaviour for Robert's underwriters, men whom he sought to reward or press into service; it had been rowdy, fortunes had been won and lost, a man called Wilmot-Greaves had been rude; not her sort of fun. She had grown tired of wearing expensive dresses.

'Robert,' she paused, frowned, hesitated. He smiled, waiting for her to finish. 'Are you a crook?'

He laughed, too heartily. 'No!' He coughed. 'What on earth makes you think that?'

'Just something my father said.'

Now he was roused. 'What was that?'

She ignored the question. 'All this entertaining, the wine, the food, the money . . .'

He took her hand. 'I just play the game. Within the rules. For our benefit.'

He nodded at the room, implying the house, implying her. She persisted, refusing to be drawn into the implication. She had protected him by lying to Inspector Wilson.

'What about the Monet – is that within the rules? What about all these people who have lost millions? Is that within the rules?'

He was silent. She looked at him and, despite herself, leaned forward and stroked his face.

Then he asked her whether Urs was to stay long, and she saw what he meant and said she did not know, barely concealing her annoyance. That was for Urs to say.

Still she asked him to rest at home and recuperate. He refused vehemently. Today was special; there was to be an election, Robert might become a member of the ruling committee of Lloyd's to which his father had so wanted to belong; there were deals to be struck. He had to be there. This was what he always said. Again, she asked him to stay at home, for her sake. She thought of how she had seen him, queuing at Lloyd's with a slip of paper in hand, waiting for a signature. He could have been a newspaper boy, a postman, anything. With his little bits of paper in hand, he might have been shopping for vegetables.

She did not understand why he should be paid so much – millions, just for bits of paper.

That was, probably, why he wanted to continue. Money. Ultimately, he could always find a fashion model.

She looked out of the window, as the countryside was starting to take grey shape before her eyes. It was so beautiful. She tried again, resorting to one of his favourite saws: 'Hell is filled with the souls of irreplaceable men.'

He laughed again, but easily. By now, dawn was lighting the tree-bound horizon and blackbirds were starting to sing the world to order . . .

After a long week without him, one Friday late in July, she took a decision. She packed two cases and a mini-cab took her to the station. A letter, left on the hall table, said: 'If you want, you know where to find me. Give Veronica Cantor my regards, all my love, Thérèse.'

This was unfair, Robert thought; he had not seen Veronica since October, although he had had flowers sent.

THREE

THE JOB OFFER from the Marchwoods came as a bolt from the blue.

Of course, Kevin Vaughan had suspected that it might occur to Ray that he could be useful. Of course, he knew the Blighter and Tony MacNulty and their friends would not like the idea. That was their problem.

It had all started when he had trudged off to see Ray, not for any devious reason, only because they were both into computers and because Kevin was interested in bee-bop, jazz and suede shoes, too. They met every so often, perhaps every other weekend, he would often show Ray work from his computing classes at the City University – stuff that Ray more than often knew. Although Ray was entirely self-taught, he was astonishingly good. He also had a personal museum of the micro-computer – every obsolete widget and gadget you care to mention – which was a laugh. To think man had landed on the moon with a mini-mini-memory, with a pea as brain! Computers were one technology where you really could see progress, almost daily . . .

One Saturday in July, they were sitting in the back bedroom-cum-loft, which Ray had converted into an all-white computer den, with printers, modems, mice, old drives, new drives, and the very latest, the most expensive, hottest micros. A multi-millionaire could afford to junk a micro every other month. It was Ray's sole area of conspicuous consumption.

He was looking through one of Kevin's programs: 'Very pretty, very neat, very fast,' he commented. 'Wrote something similar myself once . . .'

Charlie Parker was winding up on the old saxophone. Kevin drank some medium-tepid tea, looked out of the window, letting the tiredness of a hard week slip pleasantly by. He half-heard what Ray was saying.

'. . . It imposed a pattern upon immense amounts of data, while letting them seem random to the untrained eye. The clever thing was, the pattern generated six or seven lines of code, which showed what had to be done with the data and proved that the pattern was working. It actually worked . . .' Ray's voice trailed away.

Kev glanced over to Ray, who had pushed back his metal-rims onto the bridge of his nose. He was surprised; Ray rarely boasted about anything.

'So what did you use it for? Why the secrecy?' Kev asked, idly, but only received one of Ray's long silences by way of reply. He'd learned when to let well alone – Ray had his no-go areas – so he dropped the line of questioning and instead told Ray about his latest conversation with the Blighter, about the offer to join the friends of Lloyd's. 'For months, the Blighter has been dangling his invitations. Now he's provided me with a pile of information and there's an induction ceremony lined up within a fortnight.'

Ray laughed, lightly. 'So?'

'Not my idea of fun.'

Kevin did not believe in God, not even in a vague, all-encompassing way, so he disapproved strongly of Popes, bishops and shirt-lifting vicars. And weird ceremonial. The book the Blighter had given him was filled with all sorts of rituals and imprecations and gestures.

Ray said: 'Ever thought about being a broker?'

'Could do,' Kev answered, ungrammatically.

'You could do worse than join our shop.'

'True.'

So that was settled. Ray talked to Robbo who interviewed Kev with a bottle of champagne and two glasses – but Robbo trusted Ray's judgement, left the details and the contracts to Ray. Robbo said he would explain everything to Tony and that Kevin could join straight away, no problem.

Ray had been excluded from the room, by decree; now he could only supervise the broking operation from Knowle's offices; they desperately needed new blood.

Payment was very generous, heavily skewed to performance, with neat extras such as fees for the course, a new computer and software, cheap mortgage and car . . . but then, Knowle & Co was unbelievably loaded – with a staff of twenty to twenty-five regulars, the company had accumulated a cash pile of eighty million. It was your above-average gold mine. No, it was the best gold mine in Britain.

A neat place to be number three.

Before he left Wordsworth, he was to have a holiday in Spain. He also needed to consult Alice Montfort on sartorial and other matters; as a result he acquired new clothes from an expensive tailor in one of the streets that curl alongside Leadenhall Market: braces, silk ties, two or three designer-labelled suits. After a further heart-to-heart they agreed that people were talking, so it was goodbye-and-I'm-on-my-way-to-Spain. She gave him a final kiss and he promised her lunch, some time after he returned. Neither of them wept.

Spain meant a resort not a million miles from Benidorm, with a bunch of fellow escapees from his comprehensive school who were brokers or futures traders or forex dealers and their assorted mates. One of the guys had chosen an expensive hotel in this wonderful high-rise resort. Kev had not been pleased, but was not in the habit of holidaying alone, certainly not abroad. That might yet change.

The first day and a half were OK – until they all drank too much and there were bangs, shouts, rudeness and, finally, the hotel manager fuming at the room door. Kevin had already evaporated. He became a semi-detached member of the group, and ended up with a fortnight of sangria, sun, sand and more sand.

You could say it gave him time to think. Time to consider his options. Time to read books he did not want to read, sit in high-powered places with high-powered people. Certainly, the beach gave him time to speculate on the reactions of Tony MacNulty and Alan Denbigh-Wright to his departure. They were not likely to be happy. But Robert Marchwood had insisted that there was no problem, telling him: 'I'll sort everything out with Tony. Don't you worry about a thing.'

Still, as Kevin contemplated his future, he wondered if he had not been over-hasty.

FOUR

DETECTIVE INSPECTOR STEWART Wilson was near to despair.

Normally, he could console himself, tell himself he was on the verge of a breakthrough, that patience would be rewarded. Something, somewhere just had to give.

But now he had ceased to trust those around him; the loss of the file had been a blow from which he had not recovered; everyone who worked near his desk or in his office had to be watched. Even Tomlinson was impossible to fathom.

The investigation had died on him. This was the norm when research rather than leg work was needed; there was always a desperate point where the pieces fell apart and he seemed to be faced with the remnants of unrelated games, a chess endgame played with half a pack of cards. Over the years, he had patented ways of coping: a new haircut at his old barber, a game of chess, in the past a weekend fishing expedition or a night out with Rosie had helped pull him through.

This time they had not worked, so he decided he needed a holiday: out of habit he booked a hotel room in Magaluf, Mallorca, then told Rosie who seemed, as ever, grateful enough. Magaluf had been her idea, the first time they went there, and over the years they had had many rattling good holidays there.

Now, however, Rosie was no longer in the mood for their old haunts, for the tapas bar, the disco and the sleepless siestas. OK, Stu thought, that's fine by me. But it wasn't.

Of course, Rosie was at a difficult age, so she said, but was not every age difficult? That was no reason for the world to come to an end. He tried not to complain and hoped the sunshine would cheer her up.

And Rosie did not complain, nor criticise over-much, but she brooded, almost audibly. Not that they even had words when there was a problem: they never really rowed, they always rubbed along, that was the general rule.

So they still held hands as they walked along the promenade, which had been cleaned up, and visited Palma, a little town crammed with art galleries which appealed to them both. It was terribly civilised, very nice. But it left Stu feeling as if he was fifty-turning-seventy rather than the fifty-could-be-forty he saw himself as. The Good Lord gave us just the one life and the idea was to make the most of it.

When Stu repeated this jokey dictum to Rosie, over a rioja-washed meal beside the bay, she all but turned on him: 'That is most unchristian, Stu.'

Since he had never professed to being a Christian, this did not seem to matter. Stu said nothing. Yet it evidently irked Rosie, she left her meal and retired for the evening, on her own.

In the past, even without children, there had been no shortage of things to talk about; she had her books, her library and her church; he had his work, his dealings with all manner of folk. They were different, sure, but he liked to think they complemented each other. For years, for twenty-six years in fact, they had been lovers and the best of friends.

Now there were silences between them. Differences of opinion and temperament. Well, there were worse things. So he put Magaluf down to experience and hoped for better times.

But on their return, things were no better. His morale was not high. The job was to blame. He took to waking between three and four in the morning, Rosie found him sitting bleary-eyed in the kitchen with a cup of tea and her latest agenda from the Green Party or a chess book. He had always slept like a tomcat fed on cream. Now he was worrying about the ozone layer, the destruction of his position as he knew it.

There was nothing Rosie could do, it seemed. Yes, she tried, gave him a kiss and a smile.

He was more than just preoccupied. He turned Lloyd's over in his mind, again and again, the interesting things, the uninteresting things and the junk that simply did not fit. He wondered, once again, if he should question the key men but decided, once again, that it would just alert them, close down potential lines of enquiry. It was, however, a narrow decision. Weeks drifted past in menial work for Tomlinson and fear of contact with the DG.

Finally, Stu Wilson wrote his report, knowing full well that it promised much and delivered little. A Monet had probably been imported by MacNulty and Devies, and had probably been given to Marchwood as payment for rigging the Lloyd's insurance market. Which was why the outside names were now screaming blue murder. Yet he could only come up with a Probably. Which was why the DG was likely to roast him alive.

He read and re-read Welsby's affidavit. Talked to Keef. Finally, he took another trip over the Solent, to Ventnor and Welsby, just to be certain. Welsby had recognised the third Englishman on the boat that day. It was Stephen Grote, chairman of Lloyd's of London and art-smuggler. Probably. This could be severely embarrassing to Lloyd's, if true.

There was, however, no Russian collector seeking a Monet, he had checked through Interpol. No explanation for the theft. No record of the picture either before or after it appeared on the wall of Mr Robert Hugh Marchwood. In short, the case remained a mess.

He wondered who or what he was fighting, for whom. The financial discomfort of names he found uninteresting. The Government might lavish love and attention on the rich and famous, but Stu had seen too many who had too little. The names' plight was not tragic, not to him.

Admittedly, they had been robbed. They had entrusted their wealth to smooth-talking strangers, and they had been nobly mugged, royally ripped-off. Perhaps you should not believe everything people tell you, particularly when money is involved? Through the Marchwood deal on the rigs, tens of millions, perhaps hundreds of millions had been snaffled; it could not be easily quantified, it was not like a video that fell off the back of a lorry, but still it was theft. On principle, therefore, he did not want it to succeed.

The hypocrisy was galling, too. The guys who had stashed away millions were honoured members of the community, the salt of the Tory earth, the officer class. These were the people whom the police went out of their way to protect. These were the guys, in the great global cricket match, who were batting for Britain. Yet that was a lie, too. The more Stu thought about them, the more he was outraged, the more he wanted to nail the blighters.

That, in those days, seemed remote.

Digusted with himself, angry with Kevin, he threw his report into the DG's pigeonhole on a dull Friday afternoon in August, sure that he would be carpeted on Monday the thirteenth. He included Welsby's testimony in the report. He did not like to; but he had no choice.

He planned to take the weekend off, go fishing in Norfolk, unwind beside some stream or other. There's nothing like a fishless day in the rain to cheer up a washed-out inspector.

Rosie, however, insisted he stay and have Sunday lunch with Jenny and Kevin. It was to be one of those patch-up affairs because Stu and Kevin had found it easier not to see each other since the previous October.

On Saturday afternoon the doorbell rang.

This was the worst possible time and Stu was in the worst possible mood; he should have been fishing and Monday loomed as large as his failure.

At least he had been asked, at the last minute, to play that night for the Essex chess league.

Stu opened the front door to find a tall, heavily built man somewhat younger than himself. Derek Tomlinson.

'Sorry, mate,' Tomlinson said, apologising for some unspecified misdeed.

Stu was cool. He stood by the door and explained he was on his way out.

Tomlinson, known to his friends as Tommo, seemed to think he had a right of entry to the Wilson household. 'There's talk about your report. We need to have a word.'

Stu ushered Tomlinson into the kitchen, without apology or offer of tea.

'Since when have you been reading the DG's mail? I left it in her pigeonhole, yesterday.'

Tomlinson took a chair, then hesitated. 'Let's say I've heard things. Are you sure about Grote?'

Wilson was silent.

After the first batch of photographs vanished, Stu had kept his desk clean and orderly; he had avoided leaving anything of significance in the office overnight or unattended during the day: he kept the affidavit from Welsby, tapes, computer data and the rest snug in Capri. He had neither suggested, mentioned or hinted at Kevin's name. Yet because everything was so neat, he could not always see if someone had rifled through his desk drawers. He felt watched.

Tomlinson said: 'You're on a hiding to nothing.'

'Meaning?'

'You're involved in a game that goes, well, deeper than you imagine.'

'Do you have to talk in riddles? I don't understand,' Stu steadied his wrist to look at his watch, even though he could see the kitchen clock. He had done the job to the best of his ability and, so it seemed, had failed.

Tomlinson produced a clipping from that day's newspaper. He scanned the headlines, the first paragraph or two. About the Banco Cristòforo, the banker Scrivano, who had died last year in the Thames, and the Italian Freemasons. No, he had not seen the newspaper; nor did he mention that he had spent a fruitless morning, looking for a decent new variant in the Caro-Kann defence for that evening's game.

'That's been leaked from on high. To my knowledge, the City police are sitting on that murder. And there's a definite link to Lloyd's. So what about Grote?'

Murder? Not accident? Not suicide? Ah, the newspaper was suspicious. And Lloyd's?

'A mate of yours is in the know?' Stu asked, unruffled by his lack of knowledge. He had heard lots of 'good stories' in his time. Every policeman with a long service record had his own store of half-open, half-closed files and cases, where the chief super didn't like it or the witnesses suddenly agreed to disagree. Such stories were like the fish that get away: there were shoals of them and they tended to be larger and smellier than the ones that landed in the courts.

'A mate? You could say that.' Tomlinson smirked.

Stu saw the smirk and a wise guy who was full of hot air. Certainly Stephen Grote, chairman of Lloyd's of London, formed part of his investigations into the theft of a Monet. But so did everybody down to the Archbishop of Canterbury's cat.

Tomlinson held up a hand. 'Look, I haven't come here just for fun.'

Inspector Stewart Wilson looked at Inspector Derek Tomlinson and waited.

'They may ask you to move in. When you do, just make sure you've armour-plated your spine.'

Thanks, thanks a million. Bland stuff and nonsense. Go chew some scrap-metal, Tommo.

'What's it to you?' Stu asked.

Tomlinson shrugged large shoulders. Perhaps, Stu guessed, the visit was well intended; perhaps Tomlinson genuinely had a contact he couldn't talk about. But whatever his motives, Stu was in no mood to run for cover. Without another word, he showed Tomlinson the door.

FIVE

ALL AT ONCE, Connie realised where Ron had kept the key.

The idea shook her from a dull, drug-induced sleep, all but flung her out of bed; in her nightshirt, she threw open the bedroom door, hunted, then found the upper landing light, her feet were surprised by the carpet pile; normally she wore slippers. Shadows thrown by a solitary street lamp waved in the stained glass of the staircase window. She headed downwards, rushing across the hallway, flicking on another light switch, until she stood in the front room, where everything was still firmly in its place.

She had not been there for months, it was as if she had left it behind, in another life. The clock on the mantelpiece no longer ticked, a drooping wood semicircle, a 30s mixture of geometry and architecture. Ron had wound the thing up, once a week, placed the key in a china dish next to the clock, above the tiled hearth.

She switched on the light, closed the curtains, tipped the contents of the flower-rimmed dish carefully onto the dark stained-oak coffee table, to avoid scratches.

Found it!

In the kitchen, which was cool, the tiles chilled her feet. There in front of the dishwasher was a grey metal filing case, locked. More an expanded briefcase than a filing cabinet, it had stood in her kitchen for weeks.

'The boss kept this in the stockroom,' her head mechanic had said, presenting her with the box, pointing to a padlock. 'Do you have a key?'

Of course she did. Admit that Ron liked his little secrets? Never. She needed no help, none at all.

True, she had not sold a Bentley for months. She had not sold a Bentley, period. Not a happy position. To sell the garage, she had to sell cars and, please God, make a little profit. She needed, desperately, to sell the garage, to clear debts, losses, just to re-surface, but the omens were not favourable.

Of course, she still had her school, her friends, but at the moment teaching was a more than a full-time job, there was a Bentley franchise for her spare time, an estate to wind up as a hobby – and Lloyd's to ice the cake.

She had lost so much. Within nine months, since the day of the storms, she had lost two hundred thousand pounds as a Lloyd's name. She earned only twenty-five thousand as headmistress of Lime Grove, so she had been shocked by the first demand – for forty thousand. Then the next, for twenty. Then the next, for fifty. And again, and again. That was what unlimited liability meant, that you kept paying until there was nothing left of you, not even the hand to sign cheques.

About ninety thousand ago, she had stopped paying the bills sent by Wordsworth, by that nice man Mr MacNulty, and joined all the action groups and litigation committees she could. Not that she had much hope – they were all crooks and rogues at Lloyd's. Only herself and others like her were paying: she now knew her syndicates were by far the worst, avoided by everyone inside Lloyd's.

That man MacNulty had known. When she thought of him, she thought of a fly one might splat to death. When she thought of MacNulty, she thought DDT. His so-called professional advice had cost her more money in a few brief months than Lloyd's would ever earn her in a lifetime.

MacNulty had said: 'Oh, don't worry, my dear. Most unfortunate. Next year will be much better.' Connie did not have many more years and she certainly had no more money; this she did not say.

Then that dapper little man Grote, so smooth, so reassuring and so concerned, at the annual meeting in July he had said, to general applause, 'The hurricane of last October, the wholesale destruction of North Sea oil rigs represents a great crisis for all at Lloyd's. Yet we have the will and the strength and the history to survive.'

The applause still rang in her ears.

Luckily she had a lovely GP who ensured she did not overdo the sleeping tablets, gave her a course of hormone jabs to keep her hopeful, and cracked good jokes. 'Come and see me any time, if you want anything,' the doctor said, which meant he was concerned.

She breathed deeply. Outside, a solitary car drove past, beyond the kitchen windows lay a dark garden. She looked at the safe and hesitated, key in hand.

She needed a lucky break, even more than a guardian angel GP. A flood of filthy lucre, a hidden deposit book. She needed something, just to cheer herself.

The key scrunched in the rather pathetic lock and the jaws of the safe were prised open. There were no building society savings books, no national savings bonds, not even a decent set of accounts to explain how Ron had made his money. Instead, there were a few bills. Paid, fortunately, and with cash. Mostly from some stables, a few from a farrier, a vet, a blacksmith. Apparently Ron had kept a horse for several years; she was astonished; she knew about the hunt madness, but this was ridiculous. Why did he not tell her? In a metal compartment beneath the bills she found a bundle of newspaper advertisements that Ron had placed in the *Sunday Herald*, week in, week out, for nearly a year. They were odd; long advertisements for car numbers and Ron did not sell car numbers. Some of them did not even look much like car registrations, more like some jumbled code, but still they were all under the garage's name. Here were the receipts, too. An expensive business. This was ridiculous.

At least there were no love letters.

She must ask her chief mechanic. The man knew more than she ever had and remained faithful to Ron, even when he was in the grave. Men were a pain. A pain.

The tap was dripping. She stood up, picked the papers from the floor and placed them on the kitchen table; she felt cold, she decided to boil a kettle, put some muesli in a bowl. She climbed the stairs, showered at a leisurely pace, dried her hair, did her make-up, the usual foundation, rouge and red lipstick, then dressed for Sunday morning communion and a chat with the vicar: a dark blue suit, white silk blouse and slightly raised heels.

The milk was on the step. She walked back along the hallway, her shoes clattering against the parquet floor. In the kitchen, the tap was still dripping. She drank a cold cup of tea.

SIX

SOMEWHERE BETWEEN MARSHALL'S birthday chowder and the Chicken Maryland, Mary-Ellen Lemke paused and looked out of the study window and admired the pleasant sunshine, the way a light breeze ruffled countless chestnut leaves.

Marshall was with the kids, playing softball in the neighbourhood park. The kids, that ramshackle term, meant four children with partners, spouses or not, and their ten grandchildren and step-grandchildren.

The front door squeaked in its unoilable way, as it had for twenty years, and she rushed downstairs, headlong into chowder and watercress, chicken and relish, burger and batter and the clamour of hungry folk.

Normally, she did not cook much, just weekends and when she absolutely had to. For Marshall's birthday, however, she made a special effort, though nowadays daughter number one would cook the relishes and daughter number two sorted out the chowder and number three avoided the kitchen because she was a professional cook and professional cooks lived in a world full of better and brighter food.

The table was set up in their large, irregularly-shaped dining room, which was really two rooms plus a conservatory that Mary-Ellen loved and was very English and very Victorian and filled very full with them all. The food was homecooking – everybody ate either beef or chicken and those that didn't dared not darken Marshall's door. Marshall was in the vanguard of unreconstructed males who thought vegan was another word for dyke. She was glad, seeing Marshall in a new Cleveland Indians hat and a Browns shirt someone had given him, that he had still wallowed in the simple things, like homecooking and old-fashioned prejudice. Sometimes, Mary-Ellen felt, you just needed straightforward answers to straightforward questions.

Did she love Marshall? Sure.

Did she think Lloyd's crooked? Sure.

What did she think of Grote? No answer.

Marshall, who had lost half a million dollars that he did not really have, with more losses to come, still smiled at her as if nothing had happened. He sat at the head of the table, a thickset, stocky presence with a broad grin and booming laugh. All the girls helped carry and cook, there were jokes about softball and the Rolling Stones and the family dog and fake Rolexes from Hong Kong; then everyone sang 'Happy Birthday' and she could see he was moved.

Speech, speech. Then the toast to her, too. Then the one to everybody else, excluding Red the aged setter, who was in the kitchen, whence Mary-Ellen returned to sort out the dishes, and where he came to find her and hold her tight for the first time that afternoon, to thank her for all her efforts, for being his little Cherry Sundae and other impossibilities.

When the phone rang, Marshall and Mary-Ellen were locked in an embrace, while the kids came in search of maple syrup. It was Embassy Joe, not *their* Joe, who had booked a table for that evening for serious eating.

'OK, you guys,' Marshall said, back from the hall phone where everybody had heard a long silence. 'Scram. Pop has to talk the next play with Mom.'

Jeers, wolf-whistles.

The door closed, he switched on the dishwasher, long since filled, and gestured that she should stand beside him.

'That was Joe from the Embassy.'

'I heard.'

'Bad news. I've got to fly to Milan. Now.'

Mary-Ellen cursed loudly and with her usual directness.

He said, 'Honey, there's a crisis.'

'There's always a crisis. This one can wait till Monday, like all the others.'

He smiled and she saw that it was serious.

He started to talk about Italy, about the Mafia, about the CIA and the Freemasons, stuff she had heard before and, well, half-believed. Joe was in Italy and, it appeared, staring into a black hole that even Washington called a black hole and into which any number of butts were likely to disappear because Washington had suddenly discovered that it had been investing for years in the fusilli Freemasons to keep Italy safe for the Mafia and because, moreover, the Freemasons and the CIA had seen their investments go walkabout . . .

Mary-Ellen shook her head.

Look, Marshall insisted, ever since the war, when the Yanks cut a deal with the Mafia to dethrone il Duce and Lucky The Thug had been given a complimentary oneway ticket from Manhattan to Palermo, ever since then there had been a battle in Washington between those guys scared of the reds and those other guys picking dead-heads off the streets of New York. And ever since then he had been finding company money, paid to do honourable things like blow up train stations or kill a bunch of politicians, being diverted instead into nice honest enterprises like heroin or cocaine or crack or whatever shite dope fiends needed to turn their bodies into skeletons. Of course, company money did not really matter, the US taxpayer did not really matter, the dead-heads were hell-bound anyway, but it was his job, on occasion, to sort out something. It was for Washington to decide what it really wanted, not him. He was just the hole cleaner.

She realised his argument was drifting, but she let him go on.

Anyway, this time the black hole was in a Riviera-based bank called the Cristòforo and the company had lost tens of millions, placed by Washington through Rome through Milan in the principality. The irony was that the Freemasons themselves had been duped by the head of the bank, a Mr Scrivano who had been found last spring . . .

'In St Katherine's Dock, by the Tower of London,' she said, just to show she was still on her feet and fighting.

'Killed by the local talent.'

Freemasons? How did he know?

They knew. In a way, that did not really matter, everybody was kind of happy to see Scrivano sing to the fishes, even the Pope had blessed his soul swanning off to Malebolgia, he had lost dough too. He had been investing in things Popes don't usually.

So?

In the week before Scrivano came to London, in the spring of last year, several Lloyd's firms had moved large cash holdings

145

out of Cristòforo accounts. Indeed, up to his death, up to the very day his bank collapsed, money was being transferred out. My God, Marshall wished he had such investment foresight. Wished he had Grote's investment foresight.

'My God,' Mary-Ellen said. 'And what about Donna?'

Marshall smiled. 'That's not the sort of question that's being asked in Washington. They're much more interested in what's happening to the Vice President.'

'The man who's a heartbeat away from a big mistake?'

'The man who has managed to lose even more money at Lloyd's than Marshall D. Lemke. So you better believe Washington is becoming kinda itchy; at the moment, the company just looks at Europe, sees holes. It doesn't know who created them, it doesn't care who created them, it just wants them stopped.'

He would have a coffee after he had packed.

SEVEN

STEPHEN GROTE HAD hoped to be invited to Chequers under other circumstances.

The invitation had been for Sunday lunch, which turned out to be a solitary plate of curled sandwiches in the long gallery.

He ate nothing. It was as if he was waiting to see his housemaster.

He strolled to and fro, admired the display cabinets, a William Moore gold timepiece bearing the arms of Nelson; the books included some fine early editions. There was the first illustrated volume of *Paradise Lost*, showing the defeat of Satan and his devilish machines.

When the Prime Minister arrived, begging his excuses, Grote managed to be extremely civil. He pointed to the timepiece and told him how Lloyd's had rewarded Nelson during the Napoleonic wars.

The PM responded: 'Chequers even played a small role during the last war. Churchill had the gallery converted into a cinema and watched *Lady Hamilton* here, many times.'

He signalled to his aide that he would not, for the moment, be needed.

'Grote, I'm sure you don't have to be told that we are in a hole.'

Stephen nodded, then waited, certain that a litany of complaints would follow. He was not disappointed; the economy was in a mess; the Conservative party was divided; an election was due within two years. The analysis was not surprising, but Stephen had hoped he might learn something that was not in the newspapers.

The PM then sprang a surprise: 'Have you ever considered what it might be like to be called Sir Stephen . . . ?'

Grote tried not to smile: 'No.'

'Well, if we hear the right answers, at the right time, we could move on the matter.'

Stephen asked: 'What do you expect?'

'The whips tell me that we have seventy MPs who are names at Lloyd's, of which forty appear to have been holed, including three junior ministers; we wondered if you might not move those threatened from the disaster zone.'

'People would know.'

'Think about it,' the PM continued. 'After all, the last chairman of Lloyd's was knighted, was he not?'

Grote said nothing, looking down the gallery at the stained-glass windows. He could see that he had not given the right answer.

'Have you eaten?' the PM murmured.

'Yes, thank you. More than enough.'

The PM changed tack, backed by a handwritten memorandum. It was clear the knives had been cleaned and sharpened. Speaking somewhat mechanically, the PM told him: 'Lloyd's is supposed to be whistle-clean, yet the whole place reeks. The White House is shouting about unfair treatment; the Vice President has lost money. I ask you, as if I didn't have other matters to discuss with the President!'

Grote listened in silence. The grey man demanded: 'I think you will have to ring-fence the Vice President. Then, to encourage everyone else, I want to see a beheading or two. Which name do you have in mind?'

Grote baulked at nominating a culprit. 'We are considering every option. There is a great crisis in world insurance; I should remind you that the American insurance market is little short of a nightmare. We have always met our liabilities towards America.'

'I want a name, Grote. Robert Marchwood is a name that the newspapers might recognise. The world's greatest broker and all that jazz.'

They could not discipline Robbo again. Not again.

Stephen fought for time, emphasising the freakish nature of the hurricane, perhaps global warming was to blame; the future was bleak for all insurers.

'You mean, Mr Grote, that this is the end of civilisation as we know it?' With a peal of unlikely laughter. Stephen had seen the PM grin, but never laugh.

148

He nodded, at the risk of looking absurd. 'The effects could be severe. Just imagine driving a car, owning a house or running a company without insurance cover; long-term planning would be impossible.'

The PM smiled. 'You mean, there would be a continual threat to corporate health, that sort of thing? Golly, that's something else to keep me awake at night. Lloyd's is unique, Grote. Uniquely bad. Do something, Grote. Get my men off the hook, get the Vice President off the hook. I want to see it happen. Then I want you to find me a name.'

Stephen Grote was shown out of the house by a policeman.

EIGHT

THE KEY CRUNCHED in the doorlock and Stu discovered he was still in bed.

'Stu?' Rosie called and he knew that she reproached him for his laziness. After all, she had already been to Sunday communion. He muttered something and Rosie appeared in the bedroom door, her hair drawn back in a bun, which gave her a severe air.

He could tell she had news for him.

He rose and dressed and they shared a pot of tea while she prepared Sunday lunch, to which Jenny and Kevin had been invited. He watched her peeling and chopping vegetables and felt tired, flicking through the Sunday newspaper, looking for something in the mass of newsprint that he knew he would not find, especially since he did not know what he sought. So he admired the pictures instead: a natural disaster, advertisements for cars and computers, a war.

Then he heard Rosie saying: '. . . they're going to renew their marriage vows. After fifty years of marriage, imagine that!'

That was it. This was her news, involving two of her friends, retired schoolteachers. Stu said sourly: 'I guess they gave Magaluf a wide berth.'

'What was wrong with Magaluf?' She was astonished, gaped at him, potato-peeler in hand.

'Didn't you notice? Don't imagine that you'll ever get me through that rigmarole again.'

She fended him off. 'I wasn't thinking of asking you . . .'

'Good. Rosie, I really must tell you . . .' He did not know why he had started but now he could not stop. He made a dismissive gesture. 'There's no way you're going to see me march down the aisle again.'

'Well, don't. I didn't suggest it. I don't know what I have

done to deserve . . . I really don't know what your problem is.'

'Don't you?' he demanded, angry with her, seeing her close to tears, angry with himself, angry with the world. 'What the hell does it matter what other people do? We have to do what is right for *us*. At the moment, we – ' He never finished the sentence because Rosie had run from the room.

He prepared the meal, while she sobbed upstairs, and mustered a cheery smile as he saw Jenny, sporting a summer frock and new hairdo, with a suntanned Kevin.

He offered them both something to drink and Rosie put in an appearance. For once, she accepted whisky while Jenny contemplated her sister and her brother-in-law. Cheers.

'You look well, young man,' Stu said to Kevin, who mumbled something about Spain then placed a bottle of decent red wine on the table.

Lunch was swiftly served, while Stu and Rosie avoided each other's gaze. The beef was excellent. If Rosie was subdued, Stu was excessively cheerful and, with the dessert, the conversation turned to ordinary tales of City folk.

Kevin took over. 'Since the stockmarket crash,' he told them, 'sacking has really come into fashion. Each nation goes a different way about it. The Americans talk about "downsizing" their workforce. The Swiss use the tannoy system to announce who is to go. You just have to imagine the silence on the trading floor, where several hundred people work, as the victims are despatched to the exit.'

'And the Brits?' Stu asked, sipping his wine.

Kevin laughed: 'One British bank gave its unloved a black bin-bag each. To carry away personal items.'

Jenny and Rosie seemed to agree that this was hilarious.

Jenny said proudly: 'Kevin has a new job.'

This interested Rosie greatly; Kevin rubbed his nose and admitted that he was to join Knowle & Co.

'Do you know them?' Rosie turned to Stu, for the first time during the meal. He was silent. 'Are they good people?'

'I'm sure they're good at their jobs,' Stu said, after a while. 'And I'm sure Kevin will be well-paid.' He smiled at Rosie, whose smile froze somewhat.

The me-too, grab-it-all eighties had passed her by; Rosie was an idealist; Stu only need mention pay to arouse her suspicions that the new job was not a Good Thing. He did not dare breathe a word that Kevin was working for a suspect. In ten years, he mused, Kevin could be a suspect himself.

Jenny was relating tales from the north-east, when she and Rosie were still girls. In those days she had only earned half a crown a week, as a typist in a typing-pool, while Rosie received a bit more, as a bookkeeper and filing clerk. Kevin, who had heard the stories before, dared to ask to see football on the box.

Rosie asked Stu: 'Did you have a visitor yesterday?'

Stu hesitated, then lied, out of indolence, because lying was sometimes easier and he could not be bothered to explain a truth which he only partly understood: 'No. Why?'

Rosie placed a golden trinket on the dinner table. She had found it in the kitchen. 'Joined the brotherhood of friends?'

Stu flushed as he saw a tiepin with a compass and square-rule motif. He cursed Tomlinson beneath his breath. It was either a joke or a warning and he had no explanation. Rosie did not believe him but said nothing.

Coffee was brought. Rosie loaded the dishwasher.

This was the moment Jenny had been waiting for, evidently. 'Stu, you're not doing anything, you know . . . dangerous for Kevin?'

Stu laughed at the question. 'No, we no longer work together. His career is safe in my hands.'

Rosie played a record of German operatic highlights and washed the fruit. The telephone rang; Stu went to answer it. When he returned, the dining table had been cleared and the patio doors opened.

Rosie lost her smile when Stu told her the news: 'The DG has read my report and wants to see me. Now.'

Within the hour, Stu had found his way past dozy guards and through empty corridors to the DG's office. On a coffee table there were flowers, and on the wall there were pictures, prints of sailing ships. It was the plushest room in the biscuit tin. Carnations, would you believe.

Someone loved the DG.

At her invitation, he took a seat and watched her, in unusually uncertain mood, prowl the room then sit on the edge of the desk and stare out of the window at the City skyline. Finally, she spoke: 'Wilson, we're going in. First some last-minute number-crunching, then we're going in. I hope you have some nice handcuffs, Inspector.'

NINE

IT WAS MONDAY morning. The meeting was urgent and Stephen Grote, of all people, was late.

This was so uncharacteristic that it might have given some cause for concern. Waiting in the chairman's office, Tony MacNulty knew that the situation was desperate.

Stephen was their best bet. He had led them through all the trials and triumphs of the past: Cristòforo, and a host of others. Even Baden-Baden had hardly been to their disadvantage. At the annual Lloyd's conference, a fortnight earlier, he had been brilliant. Stephen could find answers when others saw none.

On that Monday morning, despite everything, nobody worried out loud. Henry Stone had enjoyed a very talkative weekend on the Riviera, discussing the past of the Cristòforo and the future of Anglo-Italo-French cooperation. Ever since Stephen, over two decades ago, had struck a deal with Ioannis Kolokotrónis, the Cypriot owner of a huge tanker fleet, they had enjoyed excellent, hugely profitable relations with friends based in the Mediterranean.

This was another reason why everyone deferred to Stephen, everyone expected him to come up with an answer. They knew he would not announce anything formally until he was certain; but they knew he was preparing something grand, that Henry Stone and John Devies were involved.

Not everyone had found it easy to make the meeting on time. Neil Fortescue had returned from New York on the 'Red-eye' and was trying to forget the night lost between JFK and Heathrow; Alec Wilmot-Greaves kept himself to himself, hiding behind a newspaper, after a heavy weekend with Marchwood. Tony MacNulty felt restored after a weekend sailing at Cowes; besides, he had not touched a drop for weeks.

A reddened rather than bronzed John Devies, who had sailed with him on Saturday, stomped across the room, placed the two electronic devices on the table and watched their lights turn from red to green.

MacNulty knew there was an ugly report from services division in Devies's briefcase.

Everywhere there was grief.

Time seemed to tick gently. The losses caused by the stockmarket crash had, by and large, been made good but the hurricane had devastated Lloyd's, leaving them with difficulties on an unknown scale.

Tony was always surprised that so little resistance had been encountered. But this was changing: unhappy and bleeding names, an unfavourable press, a difficult annual meeting, litigation starting to turn malignant . . . and now the politicians.

Losses of two billion had been announced at the annual meeting, but there was worse to come. Perhaps five next year, five the year after. Perhaps a loss of £400,000 a name, if every name lost equally; they had not.

'We'll give them a couple of billion to think about,' Grote had said. 'That will prepare them for next year and the year after.'

It was possible that Lloyd's might not survive. In the chairman's office, it was not a thought that could be uttered. Everyone behaved as if everything could continue.

Despite his sailing holiday, Tony MacNulty felt jaded by the mere thought of work. He was sick of consoling widows, orphans and retired colonels about losses; he hated the business people whom he had recruited during the last years, people who thought Lloyd's owed them something. They shouted, threw tantrums and generally misbehaved when confronted with their losses; a rugger-playing hotelier from Swansea had even tried to head-butt him; he expected a flood of legal actions, shortly, from such persons.

Tony turned to Henry Stone. 'Good trip, Henry?'

'The weather was spectacular. Blue skies, good food and wine . . .'

'And the company?'

'Interesting. A good discussion.'

Henry was rarely specific, until something had to be done; his contacts tended to be excitable and rather unreliable. MacNulty was glad not to have Henry's task: he was decidedly happier sailing with Sue, now his fiancée, and other friends.

He said: 'Heard you were racing at Cheltenham on Saturday, Alec . . .' Alec Wilmot-Greaves looked up from his newspaper and marvelled at the speed with which Tony had been informed of Marchwood's day with a posse of underwriters. '. . . must have been rip-roarious.'

Wilmot-Greaves blinked suspiciously. He had a reputation as a man who tended to buckle badly on the third glass of champagne; Marchwood had lent him an American blonde to keep him vertical.

Tony teased: 'Alec, old boy, I was told you lost a small fortune on a Yankie . . . How was Robbo?'

Wilmot-Greaves sipped his coffee. In fact Marchwood had paid all his bets, including a ten-tonner that came home at ten-to-one, a start at compensation for the deal that went awry. He responded easily: 'His usual self. Seems nothing affects him. His Swiss wife has run off. God knows where. Not that I could ever stand the woman.'

'At least she had a touch of class.'

'Too much for our Robbo. Looked happier without her. There's some other filly in the saddling enclosure now.'

Once again, however, Robbo Marchwood was causing grief. The others did not know, not yet. Tony had been looking for a quiet word with Grote. Last Thursday, Marchwood had clapped his hand on MacNulty's shoulder and said: 'Kevin is joining Knowle next Monday. Hope you don't mind.'

Tony was walking through Leadenhall Market at the time, thinking food, and was left no time to reply. Robert Marchwood had, in his self-satisfied way, decided.

As a matter of fact, MacNulty *did* mind. Kevin Vaughan had proved a success; started with the Blighter, learned all the tricks of the trade, then worked well with their finance director, helped complete the transfer of data to a larger and faster computer, which proved not to be large or fast enough, although that was not Kev's fault. Recently, they had been contemplating other solutions and Tony had trusted Kev's judgement, ordered – and been proved right. The decision saved them money, saved space, made upgrading cheaper, moreover, the thing actually worked from the off.

Tony liked Kevin, even though he was a bit of a rough

diamond. For a computer specialist, Kev was commercial, and that made him special. There were innumerable fellows who knew about computers, but they lived in their own computer world and communicated, no, interfaced only on their own terms. Kev was different; he could explain everything to the cleaning lady, charm the guys and make money for the firm. So he would be difficult to replace.

That was not the problem. The more Tony MacNulty thought about the problem, the more his heart sank.

Stephen Grote arrived, perturbed. This was a rare sight, one that ought to have warned them. Now, he even apologised: 'Sorry I'm late,' he said.

The group exchanged their solemn handshakes.

'You look flustered,' Fortescue commented, coldly. He was always willing to show he was his own man.

'Oh, just a problem with my chauffeur.' In fact, Stephen had had a slanging match with Donna about her darned interfering sister; since she joined Lloyd's committee, Mary-Ellen Lemke worried at him like a bitch at a bone: now she had lost a small fortune, and so had her husband. Not his fault, but Donna was not in a listening mood.

'How was Buckinghamshire?' Devies asked.

Grote gave a crisp reply: 'The PM wants us to ring-fence the Vice President.'

MacNulty said: 'Difficult. It will leak out . . .' He had recruited the Vice President as a Wordsworth client when he was just another fresh-faced Republican from a well-heeled family.

'There'll be hell to pay with other American names,' Devies grunted.

Stephen Grote nodded: 'Perhaps he wouldn't notice a special deal. Reduced losses, a rebate, that sort of thing. Tony, think about it, please.'

MacNulty assented and Grote continued: 'The PM wants protection for his party friends, too.'

Everyone protested at the very idea. Nobody blabs to the press sooner than an MP; they would be hauled over the coals by the other names; it was impossible.

Grote listened to them all, in silence. Finally, he said, acidly: 'Then the PM insisted he wanted a head to roll. A trophy for the mantelpiece. Yesterday, if possible.'

For once, Grote looked to his friends for an answer. If they could not save the Tory MPs, they could, at least, find a name, a culprit, a whipping-boy.

'Marchwood,' Wilmot-Greaves said, simply. 'Blame it on him.'

Grote said nothing; MacNulty almost pitched out of his chair: after Cheltenham, he thought, this was ingratitude of the grand order.

Devies, his hands on his stick, coughed: 'It would be dangerous and unwarranted. Our search of Knowle's offices drew a blank, remember. After the last action . . . We don't know what Marchwood might do. He does have his supporters.'

'Everything seems too difficult.' Wilmot-Greaves paused, then looked at his friends. 'We're frightened of getting our hands dirty. Frightened of everything. If we need a victim, Marchwood's our man.'

Fortescue demurred, flushing red. 'How has Marchwood's record been since last year? The distribution agreed at Baden-Baden, the protection of our syndicates, has worked well. We found no evidence of surveillance or data collection at Knowle.'

Stone pursed his lips and fingered his moustache. In truth, he did not know what to say; they had played poker with Marchwood as dealer in recent times, and won heavily. It was not a good idea to deal afresh. Even Grote seemed to agree.

Wilmot-Greaves, however, insisted. He was determined that Robert Marchwood should not survive.

Grote knew this would be a crass mistake. He remembered a body, suspended improbably in the air, the watch on each of his wrists showing beneath his dragged-up shirt cuffs. Rex had always been a man who mocked himself – a watch on either wrist like the wide boys, spivs they'd been called in those days, street traders with watches up to their elbows. It was a joke that, in death that day, had seemed less than amusing. Yet, for once, he hesitated.

Then, too, a Marchwood had been a threat. Then, too, he had saved himself and gone on to flourish. Yet he had not forgotten; he heard himself remind them: 'The PM suggested Marchwood. Claimed the press would like it.'

Stone observed: 'Sounds like a good recommendation to me. Perhaps he will forget the MPs, if we do it. As for the Vice President, we can reduce his losses. Perhaps.'

Fortescue lit a cigarette and shook his head.

157

The group fell silent again.

Devies tapped his stick against the table edge and said to MacNulty: 'Tony, I think you have something to tell us?'

MacNulty looked at John Devies, who had raised a perfectly innocent, perfectly knowing pair of eyebrows. You bastard, Tony thought; just where had services division heard the tale? Perhaps the Blighter had had a word in his ear. He knew, of course, that everybody was allowed to spy on everybody else; which did not mean he enjoyed it.

His voice was, however, calm: 'Kevin Vaughan is to join Knowle & Co, today.'

Grote, for no apparent reason, turned to Stone and asked curtly: 'Italy OK?'

Stone flicked back his hair and nodded.

Then Wilmot-Greaves reeled off the catechism: What did Vaughan know? How did he know? Where was that knowledge stored, if at all, was he taking any data with him? If serious, could the information be deleted? Would the problem always remain a problem?

Tony MacNulty responded with apparent calm. He had trusted Kevin Vaughan and he had no reason to believe that trust had been betrayed. Of course, Kevin had worked in the most sensitive area of the business; of course, he could not watch his every move. Implicitly, Tony admitted serious damage might have been done.

Grote glanced out of the window, then responded: 'I want full surveillance. But discreet. No blundering around Robbo's office looking for disks.'

Devies smiled: 'Of course. Services division is looking at Vaughan.'

Tony was clearly supposed to say more. He talked generally about Kev's work on the computer-systems, insisted he had no access to the safe.

'I don't think Marchwood hired him as a way of spying on us. He's just a clever young chap making his way in the world.'

This provoked further questions. Since when had Marchwood been talking to Vaughan? Had Vaughan not been told to avoid Robbo? Had the data in safe storage been touched? Definitely not, he insisted. No, he repeated, he was sure not. If the safe had been tampered with, he would have known.

Who were Vaughan's friends at work? Everybody, anybody, he was your friendly guy.

Wilmot-Greaves had heard a rumour: 'How is your secretary, what's her name?'

Mrs Montfort. MacNulty shrugged. He did not know. He did not, in all honesty, care: 'I think that's neither here nor there.'

Everybody else seemed to disagree.

In any event, everybody knew that Tony and Robbo, despite their differences, went back a long way. His father and Marchwood's father had been good friends, the brothers had shown great guts in building the brokership, everybody knew there had been innumerable favours in the course of the years. Now this.

Devies said to Grote: 'We can always find a way to suspend Robbo and Knowle & Co from the market.'

They did, after all, control the committee; the committee ruled Lloyd's. They could blame Marchwood for the oil rigs, for the North Sea, perhaps.

There was enthusiasm for the idea.

Fortescue, sensing the tide of victory, went too far: 'Is there something for the SFO?'

There were some chuckles.

Very quietly, so that a pin might drop and still its thud on the carpet be heard, Stephen Grote pointed to the obvious risks in closing down Knowle, stated that the Marchwood deal on the oil rigs, struck at Baden-Baden, had held. By the time he had finished, nobody dared contradict. To articulate the self-evident is a great gift; it made Stephen a leader of men.

'Look at the Irwell trial,' Devies agreed, perceiving his mistake. 'Downing Street wanted heads to roll. Now the whole thing is an embarrassment. They want to make the same mess of Lloyd's and I, for one, intend to stop them.'

Stephen Grote looked at his Tompion. Nine, just gone. He was letting a knighthood go; even if he was just stating the obvious, he was still protecting Robert Hugh Marchwood. The opportunity he had so long wished to grasp was simply dangerous and irrelevant. Whatever his anger might tell him, Stephen had to decide otherwise. He had to fight for time, until they had a replacement for the Cristòforo, until they had a new international financial network up and running. Then they could move. Until then, they had to be careful.

Grote turned to them, again, and emphasised his logic: discretion, simplicity, order, control.

Devies nodded; Wilmot-Greaves, however, remained truculent and proposed instant action; Fortescue seconded him, but that was inevitable. Stone the mild had, however, become Stone the bellicose.

The Tompion ticked. Ten, and time for work, for bread-and-butter business. They knew their employees were trailing to work, heard appointments and duties gently ticking into their lives.

Finally, Stephen had his way; the majority accepted the hesitant wishes of the non-voting chairman and no decision was taken. It appeared Stephen Grote had finessed them, even finessed himself; everyone sensed that he had hesitated. Alec Wilmot-Greaves and Neil Fortescue waited until Tony MacNulty and John Devies left.

Wilmot-Greaves was outraged. Fortescue, who had flushed red beneath ruffled red hair, agreed.

Grote remained silent. One could have said: a surprised silence. Then he said to Fortescue: 'I am sorry if you felt your trip from New York was not needed.'

Fortescue conceded. 'Just one more time, Stephen. The merest hint, and . . .' He snapped his fingers.

Wilmot-Greaves polished his glasses and said: 'Yes.'

Stephen Grote nodded, at ease with himself. That much had been agreed. One last chance for Marchwood. In the meantime, Stephen decided, the Lloyd's data storage centre should be properly protected, guaranteed tamper-proof. Then it was up to Marchwood.

TEN

MONDAY THE THIRTEENTH of August, was the day when Kevin Vaughan became a Lloyd's insurance broker.

Sunday with Stu had been uncomfortable, rather than unpleasant. Fortunately, it was history now, and Kevin had already converted his motoring allowance into a flash Japanese sports car, which no normal insurer would touch, but which Robbo had promised to get covered.

All in all, a great future beckoned. Now, the rules of the game were simple: follow Ray's advice and Robbo's example. He could forget all that nonsense about whether or not his accent was right or he rolled his trouser leg. It was work, work and work, which was, for him, just fine.

His task was to do the bog standard stuff, showing small risks and small premiums to the underwriters. It was important to be swift, efficient and accurate – this would prepare him to help Robert on the big deals. He could see that he was destined to replace Ray who had depended since his banishment upon stopgap guys who had proved unreliable. The essence was to keep the cash flowing, day in day out, covering back-office overheads and the odd extravagance, leaving Robbo to pull off the big ones, to bring in the cream.

On that Monday Kevin and Robert Marchwood had met in the Lime Street underwriting Room on the black-and-white marble floor of the room, they stood beside the rostrum, a columned, temple-like construction topped by a clock and bearing the Lutine bell. Kevin had never heard the bell being rung: in earlier times, it was used to signal the loss or salvation of ships and their cargoes.

The underwriters, their customers, were still making their way to the boxes; Kevin's eyes were drawn upwards from the ornate columns of the rostrum, to the plain columns of the building, followed the lines of the columns as they soared upwards, upwards, becoming a glass and steel vault.

Marchwood saw the gaze and grinned at Kevin: 'I bet you've bought new braces.'

Kev nodded, showing him broad stripes of red and blue beneath the black-and-grey herring-bone cloth of a new suit. He also had a new haircut; he was bronzed from two weeks on a Spanish beach; apart from a wrist bracelet marked Kevin, he was a new man.

'I bet you didn't choose those on your own.'

'Don't know what you're talking about, squire.'

Groups of case-carrying men, with the occasional woman, rode up the escalators that zigzagged upwards through the atrium, from floor to floor.

'Knowle, Vaughan.' For the first time his name resounded round the Room, Kev started and sensed a flush of pride. Robert had left his name with the caller, a portly chap, who had just started his stint inside the rostrum.

'Knowle, Frankie Vaughan.' The so-and-so. A nickname already.

Robert laughed 'It's your calling card, a sign you're part of the market.'

The first caller, a hundred years earlier, had been a railway porter with a distinctive, all-stations-to-Birmingham lilt which made every name ring clearly; this guy sounded more like a priest, intoning as if he were reading lists of those fallen in action.

The same names recurred again and again; the sons and grandsons echoing their fathers and grandfathers. Even Marchwood was his father's son, though some joked that his father once wore a blue peaked cap, a blue uniform and worked at a boating lake.

This was not true. Few knew the truth, knew what had happened all those years ago; nobody had told Kevin anything. A market survives on today's business, not on memories. Whatever they said about Marchwood – and it often was not true – he had established himself in the market, his own name resounded with meanings: Knowle, Marchwood. Everybody who counted knew who was meant by that call. He was someone.

Kev said, 'Must be off. I think I saw my underwriter.'

Robbo winked: 'Be polite and give him hell.'

Robert Hugh Marchwood felt well, surprisingly well, considering.

On Sunday MacNulty had rung him at Golden Rain, one of his late-night efforts, blathering on about Kev and Wordsworth and Knowle and the handshake brigade. Robert had fallen asleep early in the evening, lying fully clothed on his bed; he was completely exhausted after a Saturday racing horses and plying underwriters with drink. On Thursday and Friday, he had been abroad, from which he had not really recovered.

When the phone roused Robert from deep sleep, he was surprised by the voice of Tony MacNulty.

Did he realise this, realise that? The voice sawed away for a good fifteen minutes, until Robert was wide awake and restless and saw it was midnight.

Tony was unhappy about Kevin. 'I think you should let him stay with Wordsworth.'

Robert grunted: no.

Then there were trade secrets. People did not like other people knowing things. Kevin knew things.

Is that right? There was nothing he and Ray did not know about the place or could not find out, on their own. Nothing. Who did they think they were?

At this, Tony was silent.

He finished the call by screaming at Tony down the blower: 'What's the bloody time? It's calls like this that have made my missus leave.'

Tony, who knew a thing or two about the subject, said quietly: 'I didn't know you were the missus type.'

Wrong.

'I'm trying to warn you, Robbo. Try listening.'

Then the telephone went dead.

He rose, undressed, showered, changed into slippers and sleeping gown, went into the kitchen where a salad was growing soggy in the fridge. Damn Thérèse, damn Tony.

Robert felt he had more than enough problems.

He had heard Veronica had given birth about a month, no, over two months ago, he had sent flowers, a card, but had not been able to face seeing her, with the little boy, in the hospital. So the Marchwood dynasty had its illegitimates, too. He almost laughed, almost. At one time, he had been desperate for another son; now, the idea terrified him. He would sort out some money, something.

For weeks, he had only had one thought: Thérèse. He fervently hoped she did not know about the child. Her letter had not said anything. Just mentioned Veronica's name; probably some drunk underwriter had kindly talked about Robert's girlfriend to his wife. Wilmot-Greaves was vicious enough to do it; the man had problems.

Yes, Thérèse mattered to him. He had fired off a handwritten letter, sent by courier, to Zurich. Thérèse had signed for the letter, so he knew where she was. He had just written: 'See you sooner, rather than later, all my love, Robert.'

Love.

He had to think about things, she had to think about things; he could not treat her as a mere addition to his life. It was partnership or nothing. It was fidelity.

It was midnight and beyond.

He helped himself to a bottle of cold beer. Too tired to get a glass. The beer tasted smooth and dry and bitter for two, three swigs, then just became a pleasant coolness in the mouth.

She would, he thought, return. On her own terms.

He did not know if he had the strength.

Fidelity, the less well-known F-word, was a particular problem. Even Ray, when he heard of Thérèse's departure, had told him to grow up. After all, he was fifty or nearly fifty, an age when only grizzled pop stars were still pretending to be twenty.

He extracted another beer from the fridge. Make him fat, make him sleep.

He had bought an open first-class ticket to Zurich, it was in his briefcase, always with him, at home or at work. Perhaps he would slip into Zurich, unannounced, see what Thérèse was doing with herself.

It was not as if he had not been here before. At first, he had vowed to change, then to be careful, then he had thought she would never notice, then he thought she did not mind, then she left him.

So there was reform or there was divorce.

Divorce was a nasty sport; he had played once, and lost. He had been at their son Rowan's hospital just once before his death. Hospitals, particularly intensive-care wards, were hell holes.

Ex-wives were a costly luxury. Jane was an expert sailor, a wonderful competitor, but the marina on the Hamble was a non-paying luxury. He did not enjoy sailing any more, not since Rowan's accident. . .

Sleep had been fitful, disturbed by the beer he had drunk, and his evening snooze.

Now Monday morning found him up to strength again. He scoured the noticeboards in the room for news of ships and tankers, for lost cargoes, scuffed his leather moccasins on the smooth marble floor.

The Cronin box was still empty; 'Ropey' Robey had yet to arrive. He surveyed the Room. Where was Ropey? He nodded to a couple of aviation guys as they rode up the escalator, had a word with a couple of non-marine fellows, waved to others; he drifted around the rostrum, which was really a monstrosity, but much loved. At the Cronin box, there were a few signs of life. The claims clerk had arrived, a happy little robot who paid up when the risks became losses and the losses became claims. Where was that rabbit Robey?

One day, he would retire; then, perhaps, he would be right for Thérèse. A nice, tame, civilised Robert. Better that than, like some of the old guard, to be carried in a black box from the Room, having spent his twilight years reading the obituaries of competitors.

He winced at the thought of the oil-rig deal. Annan, Mite Leven, Salter had lost billions, having signed his slips of paper. Still, Grote and his merry men now had every reason to be happy; they had been protected. And, of course, Knowle had taken its cut. Even so, he still winced.

They should let him and Ray and Knowle thrive and survive. If they needed Kevin Vaughan, that was their problem, whatever MacNulty said.

On Saturday, he had treated Robey, Alec Wilmot-Greaves, all the lads, to the works at Cheltenham. It was one of the big races of the season. Alec Wilmot-Greaves went past, with a wave: 'Hi, Robbo.'

Robert nodded. You just have to take some risks. Breathing was a risky occupation, life a deadly one. You could not cover every eventuality, syndicates had to take risks, to take premiums, to make money; even he had lost money on one or two syndicates, not a fortune; Wilmot-Greaves had taken some business that turned sour, a mistake. He could not surely still be sore? Most names, who took blind wagers at unknown odds, backing some underwriter or other they could not know or judge, were simply crazy; but then, that was tradition, that was their business, that was life.

Now everybody seemed to be bleating.

They'd nicked his stupid picture, thrown his brother out of the Room, kicked him, metaphorically, in the oojits, turned his wife sour and still he was polite and useful. So, there are a few knocks to take, comes from living.

Marchwood would, if need be, take things into his own hands; they should leave him be. With time, they would learn to live with Kevin. After all, they had learned to live with him.

Above the glass vault, clouds rolled by; there was a hint of sunshine amidst wind and perhaps rain.

More sober suits, more waves and smiles. What was Thérèse doing now? Talking about cooperatives with Urs? He did not want to live in Zurich. He blamed Urs.

He saw Kevin Vaughan leave a box, flushed with success. Good lad.

Then he smiled broadly, seeing a bespectacled individual in a blue pin-stripe suit take his seat. Robey had been to the dentist, so his usual grin was frail or missing. Robert thought briefly about trying again the next day.

'Sorry to see you off colour,' he said. Ropey, he thought, was too nice a guy for his own good.

'I'll be fine. You're probably still groggy, yourself, Robbo?'

'Nah. Had a good rest since Saturday.'

'You certainly know how to give parties.'

'It's a big secret. Lots of champagne, lots of crumpet.'

Saturday had been heavy on the drink; over two bottles of best bubbly a head; yet he himself had hardly had a drop. They could have raced ostriches and nobody would have known; yet there had been a great day's racing. Even though he could no longer bear to watch showjumping, he loved watching fine horses race, adored the pageant and ceremony, the gambling. He had an eye for good horseflesh, there had been years when he did not want to see a nag; but you pick yourself up, dust yourself down and get on with things, including racing horses. One filly, named Smart Theresa, in honour of someone he once knew, finished down the field in the big race.

Robey had every reason to grin. 'What's the deal today?'

Robert slid onto the bench beside him, and explained the numbers, swiftly. Cover for oil pipelines, in the North Sea. Robey tapped them into his computer, frowned.

'Not much in it for me, at that price.'

Robey was unusual. Thanks to Robert, he had not been burnt out of the disaster market; he had taken some other nasties from him, instead. Slow fuse stuff which might just explode, asbestos, industrial pollution – grim. Now, Robey had grown cautious; he liked his farm out in the Welsh Marches; Cronin was a well-respected, slightly old-fashioned outfit with a once-glorious past. Robey looked solid, dependable, could talk about wheat and sheep and stuff; people said he had been close to Grote. Well, that was not unusual in these parts, and the mere fact of survival had given him a soundish reputation, unlike Salter, Annan, Mite and Leven, who had met a grim end. Salter had just taken refuge in the loony-bin, with a severe case of crossed wires.

Robert persisted with Robey, argued that the cycle was due to turn, that the litigation in the States was turning to Lloyd's favour, that Robey should neither forget past favours nor future deals.

Robey remembered. Without Robbo, he would be out of business. He looked at the paper slip. Three oil pipelines, ten to fifteen years old, the biggest in the North Sea, record indifferent. The risk was valued at £500m, the premium at 10 per cent was £50m, of which Robbo would take 10 per cent, £5m.

'I'll take ten per cent.'

There, Robey had placed his bet. A premium of £5m, 30 per cent to him. First signed, then stamped. Robert leaped up. With Robey's name, he was off – the £5m would soon be in the bag. So much for grief.

Eleven

THÉRÈSE POURED HERSELF a small black coffee from a small metal contraption, watched the light ripple across the lake.

Last week, there had been a boat, a white boat moored on the water below her flat. There had been nobody aboard, but the boat was there, unusual, silent, white, a mystery.

Now, on that Monday morning, the mystery was gone.

There was no reason to return to Golden Rain and England, none at all. She knew he was dishonest, she had told her friends: well, he had not turned out as she had expected. Some friends disapproved, even though marriages fell apart easily nowadays, others had already become distant. Urs was surprised. For a businessman, he said, Robert had seemed uncomplicated – Thérèse should meet some of *his* clients!

Urs had a new girlfriend, of course. Thérèse felt older than she was. Her father was not well. She should leave Zurich to see him, but had postponed her journey.

The white boat that had disappeared irritated her, too: even here she felt observed, even if she was not.

The flat was perfectly neat, perfectly tidy and full of flowers; she had started doing some freelance interpreting, but found it taxing work. Still, there were evenings in the cinema, concerts, *Kneipenbesuche*, walks with friends, a visit to Einsiedeln, in a month the clear blue days would turn, glowing, to long autumnal reds, she loved this part of the world then.

She had started a letter or letters: 'Dear Robert . . .'

Yet there was not much she could reproach him with, not really. 'I'm just playing the game,' he had said. 'I don't make the rules.'

People here played games, too. There was the Swiss Army, prepared to fight the last fight in the Alpine valleys; there were the banks, holding secret money from dictators, drug dealers and arms salesmen; there were the weapons manufacturers, who made weapons for the dictators; there was Swiss neutrality, which so nearly disappeared during the last war . . . Yet she loved this country, her country, the basic decency of the man-in-the-street. To live, you had to compromise, nothing and nobody is perfect.

Not that Robert was always the great player he imagined. Sometimes, he was as credible as an elephant disguised as a zebra crossing; she thought of the whispered telephone calls, the poor excuses for late-night sittings. Some would say, perhaps, that this was part of his charm.

She did not understand why the police seemed to have disappeared from the scene. His answers were, well, quite incredible, really. She vividly remembered the first interview: her father, she thought, would have been appalled by the lies.

'Where did the painting come from, sir?' Inspector Wilson had asked.

Robert had been indifferent. 'I told you, it was a gift. I didn't realise it was worth anything, it was just a daub, with hills and a river. Nothing special, in my view.'

The terrible thing was, she doubted him now even when he told the truth. She knew he had loved the picture. She had heard him speculate with his brother about its meaning, about the meaning of the series. He had been proud to own a Monet.

Every so often, in the sounds of the building, she heard his ghostly laughter and knew why.

She sat down at her desk and wrote a long letter, in her slightly edgy Gallic hand. Now it was up to him.

Two days later, the boat reappeared.

TWELVE

OF COURSE, IT was only money. Connie slept fitfully, as usual, rose early, bored by the play of light on the bedroom ceiling, the contest between birdsong and the internal combustion engine; commuters had to rise early, here. She wrapped herself around a large mug of dark tea and looked at the lawn, which was tidy, and the flower-beds, which were not. Nevertheless, she had had the roof repaired, the house redecorated – the insurance had paid. Inside, order was restored; outside, she had learned to work Ron's much-loved motormower and cut the grass. The beds, however, were quite beyond her. Then she heard the familiar sounds of someone playing with the letter box, followed by various thuds. The postman, depositing the post on the hall floor.

The letter was an abomination. Dear Mrs Cornelia Sanderson. We are very sorry, etc, etc. Please pay us, etc, etc. A sharp pain exploded in her abdomen, like an appendix rupturing. Yours, etc, etc, signed in absence by someone who was not Tony MacNulty. Mountebank, de Montefort. This was the third letter of this sort within as many weeks. She had sold her investments, emptied her bank, she only had the garage or the house left.

She was facing ruin. To think that, only two years ago, she had been contemplating early retirement, a Caribbean cruise with Ron to celebrate their fortieth. She made sure she did not whinge; she wrote a cheery letter to Jonathan, saying that Lloyd's had bowled her a googly, that her finances were quite dicky and that she could not, as yet, see a way to visit them all that summer. In the meanwhile, they should enjoy the sunshine, love and kisses.

Of course, she was going to fight this, all the way; her last hope lay with the action groups; Wednesday's child loves litigation.

The omens, however, were not good. Although the lawyers were fine gentlemen, none so far had landed a real blow against Lloyd's in the courts. It was not certain what the basis for litigation might be – MacNulty had certainly lied to her on the day of the storm. But this did not seem to be enough. There was much talk of unfairness, a great many statistics, dark mutterings about that man Marchwood. Well, so what? Even if she had a strong case, it would be vastly expensive, anything gained would be frittered away in fees, take years to resolve. In the meantime, her life was slipping by.

It was the fourth Wednesday in August, a fine day for the meeting of the action group of the Mite Leven syndicates, some of her syndicates, which someone had conspired to load with losses. Held in one of the City Guild halls, a mournful Victorian Gothic frolic, the meeting was quite well attended. Out of two thousand names on the Mite Leven syndicates, there were four hundred people present, mostly older men and women in fine clothes, discreetly elegant dresses and double-cuffed shirts. These were the people who took hampers and champagne to Glyndebourne, the people that Ron wanted to emulate. Well, he had done even better than he had imagined. Mite Leven had lost half a billion pounds on the oil rigs, she silently repeated the words, half a billion pounds, an average of a quarter of a million pounds each – and that was just the one syndicate. The sums were absurd, her bills were absurd, no wonder everyone here looked grey and tired and old, and people coughed.

She was determined this should not happen to her. Nowadays, Connie went once a week to the hairdresser, spent extravagantly on clothes and make-up, in a way that she never had done before. She had introduced power-dressing to Lime Grove Primary School. She had no money, so money did not matter. Unfortunately, she could not buy sleep.

On the dais at the front of the hall was the Mite Leven names' action committee, headed by the most suspect striped-shirt Tory Connie had seen in a long time, a prospective parliamentary candidate called Dominic Cheever-Hope. She had been told, very believably, that he had exceptionally good contacts. Sitting next to Cheever-Hope was their lawyer, a bright-enough, smart-enough fellow, accompanied by a decent array of fellow-sufferers.

She wished she could be optimistic.

She recalled the message of Stephen Grote at the annual meeting of Lloyd's. It had been a robust performance, despite heckling, despite anger from disgruntled names. His message had been blunt: those who had lost money had to pay. That was the rule of the game.

Losses were God-ordained.

Yet Mitel Leven was not a divine story. The lawyer explained that the syndicate's funds had been systematically raped, that profits had been overstated for years, that the managing agent, a Mr Mite, and the underwriter, a Mr Leven, had departed with millions in commission, quitting the syndicate just as the oil rigs exploded.

If that was not enough, it appeared they were one of a select handful of syndicates, insuring against losses from the North Sea. Among this happy élite were the Annan and Salter syndicates, of which Connie was a fully-paid-out member. The lawyer called them dustbins, because they contained everybody else's rubbish. And that rubbish, he claimed, had been directed there by Knowle & Co.

Mr Robert Marchwood, Ron's very good friend, had helped.

So Connie stood up and asked whom they could sue? They were already fighting Lloyd's itself, the lawyer replied, but then there was Mr Mite and Mr Leven, their members' agents . . . his fingers were raised, one by one, for ever more fun and games. Connie could see that the possibilities were endless.

Coffee afterwards was a sombre affair. Connie chatted animatedly with whoever happened to have a minute or two, she was curious about her fellow walking-wounded: there were some grand businessmen, several farmers, three solicitors, an accountant, a hotelier, a retired colonel. The backbone of the country. It was the same story, again and again. People were selling up, life savings, retirement homes, farms and livelihoods were going, and for the most part, they were too old to start again.

She saw things differently; for Connie, there was a life outside; tomorrow, the children would sing in assembly and the classrooms would fill. Sometimes, though, it was not easy to make yourself believe what you knew was right.

She crossed Long Wall by Wood Street, overwhelmed by mounds of concrete and metal and marble which were offices or about to become offices, walked past the police station into Cheapside, caught sight of St Paul's, turned left past St Mary-le-Bow, enjoying the hazy sunshine of a late summer day. She looked in her handbag and found the advertisement clippings.

She had decided to have a little fun. She was going to have words with Mr Robert Hugh Marchwood, chairman and chief executive of Knowle & Co, broker at Lloyd's of London, purveyor of dustbins to the monied classes.

The offices of Knowle & Co were less glamorous than she had expected, with old-fashioned metal cupboards and old-fashioned metal files. The main office had modern equipment, computers and suchlike, yet the desks were at least twenty years old. It was, she reminded herself, a private company.

'Can I help you?' It was the chairman's secretary, a willowy, elegant woman in her early thirties.

She explained herself. Her curiosity about the advertisements she had found, her desire to speak to her deceased husband's friend.

Connie did not bother the younger woman with the details; her chief mechanic had confessed all he knew. Apparently, the advertisements had been faxed down to the garage or sent by bike from Knowle & Co on Monday or Tuesday, so that they could be placed in the *Sunday Herald* on the following Sunday, along with all the car registration numbers. Sometimes, a bike came separately, with cash, to cover the cost of the advertisements, and more.

The elegant woman responded to her question: 'This is most unusual. I'll ask the chairman whether he can spare a moment to see you. Please wait here.'

Connie took a seat by the reception. Just at that moment, Kevin Vaughan, looking tanned and very swish, walked past. They both hesitated, and the secretary returned: 'I'm afraid the chairman cannot see you just now. He expresses his regrets about your husband and says he has no recollection of the advertisements. We do not, as a rule, advertise in Sunday newspapers. Now, if you will excuse me . . .'

She was excused. Kevin, who had busied himself at the reception desk, showed her to the lift.

'If you had not been there,' Connie confided, 'I would have misbehaved, and that would never have done.'

He pushed a button and smiled. He knew Marchwood was not in the office, that she had been told some lie or other.

'Are you still at Lime Grove?'

She laughed: 'Yes, for my sins.'

He asked: 'Do you want to talk?'

She nodded.

The nave of St Paul's Cathedral was the only place she could think of. The echoes were suitably confusing. He slid into the wooden pew beside her.

'A mathematician's view of heaven,' she said. 'I thought you would like it. Maths was always your thing.'

Behind them stalls sold books, postcards, tour guides. Groups of tourists entered regularly, through the glass-plated revolving door, their guides vied with each other in stridency concerning Christopher Wren's masterwork.

'Never been here before,' Kevin told her. 'Not my usual scene.'

'Not impressed? *Si monumentum requiris circumspice.*'

He looked puzzled. She explained that it was the Latin epitaph of the architect, engraved on the floor under the dome. It meant 'If you seek his monument, look around you'. A proud boast she thought, but justified.

He responded with a question: 'What could I do to help you?' He was a busy man.

She explained her position, the actions of Ron, the so-called friendship with Marchwood, the loss of all her money, her curiosity about the advertisements, about Lloyd's.

He listened in silence, barely looking at her.

A priest, speaking through the public address system installed in the pulpit, thanked everyone for coming, said the church was grateful for its visitors, reminded them it received no money from the state and asked for a suitable donation, before offering a short prayer. Amen.

'Pathetic,' Kevin said. She raised her eyebrows and he added, with an upward nod: 'It *is* magnificent, even if it isn't my thing.'

She looked at him, still seeing the gawky child behind the young man's face, and sensing the passage of time, through her life as well as his, from then to now.

She told him the core of what her chief mechanic had said when confronted with the advertisements.

'The cash used to cheer him up no end,' the man had said, with a grin. 'But he didn't like the phone calls.'

For a day or so, if anyone rang who wanted to buy one of his impossible numbers, Ron used to claim the garage was a dairy. The whole thing was crazy, undertaken presumably because Ron was permanently short of cash.

Kevin smiled, leafing through the advertisements, sent by Knowle, staring at the numbers and letters. He remembered Ray's words about 'four or five lines of code' and a computer program that could be used to manipulate a large amount of data. He would have to think.

He looked at Mrs Sanderson, smiled, and said: 'Sorry, I really can't help you,' even though he knew that he could. Even though he felt he owed her something. But he owed Ray something, too.

Ray had pronounced himself pleased with Kevin's first efforts. His very first slip, swiftly filled, was neat: worldwide travel insurance for the instruments of the National Philharmonia Orchestra, for several million.

'Anyone upset?' Ray had asked, with a smile.

'No,' said Kevin. 'I said there was only a problem if the violinists were mistaken for the Mob.'

Ray had the slip framed. Kevin sensed he had a great future in his grasp; he just had to follow Ray's instructions.

So he pocketed the advertisements and promised nothing. Leaving Mrs Sanderson sitting in the low wooden pews, he waited by the bookstand, browsing until he saw she had left. Then he bought a tourist guide, turned back along the nave towards the altar, letting the echoes wash around him. The newspaper clippings weighed heavily in his pocket and he wanted to think.

The cathedral seemed grand and stern. He turned and found the Duke of Wellington on horseback. Funny that a dead man should be portrayed on a horse here, clattering his way to the altar. He looked in his guide and discovered that, in the crypt, Nelson had a black marble sarcophagus all to himself, lucky man. And Wellington's bones were nearby. So the Iron Duke had a monument and a tomb, from a proud and grateful country.

Kevin clicked his heels on the marble floor, admiring the sound. The cathedral, he conceded, was wonderful. He took the

259 steps (a useful fact contained in the guide-book) to the whispering gallery under and inside the dome, where he paused to contemplate the murals. The dome itself was a sweeping expanse of black, grey and white. Saint Paul. Not his sort of thing. The view of the nave and choir below, the sounds of hushed and half-hushed voices forced themselves upon him, as if he were being impacted by sounds and great swaying masses of air. He was reminded of the Room.

He stepped back from the balustrade, took a bench seat against the wall and considered Mrs Sanderson's newspaper cuttings. The truth struck him: of course, they had never trusted each other, the Marchwoods and the others, the friends of MacNulty. Certainly not enough to put anything in writing between them. So they published what had to be done, what was going to happen, in a code they could deny, a code only they understood. Nobody else could know what was going on. Nobody else had the program that controlled the computer pattern of the major deals, the program used and owned by both parties, one that had been agreed upon, perhaps, at Baden-Baden.

He rubbed his nose and peered at the advertisements. They looked as if they were encrypted *Pascal*, a programming language. He glanced up and there was nobody near.

On the truly enormous deals, such as the North Sea oil rigs, hundreds of separate deals had to be brokered throughout Lloyd's. So, Kevin reckoned, the advertisement codes generated the details of these deals when inputted into the relevant program. And that was the way MacNulty and friends controlled the deal: the codes, published on a Sunday, would, once inputted, show the work for the coming week and the overall pattern needed to rig the market. To make good, safe money for them all.

This was Ray's handiwork. He rose and grasped the balustrade. The codes represented a promise, a contract for the coming week. The friends could see what would happen and know why. They could watch Robbo every step of the way . . .

The very idea. He was ecstatic.

To prove this theory, he needed to get at the hard disks in MacNulty's safe. But this was impossible. Or find the same program still in Ray's possession. That, too, was a tall order. It could be anywhere, in a safe at Knowle, hidden at Ray's house, buried at Golden Rain.

He became aware of people, walking round the gallery. He let them pass on their way to the top of the dome. A ray of sunshine crossed the space beneath the dome, entering by the lantern, revealing airborne dust.

Alternatively, Kevin thought, he could transcribe the advertisements into *Pascal* himself and try to relate them to the business that had been transacted by Marchwood in the following week. He could do this at Lloyd's data storage centre, in South London; it had all the records for the market stored on computer tape and an old-fashioned mainframe. A mate of his, who sometimes needed to get to the data, had a key hanging in his office which Kevin could easily snaffle.

If he could relate Robbo's deals to the adverts, that would be proof: proof of a marketwide agreement between the Marchwoods and the friends, proof that the market was rigged. That was what his uncle Stu needed. Proof. Mrs Sanderson too.

He looked at his watch; there was still time to grab his mate's key, if he wanted to give it a whirl. He took the 259 steps down from the gallery at a run.

THIRTEEN

THE ROAR OF a late train through a lattice of iron beams; the lone man on the Hungerford footbridge over the Thames glanced into the water below, drowned in the noise, then in the distance an alto saxophone emerged, busking the last notes of its song outside the Festival Hall. North of the river, the Savoy was silent, Somerset House, the white steeple of St Bride's, St Paul's, the blue outline of Lloyd's, its cranes and metal frame visible beneath the NatWest tower with its intricate rectangles of light and dark, beside Kleinwort Benson, Baring Brothers and, in the distance, the tower of Canary Wharf with its light. Blink, blink, blink.

The man shivered, leaned on the metal and wood balustrade, watched the force of the river churn the lights of the city, of the embankment and bridges, onwards, towards an invisible sea.

'Sorry to disturb your meal –'

'You said it was urgent.'

Another man, an older figure with a walking stick and gammy leg, John Devies, had joined the first; they stood on a widened section of the footbridge beside the railway bridge, a section that thrust out over the river.

There was no one else on the bridge. Then the saxophone player appeared from his spot in front of the Festival Hall, carrying a black case and bearing small change. Or not so small change, for he wished the two figures, barely lit by the footbridge lights, a jaunty good night. The younger of the men might have nodded.

'Yes, I'm sorry about the dinner,' he murmured.

Devies, in dinner jacket and bow tie, appeared to have been at an official function; he said nothing, waited. His companion said: 'They are going to move tomorrow.'

'Specifically?' Devies looked at the policeman, a senior figure in the SFO, a fellow mason; despite this bond of friendship, he did not even admit to a name. That was the way things had to be, if they wanted them to work.

'I can't be specific. Something will happen. The DG has been closeted with Wilson, not a pretty sight. He's been given a few number-crunchers of the young turk variety to play with.'

A train passed, a dark sound, a rattle of lights behind their backs, on its way to the depot or to the suburbs tightly packed with sleeping homes, and suddenly there was nobody on the bridge. Perhaps the few tramps bedded down on the embankment steps had seen a man in trenchcoat and evening dress, perhaps in his late fifties, in a great rush, but they had not seen him turn right at the foot of the stairs, then right again, at traffic lights, in front of a vaudeville-playing theatre, where there was a silver Rolls waiting, a chauffeur to open the door, a brandy to warm the soul.

Outside the Lloyd's building another Rolls waited, a Bentley, a Jaguar XJ6. Services division had been felt to be too spartan.

For once, Devies thought, at least it is not a false alarm. For once. You're damned if it is, buried if it isn't.

MacNulty and Fortescue were awaiting him, on the twelfth floor, in various states of evening dress. Grote, incongruously, wore a cardigan and corduroy trousers.

The debugging devices had been placed, switched on; they were free to talk. Alec Wilmot-Greaves and Henry Stone were not available at such short notice. Hands were shaken.

Devies, tired and not a little worse for wear, let himself down into a leather sofa and blurted out the news: 'Kevin Vaughan is the nephew of Inspector Stewart Wilson! Services wanted to be absolutely sure: it took them a few days to confirm it, but there's no doubt: visits to Ray Marchwood on Saturday, Wilson on Sunday.'

There was a silence. Fortescue removed his tie and lit a cigarette, waiting for someone to say something.

'Vaughan never told us,' MacNulty observed, a green shade of white, then added. 'Clearly . . .'

'Clearly nobody thought to ask.' Grote finished the sentence. Fortescue formulated an intricate obscenity.

He meant: it was an inexcusable error.

With some difficulty, Devies rose to remove his coat, grab a decanter of something or another, a light brown liquid. He poured for himself and, without being asked, all the others except MacNulty. Tony was given soda water.

'This is not the reason I called you in at short notice. My source knows the Serious Fraud Office is to move tomorrow. The target is Lloyd's. He is sure.'

MacNulty held a lit match against his filled pipe.

'What does that prove?' Grote asked, implying that no informant could be trusted completely – in the past, there had been false alarms.

John Devies snorted. Sometimes, too, he had been right. 'Mrs Rainsley and Wilson have something significant planned for tomorrow.'

'A love nest, perhaps,' MacNulty suggested, wafting pipe smoke. 'This is all too vague. We're not involved. They have no proof.'

Devies avoided looking at him: they could not know this for certain.

Fortescue joined the sceptics. Nothing to say that it was not a false alarm. Everybody was tired; this was, perhaps, one emergency that could be left in the in-tray. At least he had not had to fly here from New York, this time. He was, however, sure of one thing: 'We will have to deal with Kevin Vaughan.'

Devies looked at Grote, who said: 'As far as the SFO's concerned, it's a case of suck it and see. As for young Vaughan, well . . .' His voice picked up. '. . . perhaps even Robert Marchwood doesn't know about Uncle Plod.'

MacNulty gave a guarded response: 'Perhaps someone should have a word with him tomorrow. Stephen?'

There was a silence while they sipped their drinks.

Then Devies said: 'I think, Tony, that it's someone else's turn to do that.'

MacNulty stared at Grote's Tompion, apparently impassive, while Devies continued: 'Robbo's been abroad, again. Back on the late flight from Zurich. Ready to take his place at tomorrow's meeting, I don't doubt.'

Fortescue blew a smoke ring: 'It's rather embarrassing to see him join the committee, isn't it?'

Grote shrugged: 'Not really. I only hope he's not in Zurich to examine our relationship with the West-Europa-Bank.'

'I think not,' Devies said. 'He's taken to hiring a boat, a small white launch. Long way to go for a little pleasure cruise. Nobody knows what it means.'

MacNulty said: 'Robbo's popular, for all his faults. People were bound to vote for him . . .' His voice died as he saw the less-than-amused faces of the others. It seemed that any attempt at conciliation was doomed.

Fortescue groaned. No sooner had Ray been banished than Robert bounced back as committee member! Besides, there was the Vaughan connection. All in all, it looked very grim.

Grote smiled. He again outlined his plan for the committee meeting, which should do the trick. His sister-in-law, Mary-Ellen Lemke, was on the warpath and could be trusted to explode. 'We just have to re-direct the force of the blast,' he murmured and the others smiled.

Then Grote returned to the key issues: the idea that Marchwood might work with the SFO was unlikely, but horrific. The idea that Vaughan might do so, not quite so awful, was more plausible. All too plausible. Then there was the question of the impending raid, wherever it might happen.

'If you put everything together, it's a nightmare for us,' Fortescue observed. 'And no easy remedy.'

If the position was unclear, the dangers of precipitate action were all too obvious. Grote turned to Devies: 'The door to the data storage centre can, if need be, be slammed shut? Electronically, I mean?'

Devies nodded: 'Just as you decided. We've installed a new remote system. Very clever.'

'So it's wait and see,' Fortescue mused, extinguishing his cigarette. 'I don't like it.'

'Nobody does,' Grote snapped.

It was late.

No vote was taken; they all knew that this meeting would not be the end of the affair.

They shook hands. MacNulty and Fortescue made their excuses; Fortescue was off home, MacNulty wanted to slip back to his office at Wordsworth, just to check on a few things. Devies and Grote elected to drink another nightcap.

Stephen placed his cognac fine champagne on a glass display case while Devies complained about his evening. He had been at a charity event, raising money for some good cause about which he did not, if he admitted the truth, give a dried monkey-nut. In a way, he had been quite glad about the unexpected call from his source, even if it meant Lloyd's was under attack.

Stephen Grote smiled; he, too, had endured agonies that evening, losing his composure and his temper.

Donna and he had invited his cousin's son, Jamie Forrestier, to dinner. There was some suggestion that Jamie might one day become a director of Cecil Russell & Grote, the family business, though the good Lord alone knew how. Stephen wished him well, but wishful thinking was not really his strength. Jamie was to start as a trainee on a syndicate next week, but the boy seemed totally spaced-out, as if high on drugs. No wonder that the universities had not wanted him. Stephen had lost his rag, told him that he had to pull himself together. Jamie's look of injured pride had merely served to provoke him still further; Stephen then suggested that Jamie should go off and sell wallpaper to Sloanes. A suggestion which, surprisingly, was not treated as an insult.

Stephen remembered how he himself had rescued CRG from the brink all those years ago, making his native wit count; how he had, behind the scenes, played rough and tough to turn round the firm's finances, how he had blocked someone who knew and noticed too much, a Mr Rex Marchwood, father of Robbo and Ray; how he had thereafter talked long and hard and politely to some grey-haired men about the benefits of retirement until he had altered half the staff, in just four years, without anyone seeming to notice. It had been an immense effort. He could not quite conceive how Jamie would ever manage to cross the road on his own, let alone emulate it.

John Devies, who had four sons and several grandsons, smirked at the cut-glass balloon in his fleshy paw when he heard Stephen's description of Jamie. Finally, he sighed. 'Must be off.'

Yes, Stephen would sort out the mess. 'Bye. The door shut.

Stephen sipped his brandy. In one of the display cases, he saw the cutlasses that had been distributed at the Lloyd's Coffee House two hundred years ago, during the Gordon riots; they were given to the gentlemen of the coffee house to protect themselves against 'King Mob', the rioters who had turned on Wealth itself. It was not certain whether they had been used, but they certainly testified to Lloyd's heart of steel.

History showed that the gentlemen of Lloyd's were always willing to tough things out, particularly if a profit could be made. To guarantee a cargo of pelts, saltpetre or slaves, to insure a wherry or a tall ship, Lloyd's was the place to go; sitting at small desks in their tails, with top hats placed by their sides, the gentlemen would underwrite the business, enabling the East India Company to bring spices and tea to Britain and slave ships from North Africa to be scuppered with their live cargoes still on board, their none-too-scrupulous owners claiming from Lloyd's. In its long history, Stephen reflected, there was little that Lloyd's had not seen and outlived. That would not change now.

FOURTEEN

WELL, THE NUMBER-crunching over, at least he had to act.

That had not been Stu Wilson's first reaction, nor yet his second, after the DG had given him his marching orders. But he came to it finally.

He was reminded of the Hilton job. Politics had brought him low then: he had vowed never to let it happen again. He thought about the insignia in the kitchen at home, about Stonecot, about whoever it was who had removed the file and rifled his desk.

The DG had insisted on certain details. Time, date, place. He could have gone in any time, why then . . . ? She was unwilling to answer.

Then she had a further demand: Inspector Derek Tomlinson should accompany Wilson while making the arrests.

He looked at Mrs Rainsley QC, contemplated her owlish glasses. Although he did not express his reservations, his disapproval must have shown.

'You have to remember, Wilson, that this is an SFO operation; you are not a one-man band, d'you understand? I needn't remind you, I think, about your past.'

He still said nothing. She looked up and considered him: 'If this goes well Wilson, you'll be rewarded. Good luck.'

Friday the twenty-fourth saw the second day of the final Test: England against West Indies. Friday saw the publication of a CBI survey of business confidence and the announcement of other economic data, including the latest inflation figures. Friday saw Mr Robert Hugh Marchwood join the committee of Lloyd's, thereby becoming a City grandee. Friday was a fine, late summer's day, when a man might wake up, draw back the curtains and sigh contentedly.

On Friday morning Wilson was spick and span and ready to

do what must be done. On Friday morning Robert Marchwood, tired from a late flight from Zurich, was still puzzling over a convoluted letter from Thérèse; this was a tribute to Alec Wilmot-Greaves's ability to meddle; apparently it had been he who had told Thérèse about Veronica Cantor while they were at Ascot. At least he had not known about the child.

He did not know what to do.

He had been in Zurich a few times, for a few days, watching, wondering. About her, about himself, about them. Peering through binoculars from a small boat he had seen her with Urs. Well, no matter.

The letter had arrived some time before and he still had not found a response. He knew he had to write, write before the weekend. He worked his way through two plausible answers but, in finding the words, he lost his feelings or his sense for what his feelings might be. He had to write something, and it had to be right.

In the meantime, he had work to do. He was determined to be neither tired nor ill. Today was a day for a grand celebration, for today was the day that Robert Marchwood was to join the committee of Lloyd's of London.

The Blighter arrived in the room, full of the joys of being himself. Robert slipped onto the bench beside him. He detailed the morning's first business; US building re-insurance, nothing too exceptional, nothing too exciting; it was marginal stuff, the sort of thing a good underwriter might take on his books in order to see something decent next time round. Blighter looked at the slip; once filled, with stamps and signatures, it was worth one hundred grand to Robbo; Blighter would start him off nicely.

'We're missing young Kevin, Robbo. Used to cheer up the place. Any other favours for me?'

'I thought we had had a word already?' Robbo spoke casually. There should be no problem with the deal. Nothing to do with oil rigs or pipelines.

'Yes, Frisco buildings insurance . . .' Blighter pulled out his diary, and quoted some figures. Marchwood glowered. The numbers cited by Blighter were ludicrously high. A nice joke. Blighter was pulling a fast one.

'There must be some mistake.'

'No mistake, old boy. I have it down here.'

'That must be a mistake! Those terms are simply not available.'

'Ah, well. You offered. I said I'd fix it. A man and his word, and all that. Still counts for something among some of us.'

Robert had been kicked. A man had agreed cover for the *Titanic*, when walking down the stairs, after hours. It was known the ship was holed, but news of the sinking had not reached the market. The man paid, a debt of honour, just because of his verbal agreement. Lloyd's liked to believe that a gentleman's word was his bond.

Robert shook his head: 'My clients won't deal at that rate. It's uncommercial.'

'In which case, you've made a silly mistake.'

This was too much. Robert stood up from the underwriter's desk and left the box.

Blighter said: 'Don't bother coming back.'

Robert strode past a row of boxes, brushed past some joking brokers, knocked a document case from someone's hands, entered a metal corridor, found a steel door with a porthole.

It was the underwriters' and brokers' super-loo, a wonder in steel and aluminium. He stood at a metal bowl to wash his hands. Blood. He looked in the mirror, and saw more, a bubble of crimson at his right nostril. Then it spurted out, spotting his tie and shirt. He never made mistakes. He was always as good as his word. The Marchwoods had always been able to rely upon MacNulty's outfit, upon the Blighter; for decades, Knowle and Wordsworth had worked together, made fortunes together.

This was Grote's craftsmanship, this was the end. He found he could not staunch the flow, he tried cold water, hot water, yet still the blood flowed. The tissue box was empty, he walked to the toilet cabinets, trailing red. His grey silk suit was ruined. His legs buckled, the floor met his knees, he thought he was flying, swimming, quite absurd, he would leave in a moment.

The metal wastebin punched him.

An hour later, he was fine. He refused to see a doctor, refused to go home, took a breather at his office instead. He had been ill with this viral infection for a while, on and off, he knew he could cope. His secretary brought him a new shirt and tie, he had a spare suit in a wardrobe. She gave him a kiss and he held her close.

Today was a special day.

Today was a tribute to their father, the day when the Marchwoods entered the inner sanctum, joined the Lloyd's committee. That was what he told Ray, who seemed unconvinced. He did not mention the Blighter's behaviour, there was enough excitement around the place.

The old man would have been proud to see him alongside the Grotes, the Stones, the members of the old Lloyd's dynasties. Ray shrugged his shoulders, as if to say: That's your business.

Marchwood did not, as a rule, want to feel accepted and honoured by the community at large; he did not want a gong, a raft of honorary directorships, the membership of this or that exclusive club. Yet, within Lloyd's, where he had done so much for so long, he felt recognition would not go amiss – and, certainly, protection would be a good idea. With that, Ray had agreed.

They were not going to let Knowle & Co simply evaporate. It was not some frigging oil rig.

He still felt fine, fighting fit, as he entered the twelfth floor atrium – a world of flowers and white stone and dark wood. It was like that, the virus, just came and went. One minute, he was motoring, the next he was nowhere. Now, he was back. The committee room door was open, there were people in the room. He reached for his tie, it was fine. Half a dozen members were already in the high, white, plastered space, standing around the long table lit by three chandeliers, admiring the fireplace or looking out of Georgian windows. Yes, Georgian windows, a fireplace, on the twelfth floor.

The chairman would be along shortly, someone said breathlessly. Robert nodded to Devies, Fortescue, MacNulty and smiled at Mary-Ellen Lemke, Grote's sister-in-law. Life was good, though a cup of tea might help; Robert asked for one to be brought.

Devies and MacNulty were talking yachts, Cowes and the Royal Yacht Squadron.

Robert preferred Bentleys; he had seen enough boats, recently.

Stephen Grote arrived. The sight of the chairman of Lloyd's improved Robert's mood; there were certain things in life which one just had to enjoy. Ray had pleaded for diplomacy: now was the time to forget recriminations and differences.

'My dear chap, how nice to see you.' Stephen Grote patted

Marchwood on his shoulder: 'This is the right forum for a distinguished broker like yourself.'

Robert smiled and expressed ready thanks: 'It's an honour to join the committee.'

Grote continued along the table, a word here, a smile there, a joke about the weather, a charming dinner invitation to Mary-Ellen Lemke which she evidently felt unable to refuse.

Robert reflected, not for the first time, that this was an insane way to do business: twenty cooks, too many, all cooking up one broth.

He sipped his tea. Stephen Grote was in remarkable form; standing at one end of an exceedingly fine and long Chippendale table, he spoke about Lloyd's and the wider world. In essence, insurance was in trouble, the world was troubled, yet both, with time and confidence, could prosper and flourish. Everyone there had heard this before, yet Robert found himself admiring Grote's sense for the felicitous expression, the precise turn of phrase, his dramatic timing.

Only Mrs Lemke seemed distracted, shuffling in the seat next to his; he poured them both a cup of tea, and she smiled. Finally, there was applause, the spell was broken and Stephen asked for comments.

Mrs Lemke responded. Robert breathed deeply, rhythmically, as during exercise.

'Thank you, Chairman, gentlemen.' And she was off. The stories tripped off her tongue; people ruined, lives blighted, wealth eliminated; she had a petition, signed by two thousand names, asking for changes: that the losses of the five thousand should be borne by all the names, by all twenty-five thousand of them.

Stone said there would be legal difficulties: 'The greengrocer does not pay for the newsagent's losses.'

Robert looked at Grote while Mrs Lemke spoke; he seemed completely unconcerned, although his sister-in-law was doing her darndest to undermine him. A cool customer. Robert looked at his watch, an Omega he had inherited from his father. It was twelve fifty-two and forty-five seconds, forty-six, forty-seven. He took another deep breath. Now Lemke was criticising him personally, claiming Knowle & Co was to blame; Robert waited until she had run out of steam, responding briefly: 'These allegations are not new. I have rejected them before and I reject them now.'

There, it was said. There was, at this point, a knock at the door. The room went silent, the door handle turned, and two men entered. Robert knew them both. Inspector Wilson and Inspector Tomlinson. Behind them, Robert could see uniformed police.

'Who the hell do you think you are?' For once, Stephen Grote forgot his manners; for once, the easy calm and charm had disappeared. This had not been included in the stage directions; Robert suddenly realised that the plan had been for him to exit from Lloyd's for ever, pursued by Mary-Ellen Lemke and her cohorts.

The script had been changed.

Stu flashed a glittering smile. 'My name is Detective Inspector Stewart Wilson of the Serious Fraud Office, this is Detective Inspector Derek Tomlinson, and these gentlemen are fellow officers.'

Grote was silent.

Stu continued: 'I'm sorry to disturb you all, but you will appreciate that I'm here on an important matter. Earlier today a warrant was signed by Mr Justice Richards for the arrest of Mr John Devies, Mr Anthony MacNulty and Mr Stephen Grote on suspicion of theft and false accounting. I must ask the gentlemen I've named to step forward, and warn them that anything they say may be taken down and used in evidence against them.'

Grote hesitated, as if on the edge of a virulent outburst: 'Officer . . .' Robert saw him glance around the room, searching. Yet he managed to continue, calmly enough: 'Officer, this is completely unacceptable. Outrageous.'

'And your name would be, sir?'

'Grote, Stephen Grote. I am the chairman of Lloyd's.'

'Well, sir, I'm going to ask you to accompany me and the other two gentlemen to Wood Street police station for further questioning. You're under arrest.'

Robert breathed slowly, deeply. He avoided looking at Wilson's grease-streaked hair. He avoided looking at Tomlinson. He just held the edge of the table, checked the empty pot of tea.

Certainly Tommo had given him a call, a muttered warning, but there had been nothing he could do, even if he had known the specifics. Lloyd's had taken a hit. Even so, Robert was glad he had lived to see this day. He took a perverse pleasure in seeing Grote and friends arrested. He only wished his father might have seen it too.

Quite how he and Ray and Knowle would escape from the oil rig mess, he did not know, but that was quite another matter. Maybe he could soldier on somehow, as if nothing had happened; that would be Ray's view. People forget, the world changes, time heals all wounds. Does it? Does it really? And the money? The losses?

Grote was speechless. He looked at Robert, then turned to Fortescue and nodded.

Quite what that nod meant, was uncertain. At the time, it just seemed to confirm that Grote possessed dignity, calm, and an unusual presence of mind.

FIFTEEN

A NAME WOBBLED along Lime Street on a penny farthing, for the benefit of a newspaper cameraman. He took a seat in front of the main entrance, holding out a flat cap to beg, mockingly, from the brokers and underwriters who walked past. A placard proclaimed: 'Lost home, wife and Ferrari at Lloyd's. Please give generously.'

One underwriter stopped, read the poster, and said: 'You shouldn't have joined, sir. Shouldn't have joined.'

There were boos from the demonstrators, who were, for the most part, less than demonstrative. They were trying to impress their plight on the Lloyd's committee, meeting inside that Friday lunchtime. Someone claimed to have seen policemen enter the Lime Street building; there were police cars around the place, but then there often were.

Kevin Vaughan, with three thousand other things on his mind, almost fell over the dozen or so demonstrators who were complaining about one of the dustbin syndicates; they had hired an advertising float and slapped on it a picture of a large dustbin marked SALTER. Litigation was pending. Kevin put twopence in the man's hat; everybody laughed.

A very civilised affair.

In their shoes, he thought, he would have been furious. Of course, they had been warned that this might happen, but assured, in all but the same breath, with a nod and a wink, that it would not. They had been warned, as brave men and bold women, that they risked their shirt buttons, cuff links, they risked their last dollar, cent, centime and penny as well as the cotton sheets on their bed. But it was in certain circles the necessary thing to be a name; it was a sign you had cuff links to lose. Not, of course, that you ever would.

Kevin was buttonholed by the guy with the penny farthing, who claimed to be a member of the Garth clan, North Country landowners. He had been at Eton with Tony MacNulty and Alec Wilmot-Greaves, his brother had shared a dorm with Henry Stone. 'With contacts like that,' he bleated, 'it just should not happen!'

Sometimes, Kev thought, extricating himself politely, he was quite glad to be a product of Spring Road Comprehensive. Glad of his wits, glad to live by them. That was, ultimately, all he had. What was he to feel if thousands of middling-rich to very-rich people were being bankrupted, quietly driven to the wall? They had all been warned, they had heard the words and failed to take them seriously. They had trusted Lloyd's and the gentlemen who worked there.

Someone said that there was a police raid going on at Lloyd's, pointing to the cars. This was a good joke and Kevin smiled, before strolling into Leadenhall Market.

Here, he looked at his watch; he was early for lunch; he walked round the new bookshop, looking at the book covers and posters, admired the lobsters, skate and mussels on the fishmonger's slab, ogled the vintage champagne in the wine merchant's beside the flower shop where garlands of roses, lilies, carnations and forget-me-nots in green plastic buckets spilled out over the pavement, shining brightly in the shade afforded by the wood-and-glass arcade.

Kevin was very taken with his new job, he enjoyed working for Ray; he had kept the advertisements from Mrs Sanderson's garage, but had decided not to try to prove anything at all. He had decided he would leave the data centre well alone.

The whole broking business boiled down to salesmanship, to the right mixture of banter and seriousness. He seemed to have found the tone. Ray was giving him the tougher stuff now, complicated deals which needed hours of detailed negotiation. He had had a tough morning. He noticed his hands, his heartbeat for the first time that Friday.

There were rumours that Robbo had been taken ill, he did not know what that might mean. He heard police sirens and wondered.

A finger touched his neck and he almost jumped out of his skin.

'Surprise, surprise,' a voice said. It was stylish Mrs Alice

Montfort, wearing pink. She was in no mood for a filled croissant and coffee lunch, so it was off to the tapas bar for spicy dips and delicacies, with white Rioja, cool and slightly bitter.

'Out of sight, out of mind,' she said, without a grin. 'How was Spain? How's the new job?'

Kevin shrugged his shoulders to both questions. 'Did you see the demo?'

'Yes, a bit pathetic.'

'Difficult to feel sorry for them.'

'I don't know, you should see the letters we get. My father went bust after the war, I'll never forget that, even though I was only young.'

'I'd rather not see the letters you send . . .'

Her voice broke, and he suddenly realised she was upset, close to tears. He asked, gently, if there was a problem.

She rose to powder her nose; Kev sipped wine.

'You look well,' he said when she returned. 'Pink suits you.'

'Thanks.'

Their last heart-to-heart had receded, becoming hardly more than a beautiful memory. Yet Alice was not her normal, definite self.

Kevin ate and decided, definitely, that he liked black olives, marinaded artichoke hearts, paprika-spiced chorizo sausage and hot food. He pushed some of the dishes towards her, by way of encouragement, and she picked at his offering in silence.

Finally, she confessed. Tony MacNulty had blown into the office, mid-morning, livid with rage. In front of everybody else, he had told her to collect her things and go; her services were no longer required. After fifteen years, she was out.

Kevin was suddenly unable to chew his food. He wondered what, exactly, Tony had discovered. And how.

Sixteen

DONNA WARRILOW WAS kind of hiding in Bond Street, in her den, well away from the noble black façade and gold lettering, deep inside the green warren of corridors and stairs, in the office which served as 'consulting room' for difficult cases. Yet today she had a headache.

An early early-season sale had been foisted upon her and she was under pressure: that Friday morning there had been visitors eager to view her sale collection – eighteenth-century English furniture – there were final notes to draft, last minute plans to be laid and every collector who mattered had to be found, dead or alive, and transported.

So she had tried the tablets, to no avail: even the silence throbbed.

Stephen was to blame.

She made another foray to the galley kitchen and returned with another pot of peppermint tea in her burnished steel container. Style: Swedish Sixties. Provenance: Sheffield. Value at auction: Dented.

A package arrived mid-morning, by messenger, from Asprey's City branch. She let it lie on her desk. Yes, Stephen was at fault and she guessed the little Asprey something was his attempt at apology. She would darn well ignore it.

Some of the collectors who had flown over were friends or good acquaintances, people she had known for decades. There were the Davidoffs from Chicago, the Mayers from New York – people with money and taste and time; they were interested in the Beaulieu cabinet. To her mind, a heavy, over-elaborate monstrosity, it had attracted an outcry: save an Italian cabinet for the British nation! Our heritage for sale! The nation had rarely seen the beast, which had gathered dust in a stately home with the usual leaking roof, for decades. Millions were needed for the roof, millions were therefore needed from the cabinet, and government refused to pay.

So the press would concentrate on the Beaulieu, and she would be happy if it sold well. Together with other fabulous objects from old collections, a Queen Anne bureau cabinet crafted from walnut, a Rococo library table by William Vile and much Chippendale.

In any event, hers was going to be a marvellous sale, helped, she had to admit, by crumbling masonry and death duties, especially now that some of the owners had fallen under the curse of Lloyd's.

Over breakfast, Donna had said to Stephen: 'You know, you're working for me.'

Stephen had kind of grunted; he had understood. Then he pointed at that Friday's newspaper and said, with evident distaste: 'Everyone's been talking to your sister, Mrs Rent-a-Mouth.'

Oh-oh. Mary-Ellen had been making rude comments about Lloyd's to journalists, an unforgivable offence; she had failed, it seemed, to understand that committee persons are, one, not supposed to talk to the press, two, not to utter criticism, three, not to think.

An exchange of tirades ensued; Stephen accused her of a lack of support; she accused him of neglecting her; there had been a certain harmony between them, then someone had called, late, and he had disappeared, only to return home long after midnight, asperged with cognac.

'I'm starting to wonder if you don't have a mistress.'

Besides, she suspected Mary-Ellen could be right; she had, after all, seen Stephen trying to extricate Marshall and Mary-Ellen from certain syndicates before they exploded. She said: 'Mary-Ellen has her point of view. She reckons she has paid enough and it stinks. Can't say I blame her.'

Breakfast ended with the taste of stale muffins and cold coffee; a headache was launched and Stephen was definitely to blame.

Now he had sent her a peace offering.

Not for the first time, Donna wondered what her father might have thought. Papa was a tough, rough, hardworking tyrant, a man who neither gave nor asked for favours. Yet he was honest or she thought him so, she had never heard any different. Sure,

America was not settled by the land hunger of Rip Van Winkle or the philanthropy of Rockefeller.

The package remained irritating; finally, her resistance crumbled, she removed the packaging, clicked open a long padded box and found a gold bracelet with trinkets recalling the Magic Flute – several birds, a glockenspiel, a snake, a padlock, a glass of wine, the sun, three miniature temples marked Wisdom, Reason and Nature. The inscription was taken from the famous duet: 'Stephen and Donna – man and wife, wife and man'.

In one sense, it was quite horrible kitsch. This was, she guessed, also true of a Cellini saltcellar. Besides, the bracelet was masterfully wrought, the trinkets were ingeniously designed; it reminded her of their visits to the opera, of their best times. Gratitude swept away any doubt or resentment or anger; she stretched to pick up the phone.

Inevitably, the beast rang; less inevitably, it was Mary-Ellen. Words rushed out at her; police, handcuffs, enquiries.

Donna spat anger, then organised, without pausing: Stephen's lawyer would press for bail. The auction would take place that evening, thereafter she was at war.

At least the headache was gone.

SEVENTEEN

GET THE CUFFS on Grote, Wilson.

The DG was harder than your average nail.

There had been a ruck outside Lloyd's, some demonstrators, press cameramen.

Ah, cameramen. How fortunate, how fortuitous. And there was Wilson, accompanying Mr Devies, Mr MacNulty and Mr Grote. All clad in regulation police cuffs. So far, so good.

Yet Stu Wilson felt – well, if not like a pawn, more like a knight, available for sacrifice or exchange, in a game being played by superior forces. The cameras had flashed, and he had wondered who had tipped them off.

Tomlinson had not looked pleased, either.

Detective Inspector Stewart Wilson was not, by nature, a nervous man. His bravery had, many years ago, been commended. He had once disarmed an escaped prisoner single-handed, a violent bruiser, with a history of gun use. Though there had been some huffing and puffing about his disregard for the book – he had gone in on his own – his superiors were pleased to promote him, from sergeant to inspector. He had not been nervous. He was just doing his job. Simple as that.

Everything had been simple, in the glory days.

This was not so simple.

He looked at the man sitting beside him in the car, Grote. No simpleton. A super-smart, smooth man, yet tough and proud. Stu doubted he would be able to squeeze much out of him.

They would see.

Grote and Wilson felt the need to talk. So they talked about how the way it always rained in Britain, about the terrible English cricket team and the appalling London traffic. The sort of conversation two Englishmen might reasonably hold anywhere in the world. Saying nothing was a British art form, equally suited to the casbah or a bivouac in ice, at fifteen thousand feet.

Wilson recalled the DG's words: 'I've decided you have a stronger case than you think. Take them in, and give them the works.' The works?

He had sent a team down to Wordsworth & Co, with its boss MacNulty, to get at the safe and the hard disks. DA&P, Baden-Baden . . . if they existed they might be his salvation.

He had sent a pair of guys, late yesterday, over to Cowes, to interview Welsby's boss, the head of customs and excise, who had hesitated, then confirmed everything Welsby had said. He, too, had identified Stephen Grote as the third man on MacNulty's ketch, the day that a multi-million pound Monet was imported into Britain: MacNulty, Devies and Grote, plus Monet. Mrs Rainsley had laughed at the news and told him to get the cuffs on Grote. The idea appealed.

So far, so good.

Grote hummed something, tunelessly. He caught Wilson's glance: 'Like music, officer?'

'Not much, I'm afraid. My wife treats me to arias from Italian operas, which I can just about take. I prefer Mozart to Verdi, put it that way.'

'You wouldn't mind removing the handcuffs, would you? They are very uncomfortable.'

'We'll be there in a minute, sir.'

Grote winced and wondered. His term as Lloyd's chairman had probably reached a less than natural end. An unhappy fact. This had nearly caused him to lose control, to indulge in a bravura display of fireworks. Fortunately, he had reined himself back; his behaviour and bearing had been impeccable. The police had nothing against him, of course, but his reputation was sullied. No great-and-goodmanship in old age, which was a pity; he had always half-hoped he might become chairman of the National Trust, head a museum. Still, it was fortunate he did not have a knighthood to lose.

Ultimately, the only thing that mattered was to avoid gaol. That would be difficult to bear. And in the meantime he would fight. Fight like fury, but calmly.

He turned to Wilson and asked coolly: 'How is your nephew finding his new job, Inspector Wilson?'

It was a question that Wilson, engrossed in his own thoughts, only half-heard. Ahead, in the sunlight, he could just make out the blue lantern of Wood Street police station.

He made no reply.

The media were waiting for them. Lights, cameramen, reporters jostling for position. They drove straight into the station compound.

Men holding cameras rushed into the road behind them, brushing passing cars, jostling with each other for the snatched shot. This one will stop, no, this one won't. One car had driven past, false alarm, then a camera had fallen from a flailing hand, rolled into the gutter.

It was fortunate nobody was injured.

'Which one was he in?' Someone had photographed the lead car, not the second.

'Search me. I'm only here to get his mugshot. That him?'

A picture of Grote in a suit, sitting next to a model of the Cutty Sark, was proffered. Yeah, that's the guy. Second car. Some old favours were called in, some blokes had still to be convinced, others were already on their way back to the picture desk.

There must be other cars. Someone had told them four cars. Someone had got some pics outside Lloyd's. A couple of the broadsheets had been tipped off.

'Search me. I was just told to get the camera down here, someone'll have to pay for that. A reporter's on his way. Stuck in a taxi somewhere. By the time he's here, it'll all be over, and we'll have to piss off back.'

'I heard one of your guys got killed today.'

'Yeah, Rick. Over in Romania. Car crash.'

'Shit.'

'Yeah, nice guy.'

'Here are the others.' A cheer went up. Bodies scrimmaged, two cars slowed. Then it was over. The cars were in the station.

'Any luck?'

'Could be OK.'

'The police never help. The bastards. Seeya.'

The knot of men, wielding heavy bags, dispersed down Cheapside and up London Wall. Running. The pictures might not make the first editions. It depended what else was happening in the world. More a story for the heavies, and they might bury

199

it inside. It depended what they made of it on the box. It all depended.

Someone went down Mayfair way. Yeah, the Grote mansion, you know the story: millionaire nicked.

Television lights blazed in Wood Street. Clapperboard. No, no. Try again. Nerves. The late afternoon news was evidently running it big.

'In a dramatic raid, City of London police have arrested the chairman of Lloyd's, the world-famous insurance market, on suspicion of fraud, theft and false accounting. The three men arrested were Stephen Grote, the chairman of Lloyd's, John Devies, the deputy chairman and Anthony MacNulty, a leading figure in Lloyd's. The three men are assisting the police with their enquiries at Wood Street police station.

'With a general election widely predicted for the autumn, the Government is keen to get tough with sharp City practice. Sources close to Downing Street claim the Government want to show that the City is not above the law.

'For Lloyd's of London, the arrests could not have come at a worse time. The insurance market has recently announced losses of two billion pounds and further losses are accepted as inevitable. Many MPs are known to have lost fortunes.'

The director nods to the reporter. Lights out. Fine, everybody. Thank you.

EIGHTEEN

ROBERT MARCHWOOD, CHAIRMAN and chief executive of Knowle & Co, insurance brokers at Lloyd's of London, was exhausted. The friends were sure as hell going to come gunning for him, for Ray and the business now.

What was to happen to Knowle? Damn that. What about his marriage? What was the matter with his health? He might be finished, well and truly finished, but it was time to celebrate. Man that sleeps with woman hath but a short time to live, and is full of laughter. It was bubbly time. Not time to go home; there was no home to go to.

Ah, the look on Grote's face as he saw Wilson: Robert would never forget that. The flicker of terror, anger, then nothing, blank indifference. A nod of the head. Then nothing.

Robert wandered around the City. It was mid-afternoon, when all who were not drunk or shellshocked were working. He was stone-cold sober, this had to stop.

He stumbled on the flight of steps that led to the Caves de Champagne. Today's Specials (for lunch, chalked on the blackboard) had been avocado and prawns, lobster, chocolate mousse. The staircase was painted black, enlivened only by fish tanks filled with tomorrow's fare. He pushed open the door and entered the bar, with its black, sawdusted floor, black walls and dark furniture. On the walls were spotlit sporting prints, hunting meets, days at the races; through the windows he could see the dark outline of the Great Standard Hotel. In the bar, there were ledges where people could rest and stand and drink and eat. In the restaurant beyond there were tables where people could sit and drink and eat. The bar was half-empty and the restaurant was closed. He entered a half-empty silence and, suddenly, felt hungry; the blackboard menu was history.

Some people were letting an exceedingly late lunch slip away, others watching a happy-hour slide closer.

'Did you see the cuffs go on, Robbo?' This was Robey, standing with a group of other underwriters, including the Blighter, a couple of guys from Wilmot-Greaves's outfit, a familiar face who worked for Stone. The more he looked at the Blighter, the more Robert felt like . . . but he would be polite. Be polite, Robert. That was what Thérèse always said. Be polite.

His large fingers ached to become fists; he had a little matter to settle with the Blighter, otherwise known as the man who had kicked him in the balls earlier that day.

Be polite. So, Robert offered the calm exterior of the perfect gentleman, asked the blokes for their orders; he was paying, as ever. He joked he had just read a great book: Mr Plod's Big Day in Lloyd's.

'I didn't know you knew the alphabet.' The Blighter turned to Robey. 'Just imagine. Marchwood has read Enid Blyton! Soon he'll be able to remember, keep promises and tell the truth.'

Robert bit his tongue, signalled to the barman, intent on keeping his cool.

The Lloyd's guys were unhappy; their world had come to an end; without its reputation for integrity, Lloyd's was nothing, they were nothing. Their pay cheques for hundreds of thousands would disappear.

The market lived on the mutual trust of gentlemen. That was the claim. Even if the last gentleman had died some while ago.

'I don't think the arrests are a case for celebration,' Robey observed. You could tell that his business was turning sour, that he did not like oil pipelines. Nor asbestos.

Robert had few worries. 'Actually, I'm just mourning a Monet I thought I saw once.'

He looked at the Blighter and saw no reaction.

'What are the charges?' a Wilmot-Greaves man asked.

'Cheating. Being rotten cheats and bad sports and playing dirty. Let's get some bubbly going here, if you gentlemen would be kind enough to join me.'

The guys nodded, showing Pavlovian instincts, a Lloyd's man and a bubbly bottle are seldom parted until one is empty and the other filled. He turned to the barman. 'Three bottles of Moët, and a steak sandwich with a side salad. Do me some nuts and some crisps, too.'

Robert rarely came over here, at lunchtime he struck his deals in a private room at a City club; now he looked at the blokes. They were hurt, afflicted, even grieving. Robey, who always had time for a smile, was frozen-faced.

'Come on, you shouldn't take this personally,' Robert told him.

Robey said nothing, but the Blighter snorted. His boss had been arrested; the Wordsworth offices raided. He said: 'Our reputation has been built up over decades. Now it is gone. We had enough problems, before this. Huge losses, names leaving, rancid publicity, you name it. Now the chairman is arrested for fraud.'

Robert remained optimistic: 'Look, we just have to keep to our guns, stick to our mettle. Forget Grote and the rest, they don't matter. They're up on the twelfth floor, playing power games, lining their pockets. Now they've come unstuck. So what? The blokes in the market, the underwriters and brokers don't need them.'

He sensed he had touched a chord, one or two of the guys grinned.

The Blighter was unimpressed: 'There was some talk that you were to be expelled from the market.'

'Me? You must be joking! Grote was cooing my name. Treated me like royalty.'

Of course, he thought, after Mary-Ellen Lemke's speech, there was to have been a discussion, and a vote. Grote would make a concession to his sister-in-law and Robert Hugh Marchwood would walk the plank.

That was what the Blighter had expected. Tony had tried to tell him; that was the threat behind Tony's phone call at the weekend.

The time and place had been perfect. Unfortunately for Grote, Inspector Wilson had intervened.

'What are we drinking to, Robbo?' Glasses were distributed, then filled with pale, yellow-green tinged liquid.

'To Mr Plod?'

He saw little enthusiasm for this suggestion. 'OK. To long lunches, good health and wild women.'

'The first sound suggestion you've made today,' Robey said. They all drank. Cheers. Very pleasant little number. Yes, very pleasant. Another half-familiar face entered, was given a glass, asked if Devies and MacNulty and Grote had been arrested. Yes indeed. For once, the newspapers were bang on the money.

There was another long silence. There were some wounds that even bubbly could not heal.

'If I believed all the doom and gloom,' Robert told them, 'I wouldn't get out of bed in the morning. No, in my book, the disaster cycle is over. The world is just waiting to become a saner, safer and quieter place.'

Kevin Vaughan arrived, panting, with a wodge of paperwork under his right arm.

'Frankie!' Robert said, extravagantly, with a cod-accent from somewhere: 'Glad to see you is workin' today, glad to see anybody is workin' . . .'

Kevin was not looking for a party: the office was empty, Mrs Phillips and Ray were nowhere to be seen, then this story about the police . . . He did not know what to believe.

Food arrived. No, Kevin did not want anything, apart from some answers. He took a glass of bubbly, anyway, for good luck. There seemed to be almost a dozen guys standing around, getting drunk on Marchwood's champagne when they should be working.

He asked Robbo: 'You're sure you are OK?'

'Sure. Sure I'm sure.' Robert proposed another toast: no disasters!

Robey said: 'We'll all drink to that.' Old Ropey was planning a holiday in Africa, shooting big game. Despite himself, Robert smiled. He dispensed a third bottle of bubbly.

'To no disasters.'

'No disasters.' They all slurped, religiously, except Kevin.

Robert felt a hand on his shoulder. It was Fortescue, newly arrived, looking stern and flushed, his red hair tousled; Marchwood rose and asked the English head of the European arm of the great American brokerage, King & MacLuhan, otherwise known as K&M, to join their quiet celebrations of Lloyd's wonderful future.

Fortescue, searching for a cigarette, blustered about the very idea. Some people simply did not know how to behave; they might just as well stage a jolly in a mortuary!

'I'm afraid I need a word, old man. If the gents don't mind,' Fortescue said. They did not mind. He had evidently searched high and low to find Marchwood.

Robert signalled for more of the same to the barman, then retreated with Fortescue to a ledge beside a window. It seemed strange not to be at his club, cutting deals. For once he was without pencil and papers; for once he had had more than a discreet glass, but he could still wave a hand, dictate terms to the air. Even if millions did not ride on every word, it was still fun. Besides, Ropey had made him a bob or two, earlier in the day. He breathed deeply, deliberately. There was a tightness in his chest.

Fortescue whispered: 'This is a complete and utter mess.'

'Not good, not good.' Robert could not help but smile.

'What did you tell the police?'

'Nothing. That Grote likes Monets. He's got a couple, hasn't he?'

'Clocks. Grote has clocks and watches and antiques.'

'Ah, my mistake.'

'For Christ's sake, Marchwood.' Fortescue suddenly ceased to be a cooler-than-cool sophisticate.

With a great effort, Robert tried to be serious: 'What do you want, Neil? Isn't the game over?'

There was a hesitation. Fortescue looked round the partition, then said: 'Kevin Vaughan is the nephew of Inspector Wilson, the arresting officer.'

For once, Robert had trouble with a handful of peanuts. 'News to me. Wilson was investigating the Monet. He got nothing out of me.'

Fortescue nodded earnestly, as if he really, honestly and truly believed him. He lowered his voice: 'We have two demands. No help to the police. Fire Vaughan.'

Robbo raised his glass of fizz, sipped before replying. He had done everything they asked. They had benefited; Salter, Annan and Mite Leven had lost. In return – he had been insulted, his Monet dissolved, Ray excluded, his wife driven away.

'Tell me, Fortescue, why do you think I should trust you?'

'You have to.'

Robert laughed.

'Just think what will happen if the SFO unravel Baden–Baden. They'll blow you away, too. We have to trust each other.'

Robert continued to smile. They would destroy his firm, one way or another. He said nothing. One day, they would come for him, as they had come for his father.

'How will it help if I fire young Kevin?' he asked.

'It will,' Fortescue lit a cigarette.

In the mirror behind the bar, he saw Kev joking with the

blokes. Robert was not in the habit of firing people. If staff were successful, they were rewarded; if they did nothing, they were paid nothing. Of course, if someone was a problem, the person was soon informed. Robert was, by and large, someone one noticed if he was unhappy. But there were people on the staff who did very little at all, apart from exchange jokes with the boss.

Damn.

'Frankie, come over here, will you?'

Fortescue looked at Robert, unsure whether to stay or leave. Robert effected the introductions: 'Mr Fortescue, please meet Mr Vaughan of Knowle.'

Both were delighted, delighted.

He turned to Kevin: 'Old Fortescue here wants me to sack you. What do you say?'

Kevin looked at Fortescue, who said nothing, then asked: 'Why? What's it to do with him?'

'Your Uncle Stewart is about to blow Lloyd's out of the water, smash Wordsworth and torpedo Knowle.'

Kevin laughed. The two older men did not laugh; Robert had lost his smile; Fortescue tried to recover his calm by blowing a smoke-ring.

'Inspector Stewart Wilson is my uncle. What's wrong with that?'

'Why didn't you tell me?'

Kevin flared up. 'What does your aunt do for a living? Clean floors?'

Robert's sense of humour had run dry. He swatted the cigarette smoke away. Fortescue was in a rage. There must be a civilised way to resolve this. What would Ray do?

'Kev,' he said. 'Listen, old man, it would be a good idea, in present circumstances, if you took a holiday . . . While we think about your future.'

'My future is with Knowle & Co.'

'Look, your uncle has just arrested the chairman of Lloyd's. With the greatest respect . . .'

Kevin Vaughan looked at Robbo, looked at Fortescue, turned on his heel and left the bar.

Robert turned to Fortescue who said: 'You may have done enough. This time.'

NINETEEN

DONNA MADE AN hour, where there was none.

Mary-Ellen, quite incorrigible, had stipulated the American Bar in the Carlton. There and only there, would she spill the beans about the arrest and talk about their losses. They had avoided the subject for ages; relations between the Grotes and the Lemkes were not at an all-time high.

Normally, Donna would have refused. She had no desire to risk meeting Americans on a less-than-languid Grand Tour, the Davidoffs or other heavy-hitters in London for the sale, but a sister was a sister.

She entered unobtrusively, if that were possible, through the black wood and brass revolving door of the hotel entrance. Just visible from the foyer was the lounge; here a white baby grand had been placed like a wedding cake, overarched by a white pergola and garnished with flowers. She was glad they had agreed on the American Bar instead, with its unadorned twenties style.

Despite their disagreements, they cheek-kissed. Mary-Ellen was enthusiastic. Donna worried about this, as if it contained a hidden reproach. Was she responsible for everything Stephen did, might have done?

They ordered wine rather than Daiquiris: zinfandel from California, in wide-brimmed, semi-floral cups. She had, after all, work to do, she had to be sober.

'I've an auction later. I really shouldn't be here.'

Mary-Ellen paused, then failed to commiserate: 'You sent me a catalogue, but I guess I'm not in a buying mood.'

O God. Donna sipped some wine, pecked at a nut, admired the art deco bar. She observed that Mary-Ellen had become a little too plump, she had always been too short, and she was not helped by that suit.

Mary-Ellen sure was a good talker, though.

Donna smiled in adversity, half-listening to her sister's tirade against Lloyd's, half-admiring the way she minced her enemies; it was as if Stephen's sequestration was a triumph of all-American probity over the corrupt Old World. The tale was long and rambling; a bank on the Côte d'Azur, a dead banker, Marshall in Milan, Marshall in the agency, the Freemasons, the Mafia . . .

'How did he take the arrest?' Donna asked.

Mary-Ellen hesitated: 'With dignity, I must say . . .'

Then she was off again, attacking. Donna ought by rights to have felt thoroughly miserable, but she did not; she recognised versions of perfectly innocent events she knew or thought she knew about. Stephen, for example, had indeed made several trips to the South of France and to Lake Maggiore, driving down from the chalet in Gstaad, but for no conspiratorial reason.

Donna reminded Mary-Ellen of Stephen's attempt to change their syndicates: 'You should have taken his advice,' she said.

Mary-Ellen's outrage disgusted her.

It was not as if Marshall and Mary-Ellen were whiter than white. Marshall had organised clandestine purchasing in Europe during the 60s – whatever he said and he sure would not talk much about that, Vietnam had been a mess, still was a mess, after all they had thrown at the gooks.

Mary-Ellen's morality was OK, as long as you liked everything draped in stars and stripes, but then, it was Marshall's job to think that way. His face had to fit at the Embassy.

'How much have you lost?' Donna asked.

'*We* lost, sister, *we* lost.' Given the structure of their father's estate, held in one large trust, it was difficult, if not impossible, to disentangle their interests. The money involved was large and mounting: but they were, well, very affluent.

'How much, Mary-Ellen?'

'Guess.'

Donna put the glass down. 'No, I won't. Now, you tell me . . .'

'A million.'

'You've just got to be joking . . . Bucks or pounds?'

'Pounds. Most of the losses were in Marshall's name, not in mine.' Mary-Ellen gestured. Donna understood: because Marshall was that sort of guy, he thought he should take the hit.

An absurd thing, pride, but it was the stuff Marshall used for gasoline.

'So Marshall's in a bad way?'

'He ain't chipper, that's for sure.'

Of course, Mary-Ellen knew of a bunch of other cases. A horde of dentists from Minnesota had had the gold fillings removed from their teeth. Then there was the Vice President, his grief had been conveyed in indelible ink to Marshall at the Grosvenor Square embassy.

Donna was not amused. 'Look, you pay Marshall's losses, your losses, using our trust fund. Go to the bank, if need be.' She stood up. 'I have to go. D'you know, all this fake morality has made me sure of one thing. I admire Stephen's drive and determination. In fact . . .'

She forgave him everything. Well, almost everything.

As soon as she made the Bond Street auction room, Nathan Mayer came right over, was his charming and delightful self. He had seen it all before. As senior legal counsel to one of the top Wall Street outfits, Nathan had defended thirty guys charged with insider trading: they had been frog-marched in handcuffs across Wall Street. 'Just for doing their job, for Christ's sake!'

She smiled. Later, the Davidoffs were sniffy when they saw her, so she was quite pleased when a woman friend of theirs carried off the Beaulieu cabinet for eight million; all in all, her pre-season sale was a triumph, marred only by the headlines in the evening newspaper.

She slipped away before the hubbub died away. Perhaps she could still extricate Stephen from Wood Street police station that evening.

TWENTY

THAT EVENING, FOR once, Whitehall Nigel and Downing Street William met each other in the hallway of the Athenaeum and both men were on time. They ordered much-needed sustenance and headed upstairs to the library. Here, in the quiet, a couple of acquaintances scanned this morning's papers. Rather out-of-date papers.

Whiskies arrived, with triangles of smoked salmon and brown bread; they should not eat here in the library, should not drink here, but some rules were made to be broken, even by civil servants.

William lit a cigar and observed: 'My lord and master has been hyperactive all day. A European ally in the morning, an early call from the Oval Office, followed by a Treasury presentation, then questions in Parliament.'

Nigel added soda, then raised a glass: 'To next week.'

'To next week.'

The economic data had been bad, but not dire. Some forecasters had been pleasantly surprised; the next few months should be stable, too. Something could be juggled to produce a tax cut. The Treasury had come up with something halfway plausible.

The two gentlemen nodded solemnly. They had both seen the presentation, dominated by the one, barely hidden message: a snap election, to be called in the autumn, could be announced within a fortnight.

'My wife won't like it,' Nigel said. 'Another holiday down the tube. We were planning a September break, when the boys are back at school.'

Now, instead, they had to prepare for the return of Her Majesty's Glorious Opposition (RIP), extract plausible campaign promises from the implausible, resurrect dead election-winning ideas from the morgue. Even if the task were delegated to junior staff, it had to be carried out in a professional manner, demanding time and effort.

The Lloyd's raid had been a triumph; people had jumped for joy. The presentation had been halted, everybody had piled into the next room for a look-see on the box. There they were: Grote and friends, in handcuffs. Wonderful.

Bill smiled: 'The master really loved our boys' little foray. He reckons locking up fat cats is worth at least three marginals. Only winning the World Cup ranks higher.'

'Or a royal blessing,' Nigel suggested.

'Ah, they're not what they were.'

True, true. There had been some robust comments from that quarter, too: some minor royals had been frazzled in the North Sea, thanks to Lloyd's.

'Bill, what's your feeling, do you think they'll win if they go to the country now?'

A shrug. It was implausibly plausible.

'They don't know themselves, do they? On board ship, you watch the rats. At the moment, at least half the rodents are talking to the private sector.'

There was a silence. Every cloud has a silver seam.

'So even the master was in a good mood?' Nigel ventured, changing subject.

'About time, too,' Bill responded, tartly. He had been on Chequers duty recently. Out there, usually, the diary allowed time for reflection, contemplation and an extended nap, but not this time. There had been calls from the White House, a stream of junior ministers, backbenchers and other friends of friends to see his lordship, losers to a man, all diluting their whisky with tears. Grote had not gone down well and, after the meeting, the great man had simply wanted to see blood.

He asked Nigel: 'I expect you've got enough ammo at the Department of Trade, in case her majesty's opposition gets the hots over Lloyd's?'

'My man will put them down. That's his one area of complete competence.' Nigel replied.

William lowered his voice: 'The issue will not go away. All those backbenchers slowly roasting in their juices. Several have sold their old rectories already. The White House is bitter about the Vice President. I am told that the agency has been invited to have a look. His greyness turned puce at the idea.'

'Do you think,' Nigel mused, 'that the arrests will prove more than just a quick fix? How high are the chances of a successful prosecution?'

They looked at each other. They owed their longterm success to appeasing short-term needs; both feared that government had become the art of disguising the slide from bad to worse. This did not satisfy them, but the size of the mortgage was the measure of the man. Besides, both men were due knighthoods shortly. Both men laughed, heartily, easily.

They knew the score: the desire for votes sweeps all before. So something had been done to keep people quiet. Then, when the worms emerge from the can, months or even years later, the problem has been forgotten. If the worst comes to the worst, the whole stinking mess can be buried under a mound of disinformation or a Commission of Enquiry.

A servant arrived and took another order for whisky.

'Who's on the investigation?'

Nigel hesitates. 'A good chap called Wilson, I believe.'

'Not so good that he's indispensable, I trust?'

'Nobody is that good. I've even heard talk that you were to be pensioned off, Bill.'

William cast his hands in the air, blew cigar smoke and smiled.

BOOK FOUR

ONE

THE FIRST SIGN of a problem came on the Friday evening; it seemed innocuous.

Jenny Vaughan was at home, watching the news on the television, slightly stunned by the arrests, when the telephone rang. It was a woman caller who, after hesitation, announced she had expected to see Kevin at seven that evening; she was an estate agent; she had a wonderful flat in a new development overlooking the river and if Mr Vaughan wanted to buy, he should make an effort to be punctual. Thank you.

Kevin had said nothing. Jenny knew he wanted to move out, should move out; yet he was her only son, she did not like to see him go. He should have told her.

She started to worry, as she often did, but it had turned midnight before she finally rang Rosie and Rosie, tired but troubled, rang Stu at Wood Street Police Station. Who was not there, not even for his wife. The irate switchboard operator had been run ragged by the press. The Inspector's wife, ah, she'd heard that one before.

Nevertheless, Rosie left a message. Inspector Wilson to ring his wife at home soonest.

In fact, Stu Wilson had been still in good form at midnight, sitting in the canteen at Wood Street, drinking something brown and awful, reviewing the case with Tomlinson. He could not avoid the man.

'Make a splash, Wilson,' Mrs Rainsley had said.

They had certainly done that. Search warrants had been issued, yards of black and white striped tape had been draped round Wordsworth's offices, doors had been sealed and box after box, yards and yards of paper files had been recovered. The press and, especially, the television crews had been pleased with the pictures. Meanwhile, three hard disks were extracted from MacNulty's safe and the Wordsworth computer system was placed 'in protective custody'.

Stu fought hard not to let himself get carried away. What had happened to the hard disks? He wanted to be sure that the essentials had not been overlooked.

'Formatted, inevitably,' a T-shirted accountant announced to the incident room. This meant that someone had tried to wipe the disks clean before their raid; someone had tipped off MacNulty.

'Is the data on the disks lost?' he asked brusquely.

'Depends how the formatting was done. We're trying to rescue the stuff now.'

Stu tried not to show his frustration.

They occupied a suite of white-walled rooms on the sixth floor of the biscuit tin, with views of the British Museum. Until recently, Stu had been on his own. Suddenly, there were people everywhere. Mrs Rainsley had found a dozen guys for him, and until now, everything had gone smoothly. Now someone had known, someone had tipped off MacNulty. Someone in this office, or at least in this building.

Stu prayed they could recover something from the disks; it would probably tell them everything they needed to know.

He returned from the SFO to Wood Street Station, to question Grote, Devies and MacNulty whom someone, before the raid, had named the three monkeys: hear no evil, see no evil, speak no evil. Tomlinson was waiting to join him during the sessions.

The interview room was bare-walled blue, with black plastic-padded furniture, guarded by a tape machine.

Stephen Grote was the most innocent guilty man Stu had ever met; his lawyer sat beside him, but Grote never felt the need for a consultation, talking simply, clearly, sincerely. He had sailed with Tony MacNulty once or twice, but never to smuggle contraband. He could not even recall a picture on MacNulty's boat.

Charming, simply charming. Without Welsby's emphatic testimony, without the reluctant, but incisive confirmation of his superior, Stu would have had his doubts.

John Devies was outraged and refused to say anything.

Tony MacNulty was less definite in his approach. He appeared curious about the painting, was astounded that there might be witnesses. He looked long and hard at the photograph. No, there was no painting on board . . .

'So this isn't the painting that you gave Mr Robert Marchwood?' Stu Wilson asked.

'Who told you I gave Marchwood a painting?'

'Mr Robert Marchwood.'

Stu knew he was pressing his luck. Marchwood had said, a close business associate whom he could not name. MacNulty, a long-fingered, slow-speaking gentleman, hesitated. Stu's luck held.

MacNulty said: 'That was just a daub, a mass of blobs, nothing like this.'

A daub. Next Stu asked: 'Where did you buy the daub? No, I will correct that: where did you purchase the picture that you describe as a daub?' As the tape would be transcribed verbatim, he had to observe the niceties.

'It was just a family heirloom. Painted by a cousin, or somebody.'

'So your wife would know the picture?'

Silence.

'It was definitely not this one, here?' Stu pointed at one of the photographs. Silence.

MacNulty's solicitor whispered something in MacNulty's ear. Stu became aware of a buzz from the striplight overhead. He was tired. It had already turned Saturday.

'Why did you give Mr Marchwood the picture?'

MacNulty smiled: 'We have been good business contacts for many years. Even our fathers did business together . . .'

One big, happy family.

Stu smiled at Mr MacNulty, thanked him for being so helpful, wished him a good night.

'We'll crack him,' Tomlinson crowed, when they were in the canteen.

They had several leads. The first, Mrs MacNulty who was probably quite sore with her Mister, then the MacNulty children, a housekeeper, then the Royal Yacht Club at Cowes . . . They would push for more once they had examined the documents and hard disks. Unlike his friends, MacNulty was a nervous man who would, once squeezed, talk freely. Kevin had told him he had been a bottle of gin a day man.

A desk sergeant appeared, glad to find them: a Lloyd's warehouse, south of the river, was on fire.

'What do they store there?' Wilson asked.

The young man with the round face and ready smile answered: 'The brigade say it's nothing. Just old computer tapes, a disused computer, that sort of stuff. Old tin cans.'

Inspector Wilson rose, as if stung by a much-angered wasp. A car was ordered, commandeered, a driver found and they were off, Tomlinson beside him. Light and sound. Holborn, Southampton Row, Kingsway, over Waterloo Bridge, past the National Theatre. A roundabout, another, a hospital, Lambeth Palace, their light and noise sliced its way along the embankment, while amid the frenzy Stu talked on the telephone in low, quiet tones to the brigade, his message simple: save.

Here you are, sir.

Wilson clapped a hand on a shoulder. Good lad.

Three fire engines loomed beside the light-industrial-cum-storage units, brick built and metal clad. A wine merchant, the Austro-British Patisserie Company, a Christie's storage unit, a maker of blinds . . . the Lloyd's unit did not proclaim itself with a large sign. Instead, it burned. Behind a high perimeter wire, watched by cameras and security guards, the Christie's unit stored furniture and paintings. The guards had notified the fire brigade and the police. Otherwise, everything might have been too late.

'We'll have it under control shortly, sir,' a fireman reassured Stu Wilson, as the large, square door yielded to an engine with a tow rope, and streams of artificial snow flooded through the doorway.

Gradually, the tongues of flame and soot-filled smoke ceased to gust round the yellow-black figures in masks. Beaten back, the fire was suddenly defeated, only the heat and hiss and stench remained.

Sooner than had seemed possible, firemen entered the contorted door, stepping through splayed and shattered metal.

The alarms fell silent. Voices could be heard. A train rattled past. There was no wind.

Shouts. More men in masks were drawn to the door. A stretcher was brought, and an ambulance drew past, to the edge of the heat.

'Anything in there worth saving?' a fire officer asked, not necessarily needing an answer. 'Inspector Wilson?'

'I don't know. You seem to have a casualty. Was this place guarded, was there a watchman?'

The fireman shrugged. The sprinkler system had failed, so the guys said. Once that happened, no chance.

'Do you mind?' Stu asked, gesturing to the doorway.

The fireman nodded. 'Should be safe, sir.'

They approached together. Stu had seen bodies before. The warmth swamped him; he could hardly breathe, but walked onwards, through the cutting edge of the heat, to where medical staff with useless resuscitation equipment stood in silence.

There was little left. Where hair might have been, a black frazzle of loose connections, ears turned to unspeakable remnants, the arms, the legs crumpled extensions of an excavated torso. A body of bits and bobs, residues.

'Anyone you know sir?'

Wilson shrugged. He turned on his heels and walked, until Tomlinson clapped him on the back and shouted something.

'They've found a car round the back. A constable's checking on the registration now.'

A red Japanese sports car was parked on the double yellow line, outside the unit's loading bay. Tomlinson took Stu by the arm and they skirted the heat and dust and flames. He pointed to the rear door of the industrial unit, beside the loading bay: 'Whoever it was, he or she'll have gone in through there.'

Stu said nothing when he saw the fine leather interior, nothing until he saw a briefcase that he knew, an umbrella that he knew, a tie that he knew. He could not believe what he was seeing. He said, speaking with a calm that he did not possess: 'We have to get inside this car, Tomlinson. Can someone here open it up?'

Some years had elapsed since Wilson had been on the traffic beat. He waited until a constable from a patrol car made one of his many keys fit so that the door clicked open.

Stu opened the briefcase: a diary, a letter, pens and papers, the headed notepaper of Knowle & Co, Marchwood's outfit.

Someone had been inside the unit, had been burnt to death, along with a great many records. That someone had been Kevin. For the moment, Stu had no questions, he was just overwhelmed by guilt.

'The car is owned by Knowle & Co, Lloyd's insurance brokers . . .' Tomlinson relayed the message.

Wilson felt the tie, picked up the umbrella. Both were gifts from Rosie. He shuddered at the memory of the charred and burnt corpse. He had not recognised Kevin.

Beside them, the heat from the unit still stifled him with its force.

Stu showed Tomlinson the diary he had removed from the car and said: 'My nephew, Inspector.'

Stu looked away. He had kicked a ball and laughed with the child. After a while, he realised that Tomlinson was expressing his condolences, others were by his side.

'I think you should go home, sir.' A medical orderly.

'Wilson, I'll get the driver to drop you off, sharpish.' Tomlinson.

'Always a nasty shock.'

Someone gave him a handkerchief, someone marched him over to his police car. Stu shook him off, then rejoined the fire officer with his men surveying the façade of the wrecked building.

'The dead man was my nephew, Mr Kevin Vaughan, officer. His car is outside the building, with his personal belongings. The pathologist will need his dental records to make a formal identification. I will inform the next of kin, myself.'

Tomlinson stood beside him. 'Was he working for you, Stu?'

He started to cough, his lungs bruised by the singed air and the stench of burnt paint, burnt chemicals and plastic.

God alone knew what Kevin thought he was doing. For nine months, no help, no information, nothing. Yet Stu was certain they should have raided the data store earlier in the day that had now become yesterday. Despite detailed plans, they had overlooked the obvious.

The lad had had a change of heart. A good lad, young Kevin. But what was he to tell Jenny? What could he say to Rosie? The world was not overpopulated with Vaughans and Wilsons.

He knocked Tomlinson's hands from his shoulders: 'We've got to hit Wood Street Police Station, Tomlinson. Let's move.

He found his own way to the front passenger seat, nodded to the driver, Tomlinson slammed his door. Wait; Stu raised a hand and, through the car window, shouted at the fire officer: 'Examine everything. See if you really think it was an accident.'

The car wheeled round and Stu fell silent. They had to talk to the three monkeys before they received bail, later that Saturday. He left Tomlinson on the pavement outside the station; interviews, with lawyers, would be arranged at four, five and six, that morning. Tomlinson's task for the wee hours.

Meanwhile, the police driver let Stu half-doze until the car pulled up outside his home; even though his shift had long since finished, the driver would wait, even though chauffeured cars were not for personal use. The fellow knew that rules were made to be broken.

The house was in darkness; he roused Rosie gently from a profound sleep, asked her to dress.

He never knew how to break news. This time, he found a blurt, a statement, an announcement. He was not born to be a vicar; he usually took a female officer along with him, with a supply of tissues, for that very reason.

Rosie erupted in grief and fire. He took her in the dead of night to Jenny.

They drove the few miles in silence. An empty, half-dirty high street pulled past on either side, the town hall, the magistrates' courts, rows of houses besieged by cars.

Jenny was awake when he rang. White, without make-up, she opened the door.

They followed the light into the kitchen, and huddled around the table. The words he needed were not to be found in the drawer, the cupboard or the fridge; nevertheless, he started a pot of tea, went through the motions, fresh water into the kettle, four teaspoons of tea fanning into the pot, while his wife told Jenny that her son was dead.

Odd, Stu thought, you rarely considered the time, the effort, the sacrifice that each and every one of us demanded from our parents, from whoever went before. Jenny had cared for Kevin every day of his life, some twenty years, until that moment. Stu found it hard to appreciate the immensity of her gift; her love, thin or generous, little or large, ghosted around Kevin's body whether he wanted it or not. Mostly not, at that age, yet it was always there. The young man had not been grateful, of course not; children were an indulgence, children knew they were meant to be loved; his mother should be pleased that he had grown and flown, that was reward enough.

Stu never finished making the tea.

Rosie flung him out of the house, slamming the door so that its noise quivered the length of the terraced street. She said nothing. Jenny said nothing. But, in every way, he was to blame.

At Wood Street, Tomlinson had worked wonders and the

monkeys were ready. So Stu gave them hell. He had plenty to spare: good, solid, homemade hell.

Monkey number one – Mr Stephen Grote – appeared to be quite surprised. He protested about the hour, about his treatment, about the senselessness of an interrogation at this time. He did not mention his lawyer's fees.

Stu told him first about Lloyd's data storage centre, about the fire, about the lost information.

'Oh, nothing of much import, I suspect,' Stephen Grote said. Very regrettable, but not invaluable.

He advised Stu to talk to Lloyd's data processing experts, it was not really his field.

Then Stu told Grote what else had happened that night. There was little expression in Stephen Grote's face; he regretted, wondered why Mr Vaughan should be ferreting round in the data store, not a place where ambitious young brokers normally congregate. The death was deeply regrettable, of course. 'A young death always is.'

'That's not enough.'

'I don't know what you mean, Inspector Wilson. I met the young fellow once, let me see, yes, it must have been on the day of the storm, in John Devies's office. Seemed a pleasant enough young chap.'

'You know perfectly well what I mean. I remember your question in the car: how is your nephew finding his new job at Knowle & Co?'

'So?'

The exchange continued, until words threatened to turn to blows; Tomlinson placed a hand on Stu's shoulder. Grote's lawyer asked for calm and decorum and a break.

Sure.

When Stu Wilson returned, he had observed the direction and force of the wind; he changed his tack: 'Have you ever had any professional disagreements with Knowle & Co?'

Grote fought his way around the question with the easy skill of a politician, conceded there had been an offical reprimand of Knowle by the Lloyd's committee, he could have all the documents brought during normal office hours, including the papers concerning suspension of Raymond Marchwood. However, he could see no relationship between Knowle & Co and the reasons given for his arrest.

Stu looked at Grote and smiled: 'I suggest you knew that Kevin Vaughan had discovered a secret deal between Robert Marchwood and yourself, a deal to control Lloyd's risk-taking capacity . . .'

Grote raised a hand in protest.

'. . . a deal which was sealed by the gift of a Monet, illegally brought by yacht from the continent, by yourself, Anthony MacNulty and John Devies.'

'Preposterous,' Grote pronounced. 'A ragbag of unsustained assertions. An insult to my intelligence, not to mention my honour, Inspector. You will have to do better.'

Stu watched Grote rehearse the civilised rhetoric of outrage, admired the man's self-control under stress. He sensed, too, a head of fierce anger bursting to be vented.

He pointed out that Grote had not answered one single question; so they went through his assertions, one by one, which Grote dimissed individually as feeble or untrue. Moreover, he found it intolerable to be interrogated in such a room at such a time.

The performance did not lack passion.

Wilson returned to the question of the relations between Grote and Kevin.

'An employee of Knowle & Co died this night. A young man who certainly believed that the market had been rigged. Who was trying to prove his beliefs. Who was looking for proof in the data storage centre. Let me tell you, I believe you had him killed there and I intend to prove it.'

He was jumping to conclusions. Perhaps Grote's people just wanted to destroy the records, remove the data showing their past misdeeds; perhaps, however, they had been expecting someone in particular.

Grote signalled contempt, while his lawyer protested.

The interrogation had reached its natural term. Grote knew what he knew and had no need to tell. Stu had not made him lose his cool mastery of himself and the facts.

There was no answer to be had from John Devies either, the silent monkey who stiffly refused to comment. Devies, puffy-faced, with bloodshot eyes, held himself erect with a walking stick. They batted his silences to and fro for an hour, to no avail. No comment meant no comment.

By the time Tony MacNulty was seated by the tape machine,

dawn had entered the main staircase through dirt-caked windows, accompanied by the aromas of the first fry-up of the day; Stu discovered an unshaven chin.

'This is an outrage and an impertinence, Inspector.'

MacNulty had not slept well in the cells and complained about song-lark drunkards and unwanted smells. Stu took his seat beside the tape machine and Tomlinson, then spoke the routine spiel into the machine: he, Detective Inspector Stewart Wilson, and his aide, Detective Inspector Tomlinson, were interviewing Mr Anthony MacNulty at six-thirty a.m. on Saturday the twenty-fifth of August, in the presence of a lawyer. The tape machine turned.

Neither detective had slept. Stu apologised to Mr MacNulty if cell conditions did not make for perfect sleep, but he had to tell him, a former employee of Wordsworth & Co had died in suspicious circumstances.

Tony MacNulty said nothing.

'I think you know who it is and why it was.'

A grimace. MacNulty looked at Wilson, at Tomlinson, at his lawyer. 'I know nothing,' he said. His hands interlocked, covered his mouth with one large fist.

'Kevin Vaughan.'

'My God . . . it must have been an accident, nothing to do with me – I swear . . .' As a protest of innocence, it did not lack conviction or intensity; besides, he had been in police custody at the time, a reasonable alibi. Stu contemplated MacNulty's drink-drawn features which, by day, suggested youth but here betrayed the abrading years. His grey hair was matted and lank from the cell.

MacNulty asked how it happened. 'I always found Kevin a very likeable young man.'

'So it was a pity to have him killed?'

'Inspector! I know nothing about it.'

'Yet Kev knew too much. You knew that he knew too much when he moved from Knowle. So . . .' MacNulty's lawyer protested.

Sure, sorry.

The tape machine hummed; a click and the recording continued, the tape turning in the opposite direction.

'Let me put a hypothesis to you. Kevin knew the way you and your friends ran Lloyd's, knew where the evidence was, knew about the hard disks in your safe, knew that your role behind the

224

scandals was decisive, knew that the market was controlled by half a dozen individuals . . .'

Stu was aware that his hands were perspiring; he thought to remove his jacket until he realised it hung over his chair. MacNulty did not move.

The lawyer said: 'Really. Is that a question or a hypothesis or what?'

'A fiction,' MacNulty said, and it seemed certain Stu had stated the plain, if not simple truth.

'Since it is a fiction, let us discuss the matter in detail. No time like the present,' Stu said, with a sour grin at Tomlinson.

He produced Kevin's analysis of the relationship between Wordsworth and Knowle, estimated that more than half of Wordsworth's profits came from this one source, pointed to Wordsworth's privileged position in respect of the risks from asbestosis and oil rigs. MacNulty was silent.

'The arrangement was of course recorded on the hard disks and at the Lloyd's data storage centre, which went up in flames tonight. So your accomplices killed Kevin and destroyed the evidence. Unfortunately for you, we have some more.'

On the wall, the clock clicked lightly. Past seven, breakfast time. Despite a stomach which felt as if it had been reconstituted from rope and wire, Stu thought of a full plate of food.

MacNulty nodded, just nodded, and laid his long hands, palm on palm, their tips touching his mouth in awkward prayer. Stu observed this silent submission and waited for speech. Nothing was said.

He felt that MacNulty was confessing, in his own mind, submitting to the weight of evidence and argument; if he had Grote's strength of character, he would convince himself that Stu was talking drivel; if, alternatively, he protested long and hard, then Wilson would have reason to doubt his analysis. But MacNulty was a beaten man: he only had to admit it.

After a while, Wilson pushed his luck: 'We are analysing the other disks now. The crude attempt to erase the material failed. First indications show a market-wide pattern . . .'

'A pattern is not an agreement.'

'. . . being implemented through Horcum and, particularly, Knowle, backed by the top underwriting groups like Wordsworth and CRG. We estimate you had half the market under your control and could dictate terms to the rest.

'There was a market-wide deal. It was concluded with the gift of the Monet to Marchwood. Without him, it wouldn't have worked; you gave him the picture.'

Then MacNulty laughed, a high, whining chuckle: 'Very good, a very good yarn, Inspector. I trust you have proof.'

'The proof is the death of Kevin Vaughan. You knew that he knew.'

Again, that silence. Stu heard Tomlinson breathe beside him as they waited.

With his right hand raised to his face, MacNulty appeared to palpate his cheekbone with his fingertips.

'Shit,' he said and would say no more. The word meant little, his expression said everything, but Wilson's gambit, with the white pieces, had been refuted. This time.

TWO

NATURALLY DONNA WAS in Wood Street on Saturday morning, wearing something long, flowing and extravagantly coloured, clutching sunglasses; she waved and smiled when Stephen emerged and looked towards her.

There were no real objections to bail, nothing that would be a real problem but the conditions were tough: a hefty surety, loss of passport, a daily personal appearance in Wood Street, no rendezvous with MacNulty or Devies.

Yet when Stephen stepped out into a warm, fine day to see Donna, he enjoyed the sudden onrush of daylight, traffic noise and smells, as if a peculiar wave had broken over him, covering him in something sweet and magical called freedom. And a little more. He smiled at the cameramen, kissed Donna, gave her his arm, then strode round the corner to where the Rolls was ticking over.

At their Mayfair home, Donna had had a cold luncheon buffet brought in by outside caterers, with little expense spared; black caviar (not the fake red or black-dyed stuff) accompanied smoked salmon and lobster, there were things in aspic. From the cellar there was Krug rosé vintage champagne, a Huegel gewürztraminer, a well-rounded and fruity Burgundy from Nuits St Georges and more besides. Donna had invited some friends from Lloyd's and Sotheby's for a quiet, graceful celebration.

Neil Fortescue, who had spent the morning in the pavilion at Lord's watching the Test Match, arrived early and insisted that the television should be accessible, given that England might actually win the match; when Stephen saw him, he nodded and Neil smiled, so everything was fine.

Even if there were tensions between the two men, Stephen

Grote was glad to have Neil on his side. Even if the man smoked rather too much, he had an excellent eye for detail and was a tough, forceful character: he would, in the fullness of time, make an excellent chairman.

The fact that Neil was a main-board director of an American brokership would make a positive splash in cross-pond politics, too.

Henry Stone on his own, Alec Wilmot-Greaves with his new American girlfriend and the Nathan Mayers together arrived in a flurry of taxis. The Davidoffs were due later. It was a small, select list; entertaining, rather than exhausting.

The hosts led their guests into the dining room, with its acres of food and acres of space. Nathan, who was short, bald and bronzed, still managed to fill the room with his booming voice and easy laugh, to the evident admiration of his wife.

When the Davidoffs arrived, Sam and Miriam, who both wore starched white cotton and severe black spectacles, Donna placed them either side of Alec Wilmot-Greaves so they could not be shy and refined together.

Stephen agreed with Nathan that cricket was not comprehensible and, since it could not be understood, it could not be justified. He then changed subjects, bringing Sam Davidoff into the conversation by asking if he thought a United States of Europe was a good idea and, if so, whether the Europeans needed a civil war to cement the union?

It was only afterwards in the garden, armed with coffee, fortified by wine, that Nathan seized his opportunity and turned to Stephen: 'Could you explain to me as a home-spun attorney why you've been arrested?'

Donna smiled at her husband; he would have to get used to this. He said: 'They think we conspired to defraud Lloyd's investors. If I understand what they think that they think.'

She tried to tease him: 'You were lucky, darling. Your inspector's gruff exterior hides a cultured fellow, definitely a Monet collector in the making.' Ms Warrilow had been recognised by Inspector Wilson in Wood Street and had caused him quite a shock.

'Oh, I'll see if I have another available, I have a stock under the stairs . . .' Stephen smiled at Sam Davidoff, hoping he would not take this, at least, seriously.

Neil joined them, hot-foot from the television, with the sad news of an English batting collapse, the impending loss of the match and the Test series.

It was some time later, between coffee reinforcements, that Neil took Stephen aside for a whisper. He was worried that Tony MacNulty was becoming unsound.

By then, the Davidoffs had made their excuses.

THREE

STU WILSON SIMPLY could not believe it.

Donna Warrilow was none other than Mrs Stephen Grote. She had smiled at him outside Wood Street station and he had smiled back. Old friends.

Then there was the stolen photograph and file, the wiped hard disks in MacNulty's safe, the masonic insignia left by Tomlinson, his right-hand man, in his very own kitchen. Someone had known everything all along, at every twist and turn, he was watched.

Not to mention Kevin.

After bail was awarded, Stu took a couple of hours' compassionate leave. Long enough to discover that conversation at Jenny's house was difficult; long enough to acquire food for Rosie's deep freeze. Because he had told them Kevin was no longer working for him, said there was no danger, laughed . . . He was going to be living on his own for some time to come.

There were love letters in Kevin's room from a woman, which Jenny would not let him read. Some newspaper cuttings. He did not press the point.

That Saturday afternoon, everybody was screaming for him, including the DG. A sergeant working for her tracked him down in the room overlooking the British Museum. His team, Stu observed, was more excited by the publicity than by the need for concentrated work. Sometimes, Stu felt like a grandfather in a crèche.

'Where have you been, Inspector Wilson? With respect, you know we have to be able to contact you.'

'I can't be everywhere at once, Sergeant.'

'The DG wants a word.'

'Thanks.'

He walked into Rainsley's office.

'What *are* you doing, Wilson?' Rainsley asked, as if he had arrived from another planet; a pair of cold eyes surveyed his face.

He explained himself in short, lumpy sentences, repeating the accusations he had aimed at the three monkeys. He was listened to, in silence.

'Are all of these things linked?' she asked. 'Can you prove to me that this fraud case also involves a murder? Which case do you want to investigate, Wilson? When are these men going to be charged?'

She was mocking him, not for the first time.

Her deputy, a man somewhat younger than Wilson, expressed his condolences for the death of Wilson's nephew.

Rainsley was unmoved. She did not want to see him wasting his time or distracted; she wanted results.

Wilson tried to reassure her; they had more than enough evidence; now, all they needed was compliant witnesses and confessions. The trio would be charged next week.

Rainsley emphasised her support, moral and otherwise, but she wanted to see results.

Detective Inspector Wilson contemplated her prints of ships becalmed in a Thames sunset and wondered whether he could have endured life aboard a sailing ship, could have climbed rigging in the thick of a storm.

He rose and was surprised to hear her expressing concern that the trio might now cover their tracks.

He seized his chance. 'With respect, that was the purpose of the fire at the storage unit – the destruction of the recent history of Lloyd's. We have to ascertain whether, if that was deliberate, my nephew was deliberately killed.'

The DG interrupted his exit. 'I still want the Met to investigate Vaughan's death. That is their task; they have the resources; that is an order, Wilson.'

He clicked his heels.

'This is a fraud case, Inspector, potentially the largest in English case law. I would have thought that would have tested even your ambitions.'

In other words: leave the pathologist well alone, do not visit the storage site, thou shalt not investigate, unless thou desirest punishment and pain.

All his adult life, Stu Wilson had made a point of doing his duty, sometimes to excess, sometimes to his own disadvantage. Conforming, obeying orders, doing the right thing, was not always just an option; it was duty that had allowed Stu to enjoy his cup of cocoa on the bridge in the dead watches of the night. In the police, it made him go that extra mile, just to be sure that he was not promoted.

So he nodded at the DG, smiled and, at the front desk, found the driver from the night before and commandeered a car.

Move it, man.

Lights, sound. Again they took in all the sights. At the hospital, home to the local pathologist, they had to wait. His hand tapped the rear of the seat. He was becoming too old for this game; yet it was now a family matter.

He had not been Kevin's father. Jenny had met Mr Vaughan while working in an office in the West End, after everybody had decided it was too late for her, for a family. He worked in films or advertising or something, and he had not lasted, once they married and had a baby. At some stage he had packed his bags or failed to return from a trip abroad. Landed up in the Far East somewhere; there was a rumour he made girlie films for Japanese consumption. Jenny was better off without the man, although she suffered, the boy did too, there were bad nights and difficulties at school. Rosie helped as much as she could. Stu worked and worked and worked; even so, every other weekend, he might have seen the lad, kicked a ball or played a game.

Stu had not had a son; he was nobody's father.

The hospital was a jumble of architectural errors linked by bright signs. His bleeper bleeped. He switched it off, left the car. Maternity, X-Rays, Psychology, Neurology, Out Patients. He stepped into a lift and was greeted by two cheerful customers on rubber-wheeled trolleys. It was back to the wards for them, he did not dare ask further. He winked at a nurse who became pretty as she blushed.

The epoxied concrete floor became ceramic tiles, white and dull underfoot. Metal sinks, glass cabinets, reagent glasses, electronic measuring equipment. A couple of people in white coats. Dr Reynolds, the pathologist, greeted him and he introduced himself.

'Ah, Inspector Wilson, the Met has already been here. I wouldn't have thought this was a case for the Serious Fraud Office. . .'

'Perhaps I could still have a word.'

The dark-haired man, probably in his thirties, nodded.

This way, please. Dr Reynolds might have only been thirty, but he had long been a cynic. He pulled at a filing cabinet, looked at Wilson, commented: 'The dental records match the evidence. Mr Kevin Vaughan. . . Are you well, Inspector?'

Fine, just fine. Nothing that sleep, a good long sleep, would not solve.

A white-coated woman brought a chair, and some tea. Two faces contemplated his.

'You are related to the deceased, Mr Kevin Vaughan?'

Wilson nodded. Yes, related.

The lab lady gave him some more tea; she had a ribbon in her hair, drawn back into a pony-tail. At his age, all young women were starting to seem beautiful.

Dr Reynolds was apologising. 'The young man is a bad case. The state of the body isn't helpful, there's little chance of determining abrasions and lacerations, although we're still making tests. Our conclusion, however, is clear: death by asphyxiation, caused by noxious fumes.'

There was sugar in his tea. He did not take sugar.

'There's no sign of foul play. No breaks, no haemorrhages; lungs in a poor state; high levels of carbon monoxide in the blood; brain showing signs of oxygen-deprivation. Just as you would expect.

Mr Vaughan was gassed to death. The subsequent burning was not experienced. He was already dead.'

'Time of death?'

'Consistent with the fire starting around ten in the evening.'

Stu raised himself gently and found he could stand. It all depended upon how the fire had started; he had to return.

His driver all but yelped when he saw Stu: HQ wanted him back, sharpish. They were complaining that he kept disappearing.

Sure.

First they would make certain that the trip was well and truly illicit: Lambeth Palace, Lambeth Bridge, Elephant and Castle; they hit the one-way sytem that swirled around the railway arches at some speed, and he spotted the insignia of Christie's, the high brick walls. There was the entrance to the close where the industrial units stood, where the fire had taken place.

233

At Christie's warehouse, there was no sign of security guards; the remote cameras did not turn their way when they passed. Stu looked at his watch and failed to register the time. Then he considered the main door to the unit, the fire-blackened bricks, the whole sealed from the outside by police tape. He perspired, shook and, quite humiliated, cried; it was a fever and worse. The road was quiet, no passers-by, nobody appeared under the orange streetlights. He was, he had to admit, not at his best.

He got out of the car. There were twisted beams and rafters, charred walls. He wanted to find the electrics – why had the sprinkler not worked? And the fire alarm? Behind him a police car drew alongside. Two cops.

Before unprofessional words could be exchanged, Stu explained he worked with the SFO, that this was an undercover mission. They should leave him to his work.

The two constables blinked; the SFO was, by and large, resented rather than admired. So they could afford to be reluctant. Until a second squad car arrived in the close, in search of the first, flashing blue lights on brick, metal and the infrequent window. So the SFO, eventually, would hear of this; Stu had few illusions what the outcome could be.

Suddenly, he felt absolutely awful, drained of everything, devoid of being himself.

'Let's go back to the SFO.'

The driver agreed.

Outside the railway station, a newsstand proclaimed: PM RULES OUT SNAP ELECTION.

On his instructions the car braked sharply, Stu hopped out, vaulted over a barrier, tossed a couple of coins to the vendor, took a paper. On an inside page there was one sentence about a fatal accident, a fire and a fatal accident.

FOUR

AS THE FIRST shot impacted, he was somewhere in paradise. A Saturday morning sort of paradise.

Robert Marchwood was thinking of Thérèse; that he missed her, that he would see her shortly, that she was all that he had ever wished for, even though they were so. . .

He was also, it was true, thinking of Veronica; that she was young, beautiful and had given birth to his son. She was angry with him now, but that might change. As far as he knew, she was on her own; to help, he had that morning instructed his personal lawyer to sort out a sizeable package for mother and child, subject to certain conditions, subject to silence. The lawyer did not like it; he warned non-disclosure could be a problem. Robert insisted. He did not want to raise the child with Veronica, but he did want to provide.

To Thérèse, his dear wife, he had finally sent a letter. It was as honest as he could be, it did not mention Veronica, it started with a confession of love and admiration, continued with an admission of guilt and human weakness and ended with a plea for reconciliation. Sounded good; ultimately, he reckoned, honesty was all fine and good, but a bloke needed to lie if he was to woo and win. Truth was reserved for the after-life.

Yet he wanted her back here, beside him, so he had it sent by the very last courier to Zurich, with a first-class plane ticket. Now Thérèse would return tomorrow, on Sunday, he was sure.

In its way, his letter tried to say what he had often said, but rarely meant, which was therefore best left unsaid. It sounded better in French, but that was a cliché, too: 'Je t'aime.' At least, as Thérèse would say, the accent was unmistakably his.

The first bullet had hit the far window. The swimming pool stretched out into the garden, edged by lawns, a rose-bed and encroached by shading trees; built in the ornate style of a Victorian conservatory, but with heavy duty glass, double-paned, to retain precious heat and exclude the unwanted. Thus the far window was simply punctured, with a hole, almost round, surrounded by cracks.

This was a surprise; Robert looked at the tall, wide pane, found the view into the garden and hedgerows spoiled, then let himself slip into the water. Beyond, he had seen a figure, in green and brown.

It was the second bullet that removed the pane, the jagged slabs of glass shattered, gushed as oblong splinters over the pool edge and fell into the water.

The figure, he thought, would approach now, then he would know who had come to pay their final respects. He waited, half-submerged, unable to move without offering himself.

A dog could be heard, barking. The German shepherd, he had forgotten its name.

Then there was a third shot.

The alarm went off, finally. The whole place was awash with lights and alarms. He took this as his cue, vaulted out of the pool, through the changing rooms and into the main body of the house. He thought he heard something slam into the pine wall-surround, close to the changing-room door.

At least he would have died running.

In the house, Mrs Hughes, the housekeeper, expressed Welsh-inflected horror; Mr Hughes helped make safe two doors, then peered out of the kitchen window.

'Where is he?' Robert shouted, dripping water.

'The dog's dead; he's looking at the dead dog.'

There was not a gun in the house, not even for pigeon-shooting or fox-killing, not even an air gun to frighten pestilent magpies. Thérèse would not hear of it.

Mrs Hughes had discovered how to use one of the Marchwood household's several portable phones. The police were on their way, she said. Ten, fifteen minutes. Enough time for their friend to kill them all.

Hughes had only seen the one man, far off, a tall figure in wellington boots and waxed jacket, bearing some sort of gun. A country gent out to bag a brace of pheasants.

'He's in the woods, there, you see.'

Robert peered and saw nothing; well, perhaps. He asked the

pair to watch the rear of the house, while he watched the front. They should lock the internal doors and head upstairs if the man started to break in. No silly risks; they both nodded.

He trailed water through the hall and up the staircase, across the landing carpet. He locked the bedroom door, dried himself and started to dress.

On the other side of the house, there was breaking glass, a wrenching crash, then silence. On this floor. He opened the bedroom door, looked down the white landing; closed doors. Mrs Hughes shouted something; he answered that he was fine, and turned, opened the door of a bedroom at the rear of the house. The cotton curtains had been shredded, the bed engulfed in dust, glass and wood; there was a jagged gap where once there had been a window.

Odd to be able to hear birdsong, the rustle of trees, so distinctly; the woodland setting had moved them to buy the house. A mistake.

Nobody to be seen.

In the hallway below, he could hear Mrs Hughes sobbing. The doorbell rang. Robert strode downstairs, answered an official voice through the intercom, then pressed the remote control for the gates.

A police car entered the main drive, firing white gravel into the lawn, and Sergeant Keith Peters, together with a constable, presented themselves.

'You took your time,' Robert observed, generously.

He explained the situation, and Peters called for reinforcements, by radio. There was no chance of a helicopter.

They returned to the kitchen and peered out into the grounds, which had been pleasantly laid out in the last century, with an eye for disorderly order. Where was the man? The control panel of the security system showed that there was nobody in the swimming pool or gymnasium; slowly, carefully, they worked their way into the garden, through the kitchen door; the two policemen disappeared in the woods.

Robert took the opportunity to pack a case and ring Ray.

The police returned, relieved to find the man had gone. Among the trees, there were some nice footprints, some spent cartridges, and Hughes had discovered a bullet embedded in the swimming-pool wall. If they ever got their man, prosecution would be simple; the embedded bullet had attempted murder engraved in its metal.

More police arrived, to look, measure and record. Mrs Hughes brightened up. There was so much to tell.

Peters interviewed them, individually, then as a group.

'Did you catch a glance, sir? Any idea who it might be?'

Robert wished he did. Hughes had seen someone tall, wearing a tweed flat cap, rubber boots, not waders, green trousers.

'Dog's a mess, sir,' a constable observed, entering. Peters looked at him, then understood. Someone had taken the necessary photographs, so the carcase ought to be buried, sharpish. He whispered in Hughes's ear, who nodded.

The police were working out angles, distances, pointing into the woods. One hell of a good shot, that fellow.

Security people arrived to guard the house – the Hugheses were to take the weekend off; Robert insisted they should stay in a very fine hotel, locally, until the house had been made safe, until they felt safe to return.

Sergeant Peters understood his reasons for leaving, but wanted an address, a telephone number and a commitment to ring the station tomorrow. In return Robert asked him not to tell the press, for safety's sake.

Ray was white when Robert arrived, close on the heels of his phone call from down the road.

Had he been followed?

No.

Officially, Ray lived elsewhere; he never used his private address – all personal correspondence was routed through the office, the house was owned by the company, he had a flat in a converted stately home where he was registered as voter and fly-fisherman, the telephone number was ex-directory. You could say Ray appreciated his privacy.

Now he placed small objects, flat metal disks, portentously into Robert's hand. Electronic bugs: from the office.

'Your phone, my phone, your desk, your lamps. Half a dozen, placed in the last two months. I hope you haven't been indiscreet?'

'Not recently,' Robert lied. He was always indiscreet, in one way or another. One had to live.

But the whole thing was getting out of hand, turning into gang warfare, just because their rules had been broken. Who did they think they were?

Ray removed his spectacles, checked them for dust and grease;

then he told his brother about Kevin. Jenny Vaughan had rung him, that Saturday morning; she wanted to tell him, tell someone. And now the Met wanted to talk to him, the day after tomorrow, all very leisurely, just a matter of routine.

'Fire?' Robert was incredulous. 'In a modern warehouse? Arson?'

Ray shrugged his shoulders. 'They employ professionals. I'm sure they were waiting for this very opportunity. I bet they thought he was working for us.'

Robert wondered what Kevin might have been doing inside the data storage centre. When they last spoke, as he recalled, he had sent Kevin on holiday.

They made a cup of tea, yet Robert did not feel hungry; they went upstairs, to the computer den, where Ray was fiddling with computer graphics.

Robert looked out into the garden, surveyed neighbouring gardens; Ray's minimalist garden, a lawn, roses, large bushes, was surrounded by a high latchwork fence.

'Do you think you're safe, here?'

The old sash windows had been removed and replaced by one, large, double-glazed window; the loft space above had been converted and integrated by a canny architect into the room, fitting a large skylight into the roof. Light and more light, that was Ray's idea of a comfortable room.

Ray shrugged at the question. His neighbours protected him; he did not live in an isolated mansion in the country.

'What's this all about then?' Robert pointed at the patterns on the screen, which Ray had created by repeating the same, simple calculations, using the outcome of each as the starting point for the next. The result was an infinity of coloured worlds, revealing the same basic shape, time after time. Robert was familiar with these computer graphics, known as fractals, from the office computer.

'They remind me of Monet. The same shape repeated in different colours,' he said.

There was a noise outside; a dog barked; Robert stepped quickly to the window, saw a neighbour, watering his roses. The sun was setting amidst scratched-grey clouds, a half-filled gasometer and two exuberant pear trees.

Robert took a deep breath, then returned to the screen. Ray switched software and produced another graphics program; this time the screen showed mountains, ferns, trees. These pictures had been produced in the same way: repetition of one, simple mathematical formula. They did not appear to be abstract, however, instead they resembled this world.

'It's like a dream,' Ray admitted. 'Not proof of anything, but suggestive of something.'

He proposed that much of life might be due to codes, similar to the formulae behind the computer images. Many codes were unknown, those for a mountain range, a hillside or a forest, for example; but modern biology offered an explanation for a tree or a fern or, even, a man: 'Each of the millions of cells in a man's body contains the formula for his growth as well as the need for this formula to be copied.'

'So sex is a social duty?' Robert ventured, with a grin.

'You don't need any excuses.'

Time for some microwaved pizza and something saladlike extracted from the fridge. Ray specialised in five-minute meals.

They were just about to sit down when the phone rang. The police, with some questions for Robert; he answered, trying not to show his irritation. He took his seat beside Ray, who had decided to nuke another pizza.

'Tough times, eh?' Ray said.

'We'll see them through.'

'You realise of course that your demand for a Monet, the row in Baden-Baden, was the start of all this?'

It was a rare reproach; Robert ignored it. Most times, when he overbid his hand, they made money. If you wanted to win, you had to be prepared to lose. He always aimed for the grand prizes. Besides, Ray had stirred the pot too, rummaging in Grote's data banks.

They talked about Kev Vaughan. They both had liked the lad; he was a loss; neither had known about the uncle. 'He may have mentioned it, at some time,' Ray excused himself. 'Or Jenny may have said.'

'Forget it. Hardly matters now.'

'No. We have to think ahead.' Ray could see what would happen. All good things came in threes: the bugs, the fire, the shooting. 'It amounts to a declaration of war.'

A car backfired.

Robert rose from the kitchen table, suddenly incandescent

with rage, livid with himself and the world. For once, he could not negotiate his way out of trouble.

Quietly, Ray offered him more food, wine and salad.

He said thank you, then stomped around the kitchen, apparently absent-minded. For a time, they did not speak.

Finally, Robert said: 'I don't think I want to stay the night.'

'Fine, whatever you wish.'

He was sure: Thérèse was due to arrive from Zurich tomorrow. He had played through the scene again and again: the scheduled arrival of BA flight 335 from Kloten at Heathrow. He would stand among the waiting herd of taxi drivers, businessmen and spouses, waiting, waiting. Allow thirty minutes for passengers to collect their baggage and pass through customs.

But now it was a mess. She would not accept a life under fire. He had to hide the mess, provide perfection and inspire romance.

Suddenly he noticed that his brother was furious also, in the calmest possible way. Normally, if he fell silent, Ray contrived to talk him round; they were rarely both in such a state.

'I'm going to take my car,' Ray announced, 'and examine that industrial shed.'

'I beg your pardon?' Robert stuttered. 'You realise how my dip was spoiled today?'

'Do you think the police will find anything? We have to be certain, we have to know what was done, by whom. Then we decide what we have to do.' Ray would not change his mind; he went to find his camera bag, and they left. Dusk was falling.

They collected Ray's car, a collectable two-seater, kept in one of the lock-ups reached by the path behind the gardens; bought twenty-five years ago, maintained regularly, resprayed in British racing green. Ray searched the lock-up for some tools and a torch then placed them in a grip behind the car seat.

The motor blurted into a roar, and they were away.

'How long have you known Mrs Vaughan?' Robert asked, trying not to let his brother's gear changes disturb him.

'Years.'

'Was there anything between you?'

Silence; Ray appeared to be interested in his rear mirror, but they were not being followed. Robert had accepted that he would not receive an answer, when Ray replied: 'We courted, for a time. Long before Mr Vaughan senior appeared on the scene. You were in America.'

London trundled past and Robert half-dozed, wondering about Thérèse. The drive did not help him find any answers. He recognised a vegetable and meat market, waiting for the hullaballoo of Monday morning trade. Then Ray braked by a red light under a railway viaduct and they were there.

'A neat job,' Robert said on seeing the scarred warehouse among the neat close of new buildings. They circled the unit, stopping at the rear, where a taped-up door hung out of its frame.

Ray picked up his tools and his camera-bag, without a word. He had taken a decision and Robert knew there was no sense in arguing with him; besides, they had agreed that they had to know.

'I'll wait here and watch,' Robert said, heaving across into the driving seat. There was the sound of a car siren, perhaps a police car. He switched off the car headlights and waited. Minutes went past like long hours. At least the siren had gone, but then there was another and another; there was always the possibility that it was someone coming in their direction.

Robert had to admit, for once, that he was frightened. That the shooting had changed his life; until now he had, at worst, feared the loss of money, but now his own death was a black space before him. He could not draw Thérèse into that space, he must keep her away; she would not join him. She must not know. He had asked the police not to inform the local press of the shooting and Sergeant Peters seemed a nice enough fellow.

Another car siren blared past.

Then Ray was beside him, finally. 'Got what you wanted?' Robert asked. Ray shrugged, cautious as ever. 'I took some good shots. Now I want to see the prints.' Robert smiled and drove carefully out of the close.

FIVE

STU BLAMED IT on the whisky. He had fallen asleep on the sofa after a meal and woken, screaming. Fire, fire. It was still Saturday, just.

Stu was ashamed, but there was nobody in the house to hear. He washed his face, shaved, cleaned his teeth with unusual care and attention, to prove to himself that he mattered. Rosie had not bothered to ring.

The investigation was under way. His visit to the storage unit had yet to filter through. He had spoken to the accountants, talked accounting systems, spread sheets and computers, seen the sun set over Lincoln's Inn.

A young accountant, a rapid-talker called Simon, soon had news; the hard disks from MacNulty's safe had not been properly wiped, but merely formatted, so they could reconstruct the files. Some of the data had been lost. Perhaps a tenth.

Most of Saturday, the number-crunchers had concentrated on the data on the asbestosis disk, which related to the early 80s, when people first became aware of the impending flood of pollution claims from the States. This was now costing Lloyd's billions.

Then, they had cracked it: the deals, the distribution, the pattern. Again and again, Wilder & Co was involved in the separation of the gold from the dirt: it was one, large Marchwood deal.

Stu had no doubt that the others would be the same.

Finally, they ran the numbers through their computer, transferred the shooting-match to an overhead projector – and the guys on the Lloyd's team clapped. The graphics were stamped with the truth of statistics: on certain Marchwood deals, there was less than one chance in a million that the risks had been distributed according to market forces. They could see the market had been rigged.

Now they wanted witnesses, accountants who had worked in Lloyd's, former underwriters, the disaffected but knowledge-able who would make an impact in court. This story had to be sold hard; figures alone would leave a jury cold. Even impossible odds did not amount to proof.

On Sunday morning, Stu was to see one Blythe, an ex-underwriter, who had rung to congratulate him on the arrests.

On Monday, he was going to go for MacNulty.

He turned to the crew: 'Thanks for all your efforts. The good news is that I must be off. The bad news is that I have an appointment tomorrow and I'll want to see you afterwards. Say at lunchtime. Bring your sandwiches.'

Then he hesitated: 'Simon, a word in your ear, please . . . Do we have spare hard disks?'

'No.'

Curses; the SFO used a different technology from MacNulty's outfit. They would have to wait until next week before making copies of the data. Stu said: 'Well, lock every-thing away.' They had their own store and the disks would be kept locked in a safe box.

Fine, no point in being neurotic.

Once back home, Stu shunted a deep-frozen parcel into the oven and poured himself a scotch or two. When he woke, to his own shouts, he found the cutlery and plate, unwashed, on the table beside the sofa.

He fell back, dozed for a while. Then the phone rang. Now it was past midnight. Sunday, in fact, a day of no rest. His body spoke the language of pain and tiredness.

A familiar voice: 'How are you, young man?'

He responded with a groan.

Keef laughed. 'Got news for you, squire.'

Stu, glad to hear Keef's voice, shook himself and agreed: it was to be Capri by night. They needed to talk.

The doorflap to the garage let light jut out into the darkened street. He was glad of the bike, the exercise.

Sergeant Keith Peters was admiring his handiwork, stroking the white bonnet of his turbo-charged monster, even at that hour. A man without a missus to go home to.

'Nice to see you, guv'nor. You're a hard man to find.'

244

Stu smiled, despite his exhaustion, despite everything. He briefly described the investigation so far, the interviews, the number-crunchers' success, the statistical evidence, the pain of being watched by the DG. He knew in his bones that the DG had been to Downing Street.

'I'd heard about your nephew Kevin,' Keef said, by way of reply. 'I'm sorry, Stu. Very sorry. If there's anything . . .'

Both men nodded, this was more than just a game. Stu gave Keef a present, dropping a metal something into his hand, just to emphasise the point. Keef whistled: where had he found this?

At work, inside his telephone handset; it could have been there for a fortnight; he had made a point of checking for bugs every other week out of habit, even though he knew other, more professional ways of tapping a telephone.

Keef walked to the door, looked outside, then gently drew the door shut. Then he told Stu about the attack at Golden Rain, the search through the woods, the embedded bullet. Attempted murder.

Stu Wilson was intrigued, pleased even.

Although there was no obvious logical connection between the fire and the shooting, he felt that the two events confirmed his basic conviction: Kevin's death was no accident. He had doubts about who and how and why, about details and motives, but, basically, it was murder. That conviction had forced him to batter the see-no-evil monkeys with accusations, made him overstate his case to the DG, even though he knew he would have to wait for the Met.

He peppered Keef with questions of the obvious kind. Had Marchwood not recognised the attacker? Mentioned a motive? What, precisely, had the witnesses seen?

The attack lacked logic: after the dog had been shot, the gunman had obviously paused, waited, stood off.

There was a silence while Stu walked round the garage, looking at the exhausts, the disembowelled interiors, the displaced seats. There were so many unanswered questions: why had the storage unit fire taken hold so quickly, even if the sprinkler system *was* out of action? Why did Kevin go to the store that evening? Whom had he spoken to during the day? What was he trying to achieve? Stu worried that he had had no time to investigate.

Finally, Keef spoke. 'You don't trust the Met?'

'Too much has happened. There's too much riding on this. The Met is not above being led astray.'

Keef had never seen his old boss looking so low. He said: 'Listen to old Keef, for once. It's time for a spin in the White Wonder.'

He loaded Stu in, and his bike sticking out of the back, found his way to Stu's deserted house, then turfed him out again: 'Keep your noddle down, guv'nor. And get some sleep.'

He slept badly. Two or three hours. He shaved, washed, avoided breakfast and walked into sunshine, then tried to remember. Ah, yes, Blythe. Roger Blythe, underwriter. They were sorely in need of witnesses and experts from Lloyd's itself.

East Wareham was a thatched village with an old pub, Norman church and the untroubled charm of a commuter haven. Stu saw a sign for homemade scones and high teas, drove through the village street, over a small stream with geese, down a narrow, tree-arched lane through woods interspersed with shattered beech.

'Yes, the storm caused havoc here,' Roger Blythe agreed standing in the front door, seeing him contemplate the woods. 'Would you like tea or coffee, Inspector?'

The inspector would like either, no, tea please; he had come following the phone call, because of Lloyd's. He followed the erect, slightly stiff figure of the former underwriter through the byways of his house, wonderfully crammed with memorabilia, antiques and flowers. The house was black timber and plaster, with narrow doors and inglenooks and crannies. It was illogical, and beautiful.

'Do you have a ghost, Mr Blythe?'

'I'm sorry, Inspector?' Blythe apologised, he had become slightly deaf in old age.

The housekeeper was audible in the kitchen; she was making an English breakfast, bacon, eggs and sausage. Rosie would disapprove.

'A house like this should have a ghost, did you not know?'

Now Blythe laughed, too; he wanted to show him his roses, he had to do that; every visitor had to see his roses.

Blythe took him to a walled section of the garden, which was planted with roses of every sort and size, hybrid tea, floribunda and, over a frame, a climbing rose: New Dawn.

'My wife died, you know, Inspector. Four years ago.'

Stu said he was sorry.

'I hope they feed you well in the police. Still, we'll give you some breakfast . . .'

As a keenish gardener himself, Stu was all but overwhelmed by the display, the dozens of varieties in perfect bloom.

'Greenfly is the bane, here. Do you have greenfly, Wilson?'

He did, indeed. And black spot.

'No rain, here, these past summers. And water in short supply . . .' Blythe began to mutter.

Stu was uncertain how he could broach the subject of Lloyd's without appearing to be rude. A small handbell saved him, announcing breakfast. They took their seats by the sunbright garden table laden with floral-patterned china and food.

He produced the data the guys had number-crunched on Saturday, the stuff on the asbestosis deal; Blythe placed a pair of spectacles on the end of his nose and peered.

'Ah, Marchwood,' Blythe said cheerfully, looking at the figures. 'Looks like one of Mr Marchwood's wonders. Do you know the Marchwoods?'

'That's why I'm here . . . Perhaps you could tell me, precisely, what you mean?'

Blythe lowered his good cheer to a mutter: 'Some people talk about bad blood, you know . . .'

Stu sipped his tea, so as not to have to comment.

'. . . Well, the Marchwoods were, may I say, always rather a suspect bunch. You must talk to Knowle about it all. He knows the story, see if you can get him to tell you. Funny chap.'

'Knowle? There's still a Mr Knowle around?'

'He's still a shareholder. Quite an antique, but still alive. I should have thought that would interest you . . .'

Stu recalled seeing the name Knowle as a shareholder in the accounts of the Marchwood-run firm but he had never attached much importance to it. It was just one detail among so many. He gestured to the papers again. They reflected his prime concern, the way Lloyd's of London had been illicitly run and controlled.

Blythe smiled, before returning to the figures: 'I'm sorry, Inspector, if I'm gabbing on. Now, what have we here? Yes, I remember. It was another Marchwood deal, a switch of the risks relating to asbestosis from insider to outsider syndicates. Only Marchwood could do that – with a little help from his friends, of course.'

247

'Which friends?'

'Grote, Devies, MacNulty, Wilmot-Greaves, Stone . . . you've arrested some of them. I was more or less retired, at the time. Didn't like it, myself.'

'What didn't you like?'

'Well, when they first got wind of the asbestosis problem, they recruited thousands more names and introduced them to syndicates with an asbestosis exposure. Didn't tell them about the problem, got them to pay the bills.'

'Were you approached or involved? Can you remember any meetings?'

Blythe shook his head, pointed to the figures. To him, that was proof enough; the story was well-known in the market. He said: 'It was during the DA&P mess, that I remember . . . during my last year. This problem with asbestos cropped up and then they re-arranged everything, the exposure to asbestos was moved round the market by Marchwood . . .'

Stu, despite himself, interrupted, only to be asked: 'Inspector, more tea? . . . Yes, Grote and Marchwood sort of worked together, there was a great deal of talk about that. That they might combine forces, some day. But they didn't get on. Knowle knows the story. Been sworn enemies, for years.'

Blythe was an original. In the witness box, well, they would see. He had agreed to testify, which was promising. As for Mr Knowle, it was all a question of time and effort and the potential rewards.

SIX

THÉRÈSE HAD TAKEN a deep breath when the letter arrived, with the plane ticket. It reminded her of the very first flight, the gift of the Monet sketch which proved to be an original. This time, however, the accompanying letter was not written on the notepaper of a Zurich bank, but the words themselves, the urgency imparted by the booked flight, were fine.

She had no choice. She would go.

A week earlier, Thérèse had visited her ailing father and predicted she would return to London; there were tears. She knew what the doctors had said. All her family had come and gone, as they would all come and go again, in a few weeks, perhaps a few months' time. Nevertheless, Thérèse had taken a decision, no, restated the decision that she had taken in the chapel. When she thought of Robert, she heard laughter; it was as simple as that. It was this she told Papa.

'Leaving me alone! A scandal!' But he smiled and she held his hand.

'Do you love him?' he asked, finally, with his no-nonsense directness. To him, the words had a meaning.

She nodded. There were no other questions. He caught sight of his old watch on his wrist: 'Now, it is time for you to go.'

Zurich airport on Sunday morning was all but deserted; she grabbed a coffee at a buffet bar walled in brown glass, then boarded hastily, having waited, waited to the last possible minute.

She began to think she might have rung Robert.

At least the plane flew safely, thudding down alongside a road, a row of unlovely hotels. She strolled through the grey-white fascias of customs swinging a light bag, and there was Robert.

They kissed and he held her tight and she felt there was something wrong. He took her by the arm, gently, firmly, and they started walking, through the thick ruck of waiting businessmen, past a stand selling orange juice and nuts, past the information desk, under stairs, then up the same stairs, up flight after flight, until they were standing in a windowless shop selling tracksuits, running shoes and other garish goods.

It was only then that he kissed her properly.

He was white and grave and drawn, yet he had written that he was well; he was nervous, and he had said he was calm and relaxed; his letter had been serious, touching, though blessed with wit and irony, and now he was grim and deadly serious.

Then he said: 'I have tickets for the next plane for Switzerland.'

She did not know whether to laugh or cry. It could have been worse.

SEVEN

OOPH! CONNIE EXHALED in the grand manner, after she had dropped, half-dead but unbowed, into her leather-padded chair. Tea and sinful biscuits had been placed on her table, she watched the door to her office swing slowly to, but not shut. It never closed. She looked out of the window, discovered that the sky was a grim variant of underfelt grey, then drank her tea. Ooph!

She glanced at the old, silver-framed photograph of Ron and their son Jonathan above her desk. A cough erupted, causing her to choke as she struggled to find her bag among the mess, to find her handkerchief.

That morning, Mrs Cornelia Sanderson had been for all the world her usual, irreproachable, determined self; she had managed, coped, held the fort. She was not going to be distracted by the money-grubbing letters from Lloyd's, the sad news about Kevin Vaughan; really, she had little time for speculation, her job involved more than enough puzzles and conundrums.

An early meeting had ground out its fears about examinations and curricula, about guidelines which were promised, but never arrived or, once they did, had to be withdrawn immediately. The rules were changed every five minutes, mostly to suit some theorist who had never stepped inside a classroom to teach. After a lifetime of trying to do the right thing, the questions did not go away, on the contrary, they became more pressing and she had ever less faith in surefire theories. Nobody knew where it was all leading, but it was certain teachers would be blamed for the ails of this world, while teacher-baiting politicians came and went.

If she looked at the problem with education – and there was a problem, no doubt – then she saw no easy answers, nothing suitable for a slogan or sound-bite. Sure, parents had to do more; the family was to blame; faced with a class of thirty, a teacher could not undo the harm and make good the neglect that a child suffered at home. So blame the parents, blame divorce, one-parenthood, poverty, blame television, blame money-grubbing, blame anyone or anything, as long as it was not her. She was still humping last year's recriminations and the previous decade's guilt. She had had more than enough blame.

The photograph of Ron and Jonathan was, apart from a coat and weather-worn umbrella just visible behind the door, the only personal item in her office, which was otherwise swamped by a morass of paper, papers, curricula, booklets, guidelines, timetables and bills. Every so often, she had made an attempt to clean the place up and every so often, it defeated her.

She had had to slip away early in recent weeks, to the garage, to her lawyer, to her accountant; now she worried that she was neglecting her duty, her precious charges. After all, it was not for much longer. Another term and she would be retired, out to pasture. Another term and she would have nothing to slip away from or to.

She considered the photograph. It was a nondescript, no-nonsense, happy-family-scene, the sort of thing that made everybody's life halfway bearable; every businessman had at least one such snap by his desk. For years now, it had been there, propped up in a silver frame, without a hint of reproach. Jonathan was wearing short trousers, Ron had long, luxuriant hair and thick sideburns, a garish kipper tie: this was her family, in the late 60s. She had, however, not taken the picture; it was a gift from Ron on her becoming head: remember us. The picture was harmless, pleasant; this was how Ron liked to think of himself, the proud father, and lover. That was Ron, all over. The great pretender and the snob. Now she felt that he had always somehow looked down on her – kept her apart from his expensive friends.

It was only now that she knew how much time Ron had had for hanky-panky, fun and games. Despite all his bluster about the indolent workers, the feckless poor, he had never really worked, not really, in his whole life. She had run a school, run the house, washed, cooked and ironed, shopped and organised. Ron had watched and uncorked the fine things in life. If he had been able to combine endeavour with his easy charm, he would have achieved more. Perhaps he found it more enjoyable not to work, more aristocratic.

She coughed again, her throat irritated by a summer cold.

Father and son in rare harmony. The picture must have been taken in the late 60s; by then, she had lost a daughter in childbirth. The doctors had fought for the baby, but she had known it was hopeless, and thereafter life was never the same. Not between Ron and herself, either.

She had not gone to pieces. Jonathan and Ron needed her; she had had her school work, her routine, to keep her going. Ron dismantled the waiting cot, repainted the room, changed the curtains and they had tried again, without enthusiasm or conviction, or success. It was typical of Ron that he should hide the cot in the loft, rather than dispose of it properly.

Ron insisted on sending Jonathan away 'to get a decent schooling'. The poor boy, a mere whisp of a lad, had been entrusted to the retired military man who ran Ron's old prep school. Connie had not thought to object; she wanted only the best for everybody, there were certain things, no, many things that Ron had a right to decide. Also, it had been convenient for her; she had had more time for her career, for the house, and there were always the school holidays. After some difficulty, Jonathan flourished; later he admitted to unhappiness, to regular beatings, just the thing to turn an English boy into a gentleman. But nowadays Jonathan and his family were fine, she wanted to get out there at Christmas, to celebrate on the beach.

A figure hovered outside her door, probably her deputy; she looked at the photograph, the half-empty tea cup.

A knock at the door. Yes, please come in.

It was her favourite mechanic, for once with clean hands. He was without a job and she was without a garage; the bank had foreclosed.

Another term, and the school would foreclose too. She was not getting any younger.

EIGHT

SUNDAY WENT. LIFE became Monday.

If only it had been so easy.

Half-walking or half-dozing, Stu had returned again and again to that Friday-night-become-Saturday-morning, to the fire, to the gutted brick and metal unit. Now he lay dazed on his bed, punch-drunk, until a noisy starling encouraged him to dress and to shave, to breakfast, until he appeared at work as if nothing had happened overnight. This was Monday morning.

Even though much of the work was now arduous routine, even though Sunday after Roger Blythe had been tough, the guys were still excited, still making accountant-type jokes. Stu answered this query and that, the gang was so much younger, bound for greater things, that could make a man envious. He got up to make the tea, until someone else insisted on doing the job; until suddenly he looked up and saw a ruck of guys entering yelping who then told him why.

People stopped working; it seemed that the boss had been stung by a hornet. Stu tore down the corridor, followed by the ruck and there was the store, much as it ever had been, much as it had been designed to be. Evidence in plastic bags and plastic sacks and on wooden shelves, in files, in cabinets; everything labelled, dated, signed.

'Look, it hasn't been forced.' Simon pointed at the black metal box with heavy duty flaps and largish padlock. Behind a locked door and guarded building. Such was his security system.

The door was, apart from wear and tear, in perfect condition; the metal box had never been happier. The hard disks, however, were gone. Here on Sunday, gone on Monday.

Stu had only himself to blame; he had lost a file and found a bug; his every move could have been followed; they probably knew what he knew. But this was sheer carelessness. OK, it would not happen in normal circumstances but these were not normal circumstances. Sure, he had been tired. He shook his head and wanted to weep.

He thought about blaming Tomlinson. No, that was premature. Instead, he gave orders ensuring that nothing should be disturbed; then he strode off.

Mrs Rainsley's secretary was exceedingly friendly, but firm, the DG had a tough schedule, with not a minute to spare, not even for him; Stu did not mind, he would wait until midnight if need be; he had time.

'Inspector Wilson,' Rainsley said, emerging from the inner office. 'The very man. You want to talk? Fine, we were planning to call you.'

He entered and saw red and white roses arranged in the cut-glass vase. There still was someone who loved the DG, probably not the deputy DG.

Accounts of the ensuing interview varied wildly; even Stu had to admit he was uncertain whether he had said what he thought he had said; one or two words might have cropped up, unfortunately. Usually placid and cautious, Stu had evidently imagined he could shroud that grey, impersonal room and its indifferent furnishings in black storm clouds, and enlighten its occupants with thunder-clap and lightning-crack. At least, that seemed to be his tactic, according to the DG.

Initially Mrs Rainsley had been all charm and easy smiles; the Met, it seemed, had registered its disapproval. Stu translated: some Noddy had screamed down the blower at our nice DG. An official complaint regarding his extra-mural and extra-temporal activities would be forthcoming. She had no doubts that his investigations involved insubordination and that she, Mrs Elisabeth Frances Rainsley QC, was disappointed, dis-affected and politically exposed by his behaviour. There-after, there followed a litany of his supposed errors and omissions.

'I was warned, Wilson, that you were a maverick . . .'

Tiresome, cussed, unpredictable, disrespectful, cantan-kerous. Not a team player. And besides, the Met was unhappy to see him investigating their case. She was unhappy to find him disobeying her express orders.

255

Up to this stage, as far as he remembered, he said nothing that might indicate he was a difficult or troubled soul. Her words flowed past, he surveyed the pictures, the sailing ships caught in their eternal sunsets.

But then, for some reason, he was snivelling. He was somewhere else, in a fire-burnt data store, perspiring and, well, crying.

Later, the thought would occur to him that he had wounded her pride, questioned her judgement and ruined her lunch. The DG finished with the words: 'Removed from this investigation, suspended from duty, with immediate effect.'

There was a pause. Inspector Stewart Wilson wiped his face with the palm of his hand, then responded. Corruption, incompetence, idiocy and, for good measure, corruption. Infiltration of the SFO by outside forces, by politics, politics and corruption. He liked the word. He let it turn round the room until it was jabbing away at the DG and the Deputy DG, God burn his immortal soul. He, Inspector Wilson, was merely searching for the truth, the complicated, often nasty and difficult truth; if he was unconventional, that was merely the view of organisations that adopted rigid attitudes. He wanted to succeed. Everything he had investigated was connected with Lloyd's; there was, somewhere out there, a web of facts which he intended to uncover. Lloyd's was run by crooks for crooks, and with great subtlety; someone had just nicked their hard disks out of the store, the heart had just been ripped out of the case, by someone very senior in the Serious Fraud Office.

This was, more or less, what he thought he had said; but it seemed not to produce the desired effect. Detective inspectors are not supposed to cry.

'Who could have done this?' the DG asked. 'One of our top people?'

Stu shrugged, ashamed of himself. That was for her to pursue. No, he suggested half a dozen names, including his own. And her own.

Then she attacked: 'But really, Wilson. Your tone, your manner . . . Are you quite sure you're well? Your behaviour has been irresponsible. Treat the suspension as a temporary measure. A safety precaution.'

It was only at this juncture that Stu realised he had lost. To justify herself, the DG criticised his out-and-out disobedience. This was the key point.

He laughed, despite himself, despite everything, until he found teardrops falling from his chin. This was shame, indeed. This was the first time that he really had to admit that he was no longer himself. He was crying.

Mrs Rainsley then gave him a paper handkerchief and ten minutes to move out.

'If I were you, Wilson, I would seek medical advice. Someone else, my deputy perhaps, will take on the Lloyd's investigation. I need someone with a safe pair of hands.'

It was an interview which would cause him shame and pain for days, weeks, months. He was in no shape to continue. The DG had too much at stake to support a maverick, a wimp, a failure.

This he did not tell the crèche. Time has taken its toll on your one-time leader and all questions from now on are to be addressed to a new man behind the big desk, this more or less, was his message.

Someone said: shame.

Mostly, there was a silence, a minute without a wisecrack. He walked out of the office.

Quite what happened during the ensuing days, he did not particularly want to remember. Simon rang him with the news that the hard disks had been found in his desk in the main office, this time wiped cleaner than clean, using technology that had been pioneered by the CIA. Thanks, Simon, for telling me. Don't mention it, boss.

It might have been the following day that he received an official letter from the DG, one that surprised him with its conciliatory tone. She knew he was a fine officer; she knew he was trying his best, but the death of his nephew had affected him, quite understandably. He should seek treatment. And, in the meantime, he was suspended.

Around this time, day and night became somewhat confused, he remembered nights passing as days and days as nights, watching odd television programmes at odd times; yet he woke whenever he slept, screaming at his memories. England lost a Test Match, again; he drank too much, left the phone off the hook, moved stealthily behind drawn curtains, tried sleeping, picked at tasteless food from the freezer.

One morning he rang Jenny's house to inquire of Rosie how Jenny was faring – and to see if Rosie had had a change of heart. He received polite, brusque answers, nothing more. The news about Jenny was much as one might expect, not especially good, the poor girl was pumped full of barbiturates. Rosie was near her the whole time, she was combining compassionate leave with a holiday.

That afternoon they met in a park near to Jenny's, next to the slides and swings and roundabouts, within earshot of raucous youths who should have been at school.

'You look rough,' she said, with something approaching pity. She looked, if anything, fresher than usual.

'Designer stubble,' Stu responded. 'Very fashionable.'

They talked about the youths, about absenteeism and the disorder of the world in little well-chewed bites, each knowing the other's opinion, yet hoping to be surprised.

'The doctor said he didn't suffer.' Rosie interrupted the flow of small-talk.

For a while, Stu said nothing. He remembered that the pathologist had made the same claim to him. Perhaps it was true. Yet he had seen the body, seen enough to know that doctors were only human. A knot of mothers and toddlers arrived to dare the swings. She looked as if she still wanted an answer, so he said: 'Is that what Jenny was told?'

'That was what was said.'

There was a silence. Then Rosie continued: 'I mean, what was Kevin doing there, anyway? Trying to prove one of your crackpot theories?'

'Kevin was a good lad. In this case, he'd told me nothing. He was acting on his own initiative. It was the day of the arrests, perhaps he wanted to help.'

'Will his death help anybody? After all, Lloyd's is only concerned with money. We're not going to change the world.'

Their eyes met. Stu observed coldly: 'I honestly thought that was your aim in life.' A moment later, he wanted to tread on his mouth, stamp on his lips. Rosie stood up from the bench, shook her head and left him, her decided, diminutive figure becoming smaller as she strode across playing fields still marked for cricket, although September was upon them.

Thereafter, more days drifted by; he had no mind for chess or the garden or anything; the television propped his eyelids open.

If he dozed off, then at least his cries on waking might be drowned by the homespun sounds of a quiz show or canned laughter or adverts.

The doorbell rang, it was daytime. From the sofa by the television, he rushed to the door and was disappointed to find Keef, in uniform, grinning. Stu had hoped that Rosie might, just might have come to see him.

Keef had news which neither the Met nor Rosie had bothered to tell him. The inquest into the death of Kevin Vaughan was to open within the hour. He needed to wash and shave; Keef drove with his foot glued to the floor, which had the merit of frightening Stu awake.

Keef had, inevitably, heard about the ructions at the SFO; since Stu's departure, Tomlinson had been threatened with sideways demotion as the Wansbeck affair drifted towards fiasco. And Keef's old guv'nor, Inspector Wilson, was suspected of blowing up his own investigation. At least Grote and friends had been charged.

'Well guv'nor, are you going to tell me what it means?'

'Don't think I know any more. What's happened down on the Golden Rain front?'

'Nothing much. We've not had much joy. The guys on our patch have tried hard, but with little luck.'

At least this was human fallibility, rather than politics.

'And any word on the fire investigation?'

Keef shrugged: 'The Met is not telling us anything. Nor have they been round to see us about the Golden Rain shooting.'

Both men were silent. There was no necessary link. It seemed odd, that was all, but perhaps they had unduly suspicious minds.

It soon became evident that the coroner, a large, white-haired gent with a long, horizontal strip of white hair under his nose, did not find anything at all suspicious. He had the air of a man who knew what was what in the world. He was proud of his moustache. Witnesses rose, went to the front of the court, then revealed all. Physical examination, chemical tests, all pointed to death by asphyxiation, while the Met stated that the fire had started accidentally, because of faulty wiring in the control box of the sprinkler system.

Seated beside Stu, Keef shifted his feet.

The man from Lloyd's, lowly but a computer expert, said

nobody had been in the store for days; it was not used in day-to-day operations; perhaps there had been an excess of combustible packing materials around the place. Since no one worked there, since there was a sprinkler system, it did not matter. The large computer tapes were racked, for the most part, on open storage shelves; the small number of fireproof storage cupboards had proved ineffective against the high temperatures reached by the fire. Lloyd's was unhappy to lose the details of its recent past and, clearly, sorry about the death of this individual.

Unanswered questions hung over the long, dull courtroom. Stu and Keef exchanged glances; their colleagues from the Met were satisfied, the coroner was satisfied; they had made themselves look foolish, often enough. Stu looked at Jenny, who turned her head away.

Death by misadventure, then. The white-haired gent had seen no reason to adjourn. That was his prerogative.

Outside the court, neither of the sisters approached them. Rosie had the order for burial in her handbag.

'Talk to you later,' Stu shouted from some distance, waiting for her to acknowledge his presence. Finally she nodded and he retreated, but Keef strode over, exchanged words, his large frame dwarfing hers. He was concerned.

On the long journey home, Keef told him something else: Robert Marchwood had left the country, the day after the shooting.

Stu groaned. He had intended to charge Marchwood along with Grote.

After the shooting, it seemed Marchwood had developed a funk and decided he was considerably safer in Switzerland; they could, however, reach him through Ray Marchwood, who suddenly started claiming that his brother was ill.

A convenient illness.

'Any other leads?' Stu asked, perking up.

Keef looked at his notebook: 'The cartridges were in a batch sent to a Welsh arms dealer, selling to farmers and sportsmen. A Taff who has never heard of Marchwood, thinks Lloyd's is the name of a bank and likes mud.'

'Are you going to interview him?'

Keef wiggled his head, gesturing uncertainty; a long day, one hell of a drive. He had other cases.

'You should do. Have the farmers in the area checked for connections with Lloyd's.'

'Yes, it's all in hand, with the locals.' Keef grunted, then said: 'Do me a favour, Stu. Go and see your doctor. You need help.'

At first, Stu thought Keef was joking; this was what the DG had said, that terrible woman. He was perfectly fit. Of course, there was this niggle and that niggle, but once you pass fifty, that was ever the way. Keef just smiled at the outburst.

Keef said Stu could go and see the police shrink, but it was better to go locally, if he wanted to keep his job. That way his files would not cross people's desk.

Detective Inspector Wilson protested, vehemently. Then he let his hands fall into his lap. Keef, he agreed, had a point.

Appointments were made and kept; Stu took a hair cut, bought a new suit, forced himself to sleep at regular times, even if this involved intermittent nightmares. This made his limbo seem less like hell; you cannot be dead if you can still hear the buzz of hair clippers and feel the scritch of a razor at the neck.

The coroner agreed to release the body and the funeral had to be arranged. So Stu considered the state of his uniform. Stu was a plain-clothes officer and, it was true, happier in a suit. There it was though, hanging in the wardrobe. Uniform was an oddity; every copper had worn one for years, some had never stopped; it showed they belonged and that, in turn, reassured the people who saw them.

Of course, his beat days were long gone; it was mostly for ceremonial duties, although, nowadays, people wanted to see you in uniform more often. It did not, he found, help you to think. Even so, he thought he ought to wear it, for Kevin.

Rosie returned home a few days prior to the funeral. The bell rang and there she was, with her suitcase. She had been away for three weeks and it seemed like years; they had never before been apart. Well, they were now.

'Oh, you're back,' he said, to say something, and then felt foolish. Rosie had not returned, he supposed, for his sake. Perhaps, too, she and Jenny were starting to irk each other; Jenny liked to have things buttoned down; in her own way, Jenny knew best, but Rosie was Jenny's older sister and she knew best, too. Or perhaps it was medical advice: Rosie and he shared the same doctor, a nice guy, probably he was not above muttering something to Rosie. Or perhaps the shrink, whom

Stu had told that Rosie was not at home. Then there was Keef, a fount of solid common sense, a good friend.

'Hello,' she said. 'Another person who isn't sleeping well?'

Her words did not sound like a reproach, so they kissed, brushing dry lips, and he hoped they were on the way back.

She was still kind or could force herself to be so. When he woke at night, she consoled him and made tea; he saw how she tried to listen to his anger and pain. She hid the television; she tried to stop him washing his hands. Yet, once in a while, she would say something careless, offhand or blunt and the mist lifted, revealing a scarred landscape with trenches.

He suffered, more or less in silence. She was not inclined to forgive him, not now, not ever, as far as he could see.

There was the problem of Kevin's things; he had died intestate, his assets amounted to an impressive debt, amassed largely with the help of a credit card, but also included some rather nice clothes, an unused set of golf clubs, a mountain of computer hardware and software, a dog-eared pile of science-fiction books, an expensive new hi-fi with ten jazz compact disks, which had been bought on credit. The car had belonged to Knowle. An alto saxophone, brand new, had arrived the very day he died.

Stu wrote a cheque to clear his debts. Rosie watched him sign in silence. Then he tried on his uniform; it fitted, more or less.

Kevin Vaughan was buried the following day.

BOOK FIVE

ONE

HERE IS THE gambler's paradise. On the rock high above the sea stands a white palace; its opulence calculating, wilful and overladen, suggesting the cruelty of the old gods, the blue dreams of a time before time. Between scrub-dotted hills, between the sea and the sky, rising above palms, cypresses and mimosas, the palace is more than a temple to the goddess Fortuna; its auditorium serves as theatre, ballroom and most regal opera house; its private gambling rooms are linked by secret passage and lift to the most exclusive hotel in the principality, built with other-worldly splendour to serve other-wordly wealth.

During its long history, the casino bank has been broken, shaking the principality which it finances; on the other hand an oil-maddened sheikh is reputed to have lost more at one sitting in the white palace than anyone, anywhere, ever.

To the loser, the view of sea and sky offer certain consolation; it is hard to believe that happiness will not endure where the sea elides into the blue sky.

The royalty and aristocracy of Europe flooded here once, to the Casino du Paradis, leaving their wealth like a tide mark on the shoreline; today distinctions of breeding have been discarded; now they only serve to sell glossy magazines, and the principality caters to every well-heeled wish; it is a bustling tax-haven, a royalist enclave in a republican state. Banks, finance houses, film stars and international rentiers congregate here, people the high-rise blocks, fill the jetties with exquisite yachts and traffic jam the promenade. Its roads clear only for the annual grand prix.

For some, if not all of these advantages, Le Casino du Paradis is deemed perfect for the annual insurance conference sponsored by Lloyd's. The Baden–Baden bash suffers from seriousness, is tailored for work and wife; Monte Carlo is perfect for the secretary and indolence. Older Lloyd's men remember the great coup pulled off by Stephen Grote here, during the first oil crisis in the 70s; a shipping deal struck with Ioànnis Kolokotrònis, the Cypriot magnate, which brought billions to Lime Street. Some say that it saved Lime Street from socialism. Most admit it ensured Grote would be remembered as a great chairman of the Corporation. Lloyd's has had a conference here ever since the deal was signed; an annual event staged with pomp and circumstance.

Few can resist the attractions of this place; even so, a prompt reply from Knowle & Co caused the conference organisers to whistle with surprise. Mr and Mrs Marchwood had accepted, reserving a suite at the Hôtel d'Orléans. The choice of hotel, the very best, was the only thing that was unsurprising.

Robert Hugh Marchwood, chairman and chief executive of Knowle & Co, had not been seen in Lime Street for over a year; an election had been won and lost, the British economy staggered on, and losses at Lloyd's continued to soar. Just weeks before the conference started, Neil Fortescue, Stephen Grote's successor- elect, announced losses of five billion at the annual meeting, with worse to come. The loss was visited on one quarter of the membership, some six thousand names.

The casino in Lime Street, one pundit observed, was claiming its sacrificial victims. The effects, seen across Britain, discussed in the right quarters and heard in the right places, were severe; the season, the social whirl that involved the Boat Race, Ascot and Henley was subdued. Mansions, manor houses and rectories were for sale; fine arable land, excellent shoots and the wide-open spaces of Scotland came under the hammer; thousands of names sued and were close to the edge, having risked and lost everything.

There seemed, then, little reason for Marchwood to return to Lloyd's, even if the entry was to be effected through paradise. Knowle & Co continued to survive in the absence of its great man, so perhaps, some muttered, his reputation was more effective than his presence, like a deity's.

An unfortunate newspaper article had listed Mr Robert Marchwood as one of the richest men in Britain – even though he had lived abroad for a year, some thought, in Switzerland or, according to others, in Miami. There was gossip in the market about the authorities closing Knowle, talk about the death of a young broker who worked for Knowle and, as ever, speculation about some woman or other; but most old hands saw a new, young team being skilfully built by Raymond, the great man's brother. Profits might have fallen, but the decline was less than anticipated; new markets, new clients had been found and the returns from Knowle's cash mountain offset the fall.

As for Robert Marchwood's net worth, the article both understated and overstated; he owned much jointly, with Ray, much that could not be sold; but the stockmarket and gilts had enjoyed an excellent year and their private portfolios were remarkable. Whatever the figure, Mr Robert Marchwood could risk half his fortune on the roll of a dice, three-quarters of what remained on the spin of a wheel, nine-tenths of the residue on the speed of a horse, and his remaining wealth would still be more than large enough for two lifetimes. Of course, Robert was not as rich as the great oil barons of the nineteenth century or a modern sheikh, not as affluent as the head of one of the great supermarket dynasties; he did not inherit half of Manhattan or most of Mayfair or a small, rocky principality; he was not a software Midas, barely out of teeth-braces; even so, whatever happened, he possessed enough to live elegantly, quietly, luxuriously, wherever he chose. Yet, for him, this was apparently not enough.

Having failed to banish him, Lloyd's could not afford to ignore him. So Mr and Mrs Robert Marchwood joined the list of those guests who would warrant particular treatment, champagne, flowers in the bedroom, a fine writing set with the Lloyd's insignia in the sitting room. Mr and Mrs Stephen Grote, Mr and Mrs John Devies, Mr and Mrs Neil Fortescue, Mr Anthony MacNulty and fiancée, Mr Alexander Wilmot-Greaves and guest, Mr Henry Stone and guest, these also figured on the list. The importance of Grote, Devies and MacNulty, no longer answering bail despite the continuing investigation of the SFO, was undiminished. Everyone knew that the charges were being quietly dropped. Of the leading lights of Lloyd's, only Mr Raymond Marchwood, who was still barred from the Room because of some technical misdemeanour, was missing; he had been most cordially invited to join them, but he declined as had been expected. Equally expected was the absence from the list of a certain policeman; Lloyd's was not proud of its relationship with the police; indeed, if some guests had known that uninvited Inspector Stewart Wilson was to join them on the Riviera all the same, they might have forgone even the pleasures of paradise.

TWO

THE MARCHWOODS HAD not planned to return to London before going to Monte. It was the small parcel that Thérèse collected from the tiny post office in the mountain resort which had forced Robert's hand.

The package came as a unpleasant shock. Marchwood slit open the plastic tape and found two cartridges, both engraved: Marchwood. Postmark Zurich.

Unfortunately, Thérèse happened to be standing beside him at the time.

He had contrived not to tell her about the attack at Golden Rain, there had been one solitary mention of the shooting in a local newspaper, rather imprecise, rather unspecific; the attack had been quietly forgotten. Certainly, there was no sign that the police had got their man. Until that moment, this suited Robert; he had kept quiet for fear she would leave him.

Now it suddenly became certain: they could not stay here. This was not the right place.

Even though the small, leaden parcel was imprecisely addressed: 'for collection by Robert Marchwood', the Swiss post office had no difficulty in finding the addressee; the Marchwoods lived in a rented villa on the edge of the village, where they enjoyed its famous clean air, its famous health facilities, its famous peace and quiet.

Thérèse was to blame for their presence there, for she had saved his life. No sooner had they arrived in Zurich on that quiet Sunday in August that he felt his chest heave with pain as his heart went into spasm and his fingers tingled with lost sensation. She drove him rapidly to the efficient cantonal hospital where doctors behaved as if his life were slipping away. Drips, injections, tests, examinations and more examinations ensued.

269

His heartbeat was irregular, a machine pinged by his bed, the doctors thought about intensive surgery. Then the paroxysm of pain subsided, leaving him weak and helpless.

Throughout, Thérèse was by his side, holding his hand, conferring in a low, musical voice with his doctors. She wore a faded green overall and white headband and looked pale and gorgeous; he asked to embrace her, despite the drips and probes and impediments.

He felt he owed her everything.

Barely a fortnight after their jet from Heathrow had roared low over pine forests before reaching Kloten, Robert had recovered enough to travel again, away from the heat of a late Zurich summer. Following medical advice, Thérèse arranged for a long recuperation in the mountains. Their baggage was sent on ahead, so that they were unencumbered as their train passed between the gardens and houses that overlooked Lake Zurich from its southern rim, the water basking blue and warm in sunshine, and rattled on through noise-filled tunnels.

He held her hand, though they were neither young lovers nor an old couple, and wondered that his body could have felt such pain, pain that was, with hindsight, unimaginable. The memory had to baulk at such experience; its persistence would undermine the living man.

The spa village seemed practical, unfussed and unpretentious, but it had a reputation and history. Marchwood could never have imagined living this way. Days were spent sleeping, reading, talking to Thérèse, watching the weather sweep down from the mountains and along the valley floor, hearing cow-bells, the ongush of rain. Occasionally, he turned to his 'diplomatic bags', completing Knowle & Co paperwork.

Once a fortnight, someone would fly out and deposit a thick, black legal bag with their man in Zurich, who would have it brought to their mountain retreat. He was surprised how much he could achieve here, with telephone, fax machine, pen and paper, if he wanted to. Mostly, he did not. He felt strangely tranquil and fulfilled, despite the blankness of his days and the fear of discovery.

They were together the whole time; this was a new experience, which they both found difficult. She was moody, and sometimes needed solitude; he was morose, for want of male cameraderie, an audience. Yet whenever Thérèse left to see her father, who was only just holding on, he felt weaker and less capable than he really was; her absence was pain yet she embarrassed him on her return with stories of her father's state.

The doctors had given Papa three months to live, six months ago, nine months ago; yet she remained burdened. It would not be much longer, nobody thought anything else.

This she confessed to Robert: 'Couldn't we . . .? I would like a child . . . it would mean so much.'

Marchwood was outraged at the idea. Her father had no right. Besides, he himself was too old to change nappies, to get up at night.

His refusal brought tears; he remained firm, insisted that they had an agreement, that everything had been perfectly clear, that she had no right to change her mind. His one son had been more than enough.

For a time, they slept in different rooms.

He avoided newspapers as much as he could; he remembered watching the television for a few days, seeing experts discussing some crisis; outside, the first snow of a late season fell. He hibernated and the snow melted and then there was an election which he steadfastly ignored, although his people, despite the loss of several good Tory members through bankruptcy, fortunately won. Through his diplomatic bag came a card from the party chairman, thanking him for his support, for his offshore money.

Here, in the mountains, it was the seasons that mattered, they marked the immensity of his indolence. Blue summer turned autumn gold and short autumn days became winter rain, bringing snow and brilliant sunshine, gold, blue and white. It was a new sense of time and place.

They rented a villa which, though relatively modest, proved ideal; when they needed each other, the one could find the other; they could also swim, exercise or simply disappear. The housekeeper was hardworking and a good, if simple, cook. His appetite and his weight returned, though not all his strength.

Then the package arrived and everything was different. Within an hour, he had admitted to the attack at Golden Rain, which she took in her stride, soon rising to pack light bags, while he scrutinised the Zurich postmark. The standard carton, yellow cardboard, had been bought at the post office and included a box for the sender's name: Herr X. Unknown.

She would have treated it as an abominable joke, but for his grey, grim look and his tired confession. He had consistently not told her everything. She knew he had to be discreet, that he wanted to avoid Grote; but he had not told her about the shooting. So this was the real reason why he was ill, why they were here, why he was prepared to hide with her.

Here, the only thing she had feared was the weather, or perhaps an errant skier unable to control his hurtling descent. Yet she would not stay now; she was not a rabbit waiting to be shot.

A black limousine drew up outside the villa and they left the mountains, perhaps for ever.

It was as well they had not bought the villa. The housekeeper, a solid soul, was entrusted with the arrangements; Thérèse would write.

In the sudden twilight of a spring cold-snap, their car half-slid down the mountainside, down the winding road, turning on an ice-rumbling surface, braking between white reflector marked snow piles. They began to breathe more easily as the vehicle joined the motorway, even though the sleet had become full-force snow, flakes emerging from the dark into the headlight beam, engulfing the windscreen.

'Who has done this? Who?' she asked, leaning back into the leather seat beside him.

Above all, he felt sorry for Thérèse. She had not returned to him for this. 'Grote, I suppose,' he answered. 'Friends of his friends, probably.'

'Why, but why? Tell me the truth, for once. What have you done to provoke this?' she repeated the question, watching the snow form white lines in the car headlights.

He raised his hands; he could not say.

'If you ever lie to me again . . .' She started the sentence, then looked at him; he half-protested, tried to change the subject.

Did he understand? Yes, he did. She had left him before. He tried to think about the present: where did she want to go? Hot or cold?

He had an airport timetable, a portable telephone and a credit card; it could all be solved, that evening; they opted for Nassau, Bahama, rather than Aspen, Colorado. They flew to Frankfurt, caught a connecting flight to Boston, then another to Nassau; they booked each leg of the journey separately, using different credit cards. It was circuitous, tiring, but at least they could travel first class and perhaps they might not be followed. Perhaps.

The Bahamas proved a wise choice.

The mountain air and peace and quiet had lifted his spirits, now he felt refreshed at sea level, in the sunshine. Their hotel, like all the others, was quiet between seasons. There were no other guests apart from German tourists, which did not matter too much, they played golf every day, knocking white balls onto empty greens, they swam in the hotel pool in the afternoon, slept, slept and tried to thrash things out, not always successfully.

Thérèse insisted she did not want to be a fugitive, flying from place to place, living out of a suitcase; she needed a home. He nodded. They tried thinking where home might be; another place in the mountains, or a place by the sea, among cypresses and sunshine, in Provence.

His health had improved markedly, but he still had to sleep after lunch, while Thérèse read – the letters of a French noblewoman, Mme de Sévigné, he had even bought himself a translation out of curiosity but failed to see the point.

He woke one afternoon and found himself alone. He looked down from the balcony, and saw her slight figure beside the pool, in a blue bikini. They had not made love for nearly a year, but her nearly naked, not completely naked body, close, but distant, beside warm water, in balmy air, in the sunshine, was a sight he would never forget. He waved and a moment later she entered their suite: they embraced.

From then on, he stopped waiting for something to happen, for success.

They started to travel. It seemed as good a way as any of avoiding unwanted packages, although the black bags continued to arrive, whether they were in New York, Paris or Tokyo. This was fun, for a time, but they both grew tired of hotels and the necessary obsequiousness of staff: Thérèse decided to study art history; Lloyd's was, for better or worse, Robert's life.

They would have to live with the risk, with the unspoken threat that made Robert examine emergency exits, entrances and windows.

Then the news came that her father had died; she flew to Geneva to join her brothers and sisters, to help and support her

273

mother. Robert followed for the ceremony, silently watching her sadness and admiring her animation, listening to her rapid speech. Perhaps he could learn to speak French properly.

As her sole inheritance, Thérèse had asked for an old, leather-bound copy of Racine, handmarked by her father. The rest was for the others and her mother, who was still beside herself with grief.

Robert returned to London, to make arrangements, sort out some personal matters, prepare the way. He thought of contacting Veronica Cantor, but he was ready neither for temptation nor for good behaviour. He avoided Lime Street, the offices of Knowle & Co, met Ray in hotels in the West End; yet they felt as if they were being watched.

Spring turned to summer and then, one warm-to-hot day, Thérèse was walking beside him through St James's Park. They admired the ducks, geese and a solitary black swan, avoided the joggers, policemen on horseback, and strolled easily along tree-shaded alleyways. He had something to show her; she followed his steps into a nineteenth-century apartment block overlooking the park, that had recently been gutted and refurbished.

The concierge, who observed their entry through a sur-veillance system, nodded when he saw Marchwood. They had to take the lift and the lift needed a magnetic-taped identity card and a password to reach the penthouse floor. Cameras, every-where.

Robert opened the large, black penthouse door and she entered, walking over grey-speckled white and jet-black marble, strolled from room to room, each with a view over the park. Some rooms were empty, some contained their new acquisitions. In the sitting room, which he had furnished with modern classic furniture, a Tiffany stained-glass pane hung over one window, glowing. She was speechless.

'You like it? Do you want it?' he asked, then added, almost embarrassed: 'I did a deal.'

In none of the three bathrooms, all marble and gold and whirlpooled, all totally over the top, were there any towels. So they shook themselves dry, risking mortal injury by walking barefoot and dripping over the slippery marble.

He explained, after he had caught his breath, that the penthouse was hers, a gift, a thank you for everything; there was a swimming-pool and sports room in the basement; there were

274

cameras and security systems everywhere; the place had been built for an Arab prince who had had the misfortune to be drawn into the Gulf crisis. Robert had made an offer that the developer had wanted to refuse. The documents could be signed that afternoon.

Now she would never be without a home.

He suggested that they live here during the week and, at weekends, they find another place in the country. Golden Rain could not be made secure; besides, it held unfortunate memories.

Ray arrived at six, looking harrassed; he admired the penthouse and caught a knowing smile from his brother. 'Yes, I'm thinking of moving, too. Perhaps I could retain Robert as buying agent, after his deal on this place.'

They joked idly about selling dear and buying cheap, and drank tea-bag tea, no milk, no sugar, out of chipped mugs a contractor had left in the cupboard.

Then Ray made Thérèse an offer: 'Join Knowle & Co. Become involved in the investment side of the business. That way, you and Robert will be together.'

She hesitated; she was unsure of her own abilities.

'Nonsense,' Robert insisted. 'You'll learn, just like you learn everything else.'

Thérèse was both intrigued and flattered by the offer; if she had felt frustrated over the past year, now she could feel only gratitude.

She would have a great deal to learn. Ray had had a good run recently; his good decisions had been very good and his bad ones only middling. He had appointed new people, but not always successfully; a finance director had joined, shown his worth, and left for something more demanding. The good ones go, the dogs stay to bark and bite, he claimed. Now he needed Robert, full-time, in the office. They had to start thinking about diversification; at the moment, two-thirds of operating income still came from Lloyd's.

Thérèse was not sure of the implications of this; she looked at her husband, whose expression was not easy to interpret. He was, she noticed, with some pride, looking fit and bronzed.

'Why? I mean, why do you have to do this?' she asked.

'Because Lloyd's is bust,' Ray said, then added, reassuringly: 'Not this year, maybe next or the year after.'

Robert unleashed a huge guffaw of laughter.

'Not your fault, I hope, Robert?'

This just made Ray laugh, too. He said: 'The world is turning into a disaster zone.'

Industrial claims from America, from asbestos and pollution, from increased floods and hurricanes, had followed the claims from the North Sea; the liabilities, perhaps twenty, perhaps twenty-five billion, outstripped Lloyd's capital base. The market was seized up with litigation; one half was suing the other half. It did not look to be anybody's fault, not for the moment.

Thérèse asked about the effects on the City. There was talk, Ray said, of tens of thousands of jobs being lost, hundreds of firms closing, billions in invisible exports being lost. Sure, the City's reputation would be damaged, it would slip still further behind Tokyo and New York. He seemed remarkably sanguine all the same; markets expand and contract, human beings have to adjust to the facts, that seemed to be his view.

Robert agreed. They still had to be a presence at Lloyd's, this was the base from which they would move; he was going to Lloyd's conference on the Riviera, which started next week; this would mark his return to the market and enable Thérèse to make some new contacts.

'Try not to be too. . . ,' Ray said.

'What?' she asked.

'You know, difficult, prickly.'

She laughed lightly.

Robert accompanied Ray to the front door; there was a package waiting for him at the desk, just delivered by bike. The security guard said: 'White Horse Express, sir.'

This meant nothing to him; for a second, he suspected a joke; but no, he all but gasped when he saw the package and felt its weight in his hand. With a pocket knife, he slit it open and found two more cartridges. He did not bother to look to see if they were engraved. He smiled at the guard, walked with Ray towards the door, placed the parcel in his brother's hand; Ray hesitated, then looked inside, nodded, and said: 'I went to the jeweller's this morning, to have the cigarette lighter we talked about made. It'll take some weeks, but it should be ready for the South of France.'

Robert smiled and was surprised to find himself relaxed and calm. They had expected another package, sooner or later; they knew that nowhere was safe; this time, Robert would tell Thérèse; this time, they had made their plans.

THREE

THERE WAS SOMETHING wrong, had been for days and months. Sunday breakfast was not just papers and coffee and juice and muffins, a long wait for the world to wake up to a fine August day; instead, Marshall stomped around the house, slammed doors, saying nothing.

Mary-Ellen brought him parts of the newspaper she had already read, quietly pushed the finance pages in his direction. It worked; there was a great grunt of outrage. A solicitor had strung himself up on the bannisters because of losses at Lloyd's; bankrupt, he was no longer able to practise.

Marshall, too, he reminded her, was a lawyer.

'Yeah, but you're not going anywhere without me.' Mary-Ellen kissed his forehead.

Marshall grunted again, but she took him in her arms, kissed him again and he relented enough to explain.

The problem had burned for months but only caught fire at the ambassador's ball.

Mary-Ellen fondly remembered a fine affair, filling the ballroom at Grosvenor Square with speeches and laughter, a small string orchestra and excellent food. Just as the dancing started, Marshall had disappeared, summoned for a quiet word by the ambassador. After this visit to the boys' room, Marshall returned with a smile and danced sweetly with Mary-Ellen, gliding across the floor. That night, they fell asleep in each other's arms.

'They want me out of the ball game,' Marshall now said. 'Italy's just an excuse. I'm finished.'

For the first time, he told her the truth.

Italy had not been the glorious success he had claimed. Sure, he had eaten great pasta, drunk great coffee and uncovered bag-

277

loads of hot air during a six months' stay in Milan. Did his girth a big favour. Everybody was friendly, but behind his back he could feel the smiles and shrugs and raised middle-fingers. And always in the murky distance were the Italian untouchables who had pocketed the dollar bills since the last war, since some CIA smart-ass decided to fund corruption and drug-trading in the name of freedom and democracy.

Mary-Ellen put her arms around him.

'Jesus, I didn't even make La Scala. Of course, I found some bucks here, some lira there, but most of all I found a hole. Now a fieldman like me isn't expected to be Washington's conscience. All anybody wanted was their money back, not morality or history or problems.'

'What did you do?'

'Christ, what *do* you do? You eat pasta and drink coffee and think about it! There was plenty to say which I couldn't write.'

His report had not looked good, all the same. A long silence had ensued after he sent it to the relevant powers; the response had been left to the ambassador who was in Washington over the summer. But someone had decided change was needed.

Marshall rubbed the back of his neck, ruefully.

'You could retire, you know.'

'Can't afford to. Not on, sweetheart. Not now.'

Nonsense! They had been married for near forty years, Mary-Ellen had mostly kept her inheritance because it was shared with Donna. She had spent only the dividends and interest on the children and the grandchildren, on swings and houses, on skiing and college. Recently, she had paid for Marshall.

'We'll sort this thing out.'

Marshall was infuriated: 'The worst thing is, the ambassador had met the Vice President in Washington, who's as mad as he can get about Lloyd's. Now, when the fella hears that our man in the London embassy is the brother-in-law of the chairman, who had been charged and so on and so on . . .'

'Then?'

'Then the Vice President tells the ambassador to kick butt. Which is just the excuse he's spent months looking for.'

'So he does.'

'Sure.' Marshall hesitated. 'Then there's this Lloyd's hell-hole. I just don't understand why the Brits are so stuff-assed.

You look at that Wall Street crook Milken, boom, we got him; look at Boesky, boom, we got him; these guys made millions but we kicked hundreds of millions in fines out of them, had them locked up. It's over a year since the arrests at Lloyd's and we have seen nothing. Niente.'

'Marshall . . .'

'Look, these jerks deserve everything they get, I tell you. Even if Donna is married to one.'

It was high time Mary-Ellen had words with her sister.

FOUR

FORGETTING WAS NOT Stu's style.

A buff envelope, streaked by summer drizzle, fell onto the doormat.

Letter in hand, he shuffled into the living room, found his letter opener, slit open the envelope, studied its contents, cursed until the room turned blue and Rosie, surprised, asked: 'What on earth's the matter?'

To which he found the answer: 'Grote knew the bastards . . . damn well knew the fire would happen.'

Rosie said nothing; she looked at the letter: it contained a set of four colour photographs of burnt wiring, of a scarred junction box, and a typed callbox number in Euston station, with a time and a date three days in the future.

'Stu, what does this mean? Who sent this to you?'

He showed her, cursing again. There was no accompanying letter; the postmark – West London – meant nothing.

'Look, there was an explosion, a small charge, placed in that box, you can see the scars. And that box, I bet, controlled the sprinkler system . . .'

'Do you know or are you guessing?'

'Don't you see? The charge knocks out the main line of defence and starts a fire which, with all that plastic and polystyrene and the rest, produces a deadly mixture of gases. Anyone inside would be unconscious within seconds.'

'So at least he wouldn't have felt anything,' Rosie said and returned to her book.

He turned on her: 'Don't you believe me? Is everything I say so incredible?'

She hesitated, bit a lip, then said: 'Don't make it more difficult than it already is, Stu. Please.'

His anger evaporated, leaving the doubts and despair that had, more or less, formed his daily diet of the last year. Rosie had ceased living at Jenny's house when her sister stopped needing barbiturates; she had tried her best ever since, and that was the worst of it. It was all duty and effort and strain.

Fortunately, she still had her work at the library, had to see Jenny daily and was fully committed to the Green Party, to young Christians and to church fund-raising. This left him alone with his thoughts and seemed a relief of sorts.

He understood her now, he believed, better than he had before. The grief for Kevin was shared, even if the guilt was his. However unfair that might appear, it was comprehensible that Rosie should take that view of his position.

Slowly, he came round: the nightmares became less frequent, less convoluted, less awful.

He was now allowed near a police station. He only visited the biscuit tin in his dreams. Unpleasant dreams. He spent the daytime wondering about the DG, Tomlinson and the others, a riot of useless speculation about treachery, back-stabbers and traitors. He found it intolerable that he should have paid such a high price for fighting the good fight, for doing the job to the best of his abilities. Now he was left looking at the remains, speculating about whom he could blame for his own, overwhelming sense of failure.

At the graveside he had promised: I will not leave Kevin unavenged. Little had he known, then, the hollowness of his words.

'Find something to do,' the shrink said. 'Do you have any hobbies?'

He started to play chess again, having felt unable to push a pawn or draw a bishop's teeth; one weekend in the spring he won the club championship for the first time in ten years. In celebration, he had a nice cup of tea. He felt he was recovering.

The arrival of the buff envelope, however, only served to confirm the obvious. Nothing had been solved, nothing avenged, and until it was, he could not be considered free.

He stared at the photographs for hours, with the smell of fire in his nostrils. And a name on his lips: Grote.

Yet he knew this was a pure prejudice, unprovable. Rosie said as much. Yet here was evidence; the photographs told him there is still work to be done. He could not forget, could not let

281

everything drop, the whole Lloyd's affair, the computer data, the losses, the programs, the newspaper clippings, everything that burnt before his very eyes, night after night. He would make the phone call.

At some future date, he was to face a disciplinary tribunal and, in truth, most men would have thrown in the towel now, taken retirement with honour and let other dogs fight over the bones. But he had not much left to lose, apart from his pension, so he set about proving the unprovable, once again.

It was a sunny morning in Capri when Stu knocked on a roughly painted wooden door, heard a grunt, a tuneless whistle, then discovered newly promoted Detective Inspector Peters bending over an engine, replacing a burst gasket, up to his elbows in grease and good humour. A new old banger, acquired for a song, was being returned to its earlier, noble state.

'This would've gone to scrap,' Keef grinned. 'With a new suspension, tyres and exhaust, it'll do another ten years. Bodywork's fine.'

They had cracked a bottle or two a while back, when Keef had moved up in the world, and the Marchwood shooting had been filed in the great cabinet in the sky, marked unsolved.

Now Keef had a new love in his life; the car was to be a gift to Sharon or Tracy or whoever. 'A great pair of legs, squire.' With a wink. 'You're looking well, old man.'

Yep, on the mend.

Stu had caught the sun in the garden, where he had relaid beds and lawn, faced up to pruning, weeding and seeding, planted the wonderful roses that Mr Blythe had given him. Now he placed the photographs on the spotless bonnet of the white wonder, which was more wonderful than ever, with a new leather-clad steering wheel.

'Crikey!' Keef surveyed the photographs, moving a large, oily rag up and down his fore-arm, seeming only to increase the black grease. He rubbed his nose, which added a dark streak to his cheek. 'Where did you get them?'

'Anonymous.'

'The killer?'

Stu shook his head. There was a contact instruction in the envelope.

Keef bent over the four images. Flash gun, home printed; good quality. There seemed to be flare marks in the junction box, from a small detonation, something that would not make much more noise than a car back-firing, but enough to set off a small blaze. With flammable packing materials nearby, no chance.

Well, it was a theory.

Stu found it helped; he had come to the same conclusions, more or less, after hours spent poring over these photographs of scarred fuse-blocks, disfigured switches and absent wiring.

'I wouldn't bet my life savings on it,' he said, 'but I'd take odds of four-to-one on arson and reckon to win well.'

In the coroner's court the thoroughly reputable man used by the Met had seen things differently, after looking long and hard at the actual box. But experts are born to disagree.

For Keef and Stu, there remained few doubts, merely the uncertainty of finding proof of arson or discovering whether the fire had been triggered automatically or by a calm murderer who had waited before pushing the button on a remote control handset. Either way, starting the fire was murder. Of course, Stu knew who was ultimately responsible. Felt he knew.

Keef looked at his part-dismantled motor: 'You going to make this call? If you need me, give me a bell.'

But he was busy really. With Sharon or Tracy, and why not?

Stu had his theories about the photographer, so he was surprised, on picking up the designated phone at the designated time on the concourse of Euston station (second from left, opposite the stall selling French croissants and cookies), to hear the voice of a young girl. The phone in the next booth rang, the girl's voice told him to pick it up–and an old man spoke. Neat trick, but easy – a modern portable switchboard with memory function, plus a voice-transforming phone.

He juggled, trying to transfer his microphone and tape machine to the new phone from the old.

The man's voice asked: 'Well, what do you think of the photographs?'

'Very interesting. Why did you take them?'

He did not receive an answer.

The voice responded with another question: 'How do you think they knew that Mr Vaughan was in the store? Who knew?'

Stu said: 'There's no evidence that anybody did. There's evidence of arson, but no proof. Was Kevin being watched? Was the store being watched?'

The voice stumbled: 'It was primed to go. They could easily have had small, remote cameras in there . . .'

'Who is they?'

'In the fire, they would have burned. Or could have been removed afterwards.'

'Just like you took the photographs?'

'Of course, you know who they are.'

Stu said: 'I don't know. Can you tell me? Why didn't you come forward at the inquest?'

'Suspicious.' A one-word reply: either the inquest or the speaker or both.

'Who are *they*?'

'You know; you arrested them.'

Wilson looked at passengers wearily buying belated break-fasts, the tannoy blared something incomprehensible, there was a dispute by the left luggage office.

'They were under arrest at the time,' he said.

'That place was a powder keg. Someone gave the order. Someone pulled the trigger.'

Two people, a man and a woman, emerged victorious from the left luggage queue, but were still remonstrating with each other.

'Have you got proof, hard evidence?' he almost shouted.

Click.

He rang Knowle & Co, immediately: could he speak to Mr Ray Marchwood, please? Ray had hired Kevin, was Jenny's friend.

A woman answered, his assistant. Mr Marchwood was out of the country. Then he pushed her, he was the police, for more details, until she was flustered: in the States. Yes, she was sure she was sure.

Keef laughed when he heard the story, and grinned at the tape. 'You'd have rollocked me over that, letting him go so easy.'

Of course, if he had been able to draw on the resources of the police, they could have traced the call; but since his suspension the world had changed; an election had been won. Politics can make as well as break, and the DG he had once known, had become the Director of Public Prosecutions and would, in time, become Lady Rainsley of DG and DPP; there she would not have to deal with the endgames of Irwell, Wansbeck and Lloyd's.

284

'You still going to fight, Stu?' Keef wondered.

He laughed: 'Of course. What else?'

Much now depended on findings of the tribunal; Wilson had to show himself completely amenable, willing and reliable, a team player first and last; never a maverick.

He was formally requested to appear at the Serious Fraud Office one Wednesday late in August, at ten a.m. This he took to be a good sign, believing that the tribunal would look at him seriously; ten was a serious time, when people rolled up their sleeves, devoted themselves to the important business of the day; eleven or nine would have lacked gravity; nine would mean 'before ten', while eleven would be a 'let's-get-it-over-before-lunch' affair.

At two minutes before ten, Inspector Stewart Wilson, wearing a dark suit, dark tie, blue shirt and blue collar, arrived in the new DG's office. By moving Mrs DG, the new-old government had been forced to find a new DG, a QC who was this time round a man, a Mr Mottram.

A new secretary ushered Stu into the new DG's office. Mr Mottram was a fair-haired, stocky man in his late forties who enunciated crisp greetings and smiled crisply at an empty chair. Ranged alongside Mottram, behind the large DG desk, were several faces, new and familiar, including Tomlinson's.

Ten meant, Stu soon discovered, that they had already been discussing his case for an hour. He was asked about his health, about his wishes and goals – was he still committed to the SFO? Nobody, apparently, believed it was he who had wiped the hard disks; in fact, they were not mentioned. Time heals some wounds.

The report from the shrink, top of the pile, was probably the key. Post-traumatic stress disorder was the diagnosis; a year burning in hell was the experience. Nor was it over.

Wilson looked past the faces at the wall behind; the sailing prints had been replaced by horse prints, riding to hounds and country fairs and horse races. Was Mottram a huntsman, roaring around the countryside after hounds, blood boiling at a fox? He looked a calm enough fellow.

In fact, Stu Wilson was let off remarkably lightly. Any whiff of insubordination seemed to have blown away in his absence, anything untoward was due to his well-attested illness. There was praise; Mottram read a passage from Mrs DG stating that he had erred 'largely from over-enthusiasm, from a willingness to commit himself too soon and too much.'

Tomlinson spoke in his favour; Stu did not flinch. The deputy DG, too; Stu did not let a curse cross his lips. It was almost as if counsel for the prosecution had ghosted out through the closed door, bewigged head under his arm.

Finally, Mottram expressed his condolences: 'I see from your reports that your nephew was killed . . .'

Stu nodded.

'. . . yes, nasty affair, enough to upset anyone. I want you to know we're happy to have you back.'

Thank you, sir.

There were some stipulations and conditions; someone else was now in the driving seat on the Lloyd's investigation, so he would support Tomlinson with Wansbeck, which was still proving a problem. In the meantime, he should take heed of Mrs Rainsley's strictures. Did he have any questions?

Stu asked if he might return in a month's time, in the autumn, when the office started to wind up again after the holiday season. That morning, a card had arrived, bearing a block-and-ink invitation. 'Take an exclusive holiday by the Med, join every-body at the Lloyd's conference. See you there.' Plus the dates, the address, Casino du Paradis. On the obverse, there was not, as one might expect, a picture of the sunny principality, not a vision of rock, palms and promenade by the sea, but a photograph of the burnt junction box, an essay in melted plastic and scorched metal.

Return in the autumn? No problem. Mottram offered him a hand, ever the Tory squire; well-meaning, in a middling, muddling sort of way. That was the new DG. No match for Mrs DG.

He walked out of the tribunal a puzzled hero; they could, just as easily, have sacked him, stripped him of rank and shrunk his pension rights.

So why?

Perhaps someone thought he would be less of a danger if he bore less of a grudge. Perhaps someone wanted to tidy up a few loose ends as quietly as possible: let Inspector Stewart Wilson return to the obscurity whence he came. Let the old fruit wither away, along with his memories that soon nobody will believe.

He walked down a few stairs, pushed open a door, another,

strode past name-plated doors to the open-plan office, to the desk that was no longer his.

Tomlinson, who had gained weight, caught up with him and shook him by the hand: 'Over-enthusiasm is a problem some people here could do with.'

Thanks.

He had a journey to make.

That evening, he packed a light bag and betrayed some of his plans; Rosie did not freak out, not even when he said he wanted to catch the late train to France. Even though she was tired, she took it all in her stride, she offered to drive him to central London, to Victoria, for the train. Then he told her about the tribunal, that he would return to the SFO.

She flared up: 'What sort of game are they playing? . . . I mean, I know it's not your fault.'

For once.

The phone rang; it was Keef, who had heard by the bush telegraph. Stu thanked him for his kind support, said he was off fishing and hoped his new-old banger was firing on all cylinders.

Meanwhile, Rosie pulled the necessaries together, packed his bag, foregoing an evening at the church social group.

This reminded him of their early trips to Magaluf and part of him still longed to idle on a beach, lard book pages with sun-tan oil and push his feet through sun-baked sand; he still desired warm oblivion, washed down in the evening by cheap wine or sangria or beer. Then, perhaps, a little fizz of something or other.

Rosie, he now knew, would never want that, never again.

This was a strange occasion. She had rarely packed a large suitcase, just for him. There had been conferences, weekends away, playing chess or fishing, kit-bag jobs. Since he left the merchant marine for dry land, he had rarely felt the need to roam alone. He thanked her, when she was finished, and ran his hand over the black, imitation leather case to check that the material and the seams were still holding together.

In the car, she talked with animation, she was collecting money for the clean-up in the North Sea, for the scientific work, so that the fish stocks could be replaced, the bird populations protected.

She admitted that there was an air of hopelessness, people had been shocked once, and now they just did not want to know.

The government was contributing millions, but it was not enough, much was being spent on out-of-work fishermen and oilmen; the environment did not have a vote. Seals were still being washed ashore as corpses, dead birds found in thick crude. For miles around the destroyed rigs, the sea bed was a black desert. The size of the destruction, even now, could only be estimated. Even though much had evaporated, and much had been broken up by the wind and wave, too much had escaped before the wells could be blocked. Even now, there was seepage enough to ruin the remaining fishing grounds for decades, if not for ever . . . The more she talked, the worse Rosie made it seem. Of course, fish prices had risen – you could not buy cod – but much more was at stake.

Stu listened to her anger, her concern for the sea that he knew, as much as he knew anything, far better than she. He did not disagree, he just did not feel the same way. He nodded, watched London in the early evening go about its business.

She changed the subject. They talked about his plans. He told her he was taking a trip round France, following the footsteps of his favourite painter, Claude Monet.

At Victoria they learned that the Paris train would be late. Young people wearing luminescent rucksacks and brightly coloured clothes trucked to and fro across the concourse, talking French, German, Italian. Jeans and jeans, the international language, spoken by students and school parties.

For want of choice, they took seats in a buffet where the tannoy penetrated with the resonance of truth, overcoming the spirited chatter of the foreign groups, the couples and class-loads that were waiting to stop waiting.

The dimmed table light did not flatter Rosie's face. Nobody was growing younger, but it was only on occasion that you noticed.

Did she want an awful tea, an awful coffee or an awful drink? British Rail would oblige. They had to have something; sitting was not free. He bought a pot of tea and a packet of custard creams to disguise the taste. Even so, she winced.

When would he be back?

Maybe one week, maybe two, he did not know for sure.

Her hair was greying.

He said he was sorry for, well, for everything. He had only been trying to do his best, make a contribution. He did not say to what, but she knew what he meant: to society, to the generality. It was why he did what he did, how he explained the efforts he had made in the course of the years, the sacrifices. Now he apologised.

The train to Dover was to depart shortly, platform twelve. A sleeper service was available from Calais.

In the buffet, people start to rise, only to be replaced by others: rucksacks meet in a mid-buffet squeeze.

They watch the struggle in silence, then they rise from the two-seat-one-table contraption that has locked them in discomfort.

A long queue has formed at the ticket barrier, people are worried about missing the connecting ferry; BR employees are examining the train, to what end, nobody knows, the old carriages promise little but discomfort when the train finally leaves for the sea. No bar, no heating, few lights. Yet the queue is patient, people are queuing here as they never would in their own country; midnight nears.

Rosie holds his hand, kisses his cheek, he kisses her forehead; she must go. A final kiss. The queue starts to move.

'It will be different when you get back. Promise.'

There might have been tears in his eyes; when he turned to look at the platform from inside the train, she was gone; as the train pulled out of the station, with its old-fashioned rattle and old-fashioned discomfort, he heard her words about the oil, the sea bed, the birds and the fishes.

He left the train at Dover town, took a cheap room at a seafront B&B, then caught the first coastal train of the morning. He was following a hunch.

He descended in one of the sleepier of the bathchair resorts bequeathed by the Victorians as a monument to their desire for fresh air and sunlight.

Mr Jocelyn Knowle had agreed to meet him without hesitation. The voice on the telephone had rung clear and Stu had some hope that this visit, though long-delayed, might offer an insight into the feud between the Marchwoods and the Grotes.

Though in his eighty-fifth year, Knowle was not above wearing an extravagant hat and a flowered cravat, nor above carrying a silver-knobbed cane used more for twirling than support.

They took a bench-seat in the garden, beside a neo-gothic

extravagance with extensive sea-views. The old so-and-so lived in great style, thanks to his 20 per cent of Knowle & Co. When Stu had seen the numbers in the accounts, they had seemed, at first glance, to mean almost nothing; yet this was one of the greatest pensions anyone received, anywhere.

'Why didn't you leave for one of the smarter tax havens?'

Knowle drawled a reply: 'When my mother died, I went round the world, you know, but I was always glad to return here. Home sweet home, and all that.'

The mater had died in the house; now Mr Jocelyn was pampered by a cook, a nurse, a maid and a full complement of gardeners. Given the funds available, it was not excessive.

'Mr Blythe, you know, the former Lloyd's underwriter, asks to be remembered to you.'

In fact several months had passed. Stu hoped Blythe was still hale and hearty.

Knowle smiled at Blythe's name, there were not many of his generation still soldiering on, you had to be grateful for every day.

He had reason to be grateful to Mr Robert Marchwood and his brother, Stu prompted, somewhat drily. This did not disturb Mr Jocelyn, who was happy to find someone who would listen to his life story; he had all the time in the world to remember as the morning shadows shortened.

'It could all have been quite different. Rex Marchwood, the brothers' father, steered the brokerage into disaster, having over-estimated his own abilities, wasted money needlessly and, ultimately, created too many enemies. Of course, he was very winning, in his way.'

During the war, Rex Marchwood had made the most of a junior position in Whitehall working for a junior minister and member of the nobility, Lord Yelland of Whitstable. Yelland took a shine to Marchwood, made him his personal assistant, had him accompany him everywhere, even to certain houses in Bloomsbury and Soho. 'It was there that he and I met. He had charm and charisma; people fell for him; he knew how to exploit their affection.'

He dealt, too, in everything that was not readily available, foodstuffs, whisky, wines; acted as pawnbroker and illicit supplier; knew people in many walks of life, through friends of friends, through the ministry. Kept a family in the suburbs, to which he repaired at weekends.

A smile. 'For those who knew, that merely heightened his youthful charm.'

Stu asked, steadily: 'How did you become . . . business partners?'

Unlike Marchwood, who had been excused service on some specious grounds, Knowle had always had genuine health problems and so had continued his work at Lloyd's during the war, where he ran a one-man brokership. 'Mostly car insurance and objets d'art.'

Rex brought him business from friends, unofficially, at first, becoming, after the war, first an employee, then a full partnership.

'He was not a natural intimate of the Room . . .'

This meant, Stu assumed, that Rex had not attended Eton or Harrow.

'His accent and manner had been changed during the war; he was a great man for gaining people's confidence.'

'Not a bruiser like his older son.'

'Well, yes and no.'

'How did he become a partner?'

Neither Knowle nor his mother were well; Rex managed to attract a great deal of business, moving into big ticket lines, particularly marine insurance. 'Yet he wore two watches on his wrists, so he would always have something else to sell. Apart from himself, of course.'

The old man laughed.

Even as partner, his demands did not stop, apparently. Rex threatened to leave unless Knowle gave him more equity, made him this or that or the other. Knowle had felt pressured, disappointed, claimed Rex made his life impossible, saw him undermine his authority both inside and outside the broker-ship.

This continued for some years, until Knowle felt he was only a shadow of himself, until he could see the end approaching. The partnership became a limited liability company; Knowle took an adequate pay-off and equity stake, protected by a variety of covenants, and then left, expecting to see disaster strike.

Probably, Stu suspected, he had thought to buy the business back later, for nothing, when it had all but collapsed. He refrained from making the suggestion.

Rex Marchwood had been an effective salesman, but not a

good businessman; every new contract seemed to bring new costs, new staff, a reason for celebration; he lived above his means in order to impress. The contracts themselves were often unfavourable, loss-making deals struck through sheer inattention to detail. Even as he left, Knowle saw the debts mounting, the crash coming. He skittled away and waited for the bang.

For revenge, perhaps?

'So Rex Marchwood killed himself rather than face ruin?' Stu asked.

There was a silence as both men shaded their eyes to peer at the grey sea, watching the slow, uneventful drama of the passage of container ships and tankers in slow procession through the English channel.

'He was, in my humble opinion, not a man who contemplated self-slaughter.'

Wilson tried to translate: A man desperate for money, who would blanch at little and stop at nothing. A ruthless bastard who kept his bourgeois morality locked up at home.

'I send the boys the same Christmas card every year, you know,' Knowle chuckled.

This still had not answered the question. Stu waited, patiently, grateful for garrulous mercies.

'Of course, everybody's dead from those days, more or less. A survivor like myself sees the irony. The brilliant young always seem to go first and to be lamented longest, because they have had no time to disappoint. At the end, only the boring old farts are left.'

Stu jumped at this and they both laughed.

No, Mr Jocelyn had not forgotten they were talking about Rex Marchwood. The coroner had decided: suicide while the balance of mind was disturbed. It was claimed, Knowle recalled, that Rex had behaved unusually during the last few weeks of his life – as if he were under stress. He had talked to someone about death, in an offhand way. Yet Knowle himself had seen or heard nothing of the sort – not that he had been around all that much but, a month before, he had seen Rex toughing it out with the bank, arguing with clients and underwriters and generally acting as if he was there to stay.

The ships appeared to be drawn along by the thread of the horizon, like a string of wooden ducks; the sea offered an intense calm to a grey day.

Knowle said: 'Rex wanted to merge our brokerage with Cecil, Russell & Grote, because, he claimed, they needed his financial expertise. In fact, he needed their assets. And he knew, I suspect, that Stephen Grote had been less than scrupulous when saving CRG from its creditors. In short, there'd been funny business and Rex, having made it his business to know, had a lever.'

'And that would not have been his only lever. His style was threats and imprecations, laced with charm and gifts. Yet he didn't perceive the dangers. I introduced him to the Lutine lodge and he created problems there, too, always seeking his own advantage. I saw that. People either loved him or detested him.'

Sometimes both, evidently.

'You know Grote?' Wilson asked.

'I knew the Grotes: Stephen and his father Richard. Quiet, charming people, the son had more character than the father. Their company was in trouble, everybody knew that. And Stephen saved it, by some miracle which, people whispered, involved the use of clients' funds.'

Stu asked: 'Did Rex Marchwood blackmail Stephen Grote?'

'I'm sure, if he'd thought it might help, he would have tried.'

Stu looked at the old man's face under the black hat, the eyes fixed on the sea. There were some things Mr Jocelyn would not say, not even when everybody was dead.

FIVE

DONNA GROTE WAS staying in London. Stephen had seen to that; there were to be no more arguments between them about this or any other matter. She was not going with him to the Riviera this year: her cases were staying in the basement.

She would miss it. She adored lazy days, old olive groves, watching the sun rise from a white terrace high above the sea; loved strolling through the local markets with Stephen, buying lavender, rosemary, bay-leaves. Forgetting London, for a while.

They always stayed on Cap d'Antibes, with John Devies and his wife Hettie, who had a palace, with a wide sweeping view of the bay. A place inherited from a grandfather who had, it seemed, half-invented the peninsula, filling tropical gardens with exotic plants and trees that flourished, affording sanctuary to astonished visitors who arrived from the over-filled, heat-ridden coastal road.

About to be deprived of all this, Donna invited her sister for strawberries and champagne, when the weather seemed set fair and Stephen was away somewhere. The police had even returned his passport.

Mary-Ellen accepted willingly, and they talked about this and that, by the fountain in the green-fronded courtyard garden. At least the value of gossip seemed to improve with age; it was one of those patent remedies of Dr X, tried and attested by the crowned heads of Europe, sold with a neat cork as a tonic to all ills, particularly refreshing when rinsed down with spa water or champagne.

Yet Donna knew her sister well enough to see she intended more than gossip; Mary-Ellen was troubled; so Donna let her work her way through some favourite themes until she found her real subject: Lloyd's, its victims and crimes. The list of the former was long, and champagne always brought the best out of Mary-Ellen's tongue: there was, she said, famous Marcus the Architect, with the sickly wife; there was Angus the founder and onetime owner of a perfume and cosmetics group called Highlite, who was due to be switched off; there was Penelope, bookish secretary to Alexander Wilmot-Greaves, who had started out just about comfortable and would end up old and destitute; there was Mark the Golfer, whose irons had been shortened, his fairways blocked, his holes plugged.

The list was impressive. People were being stripped, piece by piece, of everything: first, the second home would go, then the boat or paintings, the stocks, the gilts, the other savings, the pension fund, then the private education, followed by the main house with the drive and acres, then the cars, and finally the wife and children. That was the moment, someone had commented, when you noticed you were not just bust, but broken. It might be, Mary-Ellen said, hard to cry for them, but you would not wish the experience on your worst enemy; you might not like the fact, but the gutter is the gutter.

Donna did not dispute this; she was in no position to do so; the table in the room behind them would, at auction, fetch enough to house a large family in some comfort, even in London, if on the wrong side of the river. But she did suggest, not entirely unseriously, that going bust was occasionally good for the health of the system. In the States, the banks were bust, the Savings & Loans were bust, the Treasury was bust. It was the best worst-kept secret in the world; going bust had tradition in the States, it was the way the West was won and the way the Reds were beaten. So maybe a few billions down Lloyd's steel tubes didn't matter.

The polemic did not cut much ice with Mary-Ellen, who was busy working with support groups of bled-white names and, more or less openly, fighting Stephen and his friends; still, she helped herself to more of his finest Krug champagne.

'Are you locked in?' Mary-Ellen asked, lifting her sunglasses.

'No,' Donna said, 'In fact, I'm happier than I've ever been.'

There had been fewer surprises than one might imagine; Stephen had settled down to a vigorous middle-to-old age; it was a situation that had, only briefly, been disturbed by the arrests. Then, that was over now, more or less.

Mary-Ellen lifted the champagne flute to admire the handcut crystal, which was ever so slightly imperfect. Would Donna mind seeing Marshall that afternoon?

It was a strange request, but that had been the purpose of her visit, and in an hour, broad-backed Marshall arrived, wearing light grey affluence and a summer tan. Donna kissed her favourite bankrupt and he laughed lightly, well, not yet. Her sister had, for all her complaints, not fared badly with her man.

Marshall refused a glass of Krug and grasped a gin tumbler, while she fetched herself iced coffee, with ice-cream and lashings of whipped cream; to hell with it, she was tall enough to survive the consequences.

'You've come to tell me I've married a dangerous monster and that, if I had an ounce of good sense, I'd walk straight out of this gorgeous house and back to Eaton Square.'

Which reminded her, the post still had to be fetched.

She saw that she had swatted a not-yet-delivered ball clean into the outfield, but Marshall managed to smile.

Where was Stephen?

Italy, she thought, then Switzerland. Yes, Zurich.

Marshall proceeded to relate a string of quite horrid Italian stories, brutish and unbelievable, in his clipped, sardonic way.

She would just love another ice, and helped herself, consoling Marshall with a finger of colourless liquid and a hand of fizz.

'Can you prove any of this stuff?' she asked, casually, while he let ice-balls plop into his glass. A couple of blue-bottles danced around the terrace, frisky from cruising the neighbour's trash cans.

He laughed. Nobody was going to drag cardinals, politicians, the whole ruling class of Italy, through the courts; besides, the Company never prospered from publicity.

This was a weak excuse, given the scale of his accusations, but Donna remembered the name of the bank, the Cristòforo. One evening after the opera, *The Magic Flute* at Covent Garden, the name had cropped up. The boys had had their usual meeting, while the wives waited here, in the sitting room upstairs, drinking nightcaps to the Queen of the Night. Then their pampered men had arrived, their voices subdued; one of them had lost money, she thought Fortescue, and that was before the crash. By the bookcase she had heard Wilmot-Greaves express his condolences and Neil had shrugged: 'Seventy or eighty, no matter, old man.' She remembered, from later, the way they stumbled over the Italian word: Cristòforo.

They had set up other banking arrangements, she knew that; a bank had been found in the principality. It was never actually said in front of her, what they were doing, yet she overheard, this and that, until she knew. There was a bank in Zurich, too – 'la banque d'Europe occidentale'. It was all to do with transferring funds between markets and countries, across the world.

She told Marshall this, helped herself to more ice cream.

Did she know, he asked her, that her friends had moved twenty million dollars out of the Cristòforo the week before it crashed? One hundred million had poured in and out during the previous six months, from around the world.

'It was the place where they pooled funds and income from around the world, where dirty money became clean, where they could walk in the front door and draw money that nobody knew was theirs,' Marshall said. 'Now they have two places, one on the Côte d'Azur, one in Zurich.'

So the friends, for all their silly rituals and god-fearing nonsense, were just money-men, linked to Cosa Nostra, to the Holy See, financing arms deals that never existed between states which have no knowledge of each other. Siphoning money from Lloyd's.

Donna tried to feel upset about this, and failed.

After all, New York, Tokyo, London bristled with people hustling to make their million. Maybe the Americans were the loudest, the most aggressive, the toughest, but others know their way around the streets. Like everyone else, Stephen was trying to push the system as far as it would go. They did not hang around the backstreets, wait for bullion vans or rob little old ladies; they just took their cut.

Marshall sort of snorted.

She asked him – the great names of the American dream, the legends – did they earn their money by caring for orphans?

These were Stephen's arguments. He liked order; together, he and his friends provided order where the system had none, order within order. They had closed out the communists, when they were a threat; this was a historic achievement. Stephen had played his part in this, together with Johnny the Cypriot, otherwise known as Ioànnis Kolokotrònis, who helped make the Med safe for Coca-Cola. But every deal soon becomes

297

history, because very soon nobody cares who took the biggest cut on the deal before last, because there are always bigger and brighter deals to come. Tycoons die like everyone else and, some say, maybe a little sooner, but that does not matter. Freedom does.

Mary-Ellen rescued the gin bottle from Marshall's outstretched hand, substituting spa water.

'Drugs are evil,' he said, trying a new tack, as if someone they knew actually did drugs. Well, one of his daughters had certainly tried hash. In any case, everybody in Washington had been high at some time or other. Donna agreed with Marshall's qualms. She said: 'We both know that the agency would never use drug funding for operations. Or sell arms to one country Uncle Sam does not approve of to finance a covert war against a country the President loathes. A war expressly forbidden by the Senate.'

'That was necessary.'

'That's what I mean. If freedom increases the flow of greenbacks, freedom's just fine by me.'

'Well, I never. You used to be so uptight, Donna. What's happened to Miss Chalky?'

'She got laid.'

Marshall choked on water bubbles.

The door slammed, when it was not expected, and Stephen was on the terrace, suffering from the heat. A juice, please.

Words of welcome, cordial, were exchanged.

Marshall had been just going, before being waylaid by Donna's gin bottle, ha, ha.

It was only after an extensive ritual of politenesses that Stephen and Donna saw Marshall and Mary-Ellen leave. And it was only an hour or so later that Donna suggested Stephen might pay Marshall's losses, just to create peace in their time. Having defended her husband's morals, she insinuated, she thought it only fair to raid his cash. Besides, she did not want to spend her last years at war with her sister and brother-in-law.

'How much is the damage?' Stephen asked, amiably enough, as if he did not already know.

Donna thought of a large number, doubled it: 'Three million.' Then added, just to make sure: 'Pounds sterling.'

Stephen agreed that this was large, too large. In fact he was blunt: 'No, certainly not.'

298

'You are being stubborn.' She was, after all, paying half the bill already.

'No, I darned well am not.'

Well, then, she guessed he could head south without her and welcome. He thanked her for being so magnanimous.

Six

OF COURSE CONNIE had known it had to come. Ever since she had succumbed to the blandishments of the local education authority, ever since she had thrown in the towel and agreed to retire, she knew.

For weeks now, too, she had had to pretend that nothing was happening, that nothing special was being planned – even though she had her own little thing to organise, for the last day at school, her own last day at school.

Yet it all still came as a tremendous surprise. She had not been allowed into the hall for a couple of days, on pain of death or worse, while stocks of paper, paint, glue and cardboard were run down, while the teachers' common room was loud with the clatter of plans and plots.

Jill duly knocked on her door, at the agreed time, and the ritual began. Connie was led down concrete-floored corridors until she saw smiling colleagues, heard giggles, pushed open two blue swing doors – and there was the whole school, row upon row of heads turned towards her.

The newly tuned piano roared off and small voices welled to a large greeting: 'For she's a jolly good fellow, for she's a jolly good fellow . . .'

GOODBYE MRS SANDERSON. The words glared down at her from a banner hung above the stage; then beneath, in smaller letters: WE WILL MISS YOU.

More than twenty years, nearly thirty.

'. . . and so say all of us.'

Now she was standing on the stage; Jill made her take a seat, there was more to come and for once she was to sit still and listen.

Jill began by holding a large scrapbook aloft. This was the

Lime Grove and Connie Story, the tale of how, all those years ago, Mrs Sanderson came to this school and of how much, during all those years, the school had changed. In the scrapbook, the older children had painted scenes from this story and had pasted in photographs from the school archives.

She rose to thank the children for all their efforts, promised to look at every picture carefully, told them how wonderful it had been, for her to help and teach children; she hoped some of them would become teachers also. She smiled and smiled.

A hymn followed: 'Now thank we all our God, with heart, and hands, and voices . . .' A prayer was said.

A stooped, grey-haired man rose. This was the head of the local education authority.

'It is always a sad day to lose an experienced and able head teacher; it is particularly sad for us to lose Mrs Sanderson, who for so long has brought such commitment and expertise to Lime Grove . . .'

The man continued to drone on. He was not speaking to the children, but to the few parents who were sitting at the rear of the hall; Oh God. Please give me the engraved salver and sit down.

'. . . so, in conclusion, I would like to thank Mrs Sanderson . . .'

Loud applause for the end of the speech. Connie rose, slightly stiff from the plywood chair, thanked the man profusely for his kind words, shook his hand, admired the platter, returned to her seat.

Mrs Cornelia Sanderson, head teacher, Lime Grove School, in recognition of a hell of a long time.

Now Jill nodded to the pianist, who struck up a sprightly tune as a group of older pupils emerged from the kitchens at the rear of the hall, carrying a very large cake encrusted with white icing, candles and pink greetings. And there was still more to come in the kitchens.

Connie widened her eyes in delight, stood up and whispered to the hall, pointing to her girth: 'Ooh, how delicious. But I'm sure it's not just for me.'

Laughter and signs of delight from the audience.

The first cake was placed upon a table in front of the dais; the mistress of the kitchens approached, with pinny, knife and paper napkins. Connie read the inscription: GOODBYE AND

GOOD LUCK. She stepped down from the dais, cut the cake, leaving the distribution to others; classes filed up, one by one, to take their slices.

Jill stood up again. 'Just before you munch your way back to your classrooms, I have just one little thing more to announce. The children, the teachers and the parents wanted to give Mrs Sanderson a special present, to help her remember us. To help us make our choice, I had to ask Connie, Mrs Sanderson, very discreetly. And do you know what she said?'

The piano roared into action again.

Half a dozen children trooped out of the kitchen, carrying Connie's present. Suitcases! One, two, three, four, five!

Jill continued: 'Yes, Mrs Sanderson asked for some new suitcases, since she had said she wanted to travel.'

Connie was bemused, she had not expected people to be so generous. One or two would have been more than enough.

'Thank you very much, Jill, thank you to you all! You've all been terribly kind and I will miss you all, yes, every last one. Thank you very much.'

No, she would not let her eyes moisten; she would not succumb. She calmly took her seat, with a very fixed smile.

Soon, more than half the school had taken a piece of cake, wrapped in a napkin, disorder was descending, crumbs were being freely distributed, there was a queue of children bearing presents – pictures, models, writing, all in her honour. She shook clammy hands, patted heads, encouraged. By the time the queue had passed the hall was more or less empty, the kitchen staff were clearing up.

Twenty years and more were enough. She looked at the scrapbook, the salver, the suitcases, and the banner over the dais: GOODBYE MRS SANDERSON.

She picked up her trusty handbell: the End Of Term Fête could begin.

There were stalls outside in the playground; things to buy, things to sell, things to play, things to throw away. All in a good cause.

At the coconut shy, she thought of sick MacNulty, slick Grote and sleek Fortescue, in no particular order, extended her arm in anger, aimed and missed, aimed and missed again. The round hairy heads remained unmoved on their thin elongated bodies.

She was to see Fortescue and the hardship committee at

Lloyd's, soon. They would determine how much money they would allow her. Meanwhile she had to keep a grip on herself. This was her great day.

Even the sun was shining.

'You've not stuck them on, have you?' Connie joked.

'Try hitting them,' the parent-cum-stallholder said, lifting one of the nuts to show that no glue was involved. Loose heads, every one.

She bought three more balls, readjusted her cardigan, picked a victim and, with her first ball, scuffed the floor. With her second the rear of the tent ballooned. With her third a coconut wobbled in its stand, before falling.

SEVEN

IT WAS TO be pleasure first, work later.

When Stewart Wilson awoke, the train had pulled him into another world, filled with burnt-straw fields, sparse trees and dust: the South. Shuttered villages were still asleep beside vineyards and as the hazy city slid closer, as the overnight sleeper to the Blue Coast drew into the station, the early morning cool evaporated and the new day began baking the sky china-blue.

For some days, he had been living an uneasy dream, travelling by train and sleeper, staying in cheap *pensions*, eating cheaply, following the Master's steps: Etretat, Giverny, the Creuse. But this place offered peace, he knew it as he smelt the morning air, having watched the landscape arise from dawn, feeling strangely older for the sight. He left his case in a metal locker at the station, and understood why so many before him, before and after Claude Monet, had been enchanted, too.

The day was Thursday. The conference was to start near here with a ball on Friday evening, just along the coast. He wanted to look around first. He needed to think. The grey-blue sky offered him the calm before the storm. He also had an appointment. An assignation with the *poste restante*.

At a café near the station, he ordered a coffee and a *petit pain au chocolat*. The pavements were being sprayed and brushed by large machines; palm-lined roads were starting to fill with impatient motorists, yet the waking city appeared civil and very orderly.

He did not speak French. Not a dicky-bird, not even a tweet. Of course, he had his books. French in a day, in a week, in a month. The natives were, on the whole, tolerant; but he was a bit of an outcast here, which he found difficult to accept. At his age life was only bearable if he was treated with respect.

Nevertheless, he liked the country and the people. The food, even the stuff he could afford, was fine, the wine was their wine and he could see the women had style. The trains were tremendous too – clean, efficient, punctual.

People rushed in and out of the bar, gulped down an espresso before disappearing; they worked hard here. No sign of slacking in the sun.

He bought a postcard of the city for Rosie. Wish you were here. Tomlinson would have to forego his seasonal greetings, ditto the DGs, past and present; he had told Tomlinson he needed a spot of trout fishing in Scotland. He was not about to tell the office he was here, and had a job to do. Even Keef did not know.

He took a local train heading along the coast and soon the heat had him in its grasp; his clothes stuck to him, his hair was damp. Yet the sea was many washes of blue, dotted by white sails.

The four-carriage train drew into a small station, a glass-sided waiting room squeezed between track and road. He walked out into blinding light, a lone man.

The force of the sun and the heat made him seek yet another café as soon as he had found the small post office and pocketed the letter that was waiting for him. He contained his impatience until he had taken a seafront seat in this seafront town which resembled, according to his much-praised guide book, Bournemouth.

He ripped open the letter and found another photograph of the fuse-box, and a scarcely credible extract from the coroner's report. Also the address of a *pension garnie*, where he would receive further details, the following afternoon, Friday. In the meantime, he had a little time to enjoy the locality, secure in the knowledge that Grote and his friends were hereabouts.

He looked about him and, again, saw nobody take an especial interest.

It was, definitely, a beautiful spot. Remembering a visit to England's Bournemouth, Stu could see that great town was never quite like this, a fact that, presumably, had made thousands of Englanders risk the journey here, along with Queen Victoria not to mention the Russian Czar, several minor German princes, the Aga Khan, among others. Further along the coast, they had built a jetty to import English turf, just to make sure the grass was green enough for croquet.

305

He must order something.

The ubiquitous waiter in black with the ubiquitous small metal tray stood beside him. Stu breathed deeply: this was worth it. The view. He paid by ordering a café au lait.

Monet had chosen picture postcard settings, following his dealer's advice.

This was one of them.

A coffee arrived, and he ordered a slug of colourless aniseed before settling into his seat. He pulled out his bible from the bag, the Master's complete works, in plastic-covered softback. On the page the scene was flat, the colours reproduced badly, but with force: yet there was no way that Monet had painted what he saw.

He had, perhaps, tried instead to *convey* what he had seen. Stu leafed through the book, seeking answers. There had been several visits, notably in 1884 and 1888. Once with Renoir. And Monet had come here at his dealer's suggestion: to make money. Degas had said that was their sole aim. After years of misery, why not? The death of a wife. Monet had added white, that made the canvas even brighter: today, it glowed in the Metropolitan Museum of Modern Art in New York.

Monet believed he was telling the truth. The haystacks, Rouen Cathedral, the Valley of the Creuse, Marchwood's Monet. Multiple truths? The changing truth? Yet he sacrificed, worked in all weathers, convinced he was obtaining a hard and fast truth.

He was not totally wrong. You could still see, after a hundred years, a sense of place somehow contained in the brush strokes and colours. Even on the badly printed page, the image was both here and not here; a personal vision of a truth.

The Pernod arrived with two ice cubes and a bottle which could be misused on a bad night. The waiter hung around.

'Monsieur is interested in art?' The man's question made Stu feel as if he had left his flies open.

'Many painters, many writers here. Have been.'

Stu smiled.

'If you look, you can see.'

Stu nodded. He replied: 'It would be nice to take it home.'

'Ah, monsieur, it is the one thing you cannot buy here.'

The waiter was called to another table. Stu was irritated, bitten by an unidentified pest. He knew Devies had a bloody great house here, not to mention a bloody great boat. There was a mystery how he could afford these. The boat was worth seven or eight figures, the house a handsome eight, yet according to the Horcum accounts, he picked up a small six-figure sum as chairman – not enough for a decent pad in Surrey, let alone a thick slice of paradise, complete with mooring costs and upkeep. There was inherited wealth, true, and good money from underwriting on the right syndicates. Given the order of the day, Stu reckoned Devies was effectively outside the reach of the law. Under the circumstances, only the stupid were honest.

Blythe had told him he used to mark brokers from one to ten; he dealt only with the four to sixes, the ones and twos were too stupid, while the sevens were dodgy and the eights and nines were crooks. Marchwood was a ten.

Proof? Laws? Convincing a jury would even give God a migraine.

Time to move on.

He walked along the promenade, took a seat in the sunshine until a coach rolled into sight bearing the magic name of the principality. He boarded and paid. Some tourists, some natives joined him; there was space to sit alone. Other magic names drifted past, magic places, edged with palms, pines and the sea. Tired from the sun, the alcohol and too little food, his head slipped away into a bumpy sleep, the sun died in his absence, then it was time to descend. Another railway station, streets under white lights, neon signs in the middle distance. He knew that anywhere here was likely to be exorbitant; he saw the words: Hôtel de la Gare.

Somehow, he struck a deal: a room.

Somehow, he deposited his case by the metal-framed bed, locked the door, extracted a package wrapped in plastic from his case, went to the window, listened at the door before stumbling downstairs, feeling the weight of the small, triangular package in the small of his back, between jacket and waist-belt. Somehow, he found his way into the station, into a long, badly lit corridor. He slid the package into a metal left-luggage locker, found change, turned a key in an unoiled lock, quit the station.

Inside the package was a Smith & Wesson, standard police issue. Stu disliked guns, but could always find one weapon if need be. This was Keef's gun, stored in Capri, inside an old car exhaust, kept for special occasions. It was oiled and greased and there was one box of ammunition.

When he woke, sometime between dawn and the first train, he heard the sound of early traffic, discovered a pane was missing from the window of his cut-price bedroom, saw the shadow of high-rise buildings.

The locker key was still inside his shoe; he had taped it there, a small, troublesome reminder of his anger and his intent.

EIGHT

NEIL FORTESCUE, NOW chairman-elect of Lloyd's of London, had hoped to fly at midday by Lear jet to the Riviera that Friday, after the meeting of the Lloyd's hardship committee for the names who were unable or unwilling to pay their losses. Unfortunately, his plans were wrecked; others had had other ideas, others who could not, reasonably, be refused.

The Governor of the Bank of England, whom everyone called the Cricketer, summoned him at lunchtime into Threadneedle Street. The matter was urgent: the Bank of England had been informed by the banks that they were worried sick, and the Cricketer started the conversation by reeling off a few well-known Lloyd's statistics: seven billions lost in two years, more than the annual GNP of Bolivia or Oman or Senegal, four or five thousand bankrupt names, total due to the banks two billions, give or take one hundred million. Another loss, a couple of billions, perhaps, due next year. 'That more or less the size of it, Fortescue?'

Neil Fortescue had nodded, ran a hand through red hair. He could have added: total potential liabilities, thirty billions, total capital, fifteen. Finding fifteen billions from future profits or the taxman would not be easy. He did not think it wise to mention these sums.

Even without this knowledge, the Cricketer still clicked his tongue. 'If only the property business weren't in such a thorough mess . . . Anyway, Downing Street is expecting you, within the hour. Better buck up your ideas, old man. My regards to Stephen Grote.'

Downing Street had let Fortescue explain how his ideas might work; they also gave him tea. The PM and a note-taking aide named Bill listened for half an hour while the proposals were explaned: the introduction of corporate capital, greater protection for names, reduction of overheads . . . They sat in frayed armchairs in a room which might have been the directors' lounge at a firm on its uppers.

Fortescue concluded: 'We have had our difficulties; but we can fight back.'

The PM smiled throughout, then remarked: 'The Governor of the Bank of England seems to take a different view. Even though he knows only part of the truth. How large is this year's loss – another five billions, six?'

Fortescue tried to protest.

The statistics were repeated, even the crack about the GNP of Senegal, but the pay-off line was different: 'And your plan assumes you will start making money, let me see, a billion in three year's time, to wash everything out of the system. I like that: a billion profit. Good idea.'

It took some time for Fortescue to see the joke. He tried smiling.

The PM continued: 'How many billions of losses are still in the system because of the rigs?'

Fortescue failed to smile.

'What are your liabilities and your assets?'

Fortescue failed to answer.

'Look, the long and short of the matter is you're bust. You know it, we know it. You need a billion just to appear solvent, which we have not got . . .'

'I thought you might want to see this,' Fortescue interrupted, placing a document in front of the PM, who hesitated, picked up the paper and then fell silent.

The room's walls were lined with original, framed, political caricatures, some modern, some old: Gillray, Rowlandson, Low. Fortescue rose to contemplate one or two of Low's masterful lampoons of Hitler, while allowing the Prime Minister time to gather breath and his aide to read the memorandum.

'So these men will be bankrupted. . . ?' the PM said, with a gesture at the list of names. Bankruptcy would disqualify all twenty as Members of Parliament.

He knew, of course, that there was a problem, others had gone already, but Fortescue's list came as a shock because of the sheer size of the losses. At the last General Election, the

Government had been returned to power with a majority of twenty-one. Now there would shortly be by-elections, and the Government was decidedly unpopular. No seat was safe, the publicity would be awful, morale would evaporate. Yes, the list revealed something of a problem.

'As you see,' Fortescue replied curtly. 'Unless they have offshore assets unknown to us or the Revenue.'

His memorandum did not bother to state the political consequences. He recalled Stephen's dictum: the importance of power to a politician is surpassed only by the importance of beauty to a lovely woman, yet both are destined to be short-lived and to end unhappily.

'And there is . . .' Fortescue hesitated, searching for the right words '. . . the small matter of the Vice President, who has been the recipient of kindness above and beyond the call of duty. People are beginning to talk. After all, the involvement of the Vice President is known. He is not someone one can overlook.'

He lit a cigarette, found an ashtray, stared at the aide, who looked away. The PM was evidently unprepared to be despatched to a world of long-forgotten strife and stress, to the cartoonists' graveyard. Nor had he forgotten the problem at the White House.

'There has to be a way round this,' the PM insisted.

Fortescue took his seat, helped himself to a few drops of cold tea. No more, thank you.

Well, they could either provide secret backing to the individuals concerned, allowing them not to make these financial interests public, or they could support Lloyd's itself. The Vice President had been helped . . . Fortescue shrugged his shoulders.

This produced a snort of disapproval. 'You need a billion just to keep afloat; the money is simply not there; we are contemplating charging people for hospital beds, cutting child benefit, reducing pensions.'

Since the North Sea storms, the economy had been placed on a sound footing, there were no tax increases proposed, no reductions in expenditure intended, there was no balance of payments crisis; well, that at least was the truth that had won the last election. The facts could not be worse.

Fortescue looked at the PM and saw a greyer grey man. 'We want you to keep going, that's the message. Sit it out for as long as you can. If you help our people, we will see if we can help you. No promises.'

The wisdom of politicians. Fortescue refused point-blank. They could not make an exception for every politician; the Vice President was liability enough, especially since he considered himself badly treated even though his losses had been capped.

The chairman-elect of Lloyd's and the Prime Minister argued for a time, making threats and counter-threats, to no avail. And to no conclusion. They did not shake hands as Fortescue left.

NINE

STEPHEN GROTE HAD had a brief word with Tony MacNulty; they had agreed to meet at eleven that Friday in *le jardin exotique*, a mountainside garden overlooking sea, bay and the highrise principality, where exotica from round the globe flourished extravagantly, formed into bowers, avenues, summer-quadrants filled with succulents, climbers and native citrus trees, heavy with the scent of lemons.

Tony was, however, nowhere to be seen. Stephen surveyed the cacti and the prickly-pears until the sun became too much, even beneath a panama hat, forcing him to retire to a tree-shaded bougainvillea grove from where he admired the port below. The conference proper started in the early evening.

Perhaps, just perhaps, he had said twelve o'clock, meaning eleven. If he was slipping, this proved some of his great theses about life: nothing ever improves, we start as imbeciles and end as idiots.

Stephen was not pleased with himself. On the ample grey jetty of the outer harbour, he could see a dozen of the white boats known as mega-yachts: as long as ten or twenty Bentleys laid end to end, and far more expensive. Radar masts, satellite aerials, swimming pools and Lord knows what else being transported piggy-back.

John Devies had wanted to buy a white mega-toy, but Stephen had shot that down with a ground-to-air missile: 'It only takes one inspector from the Revenue, just one!' John recalled what Stephen had done to Alec Wilmot-Greaves, when he choppered his way around the Alps; even John Devies could be unnerved by Stephen's rare outbursts of anger. Like Alec, John had beaten an ungainly retreat and obeyed Stephen's laws: discretion, simplicity, security, control.

313

Hard to know whether that would now suffice.

The biggest of the monsters belonged to an American property magnate called Murphy or, rather, to Murphy's bankers. Murphy was famed for his gilded Manhattan real estate, his glitzy casinos and his pure gold debts. It was a frequently repeated canard that, before Murphy went a-wooing, he talked to his bankers to have his alimony rescheduled. In fact, he told the press so the pictures would be professional, too.

Even Stephen could not deny that Murphy's white monster shone whiter, brighter and hungrier than any other beast in sight. It was here that Murphy discovered would-be starlets and let them twinkle.

Though few spoke of him now, Ioánnis Kolokotrónis, the greatest son of a Cypriot shipping dynasty, had made Murphy look like an amateur. Stephen had known him for decades, could still recall the first offer of friendship, signed with a slug of ouzo: 'You call me Johnny, I call you Gentleman, OK?' That had been aboard an almost modest yacht, moored off Stephen's one-time North African base, where Arab contacts and politicians could talk politics, do business and drink with young friends. That had been the start of a great friendship, the basis of Stephen's greatest triumph.

Johnny's boat, the boat that was his home for decades, would have dwarfed Murphy's mega-yacht, in size, in tastelessness. The two thousand tonne *Ambrosia* had been converted from a Canadian frigate at a time when a dollar was a dollar, when a million was more than a million; Johnny had spent five or six. Just so it could moor here, they had built the deep-water outer jetty.

There was, of course, nothing simple, discreet or secure about Johnny. He gored problems to death. When Stephen first met her, Mercedes Valldemosa, the greatest bel canto soprano of her generation, Johnny's second wife was already on the way to becoming his second ex-wife, his third was destined to be Venezualan, his first, long finished, was a Frau Gräfin of Coal-and-Steel, who had cut up worse than one might imagine when Johnny captured the famous heart of the diva, celebrating his triumph by making love, it was said, in the warm waters of the mosaic-floored swimming pool.

In a life filled with deals, the *Ambrosia* was a special memory to Stephen; it was nearly twenty years ago, when Johnny (who also called himself Juan or Jean) was negotiating with four Arab ministers, including the still-secret cartel's key man and organisational genius Sheik Salman, over new transport arrangements for crude. Johnny knew, because he was Johnny, because Arabia was part of his Mediterranean world, that an oil cartel had been formed; he also saw its implications, while Washington and the West sat on their hands.

'Hello, Gentleman, you happy?' Johnny had asked, slapping Stephen on the shoulders, raising the business end of a Pol Roger bottle directly to his lips. The negotiations were proving tough, the parties were taking a five-minute break, just to clear the air; it was fortunate that Johnny had recommended the casino and Hôtel d'Orléans to his film-star friends that evening. Yet anyone with camera and high-powered lens could have photographed the preferred guests; the yacht's lines blazed out across the water to the promenade, the stateroom was bright with light. Just to make sure that the CIA knew.

'I think I will be happy when you are happy,' Stephen said, with a smile. Johnny had lit a cigar and disappeared, without another word.

Stephen had joined Mercedes, who was score-reading in the library beneath an El Greco, a portrait of an unknown Spaniard nobleman.

Mercedes was not a classically beautiful woman; short-sighted, with a pronounced nose; yet she was thin, fine, with high cheekbones and exquisitely dressed, with diamonds and pearls and graceful solitude. When she spoke French, as she did with Stephen, she brought a Spanish darkness to her speech, although her song was the purest Stephen had ever heard; and when she sang, she was the most beautiful woman anyone had ever seen.

There was no piano aboard ship. Her spectacles lay next to her glass of water, beside the score; every so often she tapped out the beat on the table.

She said she felt unwell, worried about her voice, although the clamour for her was becoming ever more raucous, her fees ever higher. There were, by then, rumours than Johnny had turned his attentions, which were seldom fixed, elsewhere.

Stephen landed beside her. Would she contemplate *Bohème* or *Traviata* in Covent Garden?

She hesitated. She knew what her voice coach and her agent

would say.

For him?

There was a silence; he smiled.

She picked up a phone, then rang Paris, her agent in New York; she had sung the parts dozens of times; she knew them off by heart, also the tenor, bass and choir, even the orchestral part. She could stay in his Mayfair house, he murmured. She could scream at her entourage, bawl at him and still receive fresh roses every day!

She laughed: 'Stephen, only you would dare to say such a thing.'

The agent was a major stumbling block; the Met, La Scala had filled the calendar, he did not like London, above all, he did not like the money. 'We are not a charity.'

Stephen offered to match the Met. Now Mercedes wondered aloud whether Covent Garden was actually planning *La Traviata*. And the conductor? How was the Covent Garden chorus? She had not always heard good reports, really, she did not know if she had the time or the energy. New York and Milan were enough, she was no longer strong and in full voice. He told her she was beautiful.

It was only when she had agreed to everything, subject to every conceivable condition, when Stephen had agreed to everything, that their little contract was sealed with a kiss. It was only when he had left her that he rang friends in London, offering to pay for half of everything, using money which he might have, but which he had not intended to spend on two weeks' living.

Meanwhile, Johnny and Salman and the others and their lawyers were about to start Sumo wrestling in the stateroom, having frayed their tempers and patience over tanker rates, port charges.

Mercedes had disappeared for the night. It must have been about two or three in the morning when Stephen chanced his arm again; this time stumbling into the cigar smoke and curse filled stateroom, only to be bawled out by Johnny.

The foul language just made Stephen smile: 'I think it's time you gents agreed a deal. Then everybody can get drunk on whatever their religion allows them.'

There was an almost baleful silence while everybody wondered who had been most insulted and why; then Salman chuckled and Stephen could retreat to the bar, crack another Pol

Roger and drink to Churchill's memory.

Johnny had been terrified of showing any weakness, knowing, as everybody knew, that his hilt-mortgaged fleet was growing rust or driving half-filled between nowhere and nowhere; so when the handshakes, backslaps and smiles had been exchanged, and the jazz band been roused from its slumbers for a dance, Ioánnis Kolokotrónis stood beside Stephen and kissed him on each cheek: 'That's for the deal, Gentleman.'

A month later, the OPEC cartel cut oil production, prices rose sharply, the world's industrial economies went into sharp decline; half the tankers around the globe suddenly became worse than useless, moored in isolated bays or hired out at ludicrous prices to a Greek-speaking shipping magnate who happened to have a long, lucrative contract to move oil across the world. For ten years, Ioánnis Kolokotrónis was the only man with a tanker fleet that was fully utilised.

If Johnny had clinched a dream deal, Stephen had not done too badly, either; the insurance for the entire Kolokotrónis fleet was placed through him and his friends at Lloyd's. The rates charged by Stephen were high, because of fears of terrorist attack, suggestions of war, the dangers of living; yet the premiums paid to Lloyd's syndicates were competitive; tens of millions were left, year in, year out, with Stephen and his friends, with their offshore brokerships and offshore bank accounts, tax free, risk free. This sleight of hand promoted Stephen to the Grand Master of the Lutine Lodge, made him chairman of Lloyd's and provided him and his friends with wealth beyond the ken of the Inland Revenue men. The only disadvantage was the need for intermediaries, the need for complex banking arrangements, which meant too much depended upon the reliably unreliable: upon the Cristòforos of this world.

Mercedes had kept her bargain, too; she came to London to sing *Traviata* as it had never been sung, bringing Gregor Stanislas, now Sir Gregor, whom she converted to the delights of London.

The great exception in Stephen Grote's life, Mercedes was the only woman he ever loved. But she loved Johnny, would always love Johnny, even though the shipowner bought and sold women like everything else, even though he had left her, only to be crocked himself by an alligator, only to run back to Mercedes

317

to whimper and complain, showering her with gold jewellery, golden flowers and gilded promises.

'Mercedes Valldemosa,' Stephen said, aloud, looking at the bougainvillea, the view, the boats. It all seemed so remote now, so predictable: her voice cracked, she had decided, one night, to take a barbiturate meal.

'Have you seen Murphy's boat?' MacNulty asked, out of breath from the climb, without any apology for lateness. Somewhere below, a bell tolled midday; perhaps Tony was not late; perhaps, Stephen thought, he was just too old for the task.

'Only from up here,' Stephen said, trying to be cheerful: 'It looks very imposing.'

He wondered if Tony had heard what he had said; it was certainly possible, for he muttered: 'The Kolokotrónis deal, we could do with a few of them, now.'

The tropical garden had lost most of its visitors to lunch and the swimming pool. MacNulty rolled up his sleeves, loosened his shirt, breathed deeply; he was still not acclimatised to the heat. For once, his pipe remained in his pocket, as if it were too hot to smoke, as if he were insufficiently relaxed.

Tony said: 'Well, you've seen the guest list; in fact, I saw the latest Marchwood Bentley in the hotel garage and heard the shrill tones of Mrs Marchwood, not an hour ago. Do we have any plans, views, intentions?'

Stephen saw that Tony, normally so circumspect, was outraged. 'Everything is sinking,' he went on, 'and we are standing on deck admiring the stars. We should be changing course, manning the pumps or abandoning ship. Doing something.'

Sometimes, Stephen murmured, you had to wait and see. He admitted that they had become peripheral recently; because of the case, neither he nor John were able to visit Lime Street, and there were limits to even Neil Fortescue's time and energy . . .

'Well, what the hell are we going to do about Marchwood?'

'That is a question I have struggled with for decades – not, I grant you, always with success.'

'Has he been talking to the police?'

Stephen looked at MacNulty's uncharacteristic pallor; his fiancée, Sue, was proving even less agreeable and even more extravagant and self-willed than his ex-wife; he was being hammered by lawsuits, hammered by bankrupt names. He had sacked most of his staff and still Wordsworth & Co was losing money. Besides which, he hated police cells and interrogations; he hated policemen.

In short, Tony had reasons to be unhappy. He had even been seen, after a time of total abstinence, drunk at work, in the middle of the afternoon. He had even had to give Cowes week a miss, for fear of meeting his clients. Now, however, some sort of fun was promised after the conference: Tony had had the latest yacht brought down to the Med and now it was hidden somewhere in the harbour, a modest thirty-metre affair called the *Lucky Lady*. Sue had objected to joining them for the cruise, with the excuse that she disliked boats. This, Stephen observed, made her the perfect partner for the deputy chairman of the Royal Yacht Club. He hoped they could save Tony from the demon thirst.

Problems, problems.

Not to show his distress, Stephen talked about the banking plans he and John Devies and Henry Stone had made, aided by service division. They had, he thought, a solution.

'All will be revealed tomorrow at John's place, on the Cap d' Antibes. But everybody will have to be there.'

Stephen had been careful never to favour one member of the group above any other; this reduced rivalries and petty jealousies: he could not, he had said, stand being at work in Japan or San Francisco and know that he should really be in London, fighting for his life.

The problem of Robbo remained, Tony observed: 'There has to be a rapprochement. Not another Baden-Baden, but a live-and-let-live agreement. Otherwise, you might as well forget your plans for new banking arrangements.'

Tony did not say: plans for a life after Lloyd's.

Yet the idea that Robert Marchwood was still, despite all they had done, able to call their plans into question was a bitter truth enough, one even Stephen had been avoiding; after all, they knew that Robbo knew or would find the means to know; despite their ultimatum Ray Marchwood continued his research, his data-bank work, and look where that had led.

Stephen blamed Robert for the data-bank fire, for the death of the young man. It had been pure self-defence, no more and no less.

Nobody had wanted Vaughan to die, God knows Stephen

was a minimalist, because violence always involved risks, but a response was inevitable as long as Robbo insisted on breaking the tenets of the Baden-Baden agreement, on meddling with their business, on watching their each and every move.

No wonder they had been sensitive about a possible involvement with that man Wilson, about a link with the SFO.

Now Robert Marchwood was back. And because he was who he was, he would interfere. Lloyd's was feverish enough without him. Stephen cordially wished that Marchwood had disappeared for good.

Tony said: 'I haven't spoken to Marchwood for a year. But it's obvious that Knowle will have to change to survive.'

'Do you think we can ever trust each other, again?' Stephen asked. 'After all that has happened?'

'We'll all have to change to survive,' MacNulty smiled. 'There's little choice.'

This simple truth hung in the heat, the tree-dampened silence of midday.

'I can arrange a meeting, this afternoon. Just a word, to clear the air.'

Finally, Stephen nodded, feeling cheered. There was nothing in his laws which justified optimism about the outcome of such a meeting. It showed, perhaps, the inexplicable strength of the will to live.

They rose, strolled downwards towards the town and the sea, over dusty paths and footbridges, between yuccas, cacti and spurges.

TEN

ROBERT MARCHWOOD HAD asked Thérèse to plan their trip to the Côte d'Azur for him.

One week's old-fashioned, chauffeur-driven motoring through France, letting the car smooth out the miles along the French country roads. They avoided motorways, large towns and, they hoped, car thieves.

Thérèse had decided that the journey in the Bentley would be infinitely more pleasant then a flight; besides, the drive would prove, to her own satisfaction, that they could live 'normally'. Robert nodded at everything. 'We'll tough this one out,' he said and she smiled.

Thérèse had not been told that they had received yet another package containing engraved cartridges.

Ray insisted they give him their itinerary and he provided them with a new chauffeur, Gary, whom he had found through a somewhat dubious agency; tall, thickset with a mop of unkempt blond hair, Gary kept himself to himself. He had served Her Majesty in places where Her Majesty's forces were not admitted to have been.

The journey was redolent of those trips in the twenties that young men made in an orgy of timeless pleasure, when there were few first-class roads and even fewer cars; now they took their chances with the crowds at Mont Saint-Michel and Chartres, but Sens, Vézelay, Tournus and Bourg-en-Bresse were deserted, calm and dignified.

Thérèse was still wondering whether she might study art history; Robert, happy to be alive, allowed her to show him all the churches under the sun, and even one or two by rain. Wherever they went, Gary followed unobtrusively.

There was much work still to be done.

In the South, they visited a small white modern church blotched blue and yellow by light filtered through stained glass suggestive of sea, sun and swimming greens.

'Matisse,' she said. 'Later on in life, when his health was failing, he made these patterns by cutting paper. Very simple, the bluest blue, the greenest green, the reddest red.'

He recalled seeing something in New York. The effect here was slightly cold, he protested.

After the first night in the Hôtel d'Orléans, the sun shone on a balcony open to a blue sea and bluer sky; it seemed artless perfection; breakfast arrived, with juice and rolls and deep bowls for coffee that smelt quite wonderful and distinctive.

The entire day stretched before them, until the Lloyd's inaugural dinner dance commenced that Friday evening, in the opera house that could be used for concerts or plays or conferences. They tried to map out the intervening hours; Thérèse suggested sights, the palace where an English monarch's brother had died en route to his Neapolitan mistress, no, the harbour, no, the tropical garden with ten thousand and more different species, no, the promenade, no.

Neither of them wanted to go shopping; churches, museums, art galleries could wait. 'I almost need a blank year to digest all that I have seen during the past twelve months. And I have shopped enough for twelve years,' Robert said. 'Besides, we are here on business.'

He expected a call.

So they talked about money, about stockbroking, about insurance, about who and whom and with whom and why; Robert's intention was simple: meet people, mingle and mix. Thérèse, in her new position, had to be herself; there were certain people, some Swiss, some German, whose acquaintance she should make. Correction, whom she had to charm, then inform. He had a list of conference participants, men of Lloyd's and their guests; all told, they placed billions of pounds of business every year, these men in suits. 'Go on a charm offensive,' he laughed. They needed one or two new, heavy-hitter clients, agreeing to place the business outside Lloyd's, if need be. They would thrive and survive, that was their motto.

By now they had drunk too much coffee, so they drank some more, contemplating the shining bay filled with shining white boats drifting in the lightest breeze.

By the time Tony MacNulty arrived, they had almost lazed past lunch, so they decided to eat together; Thérèse ordered, while the two men half-smiled at each other. Yes, the truffled vegetables would be fine, a speciality of the house.

'Been a long time, old man . . .' Tony said.

'You're getting on yourself,' Robert replied, saying no more than the truth. Through the thin paper of Tony's face could be seen the red map of his veins.

He did however refuse a drink: 'No, thanks, water with fizz.' Not even a glass of Bellet.

The breakfast table had not been cleared, but Tony still took a seat. Seeing him uncertain in Thérèse's presence, Robert explained that she was to become a director of Knowle & Co.

'Oh, congratulations,' Tony said, not bothering to hide his scepticism.

'Thank you,' Thérèse said, with prim restraint.

Robert smiled and broke some bread left from breakfast; they chatted for a while about people, about business, about rates, about politics. They avoided mentioning the police or Grote or Kevin.

Thérèse asked about Tony's family and elicited a cautious response.

The food arrived, tables were swished in and out, servile apologies made and waved away, Englishmen still sit at the breakfast table at lunchtime, it is a sign of their indolence.

Robert was still trying to encourage Tony to relax; he was, after all, among friends. Robert asked: 'Brought your new yacht down here, again?'

'Haven't been aboard yet,' MacNulty admitted, glumly.

Thérèse started a chatty monologue about their journey, telling Tony about the celestial delights of the cathedrals of France. Tony nodded, dutifully, while Robert agreed with his wife.

Finally, Tony could see that Thérèse was not going to be sent away to powder her nose, run around the shops or improve her tan.

'Grote wants to talk,' he said. 'If you want to.'

'Perhaps.'

Tony handed him his card, with a room number and telephone scrawled on the back. Two floors below, probably they could jump onto his balcony.

'If he wants to see me,' Robert said, 'I shall be gambling in one of the private rooms from four o'clock. All the rooms have dual-camera surveillance and are video-taped. To see that the bank does not run into trouble, of course.'

There was a silence; Tony remarked how delicate the vegetables tasted; Thérèse had been told beforehand that he would negotiate, try to set terms and conditions.

'There has to be a meeting of minds,' Tony said, recovering his poise. 'The warfare has to stop.'

Tony the peacemaker.

A sous-chef appeared, with a waiter, to grill fresh fish at their table, red mullet. Simple foods. All that was needed was a twist of lemon juice, a swirl of pepper and a simple green salad.

Tony invited them to a few days' cruising, after the conference ended: 'A little holiday trip along the coast, nothing serious.'

The idea appealed greatly to Thérèse. Robert, seeing her smile broaden, tried to forget his difficult relationship with boats and sails.

This plan, the food, the wine, the view that stretched to Antibes, hidden in heat-haze, lifted their spirits. Tony laughed freely, and the conversation turned to politics, to the British and, particularly, the French. Tony pointed out that every year, when he returned here, something had been built or developed, usually tastefully; over twenty years, the Riviera had been transformed from a beach and playground into a lively modern place without spoiling the *fin de siècle* dream world of the seafront towns. Things worked – trains, buildings, industry, public services – and yet there was all this talk of corruption, of Mr Twenty-Per-Cent. He deserved medals, not exile. They should visit sunny Britain.

Stephen Grote was amenable to a meeting in the Casino du Paradis; Tony confirmed, swiftly.

Marchwood looked at his watch, the old Omega that had belonged to his father. He just had time to collect a certain little something. He left Thérèse the freedom of the bathroom and rapidly quit the hotel, taking a taxi along the promenade, past the café-edged harbour, alive with yacht-business, back into the town where the taxi waited in the main thoroughfare, outside a prominent jeweller's shop. Robert entered and left the marble-and-gold emporium in a matter of minutes, clutching a wadded bag which he opened in the rear of the yellow cab; inside, he found a lighter and a message: Take care and have fun. Here's looking at you, Ray.

Robert laughed. It was a long-shot, but worth a try. Back in the hotel suite, time was pressing and Thérèse was still in the bathroom.

'Are you coming?' Robert asked, emerging from his shower and hearing a Gallic tirade of outrage sloshing over the stupid boxes of this, ridiculous jars of that and unspeakable glass bottles of the other. Thérèse did not use much make-up normally, so when the grand occasion came, she tended to lack practice; life, she said, was too precious for false eyelashes.

'*Mais oui! Merde!*'

'Then stop making me nervous.'

Either he worked with his brother or on his own, mostly the latter; this suited him best and Ray, if he came along for the ride, was cool: having to turn to Thérèse, to think what she might think, to worry about her objections and conjectures, about her flaring temper, irritated him. In Baden-Baden, he had sauntered into Grote's hotel room without a thought in the world – apart from, as it happened, Thérèse, whom he had just met.

Then they were ready; that was, more or less, it: a last glance in the mirror, one gentleman, bronzed, in white tuxedo, one lady, bronzed, with glowing red lipstick, in a rather special black-and-white suit. He patted his right-hand pocket. Ray's special lighter. All present and correct.

They strolled down the corridor to the flowery metal art nouveau lift, now fitted with a swipe-card reader and camera. This security hurdle passed, they were transported to the basement corridor that led to the Paradis; bare, cool and unadorned, the passage resounded to the crisp clip of Thérèse's metal-tipped high heels, her perfume lingered.

The private gambling room was, he remarked with a whisper, reminiscent of a high-class brothel; plush red and green hangings, an ornate mirror and fireplace, fake rococo like much of the building, swirling curled forms derived from sea-shells and the breaking wave of the sea.

Not that he had ever been in such an establishment, he added, on seeing her glance.

The croupier and his assistant were waiting; chips were being counted, piled and the wheel spun. The lights were subdued;

ceiling-mounted cameras turned silently. There would be enough witnesses, of one sort or another.

Robert presented an oblong piece of plastic, and they both obtained coloured plastic chips, identified by numbers, confirmed by his signature. Money.

They placed their first bets, idiotically, competitively, on odd and even, red and black; the zero did not transpire, so Robert's chips were raked across the marked green felt to join Thérèse's pile.

A buzzer sounded, the croupier gestured, Robert rose to look at the screen hidden beneath the table edge, nodded: then Stephen Grote entered, all smiles and easy charm.

At once, Robert's precautions seemed absurd.

'I fear this is going to prove an expensive chat,' Stephen said, obtaining a handsome sum in plastic coinage. 'Yet that is nothing new.'

Thérèse, who had never met Stephen before, was struck by his precise speech, ready smile and a punctiliousness of manner which gave him an aura of dignity; even in his sixties, he still looked fresh and vibrant. The crisis had not taken any visible toll.

As if by afterthought, Stephen and Robert shook hands across the roulette table; with the croupier waiting, they had to play. To placate the white-jacketed men, Thérèse placed two black oblongs on the red; there were red and green circles and blue triangles, too, but oblongs, she noticed, were more valuable.

'I trust you are well, Robert.'

'Couldn't be better, Stephen.'

'Thérèse is certainly the picture of health,' Grote said. 'You are a lucky man, Robert.'

'I hope we'll see your wife . . .'

'Donna, unfortunately, has an auction to prepare. She works for Sotheby's, you know.'

The north-east-south-west pointing handle of the wood and brass wheel was spun clockwise, the moving numbers blurring, then briefly staying, only to blur again; the white ball was rolled anti-clockwise around the stationary, outer rim, clicking for a time against metal diamonds which studded the rim, until it changed its trajectory. Suddenly the ball bounced between turning wheel and fixed rim, tock, tock, tock, before coming to rest in one of the metal-fretted slots known as canoes.

Neuf, rouge.

Thérèse clapped her hands, all four men in the room smiled briefly, involuntarily. Her four oblongs were on red.

Robert had been content to watch her lose; she did not. Four became eight and eight became sixteen.

'Your dear wife does not seem to realise that gambling is a serious matter,' Grote said. 'It's all about learning to lose.'

The croupier was in few doubts; any smile that might have been perceptible had disappeared.

Faites vos jeux.

Thérèse hesitated; she placed just one oblong on a column, Robert placed some petty red circles on individual numbers, and Stephen slid a green counter onto red. *Rien ne va plus.* Zero. They all lost.

'Roulette is for fun,' Robert replied, and recalled a time when he played cards in London clubs.

'You mean, you calculate odds when playing Blackjack?' Stephen asked, mock incredulously. This was intended as a compliment: Robert's memory for figures and calculations was legendary. Even so, it made him feel uneasy.

Thérèse was playing oblongs, again.

'Did you send Tony?' Robert asked.

'His idea.'

'The faithful go-between.'

'We believe in him, absolutely.'

'You have no reason not to, as far as I know . . .' Robert cursed himself: why did he mention this? To undermine Tony was the last thing he needed now. He smiled at Grote to emphasise his general, unspecified goodwill.

Douze, noir. Fifteen oblongs became thirty.

Grote looked over his half-moon glasses and conceded: 'Basically, Tony's assessment is correct. Not one of us has anything to gain from a prolonged . . . dispute. We have to put the past behind us.'

Stephen's turn of phrase was dictated by the rhythm of the croupier, the placing of bets and the knowledge that their conversation, their every move, was being taped.

It was as well, Robert thought, that they could not mention the Monet, the break-in, Kevin, the cartridges. In any case, Ray was not convinced that they were due to Grote and his friends or friends of his friends. The police had found and arrested no one. He and Robert were left in the dark; they just did not know. They had to be careful. They had to be sure.

So Robert tried his luck: 'We have been receiving some packages, recently.'

Grote looked unmoved, as he always did. He contemplated the baize, the wheel, then turned to Robert: 'What sort of packages? I don't know what you mean.'

It sounded convincing.

Having won handsomely, Thérèse was betting smaller currency, more or less randomly, feeding the wheel. Stephen disapproved; even if the long term averages could not be extrapolated to the individual spin of the wheel, she should place her bets as if there were laws.

'So, forget everything?' Robert probed, returning to Tony's suggestion.

'Yes. A new start.' The words slipped out easily. Robert restrained a smile, after thirty years of battles, strife and near-warfare, this simple offer, born of necessity, lay on the casino table between them. They both knew what was required. They should trust each other, become trustworthy; Robert should neither blow holes in Grote's business or his friends', nor should he, through investigation and research, put himself in a position of undue power; Stephen in return should not try to drive Knowle & Co out of Lloyd's or undermine the Marchwoods; the decades of strife should be ended. Hard to believe, hard to accept, even harder to sweep away, but if Lloyd's was to have any future at all they must join forces, close ranks and fight together. Everybody would have to make sacrifices; nobody could afford to have an accident à la Marchwood on his plate.

Together, Stephen pointed out, they could control the rundown of Lloyd's market, cut it down to a healthy core, then re-build it once the losses had been flushed through the system. That, at least, was the sole constructive possibility Stephen could see; billions of pounds of business depended upon it and billions of pounds of capital; millions of his own money. Without an agreement, CRG, his family business, was dead in the water. Even with one, the chances were not great.

The plastic counters were pushed to and fro. The wheel twirled, east-north-west-south, a ball knocked wood, metal, wood, before coming to rest.

Thérèse laughed; she had won again.

The two men looked at each other across the table. Robert saw a man whose personal empire was on the brink of destruction, whose reputation had been destroyed, a man who was being trussed up by his colleagues for the final fry. Then he blinked and saw instead someone at ease with himself and the world, rich, urbane; he saw a survivor. A man with plans, a man who wanted to live, who knew how to live and why. He remembered what Ray had said: 'They'll be planning a grand finale. Watch for their exit.'

But first, there was this chance of a last, desperate deal. A final attempt to save Lloyd's.

'So it's peace in our time?' Robert asked, ironically.

Grote smiled: 'I think we have no rational alternative. I propose peace and accept that there are difficulties on both sides. We each have to learn to forget and to gain each other's trust.'

Robert was silent for a while, seemingly contemplating the routine of the gambling table, actually considering the implications of these words from Stephen Grote, the outgoing chairman of Lloyd's of London.

'*Madame, messieurs, faites vox jeux.*'

There was, ultimately, no decision that could be final. They had to go on, whatever the risks; it was not over until the heavenly choir sang. Robert nodded at Stephen; his nod was his bond. A contract, made and sealed.

Stephen Grote, finding even someone else's loss of oblong after oblong to be somewhat painful, nodded back, averting his gaze from Mrs Marchwood.

'A new start, Stephen.'

'A new peace, Robert.'

They shook hands.

Faites vox jeux.

Stephen Grote saw a man who had aged; the athletic build was slighter, more frail. Though not old, and sun-tanned, Robbo no longer looked as if he still spent wintry afternoons, wind-whipped, churning mud on a rugby field. A man of contradictions; apparently a philistine, Robbo had a cultivated, accomplished wife; in one breath charming, in the next boorish and intemperate; unfaithful, yet devoted; obsessed with money, yet he would idly watch his wife fritter away –

Thérèse counted her remaining oblongs and discovered she was down to twenty. She placed them on black.

329

Rien ne va plus.

Vingt-cinq, noir.

Twenty became forty and forty became eighty. The croupier, taught not to flinch, glanced swiftly at the camera, as if asking an unspoken question.

Robert turned to Stephen Grote on the other side of the table and asked: 'Would you like a cigar, Stephen?'

Stephen Grote wondered at the question, looked at the broad-backed bronzed figure across the table, shrugged his shoulders: 'I don't normally smoke. In fact, I disapprove. Neil Fortescue insists on smoking cigarettes, which I find most trying.'

Robert removed something from his right-hand pocket, a lighter in the shape of a gun cartridge, and threw it across the table. It precisely resembled the anonymous presents Marchwood had received. Despite his surprise, Grote caught the object. This was the final test.

'Present for you.'

The assistant croupier saw the movement and informed the croupier, who pushed a button; this was not allowed; foreign objects on the table were not permissible. Nor was juggling or throwing things. It was as if Marchwood had tried to influence the roulette wheel.

Stephen Grote contemplated the lighter, which was engraved with Marchwood's name.

'A lighter?' Stephen said. 'A gas lighter? I can't possibly accept . . . But perhaps I will smoke a cigar, after all.' He gestured to the croupier's assistant, who offered a range from a mahogany humidor; he selected, snipped and used the lighter, without the hint of embarrassment or hesitation. He smiled.

M chwood had to admit that if it was a performance it was bravura, especially given the discomfiture of the croupier. Perhaps the friends really had not sent the packages. Then who?

The buzzer rattled. A man whom Stephen Grote recognised as the casino manager slipped into the room; hands were shaken, Thérèse gave an exquisite little peroration in French about a cigarette lighter and oblongs and, finally, everyone was happy.

'*Madame, messieurs, faites vos jeux.*'

All eyes focussed on her pile of eighty oblongs, placed on black. Robert said to Stephen: 'I still think sending packages was over the top.'

'Not involved, I assure you. Nothing to do with us.'

'The shooting?'

Stephen hesitated: 'Not involved.'

'Young Kevin?'

'Not involved.'

Robert had to admire the man's consummate skill. There were lies, there were truths and there was Grote. The decades of bile and hatred between them seemed to have dissolved into nothing. Peace in their time.

The wheel was spinning, the ball about to be released, Robert leaned over his wife's shoulder: 'Are you sure that is in the right spot, dear?'

She hesitated then pushed the pile onto the black. Now.

Rien ne va plus.

Deux, noir. 'Madame a gagné.'

There was laughter; Stephen turned round, to see that the manager had disappeared.

One hundred and sixty oblongs, what is that?

A flat in Docklands, plus a Rolls, plus a cheap painting, Stephen translated, casually.

She looked at him and omitted to smile.

Robert looked Stephen in the eye: 'A new start.'

Stephen nodded, pointed to the cartridge-shaped lighter that he had placed on the edge of the roulette table: 'Thank you for the gift, but no thanks. Besides, I can assure you . . .'

They shook hands again, Robert pocketed the lighter. Stephen, looking to change the subject, noticed his watch. 'Ah, you wear an Omega,' he said, 'just like your father Rex.'

Thérèse, who was turning most of her chips not into cash, but a letter of credit, payable by the bank of the principality, was surprised to hear the name of Robert's father; she looked up at the two men, and saw Grote grasp one of his wrists between thumb and forefinger, repeat the gesture with the other, then laugh.

'He always wore a watch on each wrist,' Stephen recalled. 'It was a joke, of course – during that time after the war when valuables had to be procured rather than bought. Yes, your father was quite a trader – a man with an Omega on each of his wrists.'

Robert did not smile. 'I don't know what you mean. He wore Rolexes, usually.'

Stephen wavered, momentarily. 'Oh, my mistake,' he said.

'Yes,' Robert said. 'I think it was just that.'

There was an awkward moment, then both men shook hands again and Grote left the private gambling room.

'What was the problem?' Thérèse asked Robert, when they were alone.

'Nothing,' he said, kissing her cheek. 'You were brilliant.'

She gave a long, stern look. 'Come now, Robert, I heard you say your father wore a Rolex on each wrist. But you inherited an Omega, as did Ray.'

Robert returned her gaze, shrugged his shoulders. He would say no more. She slipped him a few oblongs she had kept, should he want to play later.

ELEVEN

STU WILSON MOVED on tiptoe all Friday morning.

Breakfast, such as it was, occurred at the rear of the bar beneath the sparsely furnished rooms of the Hôtel de la Gare. There he studied the letter he had picked up on Thursday, contemplated the picture, the name of the *pension garnie*, and the coroner's report. He sat contentedly beside much-frequented pinball machines which proved that he was punch-drunk from the journey and the early hour. Car noise, police sirens, voices; station life, all had been clearly audible through the broken window.

Even while shaving, barely after dawn, Stu had found the air oppressive; after breakfast, he quietly inspected the rooms downstairs, the kitchen that led to a courtyard, the lavatories that offered no escape route. At the top of the hotel stairs there was a door onto the roof: the view was splendid and the drop ecstatic.

He bought a French newspaper from La Patronne, who was round and cheerful, then left through the plate-glass door of the side entrance, strolled along the alleyway outside, past pâtisseries, a butcher's shop selling horsemeat and a cheesery overflowing with unknown delicacies and dubious smells.

At a café beside a chemist's and a baker's, he took a seat at the bar, buying coffee after coffee that he did not want, staring past his newspaper at the large mirror that bore the brightly coloured emblem of the local hooch. Across the road was the *pension garnie*.

He might be a pawn, but only pawns could be promoted.

An hour went by, two coffees, another, he was approaching his fifth coffee when a tall, broad figure strode down the alley, wearing a T-shirt and blue jeans. The man disappeared into the *pension* that was opposite the bar, a minute or two went past, Stu preferred a large banknote to the barman who responded with a smile and small change.

The man re-appeared, looked right and left, failed to see Stu observing him via a corner of the bar mirror, then strolled off. Grey socks and brown-leather sandals: Stu felt this was conclusive. This was an Englishman, a visitor, possibly working for another Englishman, someone who took colour photographs of junction boxes, someone for whom the death of Kevin Vaughan was . . . well, what? There were so many links in the chain Stu had to challenge his own judgement. He was far from sure he could trust Ray Marchwood.

He followed the man at some distance, ducking and weaving, halting at displays of god-forsaken crockery, tasteless T-shirts and garden gnomes wearing sailor's hats. You buy, monsieur, you buy? *Non, merci.* The large man sauntered, clearly at ease, turned round two or three corners, until he vanished in an anonymous block among other anonymous blocks. Ugly, concrete, saved by bright awnings and sea views.

Wilson noted the address; he would check the telephone book at the post office, but first he would see if his guess about the role of the Englishman had been correct. Otherwise he had wasted half a morning and ten perfectly good coffees. However, the reception of the *pension*, in the road opposite the café, had a letter for him when he returned, which he ripped open on the spot, to find another photograph, some details about the conference. The receptionist confirmed that the letter had recently been left by an Englishman, one who spoke French no better than Stu himself.

So far, so good.

At the PTT, he studied the telephone directories, both personal and commercial, before retiring to his thin-walled room. He did not want to admit that he was desperate; he sensed he was being used, perhaps sacrificed, to break up entrenched positions, to ascertain the truth. He did not like being thrown into a conflict not quite knowing who, where and why; well, he knew why he was there, he opened the letter, again; another photograph of the fuse box. On the back was the time of the grand gala opening (with a chamber orchestra called the Riviera Strings).

It was, he reflected, an invitation to take his revenge.

334

He read the coroner's report again. They must think he was extraordinarily simpleminded or blind or both. He dozed off, turning names, faces, events over in his mind. He had to remain calm: the major pieces had been removed from the board, the complications of the middle game were about to break down into an endgame.

When he woke, drained, from an awful sleep, it was late; he changed into the evening dress that he associated with police social events and the Hilton penthouse suite, that desperate dash through the kitchens, decades ago, when cops were all great guys and even GBH suspects had their charm.

He left the Hôtel de la Gare by the front staircase, nodded to La Patronne, who larded incomprehensible phrases on him, apparently treating him as an especially suave and honoured guest. It was only as he strolled down an elegantly encumbered thoroughfare, past exclusive shops and well-heeled women that he saw the harbour for the first time, heaving with sails and ships and motor-yachts.

He would have to take his chances.

Twelve

THE FIDDLERS ARCHED their backs in an oft-repeated swoon, the tall, bearded conductor marked time; the guests waited to be announced, then greeted by the good and great of Lloyd's, before they swelled the milling ranks in the theatre, an essay of gold-cream-vermillion excess.

Even Robert Marchwood did not fail to be impressed. Famous for staging the Ballets Russes of Diaghilev, Nijinsky and Stravinsky, the theatre-cum-opera house had been converted for the summer conference season; auditorium seating had given way to tiered tables and chairs, with a level floor for the dinner dance; on the white stage the chamber orchestra and its maestro played Mozart. Beneath gilded stucco garlands, friezes, female-headed columns and warrior-headed rondels the royal box stood empty, behind golden drapes.

Mr and Mrs Robert Marchwood waited their turn to be announced to the theatre, then were introduced to Mr Stephen Grote, who headed the cortège of Lloyd's men greeting the guests.

Robert glanced once more at his wife, admired her fine head, her neck. So far, so good. Peace in our time.

For this evening's ceremonial Thérèse had changed into a white frilled dress, short bodiced, but with black spots, informal for a ball, more than elegant for a reception. She had only obtained the Pierrot suit after passing the scrutiny of a Parisian couturier. Yes, Mrs Marchwood could acquire those three ball gowns, these two evening dresses, and the Pierrot suit. Ten years ago, Mrs Marchwood would have thought the effort excessive, a silly game. Now her hand rested on her husband's arm, he looked the part in a white tuxedo, she was exquisite, they were the perfect couple.

336

'Mr and Mrs Robert Marchwood, Knowle & Co.'

Grote smiled as if greeting long-lost friends: 'With your luck, Thérèse, I can only conclude you have a pact with another place. . .'

She inclined her head graciously; Stephen retained her hand, mentioned some of the luminaries who had already arrived, from Tokyo, Munich, Rio, Johannesburg and New York; the Chicago contingent would soon be there.

A new start. Robert shook Stephen's hand. Shook the hand of John Devies, too, just for good measure. John and Robert were simply delighted to see each other; yes, it had been a long time.

Absence makes the heart grow fonder.

Robert found Devies little changed, propped on his stick, yet as brusque and barking as ever.

Thérèse had been blessed with a glancing kiss from Stephen Grote. She looked just a little too thin in her dress, Stephen thought. Elegant, though, most elegant. To be sure, she could carry it off.

Mr and Mrs Marchwood, Knowle & Co, strolled confidently forward, halting briefly at trays of champagne and canapés, before joining the usual crew: Alexander Wilmot-Greaves (and Sally), Henry Stone (and Lynn), Tony MacNulty (and Sue). Neil Fortescue would be flying in by Lear jet later that evening, with his consort; nobody turned a hair when it transpired that the lady would not be Neil's wife.

'Neil has been summoned to Downing Street,' Alec whispered, looking sternly through thick lenses at Robert. Earlier in the day, Neil had chaired the hardship committee collecting the last pennies of insolvent names.

The orchestra finished a scherzo, something by Haydn, the conductor directing his dozen players with a great flourish.

Robert applauded long and loudly; encore, encore; the conductor flushed at the extravagant approbation, his smile widened, he wiped his perspiring brow and Thérèse saw the white handkerchief darken with hair-dye. Instruments were retuned, a comedian in the tutti ranks essayed a few bars of Paganini, much needed for their next piece, a Mozart serenade.

Champagne and canapés on silver platters were proffered and willingly accepted; Thérèse told the ladies, Sally (with Alec) and Lynn (with Henry) and Sue (soon-to-be MacNulty), of their exquisite trip through France.

Because Fortescue was coming in the Lear later, the three couples had been forced to take a scheduled flight to the Riviera.

'You drove down in a Bentley?' Sally was surprised: 'It's a long way.'

Lynn told Henry, who had drifted out of earshot: 'They've been looking at churches.'

'Seemed a good place to unpack our sandwiches,' Robert replied, irritated.

Henry Stone rubbed his moustache and praised Chartres, Reims and Laon, feeling obliged to prove something that did not need proof. He had recently been excavating in Egypt and remarked on the fascination and grandeur of Egyptian monuments, built two and three thousand years earlier than the great cathedrals of the Ile de France.

'But they worshipped cats and birds,' Sue said, shaking her bobbed locks.

'At least they knew men's souls could be weighed,' replied Stone.

Guests' names were still being announced. It was as if the theatre, inundated with well-dressed women, had become a *belle époque* dream.

Mr and Mrs Williams-Stowe, Cecil Russell & Grote; Mr Appleby, Petteril, and Ms Cantor; Mr and Mrs . . .

'Devies, L'orcum,' intoned Robert, wearing his best French accent, causing the men to laugh and Thérèse to cringe.

He had not been in the room on Lime Street for over a year; one summer had suddenly turned into another. He had missed the life, the laughter, his stage.

'The Egyptians worshipped royalty, too,' MacNulty said, as the conversation paused, with a glance at Sue. 'Nobody is likely to make that error today.'

The conversation divided: there were those who wanted to talk about star-signs, those who talked about the future of the monarchy, and there was Thérèse, who listened and watched and worried: she doubted that the peace was real. If Robert had doubts, he did not show them.

Lynn told Thérèse that her Henry was 'forever jetting down to the Riviera.' She loved it here, it was another life; they had been here, on the Cap d'Antibes, some five weeks earlier. Robert was intrigued, but Henry did not expound on his trip, talking instead about his subsequent dig in Egypt.

338

Robert still wanted to know about Stone's interests on the Côte d'Azur, but was prevented from pursuing the point; Wilmot-Greaves rejoined their little group, having talked to some brokers newly arrived from London: 'Robey has shot himself,' he said, brushing aside all niceties.

The conversation died too. Now everyone could hear the light and airy grace of Mozart's muse.

'Killed himself, two bores of a shotgun, through the mouth.'

He gestured with his fingers, lest he had not been understood.

Poor fellow. Darned shame. There was talk of his farm, his shoot; a great hunter and shot, Robey was often seen at the Quorn, as a guest of Alec Wilmot-Greaves, who owned a pile in a middle England shire. There was, however, no word about his syndicate until MacNulty's Sue wondered aloud: 'What made Robey do such a thing?'

'Losses,' Stone said.

Thérèse looked at Robert, knowing that Robey had been one of his preferred underwriters; they had been racing together at Ascot and Epsom; she remembered someone tall and mildly spoken, who only came alive when the leading horses were ten yards from the finishing post.

Missed the storms, caught asbestosis, Robert thought, casting a glance at his watch, the rectangular gold Omega that still ticked as truly today as it had thirty-odd years ago. His father's, Ray had inherited the other one, replacing the Rolexes their father had passed on to them on the very day he died. Grote's words from earlier that afternoon had shocked him. The day of the accident was the very first time, the first and last time that they had found him with an Omega on each wrist. He was sure because the very first creditor to call was a small, dark-haired European who wore a black hat and black overcoat, seeking money for the fine Swiss timepieces that Mr Rex Marchwood had bought, just hours earlier.

Robert turned over the events in his mind, that day, over thirty years ago; the body hanging from the bookcase. Tied himself up, then removed the chair, so it seemed; kicked and flailed around the bookcase when it was too late, perhaps driven by the pain, perhaps deciding he was wrong. They had found bruising to the legs and arms, nothing suspicious.

Robert had spent years avoiding thinking about the event, working like a madman during the day, sleeping like an

339

exhausted dog at night, with his first wife Jane beside him, until yet
another accident happened, until the marriage no longer worked.
Every so often the image of the strangled face had woken him,
blue-black and distressed: the old man had swallowed his own
tongue. Robert had been in the office early that day. It must have
happened late at night or very early in the morning; during the
week, his father often spent the evening with clients, stayed in
town, hatched plans; the old boy had known so many people, from
all walks, but you could not really say his family was important to
him. It was their mother who made the sacrifices, raising the
brothers. Yet they worshipped him: Rex Marchwood was witty,
glamorous in a drab age, brought them presents fit for kings.

Poor old Robey; Robert was sorry. Yet Robey was responsible for his own actions, was his own man. He had known the
risks, gambled and lost. Robert Marchwood was not a man to
blame himself. He wondered, briefly, whether Robey had
blamed him, but dismissed the thought.

The serenade ended, to discreet applause. Grote had a word
with the conductor; no, the overture to *The Magic Flute* was too
much to ask, especially unrehearsed; giving an impromptu
speech from the stage, Grote again thanked the guests for being
guests, thanked the orchestra and its leader and its conductor.
Finally he invited everyone to enjoy themselves, referring to the
wine and indicating a buffet laden with largesse, fish and
crustaceans. He did not mention Robey.

Thérèse decided to stay beside Robert, who sat slaking his
thirst with Dom Pérignon, rather than join the Munich- or
Paris-based guests at their tables. When the time came, she
would be discreet and successful; now was not the time.

Stephen Grote joined them, taking a seat between Lynn and
Sally, somewhat to Thérèse's amusement; Stephen was charming to everyone, nobody was beneath him. Charm seemed to
come to him naturally.

After some muttered discussion on the stage, the conductor
finally waved his white stick and *Eine Kleine Nachtmusik* was
played, with great gusto and some familiarity. A waiter brought
Grote a plate, while others shuttled between buffet and table.

Outside the theatre, visible through the high-arched windows
that lead onto the terrace, the sun was setting in a flood of purple
sky above the dark sea; light glimmered beyond the horizon,
then was gone.

Thérèse was in a mood for some wickedness. 'I've heard that you can do a degree in shopping,' she suggested to Sue, who looked puzzled.

Lynn was impressed. 'I always say I've been educated in the university of life.'

'I'm sure you have.'

'Retailing, you mean,' said Sally, severely. 'You can do a degree in retail science . . .'

Robert turned to MacNulty, leaving Thérèse to extricate herself with grace; he told Tony he had found life impossible without Lloyd's.

'Well, I'm sure we're all glad to see you back,' MacNulty said. 'We have to see whether we can pull the market round. We have to get all hands on deck. I've said that to Stephen.'

Alec Wilmot-Greaves returned to table bearing two large plates, piled unscientifically, for himself and Sally, to polite applause.

'Sad news about Ropey, eh?' he said, directing his comment to Grote.

'I'm sorry, I had not heard.'

The story about the gun, the mouth and the two barrels was repeated.

Grote murmured to Robert, ignoring the presence of Lynn between them: 'Was that not your business?'

'I don't know what you mean.'

'Asbestos – you placed the worst with him.'

Thérèse dug her fingers into Robert's knee; he said nothing. Around the table, most conversations continued. Wilmot-Greaves was talking about his love of food, about the best and worst restaurants in London. Lynn was supporting her boy-friend Henry Stone, who was defending the joys of Greek food and wine against Sally, who vividly recalled an unhappy experience with moussaka and retsina and Alec.

Robert turned to Stephen. 'You saw my father, that day.'

'I'm sorry . . . ?' Grote answered.

'The watches . . .' Robert pointed to his wrist. 'The Omega watches were new; he always wore Rolexes. You must have seen him, that morning, that night, before I arrived. You were there.'

'Nonsense.' Grote was calm and trenchant. Robert almost doubted his own logic, his own memory. But Grote had understood him, he thought.

The rondo finale to the *Nachtmusik* ended amid sparse applause, and a Strauss waltz was commenced, an invitation to dance. Around the table, everyone seemed to be slowly sliding down the agreeable incline to merriment.

A deep breath. Robert winked to Thérèse, who was flagging. It wasn't her fault; the guys had not brought Lynn, Sally and Sue to explore propositional logic. He had always found being polite very hard work.

To oblige, Robert suggested to Thérèse they might dance. Someone placed an order with the twirly fellow for a Strauss waltz that did not involve a large Central European river. The fretful man with the baton smiled, the orchestra obliged and Thérèse swept Robert out onto the floor.

'God, he's a terrible dancer. Gives the rest of us hope,' Wilmot-Greaves smiled.

'Let's see if it is justified,' Sally said, taking her bespectacled charge out onto the floor and away from the champagne bottle. Other couples followed, to soothe and slide rhythmically to the sounds of a departed world.

One two three, one two three . . .

Robert had never really learnt to dance; Jane had tried to teach him, just as she had tried to teach him to sail, and had failed. He lumbered, with little regard for the calm pressures of his svelte young wife; he recalled Jane's lessons, thirty years ago, in a dance hall called the Empire, which had become an Odeon, then a bingo hall, then a DIY centre. No wonder he had failed to learn.

One two three . . .

Thérèse smiled at him, with him, without swooning. She was beautiful. He ran his hand through her hair, which was against the rules; he looked at her dress, so exclusive that he could see the exclusion zone. She caught his gaze, asked him not to drink too much, to remember their goal; be polite. He nodded.

Suddenly, among the other dancing couples, he saw a handsome, female face, her flowing dark hair held back by a jewelled slide. What a woman, what a woman. He sought her long legs among the movement of other bodies, admired their lines. She smiled at him, he smiled at her, so that was OK.

'Who was that woman, dear?' Thérèse asked, with a show of innocence. She had recognised Veronica Cantor.

'Oh, just an acquaintance. Works in the Lloyd's press office,' Robert said.

The waltz ended, his lips touched her cheek, she stroked his hair and led him back to the table, where he took a chair beside Stephen. Stephen was animatedly telling Tony and Sue about the extraordinary operas he had seen, gossiping about Johnny Kolokotrónis and Mercedes Valldemosa. A tray passed; Robert collected another flûte of champagne.

Mercedes Valldemosa had given one of her most famous performances of Carmen here, on this stage; she was then at the peak of her career and Stephen reminded Robert of how her husband Johnny Kolokotrónis, at the first curtain call, had carried the floral tribute of roses onto the stage.

'The man of means claimed his diva as prize,' Grote laughed, pointing to the stage, as if he could still see the tableau.

Robert Marchwood spluttered over his champagne: 'You should have rushed up there with a bunch of daisies.'

Only Sue laughed.

'He did look rather absurd,' Stephen Grote admitted, swiftly. 'A small, portly fellow with thick glasses beside this, this . . .' A gesture.

'Hunk-eating female. She'd have suited you down to the ground. On the ground.' Robert was, by now, flushed from the wine and the years of struggle and rage. Thérèse glared at him, across the table.

For a second, Grote looked as if someone had hit him with a wet fish; then he turned away, greeting the others as they drifted back from the dance-floor: Alec came with Sally, but Henry had been called away and Lynn returned alone, nursing a severe ladder to her tights, visible through a side-split skirt. She said that Henry had been given a message from, she thought, Neil Fortescue; he had disappeared with John Devies, looking worried.

'Oh, Neil should be along soon, then,' said Stephen Grote, with some relief, lifting his gold-and-diamond-studded cuff to see his wristwatch.

Mid-evening.

He looked up and saw Robert consulting his watch, too. His father's Omega.

'You're a loose cannon, just like your father,' Stephen commented, in a crisp whisper that was lost in the hubbub.

Robert replied: 'That why you pushed him overboard?'

'Don't be ridiculous.'

343

'You and your group of Lutine bellringers. Problem: in-subordination in the ranks – solution: man lost at sea.'

Henry Stone and John Devies with his wife, and Neil Fortescue with Cissy, arrived in a great rush of handshakes and cheek-kisses. Both Neil and Cissy were in need of a glass of something and a full plate. Stephen rose, ordered and organised; chairs were brought, tables moved, they should eat and drink in quiet and catch their breath. If anyone was surprised to see Mr and Mrs Marchwood sitting near Mr Stephen Grote, it did not show.

Both men appeared to be engaged in polite conversation. Thérèse heard nothing untoward.

One waltz died away, the conductor peered at the dancers, wiped his brow, nodded and the orchestra struck up again. Around the table Robert saw faces, glowing like paper lanterns in a balmy summer's night. There could be no peace. He wished he could take Thérèse by the arm, abandon their plans and leave the theatre and Lloyd's for ever. Then dismissed the idea.

More champagne arrived, more food: Lynn marched Alec back onto the dance floor; a cigaretteless Neil looked at Stephen across the glass and cutlery and flower-laden tables and Stephen saw, as he had expected, that Downing Street had cut up rough. Cracking lobster claws with a metal cracker, Neil Fortescue said: 'Terrible news about Robey.'

Muttered agreement around the tables.

Thérèse turned to Stephen Grote and asked for the next dance, since he had dared to come alone. Smiling, Robert waived his rights with an easy gesture and the pair left the others to make small talk about the weather.

Placing his hand in his jacket pocket, Robert discovered the black oblong remnants of Thérèse's winnings; perhaps he might give a wheel a spin himself, later. He glanced over to the dance floor, where Stephen was apparently impressing Thérèse with his easy grace.

'I don't know what your plans are.' Stephen Grote, barely taller than Thérèse, looked into her eyes. 'But I think it would be better if you both left. Lloyd's is behind you now, it is the past, not the future.'

She was astonished; she protested; they had a perfect right to continue the family business; they were still committed, neither of them was too old. Moreover, she thought there was an agreement, a new understanding, peace.

344

Her protests only served to irritate Stephen; he had gone along with Tony's attempt at reconciliation, despite well-founded misgivings, but now Robert was as rude, as out of order as ever. It was too much to bear. Good form and manners were wasted on Robert; let it not be said that Stephen Grote could not play tough.

He glowed with unspoken fury, saw someone he knew, a tall, dark woman in a chic black dress, dance past, dance near. It was an opportunity to strike that, for once, he would not let pass. He said: 'I assume you know about Ms Veronica Cantor and her young son.'

Thérèse looked at Stephen in amazement, not understanding his anger. Of course she knew about Robert's affair, but not about a baby, and she did not need to. She turned, slapped Grote's face, and left the dance floor and the music as fast as she could, threading her way out among the guests, disappearing through the high-arched door that led out onto the terrace.

The orchestra continued its waltz. Robert had been exchanging pleasantries with Fortescue when he saw or, rather, heard Thérèse's hand resound against Stephen Grote's jaw. He saw his wife depart, distressed.

As if in a dream, he strode across the room. Grote explained, denied nothing, stood his ground, seemed hardly to be present. Though impeded, Robert stepped forward and dealt Stephen a fierce blow to his body. He spoke words he would later regret, outraged that Thérèse should have heard of his son in so cheap a fashion, then struck a blow to Stephen's head. This was the man who had murdered his father. And Kevin. He had murdered them both.

There was blood, there was screaming. A ruck of dancers, including MacNulty, Wilmot-Greaves, Devies, had pinned back his arms. Now, where was Thérèse?

He had to leave.

People were looking at him, pointing, the casino manager strode across the dance floor, with a cohort of heavies. Grote lay on the wooden floor, his friends gathering round him.

The orchestra halted, the players peering down from the platform, conferring with the conductor.

Neil Fortescue walked over and introduced himself to the manager as the chairman of Lloyd's, then expressed his deep regrets.

The manager was unconvinced. 'I cannot tell people how to behave, but if they do not behave, they cannot use the casino again. It is our rule. Even if they lose a lot of money, they behave well, they like each other. They are gentlemen, you understand. No violence.'

Flushing, Fortescue ran his hand through his red hair. 'There has been a dispute, sir. Most unusual, an argument over this lady here.' He pointed vaguely, and the manager craned his neck to see.

'No shooting on the terrace,' he cried, despatching his heavies. 'That is forbidden, you understand. Nothing . . . Even if the lady is beautiful. . .'

Grote was helped away by Wilmot-Greaves, MacNulty and Stone to the men's washroom, to a washbasin and towel. Robert was unmarked.

Fortescue, finding the head of the casino less outraged, continued: 'It's a nothing, an argument over a mistress, everything will sort itself out. You understand, I'm sure, a beautiful woman, two possessive men. Unusual for the English, I admit . . . I'm sorry, please overlook this . . . We will ensure, monsieur, that you do not regret your decision.'

The hint of more money was well received. The manager looked at Robert, saw an angry man, but he bowed, signalled to the orchestra, which resumed its journey through eighteenth- and nineteenth-century Vienna.

Nobody held him back now, so Robert hurried through the gaping ballroom door onto the wide terrace above the quiet sea. She was not there. Neither were the heavies. The rock, the scintillated sea, the star-sprayed sky; Robert drew a breath, then strode on.

Grote thought Marchwood had broken his nose. Blood had dripped on the washroom floor, a white-tiled chamber with pissoir and four cabins, brass fittings, wood handles, wooden seats. Stone supported him, while Devies washed his face, produced wet napkins and found ice. Stephen's nose showed purple in the mirror. Strangely, he had few regrets, even though his anger and outrage had subsided; in a way, he was even glad that matters had come to a head. Something would have to be done.

'Inspector Wilson's here.' It was Fortescue who spoke, bursting in, with Wilmot-Greaves beside him. 'In the casino.'

'What?' Grote looked at him. This was the limit, more than the limit.

'Can I talk?' Neil asked.

'Check.'

Fortescue opened all four cubicle doors, ascertained they were empty. 'Make sure nobody enters. Keep the outer door closed.'

Natural man would have to be deprived, for a minute.

Wilmot-Greaves nodded and stood guard by the door. MacNulty had joined them. Grote tended his nose with mounds of tissue, looked at his friends' faces in the mirror. He said nothing.

Wilmot-Greaves cleaned his glasses, then broke the silence: 'Enough is sometimes more than enough.'

'We had an agreement on Robey,' Fortescue said. 'Robey should have been protected.'

Stephen said nothing. Stone, yes, even Henry Stone, nodded. The unfortunate accident of Mr Scrivano, head of the Banco Cristòforo, in St Katherine's Dock had taught him something which he had not forgotten.

Tony MacNulty did not dare to say: not strictly true, only protected as far as the rigs were concerned, the core of the deal; he did not dare to state that asbestos was a different matter. Nor did he add: Robey was a fool, and fools cannot always be protected from themselves.

John Devies ruined a hand-towel, wiping blood from the floor.

Fortescue said: 'I think we can take a vote.'

The implication was clear. There were certain limits which had to be observed, there were rules which were known and would be enforced, if not respected. Order was to be maintained. A certain order. There was the sound of Grote coughing. Someone rattled at the door, outside.

Wilmot-Greaves raised a right hand, then one by one, the others followed, Stephen Grote, Tony MacNulty last. They shook hands. Unanimity. Strength. Truth.

Fortescue shook his red hair, then spoke: 'I think, then, that someone should ring our local friends. I see no objection to that, Henry?'

Henry blinked, licked his moustached lip, shook his head, with a grim smile that recalled a dark night spent in St Katherine's Dock: 'One favour deserves another.'

This time, he was glad not to be involved; he was sure,

however, that his colleagues and associates from the Côte d'Azur well knew how to conduct their affairs.

Devies looked at his watch: 'Fine. We'll all drive to my place at Cap d'Antibes in half an hour, with all the girls. Then, it's in the lap of the gods. Stephen, you can see a doctor at my place.'

Stephen Grote smiled through the pain at his crimson-blooded hand, failing to staunch the flow.

THIRTEEN

STU WILSON HAD been drawn onto the terrace outside the opera house by the view and the hint of a breeze. He lingered, listening to a waltz being played, watching the sun disappear. The view was remarkable. Thérèse suddenly appeared on the gravelled path beside him. She hesitated, in tears, muttered something in French that Stu did not understand. Then she ran onwards, towards the hotel. Later Robbo followed, asking where she went, which way. As if he had half-expected to see him, Robbo gave Stu a tap on the shoulder and handed him a clutch of black casino chips: 'Might see you at the tables, later.'

So here he was.

Stu flipped the plastic between his fingers, glanced at the chandeliers, the mirror-and-gilt opulence of the casino. No gambler, well, not normally, he was content to watch the action and wait.

None of Grote's friends were to be seen; this worried him, but he would have been worried too if had seen them here; their absence was not in any way suspicious. Earlier, Neil Fortescue had ambled past him as if he did not exist; for the first evening, that was enough. They knew he was there.

Although there were half a dozen roulette tables in the long, high, gilded room, and tables for craps and blackjack, one wall was studded with the shoddy flashing lights of one-arm-bandits and gaming machines. This was clearly not the most exclusive part of the casino.

Watching dice being thrown, the wheels spun, Stu recalled scenes from the Met, bent casino owners, dodgy licences and bribed JPs; a world that had disappeared without leaving anyone the wiser. It all seemed so harmless, now. A lost age of innocence and purity – well, hardly.

A glance at his watch: an hour had passed. The gamblers frittered their small change, few were formally attired; he felt uncomfortable, as if in uniform.

Then Marchwood arrived, looking as he always looked, bronzed, healthy, broad-shouldered. This was the first time Stu had time to study him for a year, it was as if nothing had changed. Yet he would wait before talking to him. Fortunately, Robert appeared not see him, he spoke to staff, flashed an identity card or hotel key, a place was found for him at a roulette table. Robert started to play and people gathered. Stu could tell he was losing, sums that attracted punters from other tables.

Among the gamesters and their hangers-on, Stu recognised the man he had followed that morning, the man who had dropped off the letter at the *pension garnie*; now he wore evening dress and stood four-square under a mirror at the other end of the room.

An elegant, opulent blonde approached. 'Monsieur Wilson?'

He started, then returned her smile. Robert had seen him, after all. She took his arm, said something charming with so marked a French accent that he barely understood but found no reason to care.

Robert Marchwood rose from the gaming table, standing beside a moderate mountain of chips, suddenly dwarfing his spectators: 'Stu Wilson.' He grinned. 'It's time for bubbly. A man can't drink alone.'

So much for discretion. If the friends of Grote were watching, they could not miss them here, together. The idea would have terrified them, once; Wilson and Marchwood working together. Yet now it was just Robbo's little bluff, probably too little and too late.

He took the seat beside Robbo, who was ordering further supplies of everything, plastic money, drinks, while admiring the blonde lady. A Madeleine, apparently.

'Take care of Monsieur Wilson, Madeleine,' Robert said. 'He's a very important man. A man of . . . distinction.'

The words were spoken without irony. Stu admired the style, but suffered nonetheless. He placed the chips Marchwood gave him onto one of the piles.

'Kept them warm for you, Mr Marchwood.'

He did not know what to say about Thérèse, the earlier scene on the terrace, so he said nothing.

350

For a time, there was a silence, the ritual of betting and losing continued as Robbo fed the wheel: black, red, black, red. The spectators seemed more interested in the outcome than he.

'My luck will change. Things are just warming up,' Robert said, having lost much. He insisted that Stu drink the local red wine, the Bellet: 'It's the thing to drink. It'll keep you wise, wealthy and healthy. Then you can graduate to bubbly, like me.'

The red wine felt fine on Stu's empty stomach. Madeleine kept a calm hand on his shoulder and drank with him. Meanwhile, Robbo dispensed champagne to the onlookers around the table who appeared more surprised than grateful; bored with his own inability to win, he asked for favourite numbers, the ages of children and spouses, pleaded for good luck, for people to cross their fingers for him. Often people failed to understand, unable to speak English. Few fingers were crossed, but some numbers were offered.

'If we win, you'll get a cut. That's my speciality,' Marchwood said to someone who had named the age of his wife or his dog. The rare winning bets were distributed with swift efficiency, convincing Stu that Robert must still be sober.

'Who's that guy over by the mirror?' he whispered to Robert, who gave the man a prolonged stare. 'The one who looks like a bouncer.'

'Don't know. Do you think he's got a good number for me?'

'Been watching me all evening.'

'Don't tell Madeleine, she'll be disappointed.'

'For Christ's sake . . .'

Marchwood stood on his chair and looked, hand shading his eyes, waved, then took his seat.

'The man is my bodyguard. Not everyone in these environs is a friend of mine. Also drives for me, in his spare time. Called Gary.'

'Where's Ray?'

'Fishing.'

Stu seized his chance. 'And what was the matter with Thérèse . . . ?'

'We'd just said goodbye.'

Thereafter, the wine, the warmth and Madeleine's hand on his shoulder swept aside such inhibitions as remained. They drank, swore, gambled. As more chips were lost, more chips were brought. The crowd celebrated, the casino manager and his staff rejoiced, the other tables emptied.

351

It was humid and stuffy. Robert bought cigars for them both, which he lit with a lighter shaped like a gun cartridge, engraved with his name. Both men, unused to smoking, had difficulty with their respective cigars. Robert showed him his lighter and observed: 'Someone's been taking shots at me. Have your friends any ideas . . . ?'

'Ideas . . . plenty of them. Proof, well, that's another matter . . .' Stu laughed for want of a sober reply.

''Twas ever thus . . . So now's the time for our last bet, partner.' Robert ordered more chips, Stu was dimly aware that tens of thousands of pounds were stacked upon the table.

'Now. Think of your favourite number. None of the others count. We've had the cat's birthday, the dog's age, the number of the teeth that are still your own, then you told me you had lied . . .' Robert's peroration rambled. 'Now, I want your honest-to-God favourite number. Nothing else will do, partner. And you can have special terms. Fifty per cent of the winnings. . .'

The croupier waited while Robert re-built his piles of chips. The crowd table murmured, wanting action from the loud Englishmen. The chandeliers seemed to chink and zither like glass leaves in an imperceptible wind.

Stu laughed. 'Thirty-two.'

'Thirty-two, squire, here it is. My entire fortune.' The chips were assembled, a large, crenellated castle, next to the space marked thirty-two on the green baize. The croupier looked to the casino manager, who was among the spectators at the brass rail around the table. A solemn gesture and the bet was allowed.

Stu nodded to Robert, having drunk to everything. He felt Madeleine's grip on his arm, the subtle warmth of her body on his back. The money was toy town stuff: big black chips, big red chips, big green chips – oblongs, circles and squares.

'Fifty percent, OK?'

Stu smiled. Why did he agree to this? He was not, after all, an avaricious man. His cause was larger, ill-defined but necessary. Had seemed necessary, even vital. Yet he now had thought the fatal question, sensed the great indifference: why not? Besides, he was drunk and the drunk enjoy a special dispensation from heaven.

'Wait.' Robert gestured imperiously to the croupier, who was about to set the roulette wheel in motion. 'To number thirty-two, partner. You sure about that number?'

To number thirty-two.

They drank.

Faites vos jeux, messieurs. Rien ne va plus.

Robert directed the crowd, dispensed bubbly for medicinal and other purposes. All the other tables were empty now, all eyes on this one bet.

'I want to hear thirty-two.'

Rien ne va plus.

The whole room whispered, '*Thirty-two. . .*'

The wheel turned, the ball bounced around the metal studs, turned, spinning, before coming to rest.

Trente-deux.

The room was delirious, overwhelmed by screams, shouts of laughter. Marchwood stood up, thanked the croupier, embraced anybody and everybody, including Stu Wilson. 'Bubbly for all!'

The chips were removed, to be counted and turned into cash or cheques. Corks were popping.

'To your health, partner.'

'To your health, Robbo.'

'Seems someone has made you a rich man. I reckon that's the best part of three hundred grand, just for you.'

Waiters and attendants entered the crush with bottles and glasses; the party spread. The manager congratulated Robert: 'A beautiful woman and a beautiful game, monsieur.' He handed Robbo a bill, at which he peered, laughed and scribbled. 'Deduct everything from the cheque!' He winked, the manager inclined his head, and Stu found Madeleine's lips.

Fourteen

ROBERT RETURNED FROM the casino, from the big money and the big laugh, to an empty bedroom suite. He almost fell, opening the door, keeling over into the dark.

Sleep was out of the question.

He switched on the lights, saw the wreckage, switched them off. He opened the curtains and blinds and window, looked at the bay, the harbour, the jetties; someone was still partying somewhere, almost certainly Murphy the Tycoon.

He lay prostrate on his bed, looking at the scar on the wall and then the remains of the lamp that was its cause, shattered on the carpet. It was – or have been – mock Chinese, mock-gilt, mock-expensive. Just one half of one bedside pair amidst five hundred other such pairs, scattered through the Hôtel d'Orléans.

He had thrown it at the wall, with all his force and anger, after she had left. They had not rowed. She had sobbed, changed, packed and he had given her the car keys. Please take care.

They had even kissed; she said she loved him, but the truth was the truth. He had betrayed her. She had accepted the former mistress, she might even have accepted the child, had he told her; yet he had not and all she saw was a relationship of nothings.

He nodded, felt her skin burn against his. She had already washed her face clean of make-up; to survive the lift, she would have to wear sun-glasses. He gave her his, then listened as she reached the lift, pushed the button marked G and headed for the Bentley.

Bye. An unreal word, an unreal scene, he was not sure that it could have happened.

The lamp smashed easily. Nothing else happened; there was a silence.

After a while, he heard a door open nearby; presumably,

someone looked down the corridor, and wondered; possibly, someone rang the management and complained; the management, however, did not bother to consult him. One way or another, it would be on the bill.

He did not expect to see her again.

There were fireworks out in the harbour, clusters of bright colours and noise, the dull thud of dance music, everyone could hear Murphy was having a riot; then the police arrived down there, to tell him he had been a naughty boy. Robert watched the blue lights of squad cars spreading the length of the harbour wall. Noise, in these parts, is good. Silence is bad.

He sat on the end of his bed, craning over the balcony, just to watch the raucous fun. Nobody could be asleep.

It would all happen amicably, that he vowed; the lawyers would be kept under control and Thérèse, unlike Jane, would not attack him with the vacuum cleaner. Thérèse had once protested that she had too much, so he gave her more, just to see if she would spend it; she did not. He would be generous now. He recalled their train journey together, leaving Zurich for the mountains, then the absurd, yellow post-bus when they could have had any limousine she cared to name; she only wanted comfort, no more.

Where the hell was Ray? He really ought to call the apartment he and Ray owned, down in the town, and find out what his brother was up to. He had not had chance to speak to Gary since the morning; he and Ray had intended to consult before the conference started, but the unexpected meeting with Grote had thwarted the plan . . . in due course he would have to confess all to Ray, a less than pleasant task.

Robert only had himself to blame for her departure. He had promised her much and, ultimately, it could not be sustained. Many women would have been only too happy, but then Thérèse was one among many.

He had had a son, yet he had refused Thérèse a child. He had promised fidelity, yet there was Veronica. . .

His eyes closed and he must have slept; he shook himself, fully-clothed and cold, hearing the knock of pipes, the rush of water and then the telephone rang. He elbowed his way up the counterpane, hesitated: perhaps it was Thérèse. His fingers grasped the receiver, he heard a French voice, a woman. It took some time before he registered that it was not his wife's voice, not Thérèse.

355

He was well, thank you; in excellent spirits; he felt so dull-drowsy he did not replace the receiver and he listened to an offer he could only refuse. She was, she said, a real nice girl and would give him real nice treatment. He understood then that she had seen him in the casino and was looking for her second romance of the night. The handset did not find its way to the cradle, but fell onto the floor beside the bed. He was tired, exhausted, finished.

Perhaps it had always been doomed. Their love.

In the dark he saw the red lights of the radio alarm, blue lights from the quay.

BOOK SIX

ONE

HOW THE SEA returns the dead to shore is much discussed, a mystery. In summer, there are no tides here in the Mediterranean worthy of the name; the sea seems to thicken, to run back in silky rivulets as it retreats from shore or to push smooth-waved over pebbles and sand landwards.

Within the bay beneath the rock, beneath the white palace of the casino, below the stacked blocks of tax-saving architecture and the shunted mountains that subside into cliffs, the sea is summer-tame, barely troughs or peaks to crest a wave with white, merely eddies in close-to-silence.

An unlikely place to die.

Between the pontoons, jetties and innumerable walkways of the marina, the water seems an after-thought, occasionally spoilt by fuel oil, detritus or an inshore fishing boat returning an unwanted catch to its element. Given the lack of strong currents, given the slow and easy tides, foreign bodies are rarely washed ashore.

Yet it was here that the corpse was found.

Of course, it has been seen before; countless men had lost their lives plying these waters. Few, however, had been found within the harbour walls.

As the sun set on Friday evening when the sedate partying of the sedate gentlemen of Lloyd's burst alight in fracas and fisticuffs, the mega-yachts had lit up along Johnny's Quay where the the Kolokotrónis boat had moored for decades; now Murphy, the American property tycoon, was in town, and the party season had returned for a brief, late flourish. The alternative film festival had just ended, a high-turnover, high-profit, high-porn affair which mocked the arty aspirations of the main event, staged earlier in the year. 'This is about the serious things in life,' Murphy had told a journalist from the *Journal*: 'Taking your clothes off and getting laid.' Murphy, it has to be said, was a serious backer of anything which raked in one-hundred-and-thirty per cent within days.

By ten, the Murphy boat was happy, full of dancing lights, singing fireworks, guys and gals drinking spliced cocktails on the strength of *Steam Ice*, the festival-winning film that Murphy planned to screen for friends and stars in his boat's stateroom. At twelve, the film credits rolled before a happy audience and, by two, the ice had truly melted.

Murphy never celebrated alone. The entire harbour, the whole marina, the bay itself seemed alive with the noise, the lights, the fireworks – and, surprise, surprise, there were complaints from others who had spent a million or two in the hope of finding a quieter paradise. The prince himself, due to address the Lloyd's fraternity on the morrow, rang from his farm, the summer residence, to complain; Murphy put down the phone on him. Besides, there were two or three other yachts staging *hors de concours* events.

There are different accounts of what happened next. Certainly, there were more than enough witnesses to more than enough but, as Inspector Joubert of the local gendarmerie discovered, nobody actually saw anything.

Everybody heard screams, soon there were people from two or three boats, dozens of bystanders, party-lookers and barely-clad young women pointing at the waters beside the Murphy boat, at a body in black-and-white clothes.

Murphy, shaken, rang the prince to complain; it was nearly four in the morning, the prince rang the gendarmerie, with a plea to keep the incident, by now announced with blue lights flashing and sirens screaming to the bay, the harbour and the marina, discreet.

The gendarmerie had already arrived in four cars. Guests had to be questioned, boatowners, the partying throng. The disco music that emanated from two boats, thudding, stilled for perhaps a few minutes as a mark of respect.

Nobody knew the woman.

Murphy, for one, would have remembered: 'Not one of the chicks on this boat,' he smiled. Other boatowners made similar claims, but all, clearly, had had other things on their minds.

Joubert looked at the water beside the boat, without currents, black, slick, still. A beautiful woman in a black-and-white dress, early 40s, recently dead. Not your average gas-bloated sea-corpse.

She might easily have been set to join one of the parties, slipped overboard, taken a knock, then drowned. The pathologist would have to look.

Joubert sent down divers, with underwater lights. In that depth of water, fairly hopeless but very necessary.

It was then, in a manner of speaking, that they got lucky: the dress had an inside pocket, found by a female officer, and in it a soggy card: Thérèse Marchwood, director, Knowle & Co, Insurance Brokers at Lloyd's of London.

Within an hour, her husband, Robert Marchwood, had been found, taken from his room at the Hôtel d'Orléans and brought here; three cars jumped red lights along the promenade, around the bay's sea edge, the hint of dawn.

Robert knew what he had to know, although Joubert had said nothing. He knew the truth, having seen the grim faces of the policemen, and recognised, beneath the formal manners and the routine, a spark of anger.

He had to identify the body. A doctor was examining her, inside an ambulance; people were pushing past, still coming and going from Murphy's yacht, waiting for the wee hour celebrations to re-awaken at dawn.

There are things a man can do or be forced to do which elude explanation, more usual in wartime than in peace. This was a time of peace, but Robert would, from now on, be at war. He felt what could only be grief. Powerful lights and strange voices loomed, there were people laughing, laughing as the balmy night was drawing away from him. He was no longer his own puppeteer, watching himself watching himself, he was the dark itself, the blackness that always lay hidden in the marbled rooms where his life had been played out, where his power shook events into patterns which he could understand and to which others could conform. Here and henceforth, there was no ease to be had, the patterns had stopped reassuring, there was only a blackness which now belonged to him, which he would try to bring to life again, to revive the vanity of his strength and power.

He looked at the body. It was so small, seemed so insignificant inside the ambulance, on the stretcher. Her face was beautiful, clear and pure. He started to cry and realised, with shame, that he was crying for himself, that he would never find the grief adequate to the loss, that Thérèse was beyond help, had rejected him, and had been led here, to this.

There was no escape, nothing he could do, he sensed that spots would, from now on, appear before his eyes when he stood up suddenly, opened a door, looked out of the window, took a lift, jogged upstairs or gazed at the wall. He gasped, breathing heavily.

Yes, that was his wife, Thérèse Marchwood.

Where is the car? Where are the car keys? Her handbag and suitcase?

He explained to Joubert: she had left him. Joubert confined himself to a long glance. He turned and walked to the doctor; Robert watched them talk, understood without understanding.

'What car, Monsieur Marchwood?' Joubert stood beside him, he looked away from the ambulance interior; the doors were closed. Questions, other questions and other answers followed; theatre, casino, Wilson, champagne, bedroom. There was no laughter now. He had not left the rock that evening, that night. He stood in evening dress, the height of crumpled idiocy.

Then he played the outraged husband card, watching himself explode with accusation after accusation, scream at the doctor, the orderly, Joubert. He was good, tears fell in abundance, he was not to blame. He knew who was, though.

'I'm Robert Marchwood and that is my wife, d'you hear? Thérèse Marchwood . . . Someone has murdered my wife, killed her. I know who it was, I know, d'you hear? I will kill Grote if it's the last thing I do, the man's got this on his hands. . .'

His rant became incoherent; his breath disappeared.

A white-clad couple walking past, film stars of sorts, stopped to stare and ogle at a professional in full flight.

Robert was thrown into the back of the police car. They were angry. *Saloperie, connerie, merde*: her words, on occasion.

Joubert turned to him, spat it out, in case he had not understood. He had some questions to answer.

She had been strangled, bare-handed.

A dark, glass-fronted building. They marched him along corridors, past opaque-glassed doors, dark on either side, again and again. Behind the doors there would be nobody.

Two

THERE WAS A knock at the door.

The world was dark, awful. Stu was in bad shape, his face rasped against his hand, his eyes rasped as if rolling in sand, he stretched out and discovered a large, strange bed where someone breathed gently in the dark.

Another knock, the same imperious rhythm. Now there was a key in the lock. Voices outside.

A man who had spent his life knocking on other people's doors, Detective Inspector Stewart Wilson was unaccustomed to being in dire straits.

The body beside him stirred, spoke French.

'*Il y a quelqu'un à la porte.*'

A woman, a beautiful woman; that much he remembered. And more.

The door opened.

What had he done to deserve this? He groaned, in order to groan the world away. This failed. He retraced the events of the night. The casino. Robert Marchwood. The drink. The money. The girl. Ah, the girl.

For twenty years, he had not had such a night.

There were men in the room, lights on. Shutters were drawn, lights turned off. Dawn broke over him, over her, she ran, duvet-clad, into the bathroom.

He was naked.

Before him stood a man with a white hotel jacket and a key, a battered-looking man, with two younger men in uniform. Gendarmes. He registered a sea view, a balcony, and a room with glided plasterwork.

This was not the room above the brasserie, beside the train station; this was the Hôtel d'Orléans, one of the superlatives of

363

the French-speaking world, with stars and rosettes to recommend it. In so many ways, he ought not be here; yet he was proud that he had been. What a night.

He asked: 'Who the hell are you? Did Grote and his men send you?'

'*Vous parlez français, monsieur?*'

The tone of the older policeman was mild. Stu was glad the sarcasm appeared to have been lost on his other uninvited guests; the two men looked out onto the harbour, evidently taken with the view. All manner of yachts, boats and motor-cruisers, gently moving up and down in the warm sunshine.

Sitting on the edge of the wide, wide bed he remembered: nudity has its dignity. Only shame appears pathetic. He rose, slowly, and was the tallest man in the room. Probably with the worst hangover. He shook his head, looking for a dressing gown. Perhaps there was one in the bathroom – with Madeleine. He had to speak to her, and the rest, again.

'We are sorry to disturb you, sir.' The older policeman showed a document with a photograph. It could have meant anything.

'Most kind.' Stu gestured, and was allowed to search the wardrobe for a bathrobe. Nothing there. He heard the shower being turned on in the bathroom.

'My name is Inspecteur Paul Joubert.'

'Congratulations. Would you care to close the door?' The white-coated man with the key disappeared. He had seen enough to keep hotel gossip alive for the day.

'Is this the way you treat foreign visitors?' As he said this, Stu realised the tactic was wrong. He added: 'When they sleep with your most beautiful women?'

It worked. Joubert, a fleshy, small man with broad shoulders and tired eyes, smiled briefly. He uttered a slow response: 'A woman has been killed.'

Stu spoke as if he did not believe Joubert was serious: 'It's nothing to do with me.'

'What is your name, monsieur?'

Stu sensed that he could begin to dress without appearing ridiculous, starting with his shirt, which he had managed to locate. He saw that Joubert was more tired than he looked; that his humanity was stretched to its limits by anger and frustration and a good ration of the terror that keeps a policeman awake

364

during a long night's search. Yet Stu was not yet willing to comply.

'What are you looking for, Monsieur Joubert? If I were not a man of the world, I would say this is an outrage.'

Joubert's smile had disappeared: 'This is not an outrage. I knock on a door, see a man with a woman.' His shoulders moved upwards, his hands turned to reveal nicotined fingertips. 'An outrage is the murder of a woman, a dead body lying in the harbour. A dead body. There. *Voilà.* An outrage. What is your name, Monsieur?'

Joubert had moved, jabbing at the glass of the sliding window that led out onto the balcony. Stu, understanding his fierceness, obliged: 'Stewart Wilson is my name. Who has been killed?'

'Monsieur Wilson, it is my work to ask questions. You tell me what you know. Were you with Monsieur Marchwood yesterday?'

Stu nodded.

'Do you know the chauffeur of Monsieur Marchwood?'

He shook his head. It seemed easier to lie. Anyway, he and Gary had not met, not exactly.

Joubert became restless, rifled his jacket for a cigarette; one of the younger men tossed a light blue packet.

'Do you know Madame Thérèse Marchwood?'

Stu all but shouted: 'Is she dead?'

Joubert, receiving his answer, brushed aside the question. He knocked on the bathroom door: '*Yvette, j'espère qu'on est bien propre, maintenant . . .*'

Stu, who had managed to reach the shirt and trousers stage of decency, scrutinised the door, distracted. Socks, that was it. He had an idea that he had not removed his own socks. Rosie had never done that.

'You see Madame Marchwood last night?'

Once again, Stu nodded. On the terrace. He could recall the sound of their footsteps, the heavy, leather-soled man pursuing the light, click-heeled woman across the terrace above the sea. He told Joubert some of what he wanted to know.

'And then you . . .'

'I saw him again later, at about midnight.'

'Between meeting him on the terrace and seeing him again, you were in the casino?' Stu nodded.

'Who arranged the meeting?'

Nobody, a chance meeting. This was not a lie. Yes, the meeting was purely by chance; he had travelled here just because of Claude Monet and his desire for a flutter. He did not mention the invitation, the burnt fuse-box, Kevin. He would have come here, in any event, with or without the photographs; it was his last case.

Before there had been something of a problem; now it was a shade larger.

'How did she die? Who killed her?' Stu's throat was dry as he asked.

Showing the palms of both hands, Joubert insisted on his questions. He wanted to know where Wilson was staying, wanted to see his passport, his personal belongings, wanted to know how he had the money to stay in this hotel suite, wanted to know if Wilson had been in the vicinity of Marchwood's vehicle. The questions flowed and Stu offered answers.

Finally, Joubert exploded: 'Do you expect me to believe you? It makes no sense. You spend hundred francs here, hundred francs there, at the Hôtel de la Gare, then in one night, at the Casino and the Hôtel d'Orléans, Monsieur Marchwood and you gamble five hundred thousand francs, spend ten thousand francs! You take money from Monsieur Marchwood?'

It looked bad. Stu curled up, responded with silence.

Yvette, who had been Madeleine, entered the room wearing a white towel robe; her hair was wet, but would soon dry to a dark red-blonde, the product of a hairdressing salon; Stu wanted to kiss her, wanted the magic to return. She was beautiful, and he had forgotten what that could mean. Yet now, he was hollow and reduced to nothing.

Joubert nodded to her, offered a cigarette from the other policeman's packet, which she accepted.

'*Bonjour*, Yvette.'

'*Bonjour*, Monsieur Joubert.' She drew on the cigarette, took the hint, departed gracefully.

Stu could see Joubert was not going to provide him with answers so he tried to excuse his magic night. Never before, not in all his years in the CID, had he become involved in this way. All that temptation, all those other guys who fell and had to leave, more or less quietly, when the big investigations rolled into town. But he had always, always been clean. Now this.

'I don't see the problem,' he said. 'I won some money,

366

gambling with Mr Marchwood, and I decided to spend my winnings here. In fact . . .' His voice trailed away. He had been drunk out of his mind; he was not sure how much he had won. A plastic tower of black counters. Marchwood had plied him with Bellet and bubbly; the scene might just have been intended to frighten Grote's masonic friends, yet none had appeared in the gaming room that evening. The intention might have been shock therapy, but the patient had not responded and another had died.

That did not bear consideration; he was too tired, his eyes were too raw. What would they do with themselves now? What was left to rescue from this wreck? There could be no justification for the deaths.

Stu could not believe the degree of his stupidity, there was no excuse, none whatsoever. He should never have acquiesced to this mess, to entering a game devised by someone else, one where he did not even know the rules. He vowed retribution, silently, as he had vowed before: '. . . if it's the last thing I do.'

Robert Marchwood had not helped. He had pushed Stu into the lift with Madeleine, laughing wildly. But what had he done before, while he was gone, in the interlude between appearing on the terrace and re-entering the casino?

'I hadn't planned to gamble,' Stu said aloud, as if apologising to himself.

Meanwhile, Joubert's face was black with anger: he wanted Stu's passport, more answers, no lies. What was his full name? What was his relationship with Mr Robert Marchwood? With Mrs Thérèse Marchwood? Stu, who had found his socks, knelt and searched with his hand behind the bedside table and produced the small blue book, sign of her Britannic Majesty's goodwill, which he had hidden there: Stewart Wilson, no distinguishing features, born London, police inspector. There was a silence, while Joubert fingered the document, then an outburst of rapid French, which Stu took to be a baroque curse; the two younger men laughed.

Joubert picked up the phone.

'Please, if you're going to check my documents, be discreet. I'm supposed to be on sick leave, fishing in Scotland.'

Joubert laughed. *Ça alors. Ça alors.* He hesitated, then ordered breakfast for two, sending the two younger gendarmes outside with a flurry of words.

367

'So you are not the murderer?'

'Murderer?' Stu went white with fury. 'I have spent all my life pursuing thieves, crooks and . . .'

'OK, OK, OK,' said Joubert, running his hand over the early stages of a heavy beard. 'Now Detective Wilson, you tell Detective Joubert who did it, and we forget a little here, a little there. Policemen are not always policemen. Perhaps you explain how you come to have two million francs in the hotel safe. Perhaps we forget. Perhaps we can send you fishing in Scotland.'

Stu described, professionally and accurately, what he had seen, what he had done, what Mr Marchwood had done. He had not seen Mr Marchwood's car; he knew he had several. Yes, at least one Bentley.

'Why are you here?' Joubert asked, quietly.

Stu looked at him and wondered whether he could trust him. He asked: 'Who has been killed?'

Joubert's hands semaphored frustration. The man rose, walked to the door, talked with his subordinates, returned an envelope containing photographs.

It was Thérèse Marchwood. Or rather: it had been Thérèse. The sight of such pictures, seen so often, did not become easier.

Dear God.

Joubert looked at him, and nodded.

They had found her in the harbour, beside the yacht of Monsieur Murphy. There were marks of bare hands at her throat, but they did not yet know whether she had been dead before she entered the water or whether she drowned; they thought the former. Did he know Monsieur Murphy?

Stu Wilson shook his head; heard of the man, of course. Then Joubert suggested a theory: Monsieur Marchwood has a discussion, an argument with his wife in the casino; then in the hotel room he loses his temper, she takes the lift to the car park, where everything is badly-lit, gets into the car – no, perhaps before she gets into the car . . . Joubert raises fleshy hands to his mouth and throat; anyway, soon after that she is inside the car, she is dead. There are no witnesses in the garage, as far as they know; the man at the exit might or might not have seen someone wearing a peaked cap drive the red Marchwood Bentley away along the harbour-wall, but there are many slipways and jetties for dumping the body, while everybody is watching and listening to Murphy's party. A little tide, a little ripple drags the body across the water . . . Joubert's hands fanned horizontally; then he separated and raised two fingers, almost comically, but without humour: 'There were perhaps two men. One to drive, one to kill. Do you know Monsieur Marchwood's chauffeur?'

For a moment, it seemed he was being accused of the murder again. He stared: 'I told you – did not leave the casino yesterday evening.'

'Where you collected your money. Your payment?' Joubert was testing his reactions. Stu knew that he knew that he knew this; even so it was difficult to react naturally.

'Wrong. All wrong.'

It was, however, true that Marchwood had given him chips; true that Marchwood had been away for an hour or so; true that he had not noticed Gary the chauffeur much before midnight in the casino throng, he might have been with Marchwood for the critical period. Such a mess.

He had not pressed Marchwood about Thérèse. He had felt it was none of his business. Wrong again. Only now had he begun to question Marchwood's motives; why had he been so exuberant, quite so ebullient?

Joubert continued: 'By playing a little theatre in the casino, you make it difficult for people to remember who was there, at what time. Two could slip out, slip back, leaving a third. And there is the chance to make a little money. Perfect. How do you like that?'

'Completely and utterly wrong. Besides . . .'

'I think you will always say this,' Joubert said, tartly. 'Now you tell me the whole story, Inspecteur Wilson. This time, we will start from the beginning.'

Just then, breakfast arrived. Joubert insisted that Wilson would not object to paying, now that he was a rich man. Wilson tried to ignore the irony, rose from his seat, to discover how groggy and grey he felt; he had to wash and shave. Joubert nodded. When he returned from the bathroom Joubert, dunking a croissant in a bowl filled with milky brown coffee, offered to pour him a cup.

'White, no sugar, merci.' Stu took his seat and, despite himself, admired the unending blue of the sky over the bay and mountains. An unearthly beauty. He lifted the coffee bowl to his lips, slurped, and felt his stomach jerk, as if someone had tugged at its drawstring. Joubert ate eagerly, enthusiastically.

Bloody Bellet.

He had to say something; he tried explaining how he worked for the Serious Fraud Office, how he had arrested Stephen Grote and other leading members of Lloyd's; explained that the investigation was dying, that all the prosecutions were running into sand; most of this could be found out from the computer terminal in his office. Joubert nodded, wrote down the names of Grote, Devies and MacNulty, then asked: 'Are they the enemy? And Monsieur Marchwood, a friend? You, the agent provocateur paid by him?'

Stu tried to protest. Joubert raised a hand: 'If I were you, I would tell us. How you win your two millions.'

Luck.

The story seemed to amuse Inspector Joubert.

The heat haze was taking control of the coastline around the bay, stretching, reducing, refining the colours into shades of grey. Boats were edging out into the all-but-becalmed sea for a day of boom-rattled stillness.

Finally, Stu insisted: 'I didn't kill Thérèse Marchwood.'

This, however, left other possibilities, cannoning around the place.

'And Monsieur Marchwood? All this extravagance. . . ?'

Stu just did not know. Monsieur Robbo was extraordinarily difficult to read, to look at him, you just would not know what he was thinking. If he wanted to give you a piece of his mind, then he was able to leave you well-informed; otherwise, you would be none the wiser. Which was why he was so special at his job.

'*Et alors?*'

'Well, he didn't behave as if he had just killed his wife.'

Which was true. Even so, it stank.

Joubert laughed again, helping himself to more of the remarkably good coffee. 'Just the proof we need, Inspector. We must charge him.'

'You don't want to charge me?' Wilson was surprised.

'Not yet.'

THREE

DAWN CAME EARLY, swiftly at the Cap d'Antibes, to be replaced by a sun-filled morning, heat.

Despite the pain, the worry, the anxiety, Stephen Grote still loved this place, this time of day and time of year.

It was John Devies's good fortune that his great-great-grandfather or great-great-great-grandfather had invented the Cap or so it was said, in the days when the English found the sunshine an imperative for their ailing natures and balm for their spiritual health.

One year, when the orange crop failed, the English community had had roads built, sewers laid, to give the French peasantry work; an almost socialist idea, Devies agreed, which established that paradise had first to be found, then built. The following year, his great-great-forebear had bought a plot here, on this rock-and-sand peninsula, then started digging, planting and building with the enthusiasm of a founding father; plant species by the thousand were brought from around the world, despatched in oil-skin packets and teachests, carried by boat and train and coach, to this spot, with its glorious dawns, where they thrived in wondrous profusion and abundance: pines, palms, bougainvillea, agaves, cacti.

The result could be admired from Stephen's bedroom window; it was a wonder.

So royalty became neighbours and acquaintances: the Crown Prince so-and-so of Prussia, the Czar's brother-in-law, the Czar himself, the Aga Khan and, on occasion, the Queen of the British Empire who arrived by royal train for the mild winter months. Grand steamships, bearing royal pennants, stood here at anchor, and the grand house of the Devies clan offered a small, agreeable and discreet home to world diplomacy at a time when the British, French and Prussians wanted to meet, but did not want to be seen doing so.

Stephen Grote loved every detail of the house. Donna had thought of buying here, but they would never, ever acquire anything as fine, and John was always delighted to have their company; there was always enough room. Stephen remembered how Ioánnis Kolokotrónis and Mercedes had paid their one and only visit, arriving by motor launch at the white jetty beneath the white rocks that edged the property and its small, almost private bay. Johnny had been so taken with the house, the garden, the history, the neighbours, that he had made John an offer, in front of everybody; a very large sum, much more than anything obtainable on the open market. Mercedes had been embarrassed, Johnny had insisted. When Johnny Kolokotrónis wanted something, he made sure he got it. But John Devies, then a youngish man in his best years, remained steadfast. This was family property. The evening was ruined, of course. Shortly thereafter, Johnny took a short lease on the neighbouring property, but his third wife felt it reminded her of Mercedes, his second, so the couple only rarely stayed on land, preferring the *Ambrosia*.

The argument with the all-powerful Cypriot made firm friends of John Devies and Stephen Grote, who had risked much by criticising Johnny to his face. Thereafter, they knew they wanted to run Lloyd's, and they knew why; they started to invent the rules of the game. At the time, the Devies house had not been quite what it would be twenty years later, all the bathrooms and bedrooms renovated, the kitchen and staff wing re-built, central heating fitted, the old outdoor pool modernised and sanitised, the garden replenished and tended. Yet the old, old charm was untouched. Arriving late on Friday night, everybody started to chatter in the old hallway, animated by the sudden, giddy pleasure of being there. Breakfast, it was agreed, would be brunch and late.

It was long after dawn, but still in brunch terms early, when Henry Stone knocked on Stephen Grote's door; he had been in the gardens, sleepless, disturbed, glad to take the early sunshine and cool air with Tony MacNulty. He entered, to find Stephen standing by the open shutters, admiring the exuberant foliage.

'How did you sleep?' Henry asked, receiving a wan look from a bruised face by way of reply. The doctor would be round in due course.

372

Stephen said, however: 'It is sore, but I will be fine.'

They drew up chairs, closed the windows; Henry had been busy overnight and had distressing news. He lowered his voice. Their friends had been fitting an explosive device to the Marchwood car in the garage. They were disturbed by Mrs Marchwood. They gave chase, caught her and –

'They panicked,' Henry said, raising both his hands, turning them as if twisting something long and thin.

Frightened, the two bungling professionals had rid themselves of Bentley and body as swiftly as possible; wiping the Bentley clean of fingerprints and leaving it in a side street, they had thought to dump the body near Murphy's boat to gain time, letting the gendarmerie spend half the night interviewing Murphy and all his guests.

Stephen Grote cursed. This was the crass idiocy all violence entailed: he detested such necessities. He was also genuinely upset, appalled even, by Thérèse's death. She had been a spiky woman, but very human. His mind gave him pictures of her, strangled. He was appalled.

He berated Henry for a while, who merely listened, who had, he knew, spent hours arguing with their partners over this, to no avail. *Autres pays, autres moeurs.*

Then Stephen relented: 'It was my decision; my responsibility.' He shuddered. 'Besides, it should suffice.'

That had been Stone's conclusion, too. Particularly since Robbo had been arrested. At that news, despite himself, despite his painful face, Stephen Grote brightened.

Now, they had to be swift. John Devies was summoned and informed. One by one, the other men filed through Stephen's room to hear the less-than-wonderful news, mostly in silence. Nobody was happy, least of all Tony MacNulty, who seemed to Stephen to reek of drink – although Stephen was sure he could not, in his state, smell anything at all. Then a brunch commenced on the terrace, bright and breezy, presided over in all innocence by Hettie Devies, who was the complete mistress of polite and cheerful coercion. She had, she told her guests, made arrangements: the young and not-so-young ladies around the table were to accompany her to the local market that morning to admire the lavender, olives, bay leaves and local herbs, the smell of fresh fruit and fish, then they were to drive to the tip of the peninsula, marked by a lighthouse and a white concrete and glass

373

modernist building. It was there that the girls would have a light lunch. This was, Hettie informed her charges, the restaurant where that mad woman Zelda threw herself off the terrace because she feared her husband Scott Fitzgerald had been purloined for the night by Josephine Baker, the black dancer.

So the parties divided; Hettie took care of the girls, while the men, headed by Fortescue because Stephen Grote had to wait for the doctor, strode out into the gardens, then solemnly shook hands at a scheduled spot where English and Prussian ambassadors had once talked. Marked by a circular stone table, the place was hidden beneath shading pine and cypresses, yet overlooked the bay, with the old fort, a relic of the Napoleonic era, the Italian peninsula fading away in the blue-grey heat.

Now they felt an almost exaggerated determination to be cheerful. Despite which Neil Fortescue felt impelled to complain about the previous day's meetings with the PM and the hardship committee in Lime Street.

'We had one of your cases to deal with,' he said, nodding to Tony MacNulty. 'Mrs Cornelia Sanderson.'

One or two of the others had heard of the lady in question, a troublemaker.

'She go quietly?' Tony ventured.

Fortescue shook his head. In fact, they had had to interrupt the meeting, because the old bat had insisted on giving them all a piece of her mind and more besides. She had only come to the meeting because she had no more money left to fight. She and Fortescue had exchanged more than the odd word, before he had made her an offer, one hundred pounds a week for the rest of her life, which she immediately refused: 'I'd rather declare myself bankrupt.' With that, she was gone, even though Fortescue thought his offer reasonable.

Smiles. They were all heartily sick of the stupid people who whinged and refused to pay, so a notably ruddy-faced and amiable John Devies told a favourite anecdote about one name, a stockbroker, who went AWOL after having transferred much of his wealth into bearer bonds that he deposited in a numbered account at a Swiss bank, which just happened to be the West-Europa-Bank in Zurich, of which John just happened to be a director. Despite a false name and false moustache, he had recognised the recently-disappeared man on pictures taken by concealed cameras at the bank.

They all laughed. John squeezed a remote handset. Staff appeared; more coffee, croissants and orange juice were brought.

Once the staff had retreated, Fortescue started to tell them about Downing Street, about the latest cash-flow forecasts for Lloyd's, the business plan.

He concluded, with a wry smile: 'The good news is we can bring the government down, the bad news is the government doesn't have the money to pay, even if it wanted to.'

This account of the Downing Street meeting did not fire his friends with enthusiasm. For a while nobody spoke. MacNulty helped himself to more coffee, thought vaguely of Sue, while some way offshore a white motor yacht tuck-tuckered in lazy circles, then paused while bathers dived in bright sunshine.

Neil had admitted that Lloyd's was bankrupt, and that the politicians would not rescue them. Had he not protested to the PM? Emphasised the importance of Lloyd's to the City? To Britain? To its reputation? To hundreds of associated companies and thousands of individuals?

Devies cleared his throat: 'We are responsible for two billion in invisible earnings. That makes us as important as British Aerospace to the economy. They cannot let us go.'

Fiddling with match and cigarette, Fortescue said: 'We have fifteen billions in capital, thirty in liabilities, possibly more. People have been squeezed dry. Mrs Sanderson, bless her immortal soul, once had assets of one hundred and fifty thousand pounds; now she has losses of two million. The money just isn't there.'

Stone and Wilmot-Greaves pressed him, shocked to hear so much of their own wealth written off, their own businesses reduced to nothing.

Fortescue blew smoke and coughed: 'Financially, we are beyond the point of no return. We need Government support. That will not be forthcoming.

'So we continue for a year, perhaps two, until insolvency is upon us.'

MacNulty confessed that Wordsworth was on the brink, despite staff cuts, even though Denbigh-Wright was still making money. Then there were the costs of litigation . . . They all had the same dusty vision: the family firm based in Lloyd's, years upon years of effort and accumulated pride, was about to die. For MacNulty, Stone and Wilmot-Greaves, it was difficult to accept.

Wilmot-Greaves put a hand on a balding head and said, in an ironic tone: 'At least we don't need a deal with Robert Marchwood now in order to survive.'

Just then Stephen Grote arrived, looking unsure of his feet; yet he smiled, cheerfully, then gave everyone a solemn hand and assured them he was fine. He would leave for Zurich shortly, where (feeling he needed a pretext) he had decided to have the operation many men underwent at his time of life.

He helped himself to coffee, while others wondered aloud about the previous night's events, about the police. Fortescue offered him the Lear jet for an afternoon flight to Zurich; Stephen could be in hospital that evening.

Stephen refused, with a weak smile: 'I am not running away. There is no reason . . .'

It had to be seen through.

The others nodded and murmured; the botch had not been theirs; once again, the simple rule of separation between executive and legislative had worked. They did not deal in sulphuric acid, ship arms or manufacture drugs . . . though they might know someone who did. Grote's laws insisted on clean relationships, calm and control; rational behaviour brought rational rewards. Yet he himself, at last night's party, had neither been discreet nor self-controlled.

'I am sorry,' he said, slowly, 'for my behaviour last night. Tasteless. A mistake. All because of that darned man. But I do feel genuinely sorry for Robey.'

'My dear chap,' Devies said. 'Marchwood would have tested the patience of an angel. He's tested us all, beyond the limit.'

Wilmot-Greaves agreed, loudly: 'Hear, hear.'

MacNulty, who had not been at ease with himself since his peace efforts foundered, assured Stephen that the decision to act against Robert had been the right thing.

There had been no other rational alternative.

Nobody had seen Stephen brought quite so low. Yet even in this state he was more than a match for Fortescue, who always, in private, deferred to him. Thus it was now Stephen who produced his vision of the future, as conceived by himself, to be executed with the help of John and Services Division.

He had plans for a new holding company for their interests.

From his attaché case he produced two large sheets of photo-copied paper for each of them.

They were to create a new banking and insurance group, jointly centered on the Société Commerciale et Bancaire du Midi, based in the principality, and on the West-Europa-Bank in Zurich. The present holding structure was shown on the first page of the document; the new structure on the second.

According to the second sheet, they would soon control 84 per cent of West-Europa-Bank, holding their stakes through a web of offshore companies. The Société Commerciale et Bancaire du Midi would be a subsidiary of West-Europa, with which it would be linked by cross-holdings, for complexity's sake. Stephen said he could see them wondering how they were going to pay for this: a swiss bank, after all, is a Swiss bank.

'Tell them about the deal, old man,' John Devies said.

The first sheet showed the present holding structure: there were four holders controlling a majority: Horcum, Petteril, Wordsworth, CRG, plus several smaller holders.

The plan was to sell the bank to a management-led con-sortium ('to ourselves,' laughed Devies) for a small premium over book value. The bank itself would lend the consortium the money to buy itself, funded by the sale-and-leaseback of its grossly undervalued head office.

'We're getting the bank for nothing,' Fortescue said, fasci-nated. It was an excellent fraud, virtually invisible.

'A pleasant gift,' Stephen Grote smiled despite the bruising. Now he needed to talk to Donna.

There were some whistles of near-disbelief, some laughter. Neil Fortescue might have brought bad news, but Stephen had promised and, once again, had come up with the goods. There was, for them, a life after Lloyd's.

Horcum and Petteril had already initialed the documents relating to the sale; both firms were large, quoted companies which apparently gained little from their apparently small stakes in an apparently small bank: it was not known that its value was grossly understated by its accounts. Publicity was to be kept to a minimum, but little would be expected. The bank did not appear to be a significant asset.

Stephen Grote said: 'The outstanding sixteen per cent goes to the Swiss management. Herr Wyttenbach, who some of you

377

know, is a good friend of mine, with contacts in the right circles. He will front the operation.

'The Société Commerciale, based here, will be headed by friends of Henry. Indeed, Henry deserves congratulations on the success of his delicate negotiations at this end.'

Henry Stone folded his arms and grinned; Wilmot-Greaves patted his back.

Beneath them, the quiet sea barely rippled as it spread into the distance, dotted with sails like nuns' white cowls on a high holiday. The swimmers from the motor yacht were now back on deck, drinking, sunbathing as it drew away.

Slowly, and too late, much too late, Stephen pulled his two surveillance detectors from his attaché case. Was nowhere safe, not even here?

Oh, no. John Devies whispered anger at himself, under his breath. The house was always clean, the grounds were no problem. He had become lax; it had slipped his mind. It had slipped all their minds.

Stephen placed one detector, then the other on the table. The two lights turned green, then red.

Tony MacNulty and Alec Wilmot-Greaves, the quickest witted, started chatting about the latest yacht; Devies chipped in with gossip from the Squadron, jokes about Cowes week. A member of staff was summoned, given the remote control and told to go to the house. Still the lights remained red. The crockery was removed. Red. All pockets were emptied, the contents placed on the table: keys, wallets, pens, watches. It had to be the pens, marked with the Lloyd's logo, that had been left in the bedrooms at the Hôtel d'Orléans as gifts: simple, effective. Wilmot-Greaves had one, MacNulty another. They were left to sit together, chatting about Cowes, while the others went into the house. The motor yacht had to be checked, any cars outside the house, and swiftly. There would be time for recriminations later. Grote turned to Henry Stone, speaking in gravelled tones: 'Your friends should start a search for Ray Marchwood. Find him.' He clenched two fists, then let them fall.

Stone nodded. Nothing more needed to be said.

FOUR

CONNIE SANDERSON HAD invited her neighbours, Lucy and Walter, for a heart-to-heart talk at home.

She repeated to them the words of Mr Neil Fortescue, head of Lloyd's, which she knew by heart, would never forget: 'Please, Mrs Sanderson, I beg of you. There are many others in your situation, we have seen hundreds of names and, I must say, they have shown more understanding of their position. And may I add: more dignity . . .'

Lucy laughed nervously.

'Then I told him he was a self-satisfied, vain, patronising man! Fortescue the fiddler!'

She had lost control.

She explained: she and Ron had been worth perhaps two hundred thousand. Now she only had losses, two million owed to Lloyd's. And there were bank debts from the garage, now under new ownership.

'I am bust,' she had told Fortescue, 'and you are crooked.'

Now she needed a lawyer, a lawyer cost money, she had no money, ergo, she was asking Walter, who was a lawyer, for some free advice.

They stood for a while round the dining-room table, exchanged happy memories of the day of the storm, of Ron the demon lawn-mower, as Walter had evidently called him, wondered about the economy, which was dropping down some large hole.

Then she said: 'I think the bank wants the house, now. So I invited you round to say goodbye.'

There was a silence.

They all looked at the room, which was harmonious, in a heavy, solid-wooded, mock-tudorish sort of way; buying the furniture had involved months of scrimping and saving. Naturally, it was still worth more than a packet of Zip!

firelighters, but not much. Sentimental value, that was it; she could almost hear the ghosts of dinner parties past, the laughter of Jonathan and his friends, the Christmas lunches. Now the curtains were a once-in-a-lifetime opportunity for moths.

Walter cleared his throat and, with a notable lack of enthusiasm, said: 'If the bank makes you bankrupt, which is what you ultimately mean, I suppose . . .'

She nodded.

'Then they will sell the house, sell the contents, claim your pension lump sum, which should be due, shortly . . .'

'You mean: strip me of everything?'

He hummed: 'Well, you will be able to retain part of your pension income, but borrowing will be difficult, running a bank account nearly impossible. On the other hand, if you file for bankruptcy yourself, it could be over after two years.'

'You make it sound almost attractive, Walter.'

'Hm. But since your debts are more than twenty thousand pounds –'

'One hundred times more.'

'So in your case, with the larger debt, it would be three years. In only three years' time you –'

The debts had been gifts from a kind deity. First, there had been the Bentley fiasco, which had cost most of what she had, then there was Lloyd's, which was a wonderful example of British skill, intelligence and honesty. She found Fortescue and all his fellow rodents very inspirational. Yet it was the bank manager, not they, who had mentioned the dread word: bankruptcy.

'Walter,' she interrupted. 'Would you be prepared, let alone able, to live off fifty-six pounds a week?'

She had been told that she might be allowed the minimum to live from her pension – perhaps just her state old age pension. This made Fortescue's offer of one hundred pounds a week seem positively generous – but she had turned him down, on principle. Perhaps she was mad.

Walter hesitated. 'I know it's tough, old girl,' he stammered. 'But you'll see it through.'

Lucy asked whether she wanted to sell the cut-glass, some of it antique, for cash. Walter coughed.

Connie poured some more sherry, gin and tonic for Walter, stared at a grey-haired woman in the mirror over the mantelpiece. Cheers.

380

FIVE

'ELLE EST MIGNONNE, Yvette, non?'

Stu nodded, with a swift smile. Sweet Yvette was long gone, trailing the ghost of Madeleine like a mink wrap behind her. They were seated in Joubert's car, a black Renault with black leather seats which had turned grey from cigarette ash and dust.

In the Hôtel d'Orléans, Joubert had orchestrated everything, with the relentless energy of an important guest. He clapped his hands; breakfast was over; shouted; the table was removed; telephoned here, there and everywhere. Stu was a pawn in his campaign, poised for sacrifice.

In the marina below, yachts were putting out to sea, a motor launch arrived with a crowd of the scantily clad young. Stu thought he could hear laughter and chatter.

'OK. You pay now. Everything.' His hand signed figures on a starched white tablecloth.

'How much?' Joubert asked.

'I'm sorry?' Wilson was puzzled.

'How much for the night . . . and the day and the break-fast . . .' Joubert added, then named an improbable sum. Stu shrugged and smiled. Since he had never, ever known anything quite like it . . .

Then Joubert laughed, on the phone. 'Ah. Monsieur Marchwood has already said? Ah bon.'

Apparently Stu had a benefactor. Who happened to be in police custody. Stu ran his hand through his hair.

'Right, we leave in fifteen minutes, Inspecteur Wilson. So you must be outside the door, dressed in twelve minutes.'

He disappeared through the door in a haze of blue smoke. Stu closed the door.

Joubert was waiting at the reception, with a bill and a cheque;

Wilson signed illegibly, accepting his winnings and an exorbitant bill from the hotel. If he and Marchwood were paying twice, it did not seem to matter. Joubert nonchalantly placed the cheque for the remaining two million francs, made out in Stu's name, in his leather money-folder: 'So you come to Joubert to say au revoir.'

Joubert saw the cheque as an inducement to active co-operation. The money was as much as Wilson had earned in half a lifetime. Nothing signed, of course; no witnesses worthy of the name; no proof; Stu had, nonetheless, handed it over.

'Why are you letting me go?'

'Ah.' Joubert shrugged his shoulders. 'My job is not to prosecute British policemen.' He made judgements about people all the time. Sometimes wrong, sometimes right.

Stu said nothing. They headed for the Hôtel de la Gare. 'Since the Hôtel d'Orléans is not to your taste.'

Joubert asked about Thérèse Marchwood.

Wilson was complimentary. Goodlooking, elegant, intelligent.

Joubert rubbed his hand across his face, burst into voluble gesture, just as the car accelerated through a red light. 'Extra. *Elle était extraordinaire, cette femme . . . Ça ne se fait pas. Ah, non. Ça ne se fait pas ici.*' He hit the steering wheel, turned his torso towards Wilson, occasionally looked at the traffic.

Suddenly, Stu was dumped outside the brasserie beneath the hotel. In the bar-and-table shade, he could see la Patronne. He turned to Joubert.

Au revoir. Vague grins.

Joubert was on his way by car to the Cap d'Antibes, to talk to Monsieur Grote and Monsieur Fortescue. Meanwhile, Stu had a job to do.

He crossed the road and entered the half-deserted railway station, looking like a hung-over party-goer amid the mild-mannered straggle of bank and hotel employees still en route for work. He removed his dinner-jacket, halted at a ticket machine, observed that overnight trains from Paris and Lyon had arrived. Waited, looked.

Nobody seemed to be taking much notice. He slipped into a bookshop, admired English books at funny prices, waited, left by a side entrance, took an escalator, dashed past a barber's shop, walked along a large-tiled windowless corridor, paused by a weighing machine, strode over to a bank of metal luggage boxes, then toe-heeled off a shoe, extracted a taped key, removed the tape, grated the key in the lock. The door to the luggage box opened, he grasped the package containing the Smith & Wesson, placed it inside his jacket, pressing its weight against his ribs. He looked up, along the corridor, saw distant sunlight, to the right, the left, bored staff at the left luggage office.

He knew that Grote had friends down here, important friends. Joubert was not the only man imposing a kind of order on this edge of paradise. Stu remembered the newspaper cutting Tomlinson had shown Stu about a banker who worked in the principality, for a local bank, who had died in London, swimming face down in St Katherine's Dock. Scrivano, that was it. An accident: most unfortunate.

Stu was keen not to become an accident, too. So he took precautions. If the local heavies were waiting for him, they would be watching the hotel, yet he had to change his clothes: in evening dress, he felt like an absurd extra from an incomprehensible foreign film.

He paused at a newspaper and bookstall, apparently looking at the headlines, to catch his breath. Despite breakfast, his head still throbbed from the drink, the smoke, the lack of sleep; he ached with tiredness.

Kevin, then Thérèse Marchwood, yet still he did not understand.

He could see no reason for her death. It made no sense for Grote and his friends. They had nothing to gain, nothing that Stu could readily perceive – unless Robert Marchwood was charged and convicted of her murder, a long shot. It made more sense to kill Robert or Ray – or Stu himself. Just as it had made sense to kill Kevin.

There had been an attempt on Robert's life; it had looked serious enough, professional enough, yet the gunman had hesitated. If he had entered the pool area, according to Keef, Marchwood would have been an easy target. Thereafter, Robert had left for Switzerland, changed his life, avoided Lloyd's. If a hoax it would have been an unusual one. Stu wanted to believe in the Marchwoods, yet that in itself seemed dangerous; he felt as if he had been set up. The photographs, the telephone call in Euston, all smily Ray's, had been used to lure him down here, attract the attention, perhaps the aggression of Grote and friends, while the Marchwoods did whatever they wanted to do. He was deeply suspicious about the crucial time that Marchwood had spent between leaving the terrace and returning to the casino. Then there were the tears, the obvious distress of the woman herself. Hours later, she was dead.

Stu had told Joubert that Robbo did not have the air of a man who had just killed his wife. True, but Robbo was one of life's play-actors. According to him, he and Thérèse had said goodbye, whatever that might mean. The rôle of Gary the bodyguard-cum-chauffeur was unclear. During those hours, the two men could have killed Thérèse with calm efficiency.

He twirled a black metal bookstand containing books in a language he could not read. His arm ached, his head; he glanced around and saw one bored shopkeeper, a flow of sundry purchasers.

The Marchwoods had been more than happy to lie to him about the Monet in the past. Robbo's behaviour last night, although he had willingly played along, had seemed to mock his intelligence and his integrity. Two hundred thousand pounds, even if won at the gaming table, looked like one hell of a bribe. All those temptations for all those years that he had so easily brushed aside; now he had been turned into a fool, contemptible. Joubert had seen it all before and more besides, but seemed relaxed. That was why, Stu guessed, he was willing to trust him. Even if Stu was not willing to tell him all he knew.

Joubert had asked repeatedly why he was there, in the casino, and Stu had found no reasonable answer. A hunch, a whim, the desire for justice.

Stu Wilson wondered whether he had lost the will to fight; there were other ways to spend one's declining years. If he had the cheque in his pocket, he might have quietly disappeared: there was a golden isle somewhere waiting for him, filled with sunshine, desert palms, turquoise-blue waters, even the Costa del Cop would do. As for Rosie, well.

First Kevin, then Mrs Marchwood.

No, no. He repeated words to himself, as if they were a comfort blanket. He had to see this through . . . No surrender . . . Every defeat contains the seeds of the coming victory . . . And he would take the letters from the package containing the gun and send them to the DG and to Rosie, whatever happened.

384

He had typed them at home before leaving, struggling with a typewriter that he rarely used, fighting with correction fluid and the English tongue.

He wanted no way back. The letters, a resignation and a final parting, would confirm that, would guarantee distance between yesterday and today. Marchwood's money was no more than a later decoration.

He wrapped his dinner jacket tightly around the plastic-covered package, avoided retracing his steps, found a post-box, extracted his letters and posted them, disappeared in a subway, overtook a throng of English-speaking backpackers, was surprised by the sunshine, then entered the brasserie beneath the Hôtel de la Gare.

The fat lady behind the till said something cheerful.

Stu, not understanding a word, smiled graciously. He took the rickety stairs, between the rickety walls, two steps at a time, until he stood outside the thin-pine door. He heard someone move inside; wondered, waited, then heard high-heels on linoleum: Yvette opened. So this was love.

Who had sent her?

At first, he did not bother to ask, giving her an impeccable kiss. She was, after all, utterly beautiful. He did not want to know what he knew, just for a while. Something to do with pipers and tunes, a local woman working for local forces. He knew that trust, for the moment, was a dangerous weakness. He had trusted Robbo once too often.

'You will have to go,' he said, to Yvette. He looked through the broken pane, down onto the station. It was calmly busy with daytime activity, taxis and travellers, yet there were two cars waiting; men who were neither bankers nor tourists, dark-tanned men in sunglasses. Of course, they *could* be waiting for someone else, but he would be pleasantly surprised if they were. He could guess at a plan: pick him up, make him swallow a bullet of his own accord, plant the weapon and something from Thérèse on his body. Then everybody is happy, police, politicians and friends: one foreigner kills another. Most regrettable. Monsieur Marchwood could go free. And nobody but nobody would suspect Monsieur Grote.

He would fight. Old Kev had had no chance.

Then he asked Yvette: why had she hot-footed it here?

'*T'as bien payé*,' she laughed in response to his query; then she added something to the effect that he was a fine upstanding Englishman. One who pays. Well, there was some truth in that.

He considered his possible exits: the front door, the side entrance, the rear courtyard, the roof. He hated heights, you could too easily miss a step and fall. He strode outside the room, walked to the landing window that overlooked the courtyard behind the hotel and led to the fire escape; down below a delivery van, open-doored, voices. Everyone would hear and see him on the fire escape.

He asked Yvette to wait; in the bathroom cubicle he washed and changed rapidly into blazer and slacks, checked his gun, slipped it into a leather shoulder holster, then he gave Yvette his white dinner jacket and told her to wait for him outside, in the stationer's doorway some way down the street. A brief kiss, they would see each other later. She looked at him as if she saw through his little plan.

She left.

He heard her heels on the stairs, wooden step by wooden step. He pulled his raincoat over his blazer, put on a hat, sunglasses, closed the door. He listened. Last step, she was in the brasserie; one, two, three; she would keep his pursuers briefly interested in the main entrance, a small decoy – he hoped. He did not bother to tiptoe down the stairs, instead he took them in a hurry, strode out through the brasserie kitchen, heard a clamour of protest, responded with a 'bonjour' and a wave.

He was in luck. Two friends from the heavy brigade hit the hotel stairs, having been alerted by Yvette, presumably. A languid colleague was outside in the courtyard, concentrating on the fire escape, looking for movement from roof to roof. The delivery van was an old-fashioned corrugated metal affair with air where the front doors should have been; he could clamber into the rear. There were five, perhaps six paces between kitchen and van; he would have to move. He took a deep breath at the kitchen exit; one, two, three and out; walked steadily across the courtyard, entered the delivery van where the driver's door ought to have been, took a seat in the rear among crates of wine, water and spirits.

For an age, he waited. He removed the gun from its holster, fearing heavies around the van. Footsteps, voices, a friendly conversation between a man and la Patronne. The driver arrived, waved to the lady, took a seat. Stu ducked down behind the crates and waited, the engine stutter-roared into life and the van left the hotel courtyard, noisy with the rattle of glass.

'Taxi?' Stu asked, his gun safely stowed, showing a hundred franc note to the driver. The young man looked amazed, but did not argue. Shrugged, took the money and let Stu point the way, towards the harbour and the sun-filled bay.

Stu turned round; among the crush of cars he saw nothing that meant anything, nothing that promised to prolong the game. The man in the courtyard would, presumably, lose his promotion prospects.

After a while the driver then said something in French, offered a dark-smelling cigarette which Stu refused with nods and smiles and gestures and everything was hunky-dory. It was normal to wear raincoats when the sun was streaming brightly down. Life was kind; they drove through a couple of traffic lights, turned a corner and Stu was a free man in the bustle of thousands. Luck, calm, cheek; these were the qualities he admired in a thief. He remembered the motto of Danny Shuttleworth, conman: rush slowly. In the course of a richly rewarding career, Danny had managed to sell Tower Bridge to an American widow whose money had composted her good sense; it almost seemed a pity to have the fellow banged up.

Stu strolled into an alleyway, removed his coat and hat and sunglasses, placed them in a doorway. Patted the small, bulky object beneath his blazer.

At the end of the alleyway was a thoroughfare offering everything a tourist might desire, but not need: there were cafés, ice-cream parlours, bright junk and untold postcards.

On the other side of the street, two blocks down, stood the exclusive apartment building he had identified the previous day. Ugly, concrete, saved by bright awnings and sea views. Best viewed from within.

At the entrance, Stu cursed.

Because this was an exclusive concrete block, there was a receptionist-cum-concierge, a large, youngish gent behind a marble-clad desk, complete with signing-in book and camera opportunities.

The lift doors were open.

Broad smile. If he bounced the fellar around, eight to ten years, maximum. Joubert would not approve and his cheque would, in all probability, disappear.

So he showed his ID, said: 'Joubert, police.' And strode past, into the lift; the doors closed. He heard a delayed protest, but by then the metal box was on the move.

He had pushed the button marked six, but he dropped back to five by the fire-escape, sending the lift on to ten. They would think he had gone to seven or eight.

Five was a dark corridor, five doors, four large apartments and a broom cupboard. The nearest of the apartments according to the phone book, was Ray Marchwood's.

It was time to find out the truth. The truth was he believed nobody.

He eased the gun from its leather pouch, removed his blazer, draped it over his right arm. Lifts moved up and down, but did not halt.

The guy downstairs would call the police; if Stu had the choice between police and heavy brigade, well, you might as well go for Inspecteur Joubert.

The door was heavy, with an array of locks and a spy-hole. Stu turned back down the corridor, entered the broom cupboard where he found a mop with a head of grey rats' tails, which he placed against the glass eye inset in the apartment door. Then he pressed the bell and crouched.

He remembered his gun training. Keef had dragged him along to the range because Stu disliked the idea so much. 'Don't let the trigger-happy gun you down.' Truth was, with paper targets, he had been surprisingly good; yet he still took no pleasure in his Smith & Wesson.

The door opened, partially. The mop slid along the face of the door, into the opening, there was a cry of surprise, a very English curse. Stu rose and kicked back the door.

Gareth William Lockyer, recently employed as chauffeur and bodyguard to Robert Marchwood and Thérèse Marchwood, stood in the hallway and raised his hands. If he was frightened, it did not show; it was not the first time he had seen a gun.

Stu kicked the mop to one side, closed the door. They both moved slowly into a large room with shuttered windows; there was the hum of a radio, the chatter of voices. Ray Marchwood was operating a portable console studded with buttons and dials, a surveillance receiver, a wonder of micro-electronics.

On the floor, a bag lay open, evidently built to receive the machine, once its aerial had been retracted.

It was a moment before Ray, wearing sunglasses and baggy Bermuda shorts, looked up and greeted him with a frown-smile.

'Ah, we are just about to move. You did well to find us so swiftly, Inspector Wilson.'

Stu did not smile. 'Tell me who killed Thérèse Marchwood. Also who killed Kevin Vaughan.' He gestured with his gun: 'Because this is a . . .'

'Bleeding mess.' Ray Marchwood, who never swore, quietly finished the phrase. 'My brother rows with Stephen Grote, in front of everybody – so they kill his wife.'

It was not the reaction of a guilty man.

'Who are *they*?'

'We're here to finish them off,' Ray said.

Stu could not even manage a scornful laugh.

Then Gary, who had been less than pleased with his performance at the door, looked up and said: 'We didn't think she would waltz out of the hotel. If she'd stuck with Robbo . . .'

He could not follow them everywhere. Yesterday evening, he had planted a bug on the telephone lines at Devies's house, left a relay station in the grounds of the house; he had inserted voice-operated bugs in complimentary Lloyd's pens in the hotel bedrooms. The surveillance had worked well. 'Mrs Marchwood was not supposed to leave the hotel.'

Wilson's gun arm did not relent. The story just did not seem credible.

Ray looked at his watch; they really had to leave. *They* would be here very shortly. Given that his sister-in-law and Kevin Vaughan had been murdered and that his brother –

That was precisely the point. Stu did not care to speculate what Robert Marchwood's motives might have been, why he wanted to kill his wife, maybe money, maybe she had become redundant, maybe it was a moment of rage and passion, he just did not know. But he said, 'I was enticed here with photographs which could only have been taken with precise knowledge of Kevin's death. Whoever took the pictures was close to the murderer, knew what he was looking for.'

Ray said nothing.

'And now, I've been paid off at the casino table, just to make me the bent copper that can be easily disposed of, if need be.'

Both men shook their heads at him. He was wrong.

'I want proof,' Stu told them.

Ray mocked. 'You had the proof that we rigged the Lloyd's market. A great deal of good it did you.' Despite Stu's gun, he turned, replaced his headphones, slid a cassette into a tape machine, pressed buttons.

Stu said nothing. It had done even less good to Kevin. He shook his head: he could not believe he was there, doing this, but he wanted answers, and for the moment he could see no way forwards or backwards unless he trusted the Marchwoods.

Gary wanted him to put the gun down. Time was pressing, they really had to go.

The speakers whined and hummed with disturbed reception; then, unreally, Stu recognised the recorded voice of Grote engaged in a telephone conversation about the merits of Zurich hospitals. He needed surgery, he was flying out tonight . . . Now Grote was talking to someone he called Donna. The topic changed; the terrible weather in London; the need for a spot of global warming and a touch of sunshine. Donna did not sound especially happy.

Then there had been a terrible incident . . . Mrs Marchwood; Mr Marchwood under suspicion . . . There was a distinct lack of sorrow in the voice. Donna had not met the woman, as far as she could recall.

Stu felt tired, the drink, the hours of not sleeping, yet still he waited, rooted to the spot. Waited for proof.

Ray introduced another cassette into the tape machine on the console. Grote's voice was replaced by MacNulty's and Stone's, out of doors, walking somewhere.

MacNulty: 'This is a bloody mess.'

Stone: 'Stephen was right though. It could not continue. Not after Marchwood broke his nose.'

MacNulty: 'Well, it was his decision. Did they have to kill Thérèse?'

Stone: 'Good decision, poor execution.'

MacNulty: 'We've had too much of this. Far too much. Look at the Vaughan affair –'

Stone: 'Stephen insisted the data store had to be protected. He was right, we agreed. He ordered the trap to be set, we agreed. The Marchwoods were warned and took no notice. Then Vaughan walked into it.'

MacNulty: 'I knew the place would burn, not that Vaughan would die inside.'

Stone: 'I don't think it's right to criticise Stephen. We agreed with his decision on the store.'

MacNulty: 'Well yes, but his behaviour last night was intemperate.'

Stone: ''Fraid he does lose his rag on occasion, old man. Happens to everyone. I must see him now . . .'

The tape was stopped.

Those few words, what did they prove? Yet Wilson let the gun-point drop, nodded, holstered the weapon. Although others had done the dirty work, Stephen Grote had authorised turning the Lloyd's Data Storage Centre into a deadly trap. He was responsible.

Stu looked at the shutters, the bars of light on the curtains. He knew that there was a feud, an old feud, which had not been forgotten; now he had joined one side, the Marchwoods'; there was no other reasonable explanation left. He shook Ray's hand.

'There are still questions. I want to know about Kevin, about the shooting incident at Golden Rain.'

Ray shrugged: 'Later. It's them or us now. We have to go.'

He extracted the tapes from the receiver, telescoped the aerial so that the console fitted its travelling case, the remaining mess would have to be left. Stu grabbed the Stone/MacNulty tape, slipped it in his blazer pocket, alongside the standard-issue pea-shooter.

'They'll finish you if they find that tape,' Ray observed.

'Police evidence.'

Then the telephone rang in the room. Stu suppressed a grin; he had certainly spoilt Joubert's lunch; the local nick would have told him that someone had impersonated him, phoned through the description. He would have uncovered the only apartment in the block with a Lloyd's link easily enough. The man was downstairs.

Stu said: 'I'll get you out of here.'

Ray looked at him, uncomprehending.

Stu picked up the telephone: 'Inspector Wilson speaking. Ah, Inspector Joubert. Yes, I think I can help you with your enquiries. Could you hold on down there a moment, please, I'll see you in the lobby.'

He replaced the handset; then he told Ray and Gary what to do.

In the lobby, Joubert cut up rough; he had heard that someone with an English accent had used his name – roared over from the Cap d'Antibes, told everyone it was his case, to leave well alone . . .

'Did you find anything out from the English gentlemen, from Grote and his merry crew?' Stu Wilson interrupted.

Joubert looked away. Stu sympathised; he, too, had interviewed two or three of them in his time. Besides, Joubert said, they all had alibis; they were all together last night. Now Inspector Wilson had to explain his behaviour.

Stu said he had had to take refuge in the apartment of a friend; some unfriendly locals had tried to separate his body from his soul; despite this, he had something to show Joubert, a tape . . . He waved it, smiled.

Joubert nodded. 'But first, mon ami . . .' First he wanted the key to the apartment belonging to Inspector Wilson's friend. Stu handed him the key, wished him every success.

Joubert and his sidekick, a plain-clothed Georges, took the lift. After a time, they returned, not notably satisfied. Having access to an untidy and empty apartment is not a crime. But now it was time for lunch. Stu suggested the brasserie of the Hôtel de la Gare. 'We can ask la Patronne about my unfriendly visitors . . .'

They went in Joubert's car, found a table and Joubert ordered. Wine, it seemed, would help the questions to flow.

Wilson looked at his watch; by now, Ray and Gary should be quitting the broom cupboard on the eighth floor, packing their kit into the van in the basement. He had no choice but trust them.

'Do you smoke?' Joubert asked, offering Inspecteur Wilson a cigarette.

'Not while I eat.' Stu smiled, then placed the tape on the table, looked at Joubert's sidekick. He asked him if he was the one with a personal stereo? Stu had seen one on the car's back seat. He asked him, politely, if he would go fetch; Joubert nodded and this became an order.

Georges disappeared.

In the meantime, Stu had questions for Joubert: 'Who was Yvette working for? Who wanted to ruin my holiday?'

Yes, the wine was adequate; Joubert's fingertips touched his lips in praise, then ordered another pichet.

Stu tried again. Had Joubert had any dealings with the Banco

Cristòforo? Had he known Monsieur Scrivano? And again who was Yvette working for?

The stereo and ear-phones were placed on the table; Georges smiled, took a seat. The food arrived.

Between mouthfuls, Joubert said: 'You know a great deal about our little paradise, Inspecteur Wilson,' Joubert commented, laconically.

'Well, thank you.' Stu knew he had to wait. A shared lunch was a pledge of trust, of understanding – and Joubert had his cheque. For a time, there was silence.

'She is different, Yvette, non?'

'Pity about her friends.'

After a silence, Joubert gestured, bringing the five fingers of one hand together, pointing upwards, then covering with the other palm. Which hand rules and which is ruled? They work together, exist together. Yet, for the most part, only the one hand is visible.

Stu nodded.

Influence. Joubert gave the word its French pronunciation, carefully, then widened his arms in a sweep which encompassed everything in the restaurant. The casino, too, the police, Yvette. Everything was involved, nothing was untouched. Influence.

'Monsieur Grote has friends, Inspecteur, and these friends have influence.'

In one sense, Wilson had rather hoped to hear this; it confirmed his prejudices; in another, it confirmed his worst fears. Joubert's hands were tied.

'And in Britain?' Joubert asked.

'A green and pleasant land, not a casino on top of a barren rock. But you are right, everywhere there is influence. I would say: politics.'

Joubert flashed a broad smile, as if this was what he wanted to hear. Then Stu fiddled with the personal stereo, offering the headphones to Joubert who listened once, twice, until he was sure he had understood the words of Monsieur MacNulty and Monsieur Stone, talking about the previous night. 'Good decision, poor execution.' Then: 'We agreed with his decision.'

Joubert did not ask him how or why Stu had obtained the tape. 'Who is this Vaughan, what is this store?'

'Kevin Vaughan was my nephew. He died in a fire in a Lloyd's storage unit. He was working with me, investigating Lloyd's.'

Joubert looked at him. Shook his head, wiped his mouth with his napkin, lifted a hand showing two fingers. 'Two deaths?'

'Two decisions.'

'I am sorry for you. For Monsieur Marchwood also.' Joubert tapped the cassette player and said: 'The tape, it is not proof, I think.'

'No, only the truth.'

Joubert laughed, a large, loud, bitter laugh. It was as if he knew more than enough, for his purposes. Then he said: 'Generals do not dirty their hands. Grote is a general. He will be buried . . .' Joubert played an imaginary trumpet.

'What are you going to do with Marchwood?'

Joubert said they would have to hold him, for questioning. As for the others, he gestured at the restaurant, the casino, everything.

Stu tapped Joubert's wallet, which was lying on the table, just to ask about his winnings.

Joubert wagged a finger, shook his head: 'It is not yet the time to say: au revoir. I need you, perhaps.'

'I will not testify, not here. But I am not a coward.'

The three men rose from the table. Joubert did not bother to see the mess upstairs that had been made of Wilson's personal effects; he would want a statement in a couple of days: 'Don't get lost, mon ami. Avoid Yvette and her friends.'

It was the patronne who apologised; the gentlemen who raided her establishment were plain-clothes gendarmes, they had made a terrible mistake, they were looking for an English-man who dealt in drugs. Stu feigned surprise at the cock-and-bull tale, complained politely, then accepted the offer of another room, one under the roof overlooking the station. He moved his case with the few belongings, which had been disturbed rather than destroyed, and cursed when he discovered that his chess-set had been taken.

Through the broken window, he had spotted a solitary figure standing outside the station. The friends of Grote were watching and waiting.

Six

DAYS SLIPPED PAST, becoming a week; the Lloyd's conference had ended; somewhere, September was slipping by; Robert Marchwood barely noticed; all he saw was an absurd routine as he was shuffled from interrogation room to interrogation room. There was, on one occasion, the *juge d'instruction*, who looked at him as if he was a caged animal and did not deign to speak.

The answers were easy to find, consistent, boring. French lawyers were at hand, to protect his rights, appointed through their man in Paris. He found a thousand ways to say: he had not killed his wife. Neither directly nor indirectly. He was innocent.

He seldom lost self-control. He was not a man easily moved to tears.

His chauffeur, Gary, had disappeared. This was the area of his story which swiftly bleached grey, where the threads were on show. No, he had not known Gary well; he was reliable, a good, calm driver; he had been in the British army for a time. Joubert had understood. 'You have many enemies, Monsieur Marchwood?'

A few.

The post mortem revealed that Thérèse had been first strangled, then dumped in the harbour. For a day or more, he had not been at his best, some quack had wanted to pump him full of something or other. That was his one crisis worthy of mention.

After a time, he discovered that Veronica Cantor had visited the gendarmerie every day. Joubert told him, 'She like you.'

Thanks.

Signed statements had been made by Wilson, by Veronica, by Fortescue and friends, by hotel guests and staff; Grote's statement had been taken, but not yet signed, a formality. The man had gone under the knife in Zurich.

Veronica was persistent.

'*Elle est belle, cette femme*,' Joubert remarked, presumably hoping that something might emerge from a meeting.

Marchwood said nothing.

The food was abominable, otherwise he really could not complain. They let him keep his own clothes, brought a suitcase of belongings from the hotel. Finally he weakened and acceded to Veronica's request. He was gratified they were allowed to meet in a room with both a drinks-dispensing machine and a large window, with a view over the tumbling cliffs.

Joubert let her into the room and they stood looking at each other in silence for a while. She held out her arms, but he shook his head and gestured to the square, metal-framed table and two plastic-seated chairs that faced one another.

'I'm sorry,' she said.

'I didn't do it,' he said.

'Nobody who matters believes you did. It's been in all the newspapers, of course. Pictures of your house, your homes, you and . . .'

'Kind of them. There is no way I would . . .'

'I know.'

He looked across the table at the mother of his unacknow-ledged child. He must be the luckiest man in the world.

'How are you?' he asked.

'Well, fine. You know.' She shrugged.

His fingertips dug briefly into his palms, forming anxious fists. 'I tell you, though, whoever did this . . .' He hesitated, looked at the gendarme who seemed half-asleep in a chair by the wall. 'I'll make them pay.'

His right hand opened out and he placed his palm on the chipped and scratched table surface.

How was the young lad?

He was well; he seemed perfectly happy with her, at the hotel. She had not wanted to be there, but Grote had insisted she came to the Riviera conference.

He shook his head as if seeing something he could not contemplate for long.

The drinks-dispensing machine broke into a hum. Its presence was a luxury; he seemed to have drunk nothing but tepid water

396

for days. She gave him some change, he plied the machine, pushed buttons. Partaking of some unspoken ceremony, they each pulled back the ring-pull tops, something sweet, fizzy and cold; they sipped in silence while he contemplated his guilt as if it were a physical presence. Then it was time to leave.

He shook her hand, and then they embraced; the scent of her hair recalled a time when he was not accused of murdering his wife. She asked to see him again and he mumbled something.

Later that same day, one that had turned out to be a Tuesday in mid-September, a lawyer called Martyn Jeffery arrived from London, a partner of the well-known City firm used by Knowle & Co, in white panama hat, somewhat crumpled white suit and MCC tie.

'We'll soon have you out of here, old man; there's no case to answer, as far as I can see.'

Robert did not bother to ask if he had spoken with his French colleagues; yet he knew that Jeffery had been sent by Ray, and felt his brother's calm, methodical anger. The fight had to be continued with discipline. Robert realised his contribution had been sadly lacking, understood that Ray wanted, now, to make good this failure. Inasmuch as it could be made good.

Robert asked if there had been any success in tracing Gary, his chauffeur, who must be eliminated from police enquiries.

Mr Jeffery noted the request. Thereafter, the conversation regained the high ground of small talk; yes, Jeffery was staying at the Hôtel d'Orléans, where he had taken a suite; pleasant, very pleasant, indeed.

Robert had not protested about the release of the body; his wife's relatives had insisted; he had let it happen: Thérèse should be taken home to the mountains, and buried with her family.

None of her relatives had bothered him with an exchange of views; in their eyes, he knew, whatever happened, that he was guilty. An unspoken judgement that, night for night, in his cage, he found difficult to dispute.

Guilty, but innocent. That was his verdict.

Innocent, but guilty. That was Grote's.

The fact was, the *juge d'instruction* had asked Joubert to be circumspect, to allow a little time to elapse before releasing Monsieur Marchwood; they had a signed statement from the chambermaid on the penthouse floor that Madame Marchwood had left the Marchwood suite on the night of her murder wearing a black-and-white dotted evening dress and carrying a small suitcase; she had been crying, and she had taken the lift alone. Monsieur Marchwood had remained in the room, there had been a crash, something smashed, which proved to be the bedroom lamp. This information had to be pondered before it could be entrusted to the Marchwood lawyers who, anyway, were friends of the *juge* and liked to live well.

Robert and Mr Jeffery talked about cricket, golf and fine wine, shook hands. But Robert had taken a decision, one that Ray would approve and, if need be, accomplish without him. The matter was out of Robert's hands; it was up to Ray to deal with Stephen Grote.

SEVEN

STU WILSON HAD to travel: England, then a meeting in Liechtenstein he had agreed over the phone with Ray . . . First, however, he had to get away from the Côte d'Azur.

After the lunch with Joubert, and his return to the Hôtel de la Gare, he wiped his gun clean, removed the bullets, placed the gun in a plastic bag which he then taped inside the high level toilet cistern in the bathroom; the bullets, also cleaned, were hidden similarly next door, which was unoccupied and responded to his light burglary skills. There was, he admitted, little logic to this; Joubert had disapproved of the weapon, yet understood the need, but now . . . Well, he felt he should travel without a weapon, believing this to be the safer course. It meant, however, that he would have to return.

Finally, he clambered over gutter and roof to a neighbouring building, to its stairs and the street below. He was on his way. There was a stiff walk, a bus ride or two, a local train, then others, until he caught a train for England, for the white cliffs, the grey clouds and home sweet home in September. Kevin had been dead and buried just one year.

Both his letters, the one addressed to the DG and the other to Rosie, had arrived and it seemed they offered a solution of sorts, desired, but not sought by all.

His doctor immediately certified him as suffering from post-traumatic stress disorder, ensuring the early retirement was in the bag, although his health had never been better. With Rosie and Jenny, things had not been so pleasant and there were tears.

Rosie had refused to see him alone, as if he were some sort of monster. They met at Jenny's house, where the three of them skulked around the kitchen table. He stated his view: after twenty years, their marriage had simply died: both of them had changed, yet their relationship had not adapted to this. They were looking for things in each other that they had found years before, but which neither was able to give today.

Hurt, rather than anger, vibrated in Rosie's quiet voice when she responded. She admitted he disappointed her almost constantly; he was so involved in his work, his chess, so uninterested in what she thought or did. He was, she said, a selfish middle-aged male with (barely concealed) chauvinist views. To her mind, their marriage had become, like many others, just a habit.

'Is there someone else?' she asked, finally, her hand smoothing down her hair.

He shook his head. Jenny said nothing.

The question of his responsibility for Kevin's death was not raised, yet it lay between them too, a presence which made their relationship even more unbearable. He said: 'You can have the house . . . I do hope, after this, we can still be friends.'

'You can't just throw part of yourself away,' she observed. 'And we were part of each other, for a long time.'

Jenny, no longer dazed from psychiatric drugs, took the key proferred by Rosie, accompanied him to the house that had been their home and watched him remove a few belongings.

Jenny became embarrassed, finally gave him a kiss and said: 'I do forgive you, Stu. And I hope to see you again.'

He nodded and they both managed to smile.

Keef placed the few objects he wanted stored, a few chess books, magazines, the Isle of Lewis chess set, in the boot of the white monster.

At the Serious Fraud Office there was some bitterness. The new powers behind the investigation of Lloyd's had proved remarkably lax. The deputy DG had moved in, then moved out, the case had been given to two or three others so that nobody felt responsible. Stu could almost hear politicians muttering to the DG: 'Go easy on Grote and his crowd. We can't afford to lose Lloyd's.' Certainly, odd things had happened, not always by accident. The evidence about Lloyd's built up by Wilson had been lost or forgotten. Mottram, the newish DG, had shown himself to be boot-tough when it came to politicking: the failures of the SFO were due to everyone but him.

Well, that was the line, more or less, and since Mottram was a cost-cutter looking for a gong, he was still delighted to let Stu

Wilson slide out of the service with medals and honour and pension. The pension did not come from his budget.

So many of the old crowd had evaporated that Stu was surprised to bump into Derek Tomlinson, who was standing by the lifts and the drinks machines. The heavy-duty cases Irwell and Wansbeck had become the unspeakable investigated by the unclean. Tomlinson was paying the price of failure. The biscuit tin reeked of these major defeats, which made the Lloyd's affair seem almost a pleasant aberration. Goodbye and goodbye.

Down in sunny Capri, Keef had found some space for Stu's personal effects, not much to show for a lifetime. They stood around chatting for a time; Keef had just had some success with the shooting at Golden Rain. At least, a Lloyd's underwriter called Robey had killed himself at his Welsh farmhouse where the local police had found a suicide note, some engraved cartridges and an engraving set. The coroner's inquest was due shortly, but the case seemed clear enough. 'He wrote he blamed Robert Marchwood for his ruin,' Keef mused. 'Mean anything to you?'

Stu shrugged. Yes and no, yes and no.

The cache of Kevin's programmes, print-outs and disks that had been entrusted to a wall-hung car seat was bequeathed, with displeasure, to a local skip. This was evidence that nobody would care to use.

Keef was not given to self-doubt, but Stu recognised the symptoms. He himself had not only failed to uphold high ideals; he had failed his nearest and lost his dearest . . .

Clouds hung low over the Alps as Stu approached a small modern office building in Vaduz, the capital of Liechtenstein, which, he understood, was famous for its postage stamps; it too was excessively valuable in relation to its size.

At the entrance to the building he found a short list of the tenants, who were all lawyers, and a long list of the trusts they operated. Stu looked at his watch, then entered.

Ray Marchwood greeted him at the reception desk. Gary was there too. 'How are you? How was England?'

Just fine. Ray pushed back his glasses and ushered Stu and Gary into a bland, empty office.

'I've been considering pension plans,' Ray stated, looking at Stu.

'Pension plans?' He half-protested. That was not the reason that he was there.

Ray spoke steadily: 'I think it is important that you and Gary should both be paid, with minimum fuss and maximum discretion. We have to work together and I want you both to be satisfied that your interests have been properly considered. I know you do not view our task as a financial matter, but expenses have been incurred by you both.'

Stu said nothing.

'Sure.' Gary rubbed his close-cropped hair and grinned.

'You will each receive a million dollars . . .'

Neither Stu nor Gary moved a muscle, each avoided the other's gaze. If they were to be hired, they might as well be paid properly. Stu's problematic winnings were neither here nor there.

'Discretion is essential. By using the Liechtenstein trusts, we can preserve anonymity. The man you will see shortly, Herr Schneider, does not know your names or true identities. You should sign the paperwork using assumed names, I do not know if you have any suggestions . . .'

'Thomas Blackstone,' Gary said, quickly. Ray had evidently already explained the scheme to him.

Stu hesitated, then said: 'Daniel Shuttleworth.'

'You should use these names in every conversation here and in every dealing with Herr Schneider. Your money has already been placed in escrow; it will be paid by Herr Schneider into numbered Swiss bank accounts held by Liechtenstein-registered trusts once he receives a postcard of Lake Zurich jointly signed by myself, Thomas Blackstone and Daniel Shuttleworth. By then, of course, our work will have been completed.'

Ray summoned Schneider, who operated several accounts for the Marchwoods. A dry character, the lawyer explained the scheme, the details of the trusts and the accounts which he would administer for them; Stu and Gary swiftly completed the paperwork, giving sample signatures in their false names.

By the time they left the anonymous block in the postage-stamp country, Stu and Gary had become hired killers.

A day later, they were in Zurich, the weather had lifted and late September had turned warm and pleasant. Travelling separately, the three men arrived within minutes at the agreed time and the agreed place.

The apartment was on the sixth floor of a large block with a large underground car park; Thérèse had lived here and the place was perfect for the men's purposes, nobody would notice their coming and going; the white van Ray and Gary had used on the Côte d'Azur was parked in the car park below; they had changed its plates from French to Swiss.

That day in late September, Stu admired the apartment, the pictures, the furniture, the view over the lake, which was blue water in gold sunshine.

'How's Robbo faring?' he asked.

Ray shrugged: 'He's still being investigated. I sent a lawyer from London down to see him a fortnight back. I suppose the police want to keep him out of harm's way.'

Stu did not press the matter. He changed the subject: 'Ray, why did you publish computer codes in a Sunday newspaper?'

The memory seemed to cheer Ray. 'It was our way of ensuring that everybody knew what we were doing and why. The codes contained the deals for the week ahead and could be checked to ensure that the deals conformed to the overall plan agreed at Baden-Baden.'

'Agreed with Grote and the others?'

'Of course. They did not trust us, never trusted us, but we played fair . . .'

Gary strode over to the window, to the view, without comment.

Ray remarked: 'Keep an eye open for suspicious boats. My brother once came here, to watch Thérèse from the lake; he had an excellent view from a motorboat.'

Nothing moved on the water; the garish mooring buoys barely bobbed in the smooth water, unused.

'Did you ever meet Mrs Sanderson?' Stu asked.

'No. Should I have done?'

'She was at Kevin's funeral . . .'

'Ah. Possibly. Yes, I remember.'

'Well, her husband owned the garage which published your codes. And Tony MacNulty . . .'

Ray interrupted: 'Introduced him to Lloyd's, to Salter and all the others. . . ? Well, he placed his trust in someone who could not be trusted. Happens all the time.'

Rising to make a cup of tea, Stu said: 'Perhaps I can strike a deal with you. If you arrange a pension for Mrs Cornelia Sanderson, I'll tell you who took pot-shots at your brother.'

'Becoming mercenary, aren't we?'

There was a silence.

Then Ray continued: 'To be honest, I don't know what we are to do with all the money. It seems pointless now.'

Stu pressed the point: 'She gave Kevin the newspaper cuttings. It was for her sake that he went to the Lloyd's data storage centre, hoping to be able to work out your method, the codes, the deal . . .'

Ray said: 'OK, OK. Enough, enough. I've heard enough.'

Stu relented: 'It was the underwriter Robey who tried to kill your brother. When he committed suicide, he left a note. You'd have heard, sooner or later.'

Life in the apartment was not easy. They had to be nobodies, live invisibly, and avoid distress. Behind its half-opened blinds and curtains the place became too small and too stuffy for comfort. The highlight was the regular trip to the other side of town, to a large food store. The days dragged by, nothing happened, Stephen Grote was not at home in his mansion by the lake. Every so often, to maintain morale, they played the tape of MacNulty and Stone: 'Good decision, poor execution.'

Then the telephone rang.

Stu looked at Ray who looked at Gary who said: 'The set's not bugged. That's all I know.'

The room was covered with surveillance clutter, electronic wizardry and the mess created by three non-cooks.

Stu lifted the receiver, only to hear Robert Marchwood's voice. The man was in a box just down the road.

'Thought you'd all be here,' Robert said, when he arrived. 'I recognised the white van.'

A large hand was offered and shaken; Robert removed his gloves. 'They let me out on bail and I travelled here by train and bus, would you believe? I love public transport . . . Nice pad you've got here. Pity about the rubbish. What do you fellows have for food?'

They tidied up; a meal was made; a bottle of wine was found and, very soon they were all playing cards for bottles of bubbly that Robert did not have, not for the moment. Gary told gruesome stories about the army, Stu responded with tales from his life with the traffic police. They all managed to laugh easily, helped by the wine.

'It's all set, then?' Robert said suddenly, gathering up the pack.

Ray said: 'This time there'll be no mistakes.'

Stephen Grote was indisposed longer than expected; his London office thought he was in Zurich, but he was not here. The performances of *The Magic Flute* would be in October, so he would certainly be here soon. The man who had taken decisions would be here soon enough.

In the meantime, Robert found ways of keeping the guys cheerful. Ray prepared an anonymous letter explaining about the West-Europa-Bank, and the humour of Grote's plans: rather than stealing a bank's deposits, the friends intended to steal the entire bank, using its money to pay off its present owners. 'A neat fraud, don't you think, Detective Inspector?' Robert flashed a grin at Stu, who avoided a reply.

Ray said, simply: 'This is our revenge. For two decisions.'

For days, the shutters remained drawn at Grote's red-brown brick mansion that stood amid trees on the east side of the lake. The top floor sub-let to someone who kept an eye on the place, but this was still a holidayish season and the tenants had fled to the mountains. The shutters were old-fashioned, could be folded outwards to let in cool air on a warm day; there was a burglar alarm, sensors and trip-lights; these would not, however, deter a professional intruder.

'Piece of cake,' had been Gary's only comment, on his return and it was true: the bugs were working, yet nobody was there. The transmitter he had installed to relay signals across the lake remained silent.

Then Grote did arrive, with the sounds of bags and the scuff of cases. No wife: they had expected this, Donna was tied up in London, another big auction. Somebody helped him for a while, then departed.

They moved, the four of them. Taking the white van from the garage, they parked near the house, listening quietly in the rear until night darkened the tree- and hedge-lined streets on the steep hillside beside the water.

There were phone calls, the wooden shutters were rolled back. Grote was in a good mood; men arrived from the town in cars, one was called Wyttenbach, the head of the West-Europa-Bank, there was a measure of drinking. The four men in the rear of the white van listened to the commotion and kept their counsel.

After several hours of boredom and discomfort, three of them

405

left the van, Stu wearing an earpiece and clutching a large roll of tape and a pair of handcuffs, Gary carrying a small grip and two-way radio, Robert trailing behind; all wore gloves. Ray waited inside the van, listening.

Stephen Grote was now on his own, strolling round. He had turned up the music, whistling to an opera which, Stu reckoned, was bound to be Mozart.

Stu rang the front doorbell, and heard in his ear-piece that a door on a first-floor balcony had been prised open, Gary was now inside.

It was after midnight, yet the gateway lock buzzed open; Stephen Grote was not suspicious; he expected, no doubt, that one of his guests had forgotten something. The front door to the house was opened and Stephen Grote was astonished to see Inspector Stewart Wilson, wearing a grim smile and gloves.

He did not even slam the door in Wilson's face. He turned round, as if he had noticed something behind him. Gary. Then the opera was switched off. Suddenly he tried to close the door, too late. Stu was inside, then Stephen Grote's face clenched in a brief spasm of terror, his mouth opened to shout but found no voice. Gary's hands gagged his mouth, cuffs clasped his wrists, the three men stumbled from the doorway, along the entrance hall. Stephen fell, threshing with his feet against shinbone and muscle, falling against a shining wooden floor.

The door to the house was still open. Robert was there, too, now grasping Stephen's legs, the fight continued, the metal of the cuffs scritching as Stephen was dragged along the floor, arching his back.

'Get the tape.' Gary.

Stu loosened his grip, searching with glove-deadened hands for scissors, the end of the tape on the roll. The tape stuck to itself, he could not see, a foot caught him full in the stomach and, in the dark, he stumbled and fell heavily.

'You OK?' Robert.

Bent double with pain, Stu hobbled to the front of the hall, Ray was asking something over the radio, Stu grunted an answer, closed the door and switched on the hall light.

He turned: Gary and Robert were still engaged in battle; Stephen's mouth was still gagged, his body now pinned down by the other two, but his feet remained free to drum the floor.

'Get the tape, for Christ's sake.' Gary.

The heavy duty brown plastic refused to be cut. Stu fought the blur of imprecise feelings, you must not remove your gloves, you must not remove your gloves, then he knelt and started to wind tape around Stephen's ankles. Snip, snip. Then his mouth.

'Turn him over.' Stu.

This was easier. Two bands around the torso taped the forearms tightly to the back.

'Is he breathing?' Robert.

Stephen now lay inert, exhausted on the precise pattern of the varnished floor. His diaphragm was moving; at his neck, Stu found a pulse.

'Where do we take him now?' Gary.

'To face the music.' Robert. Gary nodded to the next door, meaning: the hi-fi he had switched off was in there.

'Fine, fine.' Stu to Ray, still in the van. Then to Gary: 'We can drag him in there.'

Suddenly Stephen's knees were free, his body jack-knifed out of his captors' hands, he pushed himself along the floor, tried to scream but found neither tongue nor breath and the others were upon him, again.

Stu cut some more tape. He was perspiring, his back and abdomen ached. He taped over Stephen's mouth and legs, again. The three men lifted the body from the hall floor, carried it through the salon door and placed it on the carpet.

'Is he breathing?'

'Yes.'

Gary placed a cassette in the tape drawer of the hi-fi, pushed a button.

'Stephen,' Robert said. The eyes were open. 'Stephen, we want you to know why you are going to die.'

The voices of Stone and MacNulty, walking through some wood in the South, entered the room.

'This is a bloody mess.' MacNulty.

Stu strode out of the room, down the hallway, opened the door. Ray was there, come to check the gloves were on and to insist they should hurry. He followed Stu back into the salon. The tape was still running.

'I knew the place would burn, not that Vaughan would die inside.' MacNulty.

'I don't think it is right to criticise Stephen. We agreed with his decision on the store.' Stone.

Robert bent over Stephen, his broad shoulders, ruddy features approaching Stephen's face: 'That's two decisions, Stephen. Two decisions too many. Young Kevin and my wife. I should never have trusted you in Baden-Baden.'

Stephen found he could shrug his shoulders. As if to say: so what? What does all that mean or prove? Look at your own glass house!

Briefly, the four men gathered round him, to stare at him. Then: 'Have you seen the painting?' Ray.

'What painting?' Stu.

Ah, the Monet from Robert Marchwood's house now hung on the wall here in Stephen's study. No doubt Stephen now wished he had never seen the thing, acquired through his friends on the Riviera, who had removed the landscape from an art dealer with a dubious past. Stu returned to the salon.

'Stephen.' This was Robert again. 'I think you killed my father. That's why you said he wore two Omega watches, instead of Rolexes. You were right, of course. On the day of his death he did. He'd wanted a change, he said, and he gave the Rolexes to us.'

Stephen shut his eyes. Stu watched as Ray and Robert raised their voices, arguing about whether or not it mattered that Stephen had killed their father.

Worried about him, Stu splashed water on Stephen's face. Stephen coughed and coughed. 'He's alive.'

'Everything ready?' Robert. 'Let's go, then. Let's get this over and done with.'

They picked him up, as if he were nothing, and carried him through into his study, with the bookshelves, the antiquarian books, Stu saw a photograph of Mercedes Valldemosa, signed and dedicated 'To my Gentleman, with love.'

Minutes later, it was all over. While threshing around Stephen kicked over the chair placed beneath his feet, but they restrained him so that his body should not be too bruised. There were enough grounds for suspicions without that. The tapes around his body were carefully removed. For reasons best known to Robert, two more watches were strapped to Stephen's wrists; nobody bothered to argue. The time for arguments had past. Elsewhere, in the salon and the hallway, little had been disturbed; Gary removed the bugs inside, the transmitter outside, Robert wielded a broom, Stu wiped surfaces, Ray waited and watched in the white van. A lamp was left burning in the study, its weak light darkening the vivid colours of 'La Vallée de la Creuse', a masterpiece by Claude Monet.

It was a calm, dark, cool night.

Finally they left, driving directly to Geneva, where Wilder & Co owned a corporate flat. A postcard of Lake Zurich was signed by Ray, Gary and Stu, then sent. A day later, Liechtenstein had wired the money through to Geneva, which Gary and Stu could collect, using the details of their individual trusts. Neither man seemed impressed.

It was supposed to have been professional. As they were parting, Ray said: 'You can contact us through Schneider in Liechtenstein.' Gary, who was thinking of life in South America or Spain, nodded. Stu Wilson, too.

EIGHT

THE TOMPION DID not tick.

Donna Grote had turned the key, thrown open the door and been greeted by a strange silence. Stephen had warned he might not meet them at the airport, that was fair enough, he had felt weak after the operation, and their mountain of cases warranted a taxi and strong driver; besides, it was still early in the morning. But Stephen would usually emerge with a smile and a pleasant surprise; so this was strange.

She stopped and listened.

Marshall and Mary-Ellen struggled with their cases, clambering the stairs to the door, whose milk-glass had been handcut in patterns of floral abstraction: the place was old and solid and self-assured; Stephen could have restored and renovated the heart out of the place, but had refused to do so. Their most expensive pieces were kept in London and Gstaad.

He was not there.

She did not show her concern, paid and tipped the driver, who left the cases in the hallway that angled its way between salon, dining room, study, kitchen, bathroom; the bedrooms were on the floor above.

Mary-Ellen and Marshall were full of the joys of a champagne-eased flight, half-laughing about their kids for whom the world seemed to turn faster than ever. The very latest was that their youngest son had met an impressive check-in girl at a HoJo motel in the Midwest, converted from Mammon to God and the fundamental-truth bible, and expected to see the Second Coming shortly. But Marshall knew: once you have been to Law School, you never really drop your belief in fees.

After Stephen had agreed to pay for Marshall's losses, Donna had rung Stephen, while he was in hospital, to tell him all the news. She had been sorry not to be at his side, but she found herself overwhelmed with work. She apologised profusely, but he forgave her; he had to suffer and preferred to do so alone, the after-effects of surgery had been painful.

Recently he had rung her from his lakeside house, missed her at the office, left a message telling her to come soon. Then she had rung and he had not answered; it happened. They all flew out here, nonetheless. Now he was not there.

Their feet echoed down the hall on the polished wooden floor. The alarm was working, but not activated.

They entered the salon where other clocks had ceased to tick or were visibly slowing. For the most part, these were mass-produced Swiss clocks of the last century, made in Geneva for export to Britain; more impressive was the small collection of watches, several by Breguet, including one of the first with a jewelled movement, another with a tourbillon, a Swiss repeater decorated by Pamina and Tamino who each rang chimes on the half-hour, then modern Swiss chronometers by Tissot, Rolex and Omega.

A large, simply furnished room with cotton blinds, black leather sofas and a picture of Stephen's father over the fireplace.

Mary-Ellen said: 'There are two watches missing from this case.' There were unwashed glasses, too, on the table, along with bottles of liquor, an opened and half-emptied soda bottle, a nearly drained bottle of red wine, a fendant de Dôle; old cigarettes in the ashtray. No sign of lipstick.

In the study, Marshall found the watches and more besides. Bellowing a curse, he racked up the blinds, threw open the study windows: the smell, checked by the study door, spread through the apartment recalling trash cans, landfills, dead meat.

Donna entered the study; she recalled looking at shelves of leather-bound volumes, first editions, fine antiquarian books, seeing the Tompion orrery which displayed the movements of earth and moon relative to the sun, then being struck by the photographs and opera memorabilia, by the painting. On the desk were his reading glasses, briefly laid aside.

The chair beneath his feet lay on its side, kicked away; rope, tongue, teeth.

Stephen had hanged himself.

On his right wrist, there were three watches.

Three watches: Donna recalled saying this, after some silence, through a block of nothingness.

She walked over to a wall where a mirror had hung which had been replaced by a picture, a Monet. Standing close, she saw blue-green paint, mottled black-purple-brown, the canvas beneath, a strip of blue-and-whisped-grey sky.

'Ah, the Monet, the Monet,' Donna said, remembering the visit of Inspector Wilson to Sotheby's, her identification of the painting. 'He will have wanted that. Expensive, though, very expensive.'

Marshall, whose professional skills were needed, examined the bookcase, the knots, the hands. Three or four days, at most. He could see no untoward bruising on the face, he wanted to examine the arms and legs, tried to lift a trouser-leg to see the ankles. Donna stayed his hand.

'I can't quite figure this out,' Marshall muttered.

It was then that the block of nothingness finally melted and Donna was swept away; Mary-Ellen held her tightly and they took her out of the study into the salon, where she was inconsolable.

Without saying another word, Marshall found rubber gloves in the kitchen and started to clean, tidy, order; he removed the glasses, the bottles and general mess from the salon, washed and dried in the kitchen, wiped surfaces clean and poured fresh drinks for all. In the study, bearing gloves and black trash-sacks, he removed the Monet from the wall, replaced the mirror, covered the picture with the sack, placed it in the corridor, then swept the study with dustpan and brush, vacuum-cleaned the rest. He dusted the photographs of opera-singers, including one of that famous diva, whose name escaped him.

He took the waste sacks to the basement, hiding them and the sack-covered painting behind the oil tank before he reappeared in the salon, dusty and cobwebbed.

'What the hell are you doing, Marshall?' Mary-Ellen whispered. Donna had removed her gold charm bracelet and was stretched out on the sofa, distraught.

'Making sure the police know what to think.' He looked at Donna, who kind of nodded. Nobody wanted another investigation.

He entered the study again, carefully removed the two Swiss watches that Stephen did not usually wear; it was only when he had replaced them in the display cabinet in the salon and taken a swift shower that he rang the police and called a doctor. A Herr Wyttenbach from the West-Europa-Bank, where Stephen was a non-executive director, was found to help with the formalities, which were swiftly and efficiently concluded. Stephen Grote, the former chairman of Lloyd's of London, had clearly been very depressed following his surgery at the cantonal hospital and a long convalescence. The press were duly informed.

NINE

THE LOCAL FRENCH train drew creakily out of the station; Stu Wilson, a dark figure in sunglasses, white linen suit and white shoes, stood alone, looking up and down the track. He carried a black leather suitcase.

The ticket office was closed, the ticket machine seemed dead, the newsagent's kiosk unused.

Stu strolled round the station where he had first arrived on the Côte. Months had elapsed.

In the sand and dirt that passed for a car park on the other side of the road from the station, a black saloon car arrived, its wheels swirling dust. A small, thickset man, Inspecteur Joubert, emerged from the cloud, coughing, a cigarette held between first and middle finger.

Stu did not rise to greet him, they only shook hands once Joubert had reached the waiting room.

'How are you, mon ami?'

'Out of a job, out of a marriage. Fine.' Stu smiled. So much was true. He had cut with his past.

Joubert offered him a cigarette.

'No, thank you.'

'You want something? Not just a talk?'

'Too true. The cheque. That's the only thing that matters now.'

The waiting room was one of those metal, glass-sided cabins that dot station platforms the length and breadth of France; even the door was metal-framed glass. It said: made in France, just as buildings in French-speaking Africa bear witness to their former colonial masters.

'How was England?' Joubert asked.

'Grey,' Stu told him. 'And it was my turn to have someone watched.'

Yet that was not in England. He recalled the signature on the photograph in Grote's study: 'For the Gentleman.'

He had been lucky, Stu supposed. They had been lucky. So far. He had left Geneva the day before and seen nothing about Grote in the English newspapers.

He explained that he found travelling tiring and hotels stressful. Particularly ones close to railway stations.

Joubert, cigarette on lip, let the ash lengthen: 'Ah. L'Hôtel de la Gare, your favourite hotel. Alors, la Patronne et moi . . .' He crossed his index and middle fingers.

'So you will know . . .' then Stu gestured. About the friends of Grote's friends.

Joubert laughed. 'Influence, my friend.'

He made again the two-handed gesture that Wilson had seen in the restaurant.

'Whose influence?' Stu asked. Crazy as it seemed, he still believed in the police, in the need to protect the individual, not just property, sustaining order and freedom within the rule of law. Yet that belief was, he had to admit, contaminated.

Joubert said: 'Influence is organised here, of course.'

'The Mafia?'

'Of course. With others.'

'Freemasons?'

'Scrivano belonged to them. The Cristòforo was their bank. Italian, French, English. And the politicians.' Joubert placed one hand on another, on another, on another.

'And the *juges d'instruction?* The police? Your bosses?' Stu asked, not expecting a reply.

Joubert said shortly: 'They will not disturb you. We have solved the case.'

He explained. Helped by the *juge d'instruction*, he had solved the sad case of the death of Madame Thérèse Marchwood, following a second post mortem examination. The laboratory had made technical errors in the first examination, it was deeply flawed . . .

Stu looked across the empty, dust-specked space in the waiting room, past Joubert, past the car park and the black car, to the mild sea.

The point was clear, Joubert said. Madame Marchwood had drowned, they had found water in her lungs at the second examination; that they had not found this at the first was

415

regrettable. Evidently, Madame Marchwood had intended to join the Murphy party that evening, join her young male friend: she was a woman in the prime of life in search of freedom and excitement. This was why she left Monsieur Marchwood, there was a lover.

Another cigarette; Joubert's smile remained unchanged.

She took the Bentley out of the hotel garage, the attendant believed he saw her leave alone, she parked the car in a sidestreet, near the harbour wall; she wiped the gear-lever, the steering-wheel, the door handles clean. As one does, on the way to a party, if you are Swiss. She walked along the promenade, hurrying to a lover, to his embrace. She passed people, many people, who would not notice her, just one person among so many seeking happiness on that warm evening, on the promenade, beneath the palms. She found the jetty she sought, ran along the wooden slats, overcome by excitement, by the desire to be with her young man. Her shoe caught, she slipped, fell, took a knock, dropped unconscious into the water. She was dragged down by her dress. Overwhelmed by the weight of water, her body drifted in the harbour currents . . .

'And the young man, fearing retribution, says nothing,' concluded Stu Wilson. An expert piece of investigation. In tune with the times: 'I congratulate you, Inspecteur.'

He gazed outside, tired of his own relentless anger. Something approaching a wind had developed; he opened the waiting room door in the hope of fresh air and was engulfed by the breath of a fierce cauldron.

Joubert continued his tale. There was still, of course, some mystery: her case, her handbag, personal items, jewellery, a diamond-studded watch, had never been discovered.

'Perhaps,' Stu helped, suddenly fond of outlandish theories, 'Perhaps she carried her belongings along the jetty, perhaps they too fell into the water. We will never know for sure.'

Joubert pursed lips, shrugged; perhaps. He preferred his own tales. In any event, the investigation was more or less complete; Gary, the Marchwoods' chauffeur, who had run away, frightened that he would be accused of the terrible act, had rung and offered to return, to make a statement. But the *juge d'instruction* was satisfied. In the meantime, Marchwood had been released; the evidence of Stu, the chambermaid and the attendant exonerated him.

Then Joubert asked: 'Have you seen this terrible thing . . . With Monsieur Grote . . . ?'

Stu shook his head. 'Nothing terrible ever happens to that man.'

'Ah, bon.'

Joubert stood, looked at his watch; the next train was due. He produced his wallet, Stu inhaled calmly, and was shown pictures of Madame Joubert, two strapping lads, both of whom towered above their father, and the family home. He received an invitation to stay, whenever he wanted; there was space. They would all sit outside in the sunshine together, eat and drink and laugh at the world, Joubert said.

Stu smiled: he would let him know when he had found a permanent base.

Joubert finally gave him the cheque from the casino, gravely shook his hand, then flat-palmed his upper arm in an expression of contempt for the wider world.

'Don't try to see Yvette.'

'*L'influence?*' Wilson stared at the cheque, which remained an extravagant amount, despite Ray's million.

'*Mais oui, mais oui.*' With that, Joubert strode out of the door, crossed the road, churned dust with his car-wheels and was gone.

The later afternoon turned to early evening as Stu reached the Cap d'Antibes; he had found his Swiss bank, paid in his cheque, removed the old case with its few belongings, the Smith & Wesson and the bullets from the Hôtel de la Gare.

He was a rich man. Quite what that meant, he did not know. Hard to believe that it was still October, the sun still warm even late in the day. There were divorce papers to sign in London. Should he bother? He would be haunted by this unspeakable and that unspeakable, for ever.

Peace is to be found in the grave. Now he would simply disappear, fade away, enjoy some sort of dream, somewhere beside the Mediterranean. At least he'd kept his word to Kevin.

He strolled along the deserted shoreline, across pebbles and sand, picked over mussel shells, crab-claws, starfishes.

He opened the case, saw his book about Monet, checked his clothing, his few possessions, the unused gun and bullets, ascertained that nothing bore his name; then collected pebbles and stones, throwing them into the case until he could barely carry it; still he managed to walk with it for a little way, clambering along a small promontory which surged out over the sea. He threw the black leather case as far and as high as he could, which was neither very far nor very high, into the waters beneath. When he left the seashore, it was dark, the pines and cypresses on the hillside swarmed with the chirp of cicadas. He was a free man.

TEN

AT THE AIRPORT, Connie bought the evening newspaper, read the story; then she almost did a little jig around the luggage and the people queueing at the check-in desk.

A gentleman and a crook.

Connie Sanderson had said those words often enough, of MacNulty, Fortescue, Grote, yet really, she blamed Ron more than she blamed them. They had merely helped a fool to part with her money.

Still, it was nice to see, she had to admit.

There was time, after some shoving and shunting, after she had finally watched her luggage bump along a rubber conveyor-belt, to drink a cup of tea in the departure lounge.

She was leaving. Yes, off to warmer climes; she had read all the tourist guides, it seemed that only two months of the year on the west coast were moderately cool, at other times it was warm, if not hot. She had debated whether or not to accept Jonathan's offer. Then there had been an almighty surprise. A solicitor, someone from a very high and mighty City firm, a gin-and-golf-type called Martyn Jeffery had approached her. He was acting for a wellwisher who wanted to remain anonymous; if she agreed, a trust fund would be set up, providing her with a pension after she had been discharged from bankruptcy. In the meantime, the money, over a thousand pounds a month, could be paid into a bank account of her son or daughter-in-law.

There was only one condition stipulated by Jeffery: she had to respect the donor's anonymity. She was at once amazed and suspicious; she told Jeffery she would have to think about the matter; he remained quite firm. His client would be disappointed if she would not accept swiftly. She tossed and turned a sleepless night on the matter, then rang Jeffery and said thanks, but no thanks. He was astonished; she said, well, in three years' time she would have a decent pension and anyway the whole thing was too odd for words. Like Lloyd's.

The truth was she was feeling disillusioned. She had become mightily suspicious of others' motives, and she was glad to be leaving. If the offer made through Jeffery was well-meant, it seemed scarcely credible amid so much meanmindedness. And besides, she still had her pride.

The very idea of Australia excited her, it had the promise of a new life. Somewhere new, unencumbered by past greatnesses or defeats.

Of course, it had been Jonathan's suggestion. He had had no real conception of her problems; in fact, she had not told him much, except to say that she had been, in the immortal expression, 'holed by Lloyd's'. That sounded, was intended to sound, halfway decent and respectable and nice. There was, of course, the law of the stiff upper lip for those who fell by the wayside: if you must be poor, pretend to be decent and uncomplaining.

Good health permitting, and she still did have excellent health, she was set to fight back. Certainly, Jonathan and Arabella had pleaded with her to come and, to be sure, they wanted grannie to play with the grandchildren, and to babysit, which she would do most willingly. But in three years she would have a reasonable pension; on the other side of the globe, she could work without telling toad.

There was much to enjoy. Jonathan had started earning pots of money, had become director of a local bank and a chemical company as well; the family had moved into a larger house which just happened to have a one-bedroom flat suitable for indigent grannies; they had been apart for too long, and life was too short.

ELEVEN

IT HAD BEEN quite a day.

Time for a snifter at the club. William pushed open the door, crossed the hallway, nodded to the porter and the cloakroom attendant, then paused to check the time by the pendulum clock that hung next to the baize noticeboard which was filled with notices he never read.

He was, as ever, punctual.

Most other members were already at dinner: the hallway echoed to the opening and closing of doors, the scuffing of feet, the movement of bodies.

Buttoning and unbuttoning his jacket in vague indecision, he opened the library door and was startled to see nobody. He peered over his reading glasses.

Nigel was late. Another departmental row-cum-intrigue, he had no doubt of that.

A waiter crossed his path and he took the opportunity to order two gins with tonic and a plate of smoked salmon sandwiches, perhaps a round of ham, too.

One day, he might diet; one day, he might be dead. Stephen Grote had not much older than he, always looked well enough when he came to Downing Street; then one fine day it was all over. Poor chap, very agreeable and a charming man. Well, Mister Fortescue had just been blown out of the water.

The memory brought a smile to William's lips. Nigel, who woke him from this reverie, was less replete with the joys of life. He dropped his briefcase, slung some newspapers over the coffee table, including the last edition of the evening rag, which William had not yet seen.

'Damn and blast!' Nigel said, rubbing his cheek as if stung by something unspeakable.

William laughed, picked up his glasses from the table; he wanted to read the rag, but it would be bad form to do so.

Instead, he gestured. 'Take a seat, old man. The refreshments are in hand. They should reduce the pain. Now what's your problem?'

'Oh, need you ask? The Lime Street mob, again. May they rot in the deepest dungeons . . .'

Fortunately, there was nobody else in the library to observe them. The waiter brought the paraphernalia of serious drinking, plus the requested sandwiches and the taste of the juniper and herbs mingled with alcohol to ease their aches and pains.

'If it isn't one problem, it's another.'

Now Nigel was dealing with Lloyd's as a trade problem; the minister had, in his wisdom, wanted to know the effect of closing down a fifth of the City, the consequences for the balance of payments, for trade, for inward investment and morale. The response was inevitable, but not quite what the minister wanted to hear.

'My dear chap,' Bill said. 'Have another, and pretend he doesn't exist. Always helps.'

Recently, all the banks had sent their chairmen to see ministers, playing the major chord based on Number 10, Number 11 and Victoria Street, indicating disaffection. A list of deficits past and future had been repeated in every available ear: a cycle of hurricanes, recession (theft and arson), pollution and storms. The fears of the banks, even when dragooned by the Bank of England, were understandable. One syndicate, consisting of some two thousand names, had lost nearly a billion. 'And most of the two thousand stopped paying some time back,' Nigel murmured. 'The banks just don't enjoy covering that debt.'

Nor would the Treasury.

'So your master took his feet off the desk and asked you to play the what if? game?' William asked, peering over his spectacles.

Nigel rubbed his forehead with a fist and nodded. In fact, the what if? game had been played, with varying success, for years. The most popular variant stated: if Lloyd's kept its promise to pay every honest claim it would go to the wall but, in doing so, it would bequeath its problem to the banks. And they would say that the Bank and the Treasury bore the responsibility. Added to which, the costs of closure, the loss of jobs, the fall in tax receipts and invisible exports would be staggering.

'Like closing down coal,' Nigel said.

Bill chuckled: 'I thought we'd done that. You can't step into the same shite twice, old man.'

Of this, Nigel was not convinced. But Lloyd's losses were at least twenty-five billion. Even if that nice man Fortescue denied the fact.

Nigel said: 'Lloyd's losses couldn't possibly be underwritten by the taxpayer.'

Another round of drinks was bought. William asked for some roast-beef sandwiches, then started to pace up and down. 'What do you think of this Grote affair?' he asked, gesturing at his newspaper.

Nigel was noncommittal. Was that Marchwood fellow still in a French prison? The tabloids had made a meal of the man; one of the richest men in Britain, accused of killing his wife. Then all the friends and ex-friends had queued up to tell all. It was rumoured that he had controlled the Lloyd's market, but he had never been charged, unlike Grote and the others.

William said: 'Neil Fortescue has heard that the French think Mrs Marchwood's death was an accident and have already released Marchwood. Seems he has good contacts on the Côte d'Azur. Bye the bye, we had the estimable chairman of Lloyd's with us today for a swift head-banging session.'

Out of his briefcase, a lawyer's bag, he produced a letter which he gave to Nigel, who smiled. He, too, had been sent the same long, anonymous letter, detailing the transfer of the assets of the West-Europa-Bank in Zurich into the beneficial owner-ship of the gents who ran Lloyd's. Gifting oneself a Swiss bank was nice work and quite illegal.

'We are still checking the facts . . .' Nigel said. 'We could, at a pinch, do the fellows for fraud.'

'Given the past record, I really would not advise it,' William chortled, despite himself. In fact, Downing Street had already acted, helped by a few late-night visits from the Party Chairman and the Chief Whip, who were forever worried that the parliamentary majority would disappear as MPs dropped off their perches, shot by Lloyd's.

The letter had come as something of a godsend. In fact, after the PM had read it he had strolled round the room, pretending to stroke an imaginary ball through the covers for four. Then he had called for Fortescue, creating an impossible appointment between appointments.

'Didn't Fortescue deny it?' Nigel was flustered to be so far behind events.

William peered over his reading glasses and winked. They had not had so much fun for ages. Of course, they had kept him waiting, then had him ushered into the PM's private study, where he had been caned, mercilessly. 'Kept the cigarette in his mouth the whole time, just to show how much he enjoyed it.'

The PM had teased out the salient details: fraud, theft, false accounting. 'It seems to me that Lloyd's is run by a team of crooks. What do you say, Mr Fortescue?'

Fortescue said nothing. The sheer detail of the letter carried conviction. By contrast, his Greyness was in the pink; he posed a question: 'Now you tell me you are going to bankrupt twenty of our backbenchers?'

Fortescue's reply was truculent: 'They have to pay their debts.'

'Amounts to the same thing, doesn't it?'

For a time, they had hacked around on the question of when not meeting one's obligations became bankruptcy; Lloyd's might not sue, but you could be as sure as hell that the butcher, the baker or the candlestick-maker would.

It was then that the PM had made his offer. He did not want to see any of his estimable colleagues brought down by Lloyd's; in fact, he felt that it would offend his natural sense of justice should any of them have to pay for their losses. He was sure that a certain Swiss bank would know how to ensure that their obligations would be met without anyone from the Inland Revenue being informed of the fact. To be more precise, a donation to every MP stricken at Lloyd's, either paid into their Lloyd's accounts or deducted from their losses . . . Well, the PM was sure that Fortescue could, given his interest in all matters Swiss, find a way of effecting a rescue of the MPs. Which in turn would also help the Treasury to extend its support for the Lloyd's market.

There had been a silence while Fortescue considered the cost of this arrangement, before agreeing. The PM later said that he thought it would swallow the bank's profits for the next ten years. And Lloyd's, well, Lloyd's might survive for a year or two, until the losses finally overwhelmed its capital base.

William grinned. Watching Lloyd's go under, the PM said, was like seeing Venice slide; it was so rotten and had lasted so long that nobody really cared anymore.

Nigel laughed at the yarn: 'Do you think Fortescue will keep his word?'

His friend picked up a newspaper. Ultimately, they could always give the matter to the SFO and let them stew in a mess of their own making. Personally, he did not believe a word Fortescue said.

Both men drained their glasses. Nigel felt impelled to go; he had promised to do some gardening before the weekend, when hordes of guests and family and screaming children were due to appear. He picked up his briefcase and gestured at the evening newspaper William held. Rum business, that. By the time William had raised his head to agree, Nigel had departed.

EX-CHAIRMAN OF LLOYD'S DEAD

Stephen Grote, the former chairman of Lloyd's, was this morning found dead in his Zurich home. The Swiss authorities say he suffered a heart attack following surgery. A much-admired personality of the Lloyd's market, Grote was known in the City for his incisive mind and forceful leadership. A notable chairman of the Council for Invisible Exports, Grote defended the City's interests in Whitehall and overseas.

John Devies, head of Horcum, the broker, said: 'Although his chairmanship was marred by the freak October storm, Stephen Grote was a doughty fighter for Lloyd's. Everyone in Lime Street will be saddened by his death: he was a charming man.'

Grote's career was overshadowed by the multi-billion-pound losses incurred by Lloyd's. Last year, with two other leading Lloyd's men, Grote was arrested and charged with theft, fraud and false accounting. As a result, Grote had to resign his chairmanship.

Grote established his reputation at Cecil, Russell & Grote, a family-owned Lloyd's agency. While a young man, he managed to rescue the then ailing agency from failure. Under his leadership, CRG's fortunes were restored and it became one of the largest Lloyd's agencies.

Outside the City, Grote was known as an authority on clocks and as director of the Royal Opera House, Covent Garden.

He received an honorary doctorate from the University of Birmingham, for his monographs about British clockmakers.

At Covent Garden, Grote was highly regarded as fundraiser and opera buff; he was credited with first bringing the great soprano Mercedes Valldemosa and Sir Gregor Stanislas, the leading conductor, to London.

Neil Fortescue, his successor as Lloyd's chairman, said: 'Stephen Grote was a great chairman. For decades, he led the Lloyd's market with wisdom and dignity; his passing will be mourned as a significant loss . . .'